"Well, Arthur, are we going to help him? Or just sit up here and watch his troops get devoured?"

"We are going to wait until the Scots are committed to attacking Urien." Again, his gaze locked on hers. "Then we will devour them."

His face betrayed no emotion save readiness for the imminent battle. Yet his cool appraisal of her sent a tingle down her spine. And prodded her into action.

"Good." If she was ever going to find out how things really stood between her and Arthur, she realized she would have to take the initiative. And there was no time like the present. "Then permit me to thank you for rescuing me."

She threw her arms around his neck and sought his lips with hers. His surprise didn't last long. He wrapped his arms around her and began questing with his tongue as though trying to probe her secret depths—a response even more passionate than she had ever dared to imagine! Desire too long suppressed welled up within her with surprising yet satisfying force, finding release at last through her ravenous lips. As he ran his fingers through her hair and she pressed her body to his, an exquisite ache flared in her loins. Her heart racing like fire through sun-scorched grass, all thoughts of enemies and battles fled, only for a moment.

But, oh, what a glorious moment!

Keeping secrets from me, are you? The grin never

Caledonia

Arbroch

Dunadd

Caer Senaudon
Alclyd

Caerglas

Dun Eidyn · Dungeldyr

Strathclyd

Dalriada

Rheged · **Bernicia**

Caerlaverock

Caer Camboglanna

Lugubalion

Maun

Tanroc

Dhoo-glass
Rushen Priory

Doann Dealghan

Tarabrogh

Sea of Hibernia

Mona

Gwynedd

hibernia

KIM HEADLEE

Dawnflight

SONNET BOOKS

New York London Toronto Sydney Tokyo Singapore

An *Original* Publication of POCKET BOOKS

A Sonnet Book published by
POCKET BOOKS, a division of Simon & Schuster Inc.
1230 Avenue of the Americas, New York, NY 10020

ISBN: 0-671-02041-2

First Sonnet Books printing October 1999

10 9 8 7 6 5 4 3 2 1

SONNET BOOKS and colophon are trademarks of Simon & Schuster Inc.

Cover art by Dave LaFleur

Printed in the U.S.A.

For Chris, Jonathan,
and Jessica

Acknowledgments

A project that has been incubating for as long as this one, more than thirty years since the day I first became enamored of the Arthurian Legends, naturally has required a lot of help along the way.

I must begin by thanking my parents, Helen and George Iverson. They were the first to have to put up with my obsession with the Legends, and they ultimately encouraged me, even to the point of letting me drag them on my Arthurian "pilgrimages."

Next on the list is my editor, Kate Collins, and my primary critiquer, Patricia Duffy Novak, as well as Dr. Norma Lorre Goodrich, from whose Arthurian nonfiction books I gleaned several key elements, the most important being the concept of a Pictish warrior-queen Guinevere. Without these ladies' keen insights, *Dawnflight* would not be the book it is today.

The decade-long road to publication I never could have survived without encouragement and advice along the way from wonderful people like Ed Gibson, Sue Ruttle, Josepha Sherman, martial artist Bruce Stewart, Caryl Traugott, Jane Vosk, Floyd Wilson, and my agent, Andy Zack. I'd also like to acknowledge my extended family—especially my late mother-in-law, Jerilyn Williams Headlee, a daughter of Celt-settled Appalachia and a fine storyteller in the time-honored oral tradition. And special thanks to the "family" that hangs out in cyberspace on the Fantasy Writers' e-mailing list, one of the best on the Internet.

Of course, this wouldn't be complete without thanking my son, Jonathan, and daughter, Jessica, for their continued love, support, and understanding . . . even though at times it must have seemed as though Mom had disappeared for weeks at a stretch. I dedicate this novel to them, and to my dear husband, Chris, who critiques my manuscripts and helps keep my logic and military strategies straight—and is my Arthur in more ways than he might ken.

Centreville, Virginia
June 12, 1998

Dawnflight

Dawnlight

Prologue

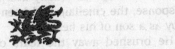

It was a wild night, the eve of Samhain. A biting gale roared down from the north, spitting snow. It tore through the trees like some mad thing, stripping away the last of the dead birch leaves and tangling in the pine boughs to make the trunks sway and groan. The snow and leaves whirled together in a frantic dance to the howls of the raging wind.

But the ghostly music was not loud enough to compete with the screams of the woman in labor.

Ogryvan, Chieftain of Clan Argyll of Caledonia, paced the circular stone room next to the family's living quarters. The midwives had refused to let him be at his wife's side during her ordeal. Now, as her cries sundered the night, his anger and frustration grew. He quickened his pace in a futile attempt to dispel the mounting tension.

The room's only door creaked open. In raced a small child. Ogryvan scooped his three-year-old stepson into his arms. The boy's eyes were wide with fear, and tear tracks stained his pale cheeks. He buried his head against Ogryvan's burly chest.

"Papa, where's Mama? Wind noisy. Me scared!"

Despite his concern for his wife, her son made him smile. Peredur hadn't reached two summers when Ogryvan had defeated the boy's father in the *dubh-lann*, hand-to-hand combat for the right to become Hymar's consort. Too young to remember his real father, Peredur had readily accepted Ogryvan, and in response, the chieftain had been pleased to treat the boy as a son of his flesh.

He brushed away the tears on Peredur's cheeks. "The baby is coming, Peredur."

"Baby! Can I go see?"

Ogryvan shook his head. "It's women's work, Son. We men must wait until it's all over."

"When, Papa?"

"Soon. I hope."

Another scream ripped the night, longer and more shrill than the rest. Peredur squirmed. "Lemme go!" He pummeled Ogryvan's chest with impotent little fists. "They hurting her!"

He squatted to set the child down but did not release his hold. "No, Peredur. You must not go. Your Mama will be all right." He hoped.

"My Lord?" came a tentative half-whisper from before him.

Ogryvan glared at the door. A young servant stood just inside the room, eyes downcast, wringing her hands. He knew her: Cynda, who had lost her bairn and her husband three days earlier to the fever.

He rose to his full height, still holding Peredur. "Well?"

"A girl, my Lord. But there was too much blood. Chieftainess Hymar is—" The woman sucked in a breath. "My Lord, she is dying."

Without a word, Ogryvan thrust the boy into Cynda's arms and strode down the hall.

The birthing chamber was swarming with women, their frantic activity reminding Ogryvan of slaughter day at the chicken pens. He riveted his gaze to the still figure on the bed. No one dared stop him as he waded through them to kneel at Hymar's side.

She was lying on her back, knees drawn up and apart, naked from her swollen waist down. Her breath came in ragged gasps. Agony etched its grim story across her lovely face. More than anything, Ogryvan wished he could wipe that pain away, and he despised his wretched powerlessness.

Gently, he gathered her into his arms while one of the women replaced the crimson-stained bedclothes with fresh ones. He laid her back down and pulled up the sleeping fur.

Hymar's lids fluttered open. "Ogryvan . . ." Her smile was as pale as her voice. "My love . . . a girl-child." Grimacing, she drew another gasping breath. "To carry on. After me. Now."

Ogryvan picked up her hand and lightly ran his fingers along her forearm, over the pair of blue doves that was the mark of Clan Argyll. "Nonsense, Hymar," he protested quietly. "Rest now. You will get well again, and—"

"No, Ogryvan. I see her. The Hag. There. By the fire."

He saw only Cynda, cradling at her breast the wee pink creature that was his infant daughter. The baby fed greedily, obviously unaware of anything save her primal need. Peredur stood at Cynda's feet, gazing up at his half-sister in wide-eyed wonder.

Ogryvan beckoned to Cynda. Slowly, to avoid disturbing the child, she approached the bed. Little Peredur marched straight to his mother's side. As Ogryvan drew the boy into the shelter of his arms,

Peredur wriggled an arm free to reach for Hymar's hand. Turning pain-hazed eyes upon him, Hymar summoned a sad smile for her firstborn.

"Here is your Hag, Hymar," Ogryvan replied as Cynda bent down with the baby. "What shall we name her?"

Hymar's face melted into joy as she beheld her daughter. "She is . . . Gyanhumara."

She raised her hand to touch the child. Gyanhumara's tiny fist closed around her finger. Hymar sighed, still smiling, eyes transfixed upon the infant. Her chest did not rise again.

All movement in the birthing chamber ceased. Silence descended. With a grief too heavy for words, Ogryvan bowed his head, pressing the limp hand of his beloved to his cheek. Peredur's soft whimpers drowned in the sleeping fur that covered his mother's chest.

The storm battered the building's stone walls, screeching its rage at being denied entry. Terrified by the noise, the new Chieftainess of Clan Argyll uttered a piercing wail.

Chapter

1

The combatants circled warily in the churned mud of the practice field, blind to the swelling audience and the chilling autumn rain. One, a giant of a figure, was the teacher. The student was neither as tall nor as well muscled but moved with the speed and agility of youth. The mud splattered on both bodies was mute evidence to the length of the session.

"Keep up your intensity!" Ogryvan swiped at his opponent's midsection. "Always! Lose your battle-frenzy, and you're dead!"

Though neither was fighting in true battle-frenzy, the younger warrior understood. Smiling grimly through the rivulets of sweat, the student danced out of reach, whirled, and made a cut at Ogryvan's thigh. The blunted practice sword could not penetrate the hard leather leggings but was sure to leave a bruise. Precisely over the wound he had taken at Aber-Glein two months before.

Although the swordmaster gritted his teeth against the pain, his opponent sensed satisfaction in the accompanying nod. The reason for the sign of approval was clear: the student had made an excellent choice of moves. Exploitation of the enemy's weaknesses was a basic tenet of the warrior's art. Mastery of this principle would serve Ogryvan's pupil well in the years to come.

"Strive to outthink your foe. Stay one move ahead," he advised between feints. The clatter adopted a dancelike rhythm as the opposing blade deftly met each thrust. The onlookers shouted their approval.

The youth answered with a powerful counterattack, silent but for the creak of leather and the hollow *thunks* as sword met shield. The swordmaster staggered backward. His disciple quickened the attack.

And grew careless. The shield sagged. Ogryvan landed a blow to the unguarded left shoulder. Startled, the youth lost footing in the treacherous mud and fell.

The laughter sparked by the mishap, from teacher and audience alike, was not unkind. Yet it did not comfort the mud-painted student.

The Chieftainess of Clan Argyll hated to lose.

And the reason rankled like that awful brew Cynda called spring tonic: she'd not done her best. She didn't need her father to tell her that carelessness had caused the fall. The loss.

In battle, such a mistake was often fatal.

She began to pick herself up, seething, only to be unceremoniously shoved face-first into the mud again. Before she could twitch, her father's foot pinned her down. His sword at the base of her neck chilled her to the core of her being. It was too easy to imagine what might happen next.

Ogryvan whispered, "Pay attention now, Gyan. This is my favorite part." His rumbling voice poised on the brink of a chuckle. "All hear and beware! The Ogre takes no prisoners!"

Had this been actual combat, her head would have

become the newest addition to Ogryvan's private collection. Such was the Caledonian way. For in this manner, not only was the foe defeated in death, but to the victor went possession of the soul. Well honored was the warrior who boasted the largest array.

Long years of training had hardened Gyan to this aspect of warfare. Yet the prospect of someday ending up on display in an enemy's feast-hall was grisly at best.

By the shifting of his foot on her back, she knew her father was posturing for the crowd. They rewarded his performance with gleeful claps and shouts. The official practice session was over, of course. But Gyan wasn't quite finished.

Her sword hilt nestled in the palm of her outflung hand. She carefully tightened her grip. In a burst of movement, she writhed and scissored with her legs, twisted free, rolled to her feet, and brought the sword up in both hands. Ogryvan toppled into the mud. The resounding wet thud of his landing was chorused by the guffaws of the audience.

Gyan grinned, holding the point of her sword to Ogryvan's throat. "And neither does the Ogre's daughter!"

No nectar was as sweet as the joy of winning. And winning before an audience of her clansmen tasted even sweeter. One day, she would lead them into battle; events like today's added another brick onto the foundation of trust. Their heartfelt adoration warmed her like the summer sun.

She sheathed the sword and offered a hand to her father. "Even?" Her voice was huskier than usual from the exertion of the morning.

Ogryvan took the proffered hand to regain his footing. "Even."

Now that the match was over, the crowd drifted back to their various duties around the settlement. One man remained at the edge of the field. Gyan strode toward him, swatting mud from her thighs and chest.

"Well, Per, how did I look?"

"Like the *baobhan-sith* Cynda used to try to frighten us with." Her half-brother reached for a glob of mud lodged in her braid.

"A fen-spirit? Ha!" Gyan playfully slapped his hand away. "You know what I mean."

Peredur beamed at her. "You did well, Gyan. I don't think I could have fooled Father like that. Or held him off for so long."

She didn't believe him for an instant. They had sparred with each other often enough to know who was the better swordsman. But she rewarded his flattery with a brilliant smile and a challenge: "Race you to the house!"

Without waiting for his reply, she launched herself down the path, bruises forgotten in the autumn mist.

The Chieftain of Clan Argyll stood alone on the practice field. Pride pulsed anew for the two promising young warriors, now racing like colts toward the family's living compound. Per, Ogryvan observed with critical interest, was gaining. Arms pumping, Per drew abreast. Too close: Gyan's scabbard bounced into Per's leg. His stride faltered. With a whoop of triumph, startling a cloud of pigeons from their perches on the timbered roof, Gyan flashed past him into the long, low stone building.

Ogryvan shook his head in amusement. She was so like her mother. Winning at any cost was one of his late wife's dearest passions. How often had Hymar played some mischief like that? When they galloped their horses beside summer-slim streams, Hymar's favorite move had been to drive her mare at full speed into the shimmering water. He could still hear her bright laughter as he spluttered his protest at the unexpected dousing.

Time had finally managed to ease the pain of his loss. Mercifully, his most cherished memories remained intact.

With a glance at the leaden skies, he hoped Hymar was somehow watching. If so, certainly she ought to be sharing his pride.

He began shambling down the path after the youths when his boot crunched against something hard. All but invisible to the casual eye, Gyan's rectangular oak shield nestled in a muddy bed. Stooping to retrieve it, he resolved to chide her about neglecting her gear.

Gyan ought to hearken well to his words if she had a mote of sense, her father mused. Per, too. They would be far beyond the reach of his guidance soon enough. The sorrow of this knowledge clutched his heart like a merlin's claw over a mouse.

To honor the treaty made after the Battle of Aber-Glein with Arthur the Pendragon of Brydein, Per and hundreds of other Caledonian warriors would be riding south after spring planting to join the Brytoni army at Caer Lugubalion. Gyan was finished with her basic martial training; the rest she would have to learn through constant practice, and in battle. But she would not be joining her brother. Her part in fulfilling the treaty terms would take her elsewhere, beginning with the Brytoni school on the Isle of Maun.

The problem was, she didn't know this yet.

Telling her wasn't going to be easy, Ogryvan realized as he resumed his course for the building. He had dodged the issue for two turnings of the moon. Now time was his enemy.

Caledonian children born into the warrior caste were raised on the heroic stories of clan lore. Battles and wars, victories and defeats, incredible acts of strength and bravery: tales as sweet as mother's milk. Gyan had devoured the teachings more eagerly than any child Ogryvan had ever known, especially the hard lessons learned from the Roman War. And, most recently, Aber-Glein.

That Gyan seemed willing to swallow her inborn hatred of the Eagle of Rome was an eloquent measure of how much she wanted to fight beside Per and her clansmen. Even though they would be wielding their weapons on behalf of the Roman warlord, Arthur.

Behind Gyan, the thudding of Per's booted feet on the corridor's flagstones announced that he had recovered his stride—and hadn't given up. Yet this time, the victory was hers! And she savored every moment.

Their laughs no more than breathless gasps, Gyan and Per clattered to a halt before his chambers. He leaned on the door to step inside.

She caught his tunic sleeve. "Wait, Per. Aren't you forgetting something?"

"Oh, aye." Per bent double in an elaborate bow. "You have bested me in a fair race, my Lady. I am yours to command forever."

"Ha! Begone, rogue!" She smiled her delight. "Save your charm for the ladies."

"Aye, but I have." As he reached for her hand, the mockery in his grin yielded to true affection. "The best lady in all the land."

He gave her braid a quick tug and fled into the room. The oaken door thumped shut behind him.

"Beast!" she hurled at the ironbound timbers. His only reply was a burst of muted laughter.

Brothers! What to do with them?

Or without them?

Chuckling softly, she set off toward her chambers at the far end of the corridor.

Normally, the afternoon would be devoted to horsemanship and mounted javelin throwing. Gyan could sit a horse better than most men could, but flinging a slim barbed shaft at a target from a bobbing back was another matter entirely. She didn't relish the idea of missing even one chance to practice this basic Caledonian battle tactic. And today marked the third day of departure from her routine.

The reason was a hard lump to swallow. A Brytoni chieftain, Dumarec of Clan Moray, was due to arrive soon. Perhaps even this day. Chieftain Dumarec was bringing his son, and Gyan was expected to look her best. Her feminine best.

Illness or injury would have been better. Without question. Let the other women strut about, Gyan thought scornfully, prettied up like overgrown dolls to snag a mate. Such was not her way.

But these days following the devastating loss at Aber-Glein could scarcely be called normal.

"Cynda," she called upon entering the antechamber.

The short, plump, dark-haired woman emerged from the bedchamber with an armload of Gyan's soiled clothes. Sighing, she rolled her eyes in a familiar gesture of long-suffering patience.

"By the gods, Gyan, you get dirtier than anyone I know! Peredur included." The accusation was delivered with a merry laugh.

"You should see Father." Gyan giggled.

Cynda, who had nursed the infant Gyan after the

death of her mother and had seen her through the bumps and scrapes of an active childhood, dropped her burden near the door.

"Very well. Strip off that leather and set it aside to be cleaned. I'll get the basin and towels. And put your linens onto the pile, there."

As Cynda left the room, Gyan moved to obey.

Standing naked in the privacy of her bedchamber, she regarded herself in the shield-sized polished bronze mirror. All her life, folks had crowed about how much she resembled Chieftainess Hymar. Yet it had always made her wonder . . .

Was she as tall as her mother had been? Or as slim? Was her hair as lustrous? Were her eyes as deeply green?

Most important, would she prove to be as wise and just a ruler as Hymar was said to have been?

She squeezed her eyes against the stinging threat of tears. These were questions she had lived with for as long as she could remember, questions destined to remain forever unanswered.

Her vision as she gazed into the mirror blurred with the remnants of her sorrow. For a moment, she saw not a lovely young woman in the bloom of adulthood but a child scampering gleefully through spring meadows, stopping now and again to climb a tree or toss stones into a chuckling brook. Her brother was never far behind; Cynda always gasped and grumbled about the pace.

Those were the special days, just after spring planting each year. Duties were light, and spirits soared high, and the sun and breeze and wildflowers conspired to lure the unwary into realms of carefree delight.

Now those days resided in the forsaken chambers of

her mind. Other matters competed for her attention. Politics. And marriage. Matters that promised to alter the path of her life forever.

There was no mystery to the timing of the Brytons' visit. To show support for the new alliance, Ogryvan wanted Gyan to select a Brytoni lord for a consort. Dumarec's lands adjoined her people's to the west, and that border had been violently disputed for generations. So his son was a logical choice.

Yet she was under no obligation to accept the suggested match. Such was the privilege of the clan's *ard-banoigin,* the woman through whom the line of succession was determined. Caledonian Law also dictated that whoever shared the bed of an *ard-banoigin* was entitled to the woman's lands. Gyan controlled more land than any of her peers. Thus, she'd been trained from the first day of womanhood to be selective in her choice of consort.

This son of Dumarec would have to prove himself her equal with sword and horse. No easy task for any man.

But Gyan was also learning there was more to life than battles and bloodshed. The serving lasses were always happy to fill her ears with stories of their bedchamber exploits. Usually, the answers to her questions came in blunt, vivid detail. Something stirred within Gyan during those times, no louder than a breeze whiffling through a pile of leaves. Soft yet persistent.

Remembering those stories, she closed her eyes and ran tentative fingers over her breasts, wondering how a man's touch would feel.

But would she ever know the true caress of love, if her consort were chosen purely for political reasons?

The sound of someone bustling into the anteroom

shattered Gyan's reverie. She wrapped herself in a sleeping fur and opened the door.

Mardha, the prettiest of the serving lasses, was bearing the water and washing linens. She greeted Gyan with a saucy smile and a wink. Cynda followed with towels and a gown.

Gyan would much rather have seen Cynda carrying a fresh tunic and breeches. And said so.

"You know your father's orders, young lady." Cynda organized the bathing implements with a practiced hand.

Gyan sighed.

The wolfskin slid to the floor at her feet as Cynda and Mardha each grabbed a wet washcloth and set to work.

Chapter 2

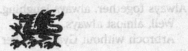

Ogryvan ducked to cross the threshold into the living quarters.

A dark smear on the gray granite flagstones caught his eye, and he squinted at the floor. The smear resolved into a double set of boot marks. One track stopped at the nearest closed door, Per's chambers. The other continued down the deserted corridor and disappeared into the shadows.

Presumably, Gyan and Per had gone to get themselves cleaned up. In Ogryvan's present mud-caked condition, this seemed like a fine idea. His daughter's lecture would have to wait. So be it.

Hefting both his shield and Gyan's, Ogryvan shouldered open the door to his private chambers. The slave tending the fire scrambled to his feet as the chieftain entered the room.

"Ah, Dafydd. Well met. I need towels and water." Dafydd bowed and started to leave. "Fresh clothing, too," added Ogryvan on his way into the inner sleeping chamber.

He left the shields against a wall, shed the muddy leather gear and sweaty undertunic, and stretched on his bare stomach across the bed, eyes closed. Memories again flooded his brain. The children this time. Not as he saw them today, but years ago. Gyan, always driving herself to keep pace with her older brother. And Per, the son of his heart though not of his flesh, forever striving to stay one step ahead. The two of them, running, climbing, riding, fighting, shouting. Always together, always laughing.

Well, almost always.

Arbroch without Gyan and Per was not going to be the same.

Creaking hinges announced Dafydd's return. The hot, moist towels soothed Ogryvan's complaining muscles. Gyan had certainly given them good reason to complain.

A pity the heat couldn't salve his spirits.

One by one, the towels came off, leaving a tingling echo of their presence. With a twinge of regret, he sat up. Across Dafydd's palms rested a thigh-length blue tunic and matching trews. Ogryvan accepted the proffered garments with a nod.

Painfully easing the trews over the purpling thigh bruise forced to mind the disaster at Aber-Glein, and he grimaced. Those memories refused to budge.

Arthur the Pendragon had orchestrated a brilliant win over Alayna and the rest of the Caledonian host on the banks of the roiling River Fiorth. How Arthur, an untried leader of men, had managed this feat was beyond Ogryvan's ken. Good men under him, Ogryvan supposed. And a small but effective cavalry squad—led by the very man on his way to visit Arbroch even now—which had outflanked Ogryvan's troop to capture the dike and help seal the victory for the Brytons.

It had been during this maneuver that Ogryvan had taken the spear wound in his thigh that, thanks to his daughter, was throbbing once again. And if the wound weren't enough, the battle itself still gave him nightmares.

After knotting the leather thong to secure his trews, he snatched the pitcher off the table, tipped it to his lips, and swallowed the dregs of the strong spiced wine. The taste wasn't nearly as bitter as the loss he and Alayna and the rest of Caledonia had been forced, by Arthur's hand, to swallow. Although, by the gods, it was no small wonder that any of the surviving Caledonians had been spared. With Alayna's men pinned to the cliffs above the Fiorth, cut off by Urien's cavalry unit, Arthur was in the perfect position to slaughter the Caledonian host. In that man's place, Ogryvan would not have hesitated.

He dragged the back of a hand across his bearded lips and surrendered the pitcher to Dafydd, who tucked it under one arm, gathered the discarded towels and clothing under the other, bowed, and left the room.

As the chieftain prepared to don the tunic Dafydd had given him, his gaze fell upon his shield arm and the Argyll clan-mark he had proudly worn there for the better part of two decades.

Picti, or "Painted Folk," was the name still used by the Brytons and other peoples of these verdant isles to refer to the Highland-dwelling Caledonians. In days long past, the name had begun among the Romans—ignorant men who'd been too busy trying to conquer the clans to be bothered with learning anything from them. The epithet had been appropriate then, when custom dictated that all clan warriors fight naked, protected by nothing but their great gleaming torcs and fiery courage and face-to-foot woad wardingmarks, blessed by the gods.

Now, only clan rulers bore the sacred tattoos. And

Ogryvan's flying Argyll Doves, once a rich blue, were showing their age. Just like the rest of him.

Perhaps the outcome of Aber-Glein might have been much different had the high old ways not been abandoned.

What a fool! With a rueful toss of his head, he chided himself for indulging in such fruitless speculation. The old ways had not helped against those first Romans, either.

The aftermath of Aber-Glein saw the drafting of a treaty between the Caledonians and the Brytons. As Chieftain of Clan Argyll, Ogryvan had been one of its endorsers. Amazingly, the terms imposed by the victors were not as unreasonable as they might have been.

For her part as organizer of the attack, Chieftainess Alayna was hit hardest by the treaty terms. Senaudon and all lands south of the fort were placed under the control of a Brytoni occupation unit. Most of the surviving Alban warriors were forced into the Brytoni army. And to ensure Alayna's cooperation, her son was taken hostage.

Argyll, the strongest clan of the Confederacy, found itself in a similar position. Five hundred warriors were slated to swell the Brytoni ranks. At least Gyan was spared from having to share the same ordeal as Alayna's son.

Small comfort.

Ogryvan pulled the tunic over his head and down into place. With a grunt, he rose from the bed and crossed to a chair near the fire, where the flames sparked even more memories of Aber-Glein.

Under the treaty, the other clans were required to provide Arthur with horsemen, each warrior and mount fully equipped with battle-gear. In exchange, the

Pendragon promised equal treatment and opportunities for advancement, an equal share in all spoils, and military assistance against Scotti, Saxon, and Angli incursions upon Caledonian territory.

Most of the other Caledonian clan leaders had voiced a preference for death rather than establishing an alliance with Arthur. The loudest dissent came from Alayna. Quite understandable, since she had the most to lose and the least to gain. But sometimes there were benefits to be had by wielding the instruments of peace rather than those of war.

Recognizing the advantages presented by this unique opportunity—despite the impact on his daughter— Ogryvan had bullied his peers into submission. He recalled that moment with a brief smile. Faced with the Ogre's forbidding glare, not even Chieftainess Alayna had dared to disagree.

The only truly bright spot in that dismal day was its unexpected conclusion. To celebrate the new-forged alliance, Arthur had feasted Caledonians and Brytons alike at Senaudon. Former enemies were treated like longtime comrades. A mountain of pork and venison had disappeared that night, drowned by a river of ale. Defeat had never tasted better.

Even Chieftainess Alayna had not acted as bitterly as she might have, under the circumstances.

Dafydd returned to the chamber with a clean goblet and the wine pitcher, its contents sloshing to the brim. The tray he carried also held a welcome surprise: a loaf of fragrant brown bread and a slab of cheese. The slave set the tray on a small table near Ogryvan's chair. Ogryvan reached for the bread, commending him for his thoughtfulness. Murmuring thanks, Dafydd started for the door.

"One more thing." Dafydd stopped and turned to

regard Ogryvan expectantly. "Please tell Gyan I want to see her in my workroom at her earliest convenience."

"Yes, my Lord." Dafydd nodded and left the chamber.

With the wine cup in the other hand, Ogryvan began to demolish the warm loaf. If Gyan truly was like her mother—indeed, most women—he would have enough time while she was bathing and dressing to finish a feast.

He took another gulp of wine as his thoughts returned to Alayna of Alban: clan ruler, warrior, mother . . . a veritable marvel of womanhood. Upon the death of her consort, Gwalchafed, seven years ago, Alayna had approached Ogryvan with a proposal to unite Argyll and Alban, which had been a sorely tempting offer. Not only because of the sensual advantages, for the flamboyant Alayna doubtless would have made an entertaining partner.

Staring into the flames, he tried to imagine just what sort of entertainment he and Alayna might have shared. It wasn't difficult.

But in asking Ogryvan to become her consort, Alayna had played to an even baser emotion: greed. What sane man would turn his back upon the prospect of doubling his wealth?

A man who loved his daughter more than all the riches this world could possibly offer. Because the mantle of chieftainship rested upon his shoulders, marriage to Chieftainess Alayna would have made Argyll cease to exist as an independent member of the Confederacy. Ogryvan could not bring himself to deny Gyan her rightful rank. Not then, not ever.

Clean and gowned—and yearning for her riding gear and favorite horse—Gyan awaited her father in his antechamber. His distinctive voice thundered outside the door as he gave instructions to the servants in charge of preparing the evening meal. Before long, the door swung open, and Ogryvan strode in. He closed it behind him and headed for his large ashwood worktable.

The summons had come as she was dressing, forcing Cynda to hurry with the comb through the last tangles. Sitting now in Ogryvan's workroom, Gyan discovered her hair was dry at last. She fingered the soft, copper-bright tresses, fragrant from the dried rose petals crumbled into the washwater. Ogryvan had taught her to keep her hair braided and pinned fast to her head while fighting, to deny the enemy a handhold. Now, it spilled freely over her pine-hued woolen gown.

"Good practice this morning, Gyan." The chair behind the table groaned as Ogryvan sat. "Where did you learn that twisting trick?"

"Per showed me. We've been practicing it for a sennight."

"Ah. Just remember to keep your concentration. And don't let overconfidence rule your actions."

"I know, Father." The morning's mud-drenched humiliation still stung her pride.

"And another thing, young lady."

His sable head disappeared as he reached for something lying on the floor beside him. He brought up a large, filthy object.

Although the caked mud covered most of the identifying marks, she would have recognized her shield anywhere. First the mud bath—now this! Only foolish warriors forgot their gear. And foolish warriors soon became dead ones. Her brow furrowed as she mentally scolded herself for being so careless. Again.

"I know you know better. I ought to make you clean it

yourself, Gyan, to make sure you don't forget this lesson." As she rose to accept the shield, he shook his head and firmly motioned her back into her seat. He leaned the shield against the wall. "But it can wait until later. No sense in ruining a perfectly good gown."

A short smile played across her lips. If muddying the gown could hasten her into more comfortable clothes . . .

Ogryvan placed both palms on the tabletop, much like a priest preparing to deliver judgment. Hesitation seemed to creep across his face—something she'd never seen in him before. It pricked her curiosity. All thought of the gown and plans for its demise fled.

"Was there something else, Father?"

"Aye." He drew a deep breath. "You and Per will be leaving Arbroch after the snows melt in the spring—"

"To join the Pendragon. Yes, I know."

"No."

"No?"

"Per will, of course, but you are going to the Brytoni school."

"School?" Gyan felt she must sound like an idiot. But surprise gave her tongue a mind of its own. "Where?"

"On the Isle of Maun."

"Maun! One of Dumarec's. Very clever, Father." She furrowed her brow. "I suppose you think that if I reject his son as consort now, I might decide to accept him later, at this—school." She spat the word like a piece of tainted meat. "Well, it won't work." Crossing her arms, she tossed her head with an air of finality.

"Now, Gyan, that's not why I—"

"I am a warrior! Not a fledgling priest to sit and listen to some mumbling old mage all day. You cannot make me go to this place if I do not wish it." The defeat in his eyes affirmed the truth of her statement. "And I do not wish it."

He sighed. "I'd hoped you would see the wisdom in this, Gyan. The advantages it could bring you. And through you, our clan."

"Ha. What can those Brytons teach me that I can't learn here?"

"Latin, first." His open, upraised hand forestalled her reply. "So you can study Roman battle tactics."

She felt her eyebrows quirk upward. A chance to learn from the army that had tried to destroy her people more than once across the span of generations, most recently at Aber-Glein . . . to prevent such a thing from ever happening again. If she could somehow bring this to pass, her name would be hailed in the songs of the clan *seannachaidhs* forever! Her lips drew back in a slow, proud smile.

Ogryvan seemed pleased to win her approval. He returned her smile.

"How long must I stay?"

"Two years, Gyan."

"I'll be finished in one." Her father laughed in obvious disbelief. "You'll see, Father. I can't let Per win all the glory!"

"What's all this about me and glory?" asked a third voice.

Startled, Gyan turned. She had not heard the door open. Arms akimbo, her brother stood on the threshold, auburn head and broad shoulders limned in dancing torchlight.

She did not appreciate being set upon in this manner—even by kin—and her voice reflected her irritation. "Eavesdropping is not polite, dear brother."

"Keeping secrets from me, are you?" The grin never

left his face. He advanced into the room and bent to whisper in her ear. "The wise warrior never puts his— or her—back to the door."

"As if I have anything to fear in Father's chambers— ha!" Nimbly, he dodged her blow. "What are you doing here, Peredur mac Hymar? Testing me?"

Ogryvan, following their banter with a smile of amused affection, called a halt. "Save that energy for the practice fields." He directed a sterner gaze at Per. "I presume you have some other purpose here than to torment your sister and disrupt our conversation?"

"My apologies, Father." Per's contrition seemed to last but a moment. "Our hunters have returned. They report seeing the Dalriadans in the hills west of Senaudon yesterday morning."

"And about time," Ogryvan replied. "How many?"

"Twenty-four, all mounted, with pack horses. They should arrive late tomorrow." Per tossed another grin at Gyan. "Will you be ready for them, dear sister?"

"More than you will be," she retorted.

"Peace, children!" Ogryvan raised both hands for silence. "That's much better. Per, how fared our huntsmen?"

"Three fine bucks, Father. And many partridges and hares."

"Excellent!" His palm smacked the tabletop. "With twenty-four guests, we'll need every morsel."

"Since they won't be here until tomorrow, there's no need for me to stay dressed in this." Gyan plucked at the neckline of her gown. "I think I shall go down to javelin practice."

"No, lass. You've too much to do as it is." Ogryvan's tone sounded kind but firm. "What with seeing that the sleeping quarters for the Dalriadans are in order, feast preparations, and the like—wait, Per," he commanded as his stepson started to leave. "You and I need to review the plans for the honor guard. Gyan, you'd best get started right away."

"Very well, Father."

Gyan knew a dismissal when she heard one and was disappointed not to be sharing in this discussion. Such subjects had always been far more interesting to her than the mundane tasks of running a large household. Yet this time she knew an argument was pointless. Days ago, she and her father had decided that she would not participate in the initial meeting of Chieftain Dumarec's party. With no heir, she had to be protected from treachery, however unlikely the source.

She rose and grabbed her shield by the straps, careful to keep it away from her gown yet toying with the notion of creating a mishap as an excuse to change. But she quickly abandoned the idea, tempting though it was. With so much else happening, the wrath of Cynda—not to mention her father—was not something to invoke.

She turned for the door. Ogryvan came from behind the table to pat her shoulder. "Gyan," he whispered. "Give him a chance."

She heard the plea in his voice and softened hers. "Him—you mean Urien?" Ogryvan nodded. "Don't worry, Father. If he's the right man, I'll know it."

Ogryvan bent to accept his daughter's kiss. Per was not so lucky. As he moved into her seat, she teasingly slapped his leather-clad shoulder. His retaliation came too late.

With a chuckle, Gyan swept toward the door.

The manner of Gyan's departure made Ogryvan recall the feast after the Battle of Aber-Glein, and how Alayna, bedecked in her costliest finery, had tried time and again to place herself in Arthur's path. Her behavior hadn't seemed odd at the time, what with the noise and confusion in the overcrowded feast-hall. Hindsight told him Alayna had wished to form a more intimate alliance with the handsome, unmarried Pendragon. And failed.

On the threshold, Gyan glanced over her shoulder. Per made an abrupt move out of his seat as though to chase her. With a mock squeal of fear, she made good her escape—and forgot to shut the door. Chuckling, Per settled back into his chair.

This time, their antics couldn't distract Ogryvan for very long.

Stroking his beard, he wondered if he had been premature to suggest the betrothal of his daughter to the heir of neighboring Clan Moray, in the Brytoni territory of Dalriada. He knew little of these Brytons off the battlefield except through his dealings with the slaves. Yet he knew enough to understand that outside motherhood and domestic duties, women played a very small role in their society.

What would happen if Gyan's consort tried to extend his influence beyond the bounds set by Caledonian Law? What would become of the clan if Gyan couldn't hold him at bay? And what would become of her? Most lasses would have been frightened to tears by the prospect of meeting men so recently counted among the ranks of the enemy. Not his Gyan, he realized with a flush of pride. She had seemed to radiate youthful confidence. He hoped it would serve her well for the decision she would soon be forced to make.

Her acceptance of Urien map Dumarec meant more than the fulfillment of an agreement. To become her consort, he had to be right—not only for Clan Argyll but for her.

Had he, Ogryvan, done enough to prepare Gyan for this fateful day? Would she be able to make the best decision and face its consequences? More to the point, was he ready to release his beloved daughter to Urien of Dalriada?

"Father? You said you had more plans to discuss with me?"

Ogryvan set aside his thoughts to regard Peredur, who, like his half-sister, so resembled Hymar that it was difficult to be angry at anything the lad did. "Aye, Son. In a moment."

He strode to the threshold and peered into the corridor, which was teeming with servants preparing for the Dalriadans' imminent arrival. Pushing the door shut, he again thought about the man responsible for all this activity. And the reason Gyan would have to marry a Brytoni lord, even if she decided to reject Urien.

Arthur the Pendragon. Unmarried. A leader whose authority was purely military in nature—not derived from one Brytoni clan but all. Such a man would pose no threat to the continued identity of Clan Argyll. Or to Gyan's leadership.

Ogryvan suspected that if the two ever met, Gyan might actually come to like Arthur. If she could force herself to see past the Roman influence. Past the conqueror's stern countenance.

Gyan marrying the Pendragon, however, would not satisfy the treaty.

Chapter
3

Arthur map Uther sat in a dim corner of the wayside inn's common room, fighting to keep his anger in check. The ale helped, but not enough. He took another pull on the flagon. To his men, he always strove to present a cool demeanor, and the room was full to bursting with the fourscore horsemen of First *Ala* who'd been recovered enough from Aber-Glein to accompany Arthur on this mission. Strong emotions never won a battle, and as *Dux Britanniarum*, commander-in-chief of the Dragon Legion of Brydein, one of the duties Arthur took most seriously was the presentation of a good example.

Which did not include throttling the woman whose stubbornness in refusing to release her son to Arthur's first envoy was the very reason for his personal excursion—a show of force, if truth be told—into Caledonian territory. The image of his fingers wrapped around Alayna's neck, however, was amusing. He felt his lips twitch in the barest of smiles.

"Want to share the joke, Arthur?"

Although Cai had spoken, Arthur's other close friend, Bedwyr, was also regarding Arthur expectantly.

Neither man was assigned to the cavalry; Cai commanded the infantry garrison at Camboglanna, and Bedwyr headed the fleet. But to demonstrate to Chieftainess Alayna the seriousness of Arthur's intent, he had invited them along to represent the other branches of Brydein's military forces. And he had to admit he was glad of this rare opportunity for their company. The press of duties took the three of them in different directions all too often these days.

The only person missing from this assemblage—though Arthur could scarcely call him friend—was Urien, former commander of First *Ala* whom Arthur had recently promoted to command the new Brytoni-Caledonian cavalry cohort. But Urien, Arthur knew, was busy conducting another affair on behalf of Brydein, one just as vital in securing peace with the Caledonians.

In response to Cai's question, Arthur shook his head and swallowed another mouthful of ale. Some things he did not share with a soul. And anything that might be construed as a breach of diplomacy certainly fell into that category.

"That's our Pendragon." Bedwyr's grin was mischievous. Little more than a year after his appointment, Arthur was still getting accustomed to hearing the title that went with the job of *Dux Britanniarum:* Pendragon, "Chief Dragon." And well Bedwyr knew it. "Secretive as ever."

That won Arthur's chuckle. "If you two must know, I was imagining what I might do to our wayward ally—and not what you might think, Cai." Arthur chuckled again as Cai, who had been ogling one of the buxom serving maids, whipped his head around at the sound of his name. He laid a hand to his neck and winced.

"Careful, my friend. One day your lust will get you in real trouble."

"As if yours won't." Cai snorted as the serving maid bustled to Arthur's side of the table and bent over farther than was strictly necessary to set before him a fresh flagon of ale, offering Arthur a tempting view of her cleavage. "You see the effect that damnably handsome face of yours has on the women."

Arthur saw. And he chose not to be tempted but kept his gaze leveled at Cai. "At least the word *discretion* is in my vocabulary."

Cai's only reply was a short bark of laughter.

Bedwyr, it seemed, was not above vying for the young woman's attentions, either. He interrupted the shy smile he was giving her just long enough to say, "But where's the fun in that, Arthur?"

Fun, indeed. Although the pleasures of female company were not unknown to Arthur, such encounters had, without exception, only satisfied an immediate physical need. The woman with whom he ultimately wanted to spend the rest of his life would not be a mere bedchamber accessory but someone he hoped would share his vision for a united Brydein and help him work to usher that vision into being. Such a woman he had yet to meet. That included Chieftainess Alayna, despite her rather obvious attempts to convince him otherwise at the feast after the battle.

Not for the first time, he wondered if such a woman even existed.

He rose from the table and addressed his friends. "You two settle this . . . matter"—he jerked a nod toward the serving woman—"between yourselves. I plan to be as well rested as possible for my meeting tomorrow with Chieftainess Alayna."

Was it his imagination, or did the woman's lips actually purse into a pout as he passed her on his way toward the door? It didn't matter; he had been perfectly serious about his intention to retire—alone—for the evening. Nor did he mind having to spend the night in a field tent, the innkeeper having informed him that all the rooms were already bespoken. As much as he would have enjoyed the luxury of a bed, sleeping in a tent like the rest of his men gave him yet another opportunity to lead them by example, which he welcomed, even in this unseasonably chilly October weather.

He never made it out of the room. The drumming of hooves sounded outside, but before Arthur could wonder who had arrived, the door banged open, and the answer became apparent. Think of the devil, Arthur mused, and he'll appear.

Urien map Dumarec swaggered into the room, flanked by his father, Chieftain Dumarec, and more than a score of their clansmen. All but Urien were arrayed in the black-and-gold-patterned wool of Clan Moray. Urien was wearing his legion armor and short scarlet officer's cloak, augmented by fur-lined boots, leather leggings, and a long-sleeved undertunic. Every man was shaking flecks of snow from hair and cloak while heading for the fireplace. After exchanging hearty greetings with their comrades-at-arms, the men of Arthur's unit made way for the newcomers.

Catching Arthur's gaze, Urien plowed through the crowd toward him. "My Lord. Well met." He did not offer a salute—which, Arthur had to admit, was within the bounds of protocol since they were in a civilian setting.

"Indeed, Tribune." Arthur wondered about the sincerity of Urien's greeting. They'd never been on friendly terms to begin with, and Arthur's appointment to the position of *Dux Britanniarum* had put even more distance between them. But since Urien was the son of a staunch ally, there was no wisdom in antagonizing him. "Your father bespoke the rooms here for your party?"

Urien nodded. "We had to. This is the last inn before we head into Picti territory. No telling what we'll find in our beds once we get there. Fleas, rats, daggers—you name it." His eyebrows knotted. "Isn't that why you stopped here, Lord Pendragon?"

Arthur saw no need to explain himself to a subordinate, nobility or not. "I had my reasons." He regarded Urien closely. "Just as I have my reasons to advise you that if you wish to be successful in your dealings with our new allies, you might consider leaving your prejudices on this side of the border."

Urien laughed. "Now you're beginning to sound like"—he tossed a glance over his shoulder at Chieftain Dumarec, who was still hunkered in front of the fire—"someone else I know." The woman who had been serving Arthur's table sidled up to Urien with a sultry smile and a frothy flagon, which he accepted with a grin. "Besides, tavern wench or warrior, Brytoni or not, these women are all the same. Even with the language differences, it shouldn't be too hard to convince this Picti chieftainess of my"—his grin widened as he patted the lass on the backside to the sound of her giggle—"charms."

Charms, Arthur thought dryly, and an ego to match. But it was no exaggeration to say that Urien was also a formidable warrior—the success of his cavalry charge had been instrumental in securing the victory at Aber-Glein—and Caledonians seemed to respect strength.

The union of Chieftainess Gyanhumara's clan with Urien's was as good as done. Such a marriage could make Clan Moray more powerful than Arthur cared to contemplate. Yet for the sake of lasting peace in Brydein, Arthur sincerely hoped it would work out for the best.

"Be that as it may," Arthur said, "I still advise caution."

"Caution, indeed." Urien's look adopted a hard edge as he ground fist to palm. "I don't trust these Picts. In fact, I still don't understand why you didn't obliterate them when I"—he stabbed a thumb at his chest—"gave you the chance at Aber-Glein."

"Do not forget, Tribune, that your charge was carried out under my orders."

Urien glared but otherwise let the remark pass. "The Picts have been a menace to our borders for time out of mind. Why didn't you—"

"The same can be said about the Saxons, Angles—and Scots." The last Arthur spat like the curse it was to him. "None of them have demonstrated a willingness to negotiate with us for peace. The Caledonians were willing, and Brydein will be getting a much stronger cavalry as a result." It was Arthur's turn to grin. "In fact, you should thank them for your promotion."

Urien grunted. "By the way, I thought it was quite magnanimous of you to word the treaty to preserve the Picti woman's customary right to choose a husband, just so long as he's a nobleman on this side of the border. So if you're so set on this alliance, Lord Pendragon, why don't you see if she wants to marry you?" He gave an elaborate shrug. "But I forget. By the terms of your own treaty, you don't qualify." His smile was so thick with insubordination that, had they been anywhere else, Arthur would have settled the matter once and for all, at swordpoint. "How clumsy of me. Sir."

"Yes, Tribune, it was." Arthur let enough warning seep into his tone to convey his irritation without alerting anyone around them. "Any clumsier, and the next time you might not live to regret it."

What irritated Arthur far more than his subordinate's attitude was the fact that, because Clan Cwrnwyll had never recognized the legitimacy of Arthur's birth, Urien was absolutely right.

"I don't like it."

Gyan glanced up to see Cynda, hands on hips, scowl at the pattern of rushes and crushed lavender strewn across the floor of the guest chambers. These rooms would soon house men who, as recently as midsummer, had been Argyll's sworn enemies.

The slave girl clutching the shallow basket of lavender looked up, startled. The basket tipped. A pile of petals fluttered to the floor. With a squeak of alarm, the girl tried to scoop them back into the basket.

Cynda softened her gaze. "Never mind that, dear, just spread them around now. Ach, that'll be fine." She pointed toward the window. "Perhaps a wee bit more over there."

The slave bent to her work. In moments, she finished and, bowing, scurried from the room.

"What is it, then?" Gyan smoothed the wool-lined wolfskin sleeping fur on one of the beds. "Have we forgotten something?"

Stepping back, she surveyed the chamber. Everything seemed to be in place: fresh linens and furs on the beds, a fire snapping in the fireplace with a generous stack of wood nearby, clean rushes on the floor, an empty trunk for clothes against the far wall, a basin and pitcher of water on the table, the lamps lit and brimming with oil. Anything else Chieftain Dumarec or his son might need could be sent for easily enough.

If something were amiss, Gyan couldn't see it.

"No, no." Cynda made a gesture of impatience with her hand. "The reason for all of this. That's what I don't like. Sheltering enemies at the Seat of Argyll—why, it's unheard of!"

"They are not our enemies now." If indeed a collection of strange scratches on sheepskin could be taken as proof, which Gyan wasn't completely prepared to accept.

"Oh, aye, if you can believe the words of a flock of thick-witted men who spend most of their time fighting and drinking and wenching."

Despite her distrust, Gyan laughed. "I'll be sure to tell Father what you think of his exploits."

"You do that, young lady. Not that he'd listen, anyway. But his 'exploits' have gotten his daughter tangled up in marriage with one of these Brytoni curs. Your mother never would've approved."

Gyan pondered this and finally had to disagree. "I imagine my mother would have done whatever was best for the clan. Even if it meant giving approval for my marriage to a Brytoni lord." She fixed Cynda with a hard stare. "But you don't approve. Why?"

Cynda wrung her hands as her eyes darkened into a faraway look. "You didn't see what those savages did to our poor brave warriors at Aber-Glein."

That was partly true. Blessed with a deft hand with bandages and a strong stomach for the sight and stench of blood, Cynda had accompanied the war-host to help with the wounded. Since Gyan had no heir, she'd had to stay behind. By Caledonian Law, the clan chieftain and chieftainess could not be exposed to the same risk of death, lest there be a struggle for succession should the worst come to pass. Since Chieftainess Alayna had more need of Ogryvan's wealth of fighting experience—although in hindsight his skill had not made a whit of difference to the outcome—Gyan had missed the chance for her first taste of battle.

Gyan had understood the reasons and even agreed in principle. But this had not stopped her from brooding over the injustice.

When the ragged remains of the host returned, she cauterized her wounded feelings to help tend to injuries of a life-threatening sort. This work gave her a glimpse of the harsh realities: the gaping gashes, the missing limbs and eyes, the raging fevers. And the broken, blood-crusted bodies of fallen clansmen who would never again feel the warmth of the sun, or hear a child's laugh, or smell the rich earth after a spring shower.

No, working in the sickrooms was not a pleasant duty. But that was a consequence of war. Whether Caledonian or Brytoni, Saxon or Scotti, the best and luckiest warriors survived with their skins intact. The others did not.

Gyan laid a hand on Cynda's shoulder. "I saw enough, afterward. That can't be the only thing bothering you about this visit."

The woman who was the only mother Gyan had ever known collapsed into her arms. "I feel as if"—Cynda drew a shuddering breath—"as if I'm losing you, Gyan . . . my wee dove."

Gyan hugged her. Words fled. It had never occurred to her that Cynda might not be able to leave Arbroch.

Having to bid farewell to her father and brother and home was bad enough. But Cynda, too?

"Nonsense, Cynda. When I leave Arbroch in the spring, you'll be coming with me."

Cynda shook her head. "Ogryvan would never allow it. I know more about the day-to-day doings of this place than anyone else."

"Then it's time you began sharing your knowledge, wouldn't you say?"

"Aye . . . Gyan, that's a wonderful idea!" Her eyes sparkled. "The winter will be more than enough time to train a replacement. But who?"

"Bryalla?"

"No, not with that wee bairn of hers. Perhaps Rhianna."

"She seems a little slow in the wits."

"Aye, you're right, Gyan. Then there's—"

A thought flashed. The woman in Gyan's mental picture was pretty and competent—and able to satisfy Ogryvan's needs in more ways than one. "Mardha!"

"Just the very lass I was thinking of." Cynda grinned.

"Gyan, there you are!"

Magnificent in his freshly oiled leather battle-gear and midnight-blue woolen clan cloak, pinned at the shoulder with a silver Argyll dove brooch, Per stood in the doorway. Gyan hoped the warmth of her smile told him just how handsome he looked.

"Per, what are you doing here? I thought you'd already ridden out with the patrol."

He shook his auburn head. "Father and I are still trying to decide which of our Brytoni slaves can be trusted to act as translator." Slaves, Gyan reflected, captured as a result of one border dispute or another, or their children born at Arbroch over the years. Either way, Per was right: not many of them could be trusted with such a critical task. He continued, "We wanted your thoughts on the matter."

"Good. Where is Father?"

"At the stables, inspecting the honor guard's mounts. He sent me to find you."

Gyan faced Cynda. "Can you finish here? And make sure there are enough pallets and sleeping furs in the Commons for the rest of Dumarec's party?"

"Ach, Gyan, be off with you!" She gave Gyan a gentle but firm shove toward the door. "I've been doing this sort of thing since before you were born—and not likely to forget anything now."

As the door thumped behind them, Gyan and Per shared a laugh.

"You know," Per said between chuckles, "I will miss that little tyrant."

Gyan made a noncommittal grunt. With luck, she would not have to miss Cynda at all.

The area outside the stables was bustling with the regular Argyll patrol and the twenty-two mounted men selected to serve as Chieftain Dumarec's honor guard. In their midst loomed Ogryvan, scrutinizing everything from harness furnishings to helmet crests. Like Per, he was impressively arrayed in his finest battle-gear, as were the honor guard and their horses.

Gyan yearned to be riding out with the guard, to see these fierce Brytoni warriors for the first time. To meet destiny headlong.

But duty tethered her to the settlement. Everything had to be in perfect readiness for the guests. This task was just as important as the honor guard's, though not nearly as exciting. She released her disappointment on the wings of a sigh.

Ogryvan looked up as his daughter and stepson drew

near. "Ah, good." His eyebrows made a thick line across his forehead as he glanced at the sky. Dark clouds were boiling over the mountain peaks, heralding a storm. "Let's go inside before the skies open on us. Gyan, I don't want you to ruin your gown."

"What's the matter, Father?" She grinned teasingly. "Afraid I might melt?"

"With you, I don't know anymore," Ogryvan retorted. "You seem to be full of surprises lately. Now, go on inside, both of you."

The three crowded into the nearest chamber to offer any measure of privacy, the tack room. Outside, the first drops assaulted the timbers of the roof.

"Did Per describe our problem? That we need to have one of our slaves act as translator?" When Gyan nodded, Ogryvan went on, "It's a big responsibility. The slightest misunderstanding could spell disaster. I don't want to trust just anyone."

"Trust, aye. We don't need someone who might say something other than what he's told to say. Although . . ." Per's face clouded with a rare frown. "I have to wonder whether any of them can really be trusted that far."

"But since none of us knows the Brytoni tongue beyond just a few words to get the slaves to do our bidding, we don't have much choice, do we?" Gyan glanced at Ogryvan. "Father, what is to be the reward if the person does well?"

Scrutinizing a spare length of saddle girth, Ogryvan did not answer right away. Nor did he look up when at last he spoke: "Freedom."

As Gyan started to voice her consent, Per broke in. "I thought one of Arthur's treaty terms was for all the clans to free every Bryton."

"Aye, Son. By this time next year, we must."

"Then why not let them all go now?"

"Think, Per." Gyan laid a hand lightly on his leather-covered forearm. "We have close to threescore men and women here, and I've lost count of how many children. We can't free them all at once, especially now with winter at the gate. The slaves own little more than the clothes on their backs. They couldn't make it to their villages on foot before the snows come. And think what the loss of their labor would do to us." She grinned to soften her words. "Would you want to be shoveling Rukh's manure all winter?"

"I suppose not." Her brother's short laugh sounded rueful.

"Very well. Let us grant freedom for the slave and his or her family and offer them passage home, wherever it may be," Ogryvan said. "We can manage the loss of two adults and a few children, agreed?"

Per nodded. "But we're still faced with the original question. Who will it be?"

Studying the neat rows of bridle pegs, Gyan pondered the options. Many pegs were empty, another blunt reminder that the fetters of duty were as strong as those made of iron. And fighting the intangible bonds was just as futile.

She abandoned her mental struggle to regard her father and brother. "We can rule out the women."

"Oh? Why?" From the surprise in Per's tone, it seemed he had expected her to suggest one of the female slaves.

"They're a timid lot." She shrugged. "We need someone who can keep his wits about him under pressure."

"Aye. Trouble is"—the folded leather strap snapped taut between Ogryvan's fingers with a loud crack—"we haven't seen any of our slaves react in a real crisis."

"What about the fire in the stables last summer?" Per asked. "Who was that stable-mucker? Dav? Daff—"

"Dafydd! Of course!" The memory of that dreadful afternoon sprang up, when Gyan had nearly lost her beloved Brin. "It was his idea to blindfold the horses so they could be led to safety."

For his role in saving the horses, Dafydd was given a position as one of Ogryvan's personal manservants. An appropriate reward, although Gyan had always wondered why Dafydd had not been set free for his efforts. In her father's place, she wouldn't have hesitated.

Perhaps now Dafydd would have his chance.

Slowly, Ogryvan stroked his beard. "Hmmm, Dafydd . . . he's so quiet and unassuming that most of the time I forget about him." He favored his daughter and stepson with a proud smile. "By all the gods, you two are right. He's got a good head about him. I do believe Dafydd is our man."

Chapter

4

"Remember, men, do not draw your weapons unless you hear the word from me. From me!" Ogryvan roared. "Is that clear?"

If the chorus of "Aye, Chieftain" sounded less than enthusiastic, it was not unexpected. They'd heard the command at least a dozen times in preparation for this special duty. But Ogryvan had to be certain of their obedience.

"I said, is that clear?" The chieftain hurled the full force of his glare at each member of the guard.

Their second response was much more to his liking. Now was not the time for youthful blood-lust. Only cool heads and steady hearts would see a successful conclusion to the first attempt in clan memory at a peaceful meeting between former enemies on Argyll land.

Ogryvan raised his fist to signal the troop's departure. As he set heels to his roan stallion's flanks, he glanced back at Gyan. The rain had calmed to a drizzle, and she had taken a step from beneath the stable roof's thatched overhang. With sword arm outstretched, she clenched and splayed her fingers in the warrior's salute. Fierce pride surged through every line of her stance. In that moment, Gyan looked more than ever like her mother. And before much longer, he would be losing her, too.

At least this separation would not be final. He hoped.

Ogryvan returned the salute. He settled the hood over his head, thankful for the rain that hid the mist rising in his eyes. To drive away the sorrow, he focused upon the matter at hand. But the image of his daughter did not fade. For that, he was also thankful.

The regular patrol split from the honor guard to take up positions behind the outermost earthen embankment. Quickly, Ogryvan inspected his men to ensure that every warrior was properly concealed, javelin at the ready.

Trust was earned through worthy deeds. Not bought by a fistful of meaningless scribbling on sheepskin. If the Dalriadans were unwise enough to display naked steel during this meeting, Ogryvan the Ogre was prepared to see that none lived to tell the story.

As the honor guard drew rein below the embankment, he watched the translator, now mounted behind Per. Like the others, Dafydd was cloaked and hooded against the relentless October rain. The iron slave collar had already been removed. Dafydd was slowly stroking his neck where the collar would have been, as though still unable to believe his good fortune.

Neither cloak nor tunic hid the angry red welts tattooed by eight long years under the band.

To use this man today was a calculated risk. If the Brytons took offense at the sight of one of their own enslaved, collared or not, then so be it. The swords strapped to the saddlebows of Ogryvan and his men had not been crafted for mock combat.

Ogryvan's roan snorted and tossed his head. The chieftain stared at the spot where the trail arrowed from the forest to cross the wide, autumn-dead meadow. Moments later, he heard the thudding hoofbeats and jingling harnesses of the approaching party. As they emerged from the dark pines, the travelers lifted their heads in recognition of the end of their journey.

The Argyll honor guard cantered forward to meet the Chieftain of Clan Moray. The two bands halted a dozen paces apart and fanned out into the meadow to either side of the cart track. Twenty-four pairs of Brytoni eyes glared at the Argyll honor guard. Most of those eyes widened with obvious surprise as Ogryvan nudged his mount a few steps ahead of the rest of the Argyll line. He often had seen this reaction from men who had doubted the tales of his height.

Ogryvan recognized two Dalriadans from the Battle of Aber-Glein: Chieftain Dumarec and his son, Urien.

At Ogryvan's nod, Dafydd slid from the back of Per's bay gelding and walked into the neutral area. Ogryvan watched the Brytons closely as they studied Dafydd, who stood stoically between both bands, waiting for Ogryvan to speak.

"Hail, Dumarec, Chieftain of Clan Moray of Dalriada," intoned Ogryvan through Dafydd. "In peace I bid you welcome to the Seat of Argyll and extend the greetings of my daughter, Chieftainess Gyanhumara." He gestured toward his stepson. "This is Lord Peredur, Gyanhumara's half-brother."

"Well met, Chieftain Ogryvan, Lord Peredur," replied Dumarec. "And you, of course, remember my son." The ebony-and-gold-cloaked chieftain glanced at the powerfully built man on his right, the only warrior wearing Roman battle-gear. "Urien."

Dafydd relayed Dumarec's words, which Ogryvan answered with a curt nod.

How could he forget the leader of the Brytoni horsemen, whose demon-swift charge at the dike had sealed the defeat of the Caledonian host? Urien's tactic had stolen victory from the clans at Aber-Glein, and now he had come to steal Gyan's heart. No, not steal it. By the terms of the treaty, she practically belonged to him already. All Urien lacked was her consent.

Which would be extremely difficult to obtain in Urien's present condition.

"Lord Urien, I advise that you change clothing before meeting my daughter. She is none too fond of anything Roman."

When they heard the translation, Dumarec and Urien leaned over to exchange a few private words. At first, Urien seemed to be arguing with his father, but he soon fell silent.

Dumarec straightened. He instructed Dafydd to convey their agreement to Ogryvan's request, adding, "Shall we take cover now, Chieftain Ogryvan?" He surveyed the dripping sky. "Your weather is most inhospitable."

When Dafydd hesitated, Ogryvan prompted, "Remember, your reward is your family's, too."

With a deep breath, Dafydd rendered into Caledonian Dumarec's unritualistic comment about the weather.

Ogryvan grinned. He'd noticed the hint of humor in Dumarec's voice. Gladness at being so near to shelter was plain enough on the craggy face.

"Aye! Let us make haste, Chieftain Dumarec, to where the fire burns hot under the mutton joints and the spiced wine mulls in the hearthpot."

After hearing the Brytonic version of Ogryvan's suggestion, the Chieftain of Clan Moray nodded his assent. Dafydd climbed back onto Rukh. Settled behind Per, Dafydd gave Ogryvan a glance of pure relief.

Ogryvan returned a brief smile, mouthing the words, "Well done."

Urien sat with his father at the high table of Arbroch's feast-hall. The host and hostess had not yet arrived, and boredom was sitting down to feast upon Urien's mind.

Absently, he stroked the red-enameled bronze brooch that was the badge of his rank, catching a fingertip on the dragon's jet eye. In deference to the chieftainess, Urien had exchanged his cavalry uniform for traditional Dalriadan dress. He was glad of the woolen tunic and trews that let him be warm and dry for the first time since leaving Dunadd. Yet he refused to go without his insignia. A brooch was, after all, a brooch. And no other tribune in the army of Brydein had one quite like it. In honor of his status as heir of Clan Moray, it bore the clan's gemstone.

But with only his meat knife at hand, he felt decidedly naked.

He squelched that thought. Showing fear without cause would likely destroy his chance to win a wife.

Urien's eyes darted around the hall as he pondered Chieftainess Gyanhumara's aversion to Romans and everyone who had adopted their ways. From what he'd been told about the young woman, it would be a challenge to persuade her to set aside this emotion for his sake. His blood raced. Challenges were his meat and drink. And no challenge yet had defeated him.

Briefly, he wondered how Gyanhumara felt about living in a fortress that had been built by the Romans. Then he remembered what Dafydd had said about her ancestors, who had driven the Romans out. The fortress of Ardoca had become Arbroch in the Picti tongue, and the victors had burned down the original timber buildings to erect their own structures within the massive granite walls. Gyanhumara probably considered the former Roman fortress to be spoils of war, nothing more.

Urien glanced at his father. Dumarec seemed at ease. With Dafydd's help, he was talking to Gyanhumara's brother about Arthur's plans for the new cavalry cohort. Urien studied the broad shoulders and sinewy arms of this man, Peredur, wondering how good an opponent he would make. Perhaps a friendly swordfight might be in order. Later, after the matter of Gyanhumara—and the acquisition of her lands—was settled.

Many Dalriadans had joined a game of dice—one of the few activities, other than fighting and sex, that needed no translator. By the shouts erupting from that corner of the hall, Urien judged his clansmen to be well entertained by their Picti counterparts. The eleven warriors who were not part of the crowd around the dice game were scattered in groups of two or three about the hall. Urien noted with approval that they kept watchful eyes upon the dais. One could never be too careful when feasting under the roof of another, even in the hall of a supposed ally. Treachery never slumbered.

His survey of the vaulted chamber brought his gaze to the rows of niches encircling the hall. This was not Roman architecture. Each arched recess contained an embalmed head. Former enemies, Urien guessed. From many years of border skirmishes, before becoming the legion's ranking cavalry officer, Urien knew that the Picts took heads, though he could not fathom why. Every so often, a Pict would glance up and point at a certain niche, as though reliving a personal encounter for the benefit of his comrades.

Even if Gyanhumara brought half her clansmen to Dunadd as a personal retinue, that barbaric head-collecting custom would never be tolerated at the Seat of Moray, not if Urien had any say.

The tall doors swung inward. The boom as timber struck stone raced unchecked through the abruptly silent hall. All eyes fastened upon the man and woman on the threshold. The crowd, Argyll and Moray alike, parted respectfully to let the couple pass.

No number of meetings with the huge, dark Argyll chieftain could have prepared Urien for the equally striking appearance of Ogryvan's daughter. Gyanhumara stood taller than her father's shoulder, matching Ogryvan stride for stride with apparent ease as they marched toward the head table. Her copper hair cascaded over her shoulders and halfway down her back in carefully combed waves. The lips framing her smile were red and full. As she drew closer, Urien noticed the eyes under the long lashes were gray-green, like the sea. She bore herself with a poise that radiated confidence and power.

His heart sang.

He barely heard the introduction, so deep was his intoxication with her exquisite beauty. Then Gyanhumara thrust out her right arm. From wrist to elbow spread an elaborate blue tattoo: a pair of birds in flight. Urien froze.

"Greet her, Son." An elbow found Urien's ribs, none too gently. He shot his father a scathing glance. Dumarec paid no heed. "The warrior's way."

Urien's mind reeled. Acknowledge this woman—this barbarian woman—as an equal? Lunacy! "But—"

"Do it." Though only a rasping whisper, the command carried the full measure of Dumarec's authority.

Reluctantly, Urien obeyed. As he reached for Gyanhumara's forearm, he expected the flesh to be rough. It was not. Her skin was as smooth and supple as that of any lady he had known.

Gowns could always be fashioned to hide that bizarre design. Besides, to display bare arms beyond the bedchamber door was a scandalous breach of the rules of modesty. Not among her people, it would seem. But if everything went according to plan, she wouldn't be living with these other Picts much longer.

Her grip was surprisingly strong. With a smile, he imagined the private wrestling matches they would share. And he tried to picture what the rest of her looked like under the bright yellow gown.

At her father's side, cocooned in the hush of the deliciously fragrant feast-hall, Gyan strode to the dais where two Dalriadans stood waiting. The younger man displayed a smile that was obviously meant only for her.

"Chieftainess Gyanhumara, I am honored to present Chieftain Dumarec of Clan Moray of Dalriada." With a glance at Dumarec, Dafydd said a few words in Brytonic. Gyan favored the aging Brytoni chieftain with a stately nod.

Dafydd went on, "And his son, Urien."

Gyan eyed Urien closely. So this was the man her father wanted her to marry.

He was handsome, beyond doubt. His rich brown hair was boyishly unruly. The dark, twinkling eyes seemed to laugh all by themselves. He was a wee bit taller than she was, no more than a forefinger's length. The close-fitting black-and-gold patterned tunic and trews hinted at rippling muscles.

Yet appearance and fighting skills were not everything. Gyan's training had been clear on that point.

Aside from the political advantages of making Urien her consort, she had to be sure of his heart. An unhappy marriage-union often birthed more harm than good.

No one would ever accuse the Chieftainess of Clan Argyll of not trying to give this relationship the best possible start. She offered her hand in welcome.

Oddly, Urien did not accept the greeting at first. Instead, he stared at her extended arm. At the clan-mark. The laughter in his eyes fled, chased away by . . . revulsion?

Surely she was mistaken. Wasn't she?

Chieftain Dumarec prodded Urien to complete the gesture. There was no mistaking the power in Urien's grip over the Argyll Doves. A chill crept up her spine.

Then his face melted into a smile even more charming than his first, as though the reason for his hesitation had never existed. Maybe that was true. Maybe it lived only in her imagination.

Gyan returned his smile, though silently she wondered how she could judge his intentions without the benefit of private conversation. Ironic that speech—a simple thing she'd always taken for granted—had become a luxury that all the gold in Caledonia could not purchase.

Chapter

5

Three days whirled past in a blur of activity. Urien participated in most of Gyan's regular training sessions, seemingly glad of the exercise after so many days in the saddle.

The journey must have been hard on him indeed, Gyan mused. He now lay sprawled at her feet. The point of the sword she had knocked from his grip rested against the base of his neck. After a moment, she removed it, and he sat up.

Firmly, Urien took Gyan's hand to regain his footing. She handed him his sword. He said something that sounded like "Good bout." Whatever it was, he followed it with a wink and a grin.

This was not the first time she had disarmed him during sword practice.

"I have a strange feeling about this, Per," she murmured to her brother as Urien strode, whistling, toward the javelin field. "I think he's letting me win." She inspected her blade for dirt and blood—though she knew there was none, it was a habit Ogryvan had drummed into her—and slid it into its sheath. "You saw our match. What do you think?"

"That you're imagining things, dear sister." Per gave her hand a reassuring squeeze. "Urien fought well. But you fought better."

Her thanks were shortened by a shout sailing from the far end of the field.

"Ghee-an-huh-*mah*-rah!"

It had taken the better part of a day and a cartload of Dafydd's patience for Urien to grasp the proper pronunciation of her name. Now, at least, it was recognizable. Barely.

Javelin in hand, he was waving to attract her attention.

She waved back. Then he shouted something else that she couldn't understand. She glanced at Per, who shrugged. Urien beckoned again.

"I think he wants us to join him, Per. Ready for some javelin practice?" As with many Caledonian horse-warriors, casting a javelin from the back of a charging horse was Per's preferred method of fighting. And well did she know it.

"Always, Gyan. Always!"

They reached the field to find Urien already mounted and armed. His javelin, like the rest, was wickedly sharp.

She'd seen Urien's chestnut mount on the first day of his visit, but this didn't stop her from admiring the animal anew. Clean of limb, deep of chest, sleek of coat, taller than the Highland horses by a forearm's length, the stallion had a build that sang of speed and strength and stamina. Its eyes mirrored courage and intelligence. Truly a mount worthy of a god. With an entire troop of these horses, no wonder the Brytons had outflanked the Caledonians at Aber-Glein.

While she stroked the proudly arched neck, Urien

controlled the magnificent horse with a casual ease that bespoke countless hours in the saddle.

Per sent a stable hand after their horses, and Urien joined the wave of Argyll warriors thundering toward the hapless strawmen. At the prearranged signal, the warriors let fly their missiles. Urien's disappeared into the center of the target halfway up the shaft.

"Certainly has an arm, doesn't he?" remarked Per.

"An arm"—Gyan's admiration was undisguised—"and an eye to match." She doubted whether she would ever match Urien's skill with the javelin.

As he retrieved his weapon and cantered toward Gyan and Per, the tone of his Brytonic words carried his excitement. With a smile, she nodded her approval. Urien's face gleamed with obvious joy.

"Come on, Gyan, let's go!" Per vaulted into Rukh's saddle, seized a javelin from the nearby rack, and nudged his mount toward the line that was reforming for another charge.

Urien dismounted. He laced his fingers as though he wished to help Gyan into the saddle. She firmly shook her head. He seemed hurt by her refusal, but her smile made him brighten again. Soon she was settled on Brin's back, javelin in one hand and reins in the other. He vaulted onto his chestnut, and together they cantered over to the other riders.

Gyan preferred the sword to any other weapon. Yet there was a certain thrill to the feel of Brin's powerful muscles bunching and stretching between her thighs and the wind whistling its song in her ears. The satisfaction of hitting a target from several dozen paces away was a feeling no swordsman could ever know.

She drew back her arm to make the cast. Her eyes narrowed on the target as she judged the distance.

Urien and his stallion pounded the turf close beside her. Too close! To her horror, she realized Urien had selected her target. The effigies were spaced to let only one horse through on either side. If neither rider pulled up, they would surely collide!

Urien didn't seem to notice the danger. His mount kept straight on course. Gyan was not about to take chances. She dropped the javelin to yank the reins with both hands. Brin slid to a stop, screaming and pawing the air. Urien cast his javelin and flashed safely through the row with the other warriors.

He came around to fetch his weapon and saw Gyan dismount to pick up her javelin. Concern colored his face. He set spurs to his stallion's flanks and raced toward her, babbling incoherently. She tried to assure him that she and Brin were all right, but of course words were no good. Finally, she remounted and cantered off the field. Still chattering, Urien followed.

Though the tone of those words seemed sincere, there was something in his manner that troubled her. Something she couldn't quite decipher.

"I don't know, Cynda," said Gyan later that evening as she prepared for bed. She pulled the sleeveless leather battle-tunic over her head and dropped it onto the floor beside the leggings. Cynda offered her the white nightgown. Gyan held it to her chest, absently fingering the soft fabric. "I think he's a better swordsman. Better, even, than Per, perhaps. Yet I beat him. Per doesn't agree with me, but I think Urien lets me win."

"He can't forget that you're a woman," Cynda pointed out, "even though you yourself like to. Maybe he thinks he'll hurt you."

"Ha! After what happened on the javelin field this

afternoon?" Gyan wriggled into the gown. "Either hurting me is the least of his worries, or he's not very conscious of danger." She wasn't sure which she preferred to believe. Neither seemed very flattering.

"Probably the latter. Most young men aren't." Cynda slapped her palm with the poker before using it to revive the embers. "Maybe by letting you defeat him in sword practice, he thinks he's being polite."

"I wish he wouldn't try so hard." Gyan sat on the bed, chin to fist, while Cynda heaved more logs onto the fire.

Cynda winked. "Never mind his fighting skills, then." She straightened to face Gyan. "What do you think of him as a man?"

"As a man . . ."

Away from the field of competition, especially after their near-accident earlier that day, he seemed very possessive of her attention. As though he saw her as an object, like a favorite horse or slave or hound, to respond instantly to his call. Surely she had to be mistaken. Didn't he realize she held the higher rank?

Gyan gazed into the spluttering red-gold flames, willing them to surrender answers to questions she didn't know how to ask. "Well, he is handsome," she admitted at last. "And . . . I think he wants me."

"That much is obvious." Cynda suppressed a grin. "Question is, do you want him?"

The Chieftainess of Clan Argyll knew what her relationship with Urien would mean to her people and his. An end to the brutal hostilities that had raged for years beyond measure. Peaceful trade between the settlements. A free exchange of goods and knowledge and ideas. No more slave raids, no more destruction. No more slaughter.

Marriage to Urien did seem to be the most logical

move for the clan. But Gyan could choose anyone she wished. Was Urien the best choice for her? Did she, as Cynda had asked, want him?

Slowly tracing the dark blue lines of the stylized doves on her sword-bearing forearm, she conjured the day of the tattoo's birth. She'd received the clan-mark two summers before, upon reaching womanhood, to symbolize her status as *ard-banoigin*. This role differed from that of the chieftainess, who shared the responsibilities of leadership with the chieftain. The *ard-banoigin* controlled the destiny of the clan.

A woman might easily be one and not the other. If not for Hymar's untimely death, such would have been the case for Gyan today.

Yet, for some mysterious reason, the gods had decreed otherwise. For the first time in her life, she felt the true weight of her dual burden. She could not in good conscience put personal needs and desires ahead of the welfare of the clan.

Like a dew-spattered web, Cynda's question hung in the air between them. So fragile, the slightest puff might drench the leaves below. And like a careless hand, the wrong answer could wreak irreparable damage.

Did Gyan want this son of a Brytoni chieftain?

Passion seemed so important to the serving lasses as they prattled about their lovers. Even Hymar had chosen Ogryvan for love, not duty. And Ogryvan had returned her love a hundredfold—was still demonstrating that love by refusing to unite with the *ard-banoigin* of any other clan. A twinge of envy pinched Gyan's heart.

Inwardly, she searched for this fabled passion and found none. Perhaps she didn't want Urien in that sense. Not yet. But this scarcely mattered now.

She was chieftainess and *ard-banoigin* of the most powerful clan of the Confederacy. Not some silly maid-servant whose only hope in life was to find a man who could bring enjoyment to the marriage-bed. And she was not her mother, who had been able to afford the luxury of a love match.

What Gyan wanted most was a mate whose gift to her would be peace and prosperity for Argyll. If Urien could grant that simple wish, she would be satisfied. She hoped.

Did she want Urien? Ruthlessly, she shoved aside the doubts. She stood, shoulders back and head high, and proclaimed, "Yes."

"I must—what?" Urien's stallion jerked his chestnut head in apparent fright. Urien stroked the silvery blaze between Talarf's eyes and lowered his voice. "Are you sure, man?"

Dafydd nodded. "Yes, my Lord. Chieftain Ogryvan said—"

"This is absurd! He can't be serious." With the iron currycomb, Urien gestured at Dumarec. "Explain it to him, Father."

Dumarec's lips cracked a wry smile. "What's to explain? It's their custom."

"Their law, my Lord," said Dafydd.

"It's barbarism." Urien resumed his work on the mane.

"Who's to say they don't think the same of us, Son?"

"We are not in the habit of painting weird marks on our bodies."

"No," Dumarec said. "But I'm sure we do a few things that would raise Picti eyebrows a fair measure."

Did he hear aright? Was his father actually taking the Picts' side in this matter?

Leaning across Talarf's withers, Urien studied the two men standing beside the stall's door. The younger was, for the most part, a stranger. The other was swiftly becoming one.

"So. I am to have blue birds drawn on my arm this evening." And doves, no less, although Urien kept that to himself. The Clan Moray priests would probably object to this, since the dove was a sacred symbol to them. Then again, with that lot it was always easier to obtain forgiveness than permission.

"Lord Urien," Dafydd began, fingering the small wooden cross at his neck, "you won't be receiving the Argyll clan-mark tonight."

"What? But you just said—"

"The clan-mark comes later, Son, during the wedding ceremony, after Gyanhumara returns from Maun. Then she will be tattooed with the Boar of Moray to make your union official." Thumbs hooked in his gold-studded belt, Dumarec chuckled. "You wouldn't be so confused if you would take your ears out of your trousers once in a while."

Urien scowled at his father before turning his attention upon Dafydd. "You told me I was to be getting a tattoo at tonight's feast. Is this a lie?"

"No, my Lord. You will receive a tattoo." Though his tone was soft, the man did not flinch under Urien's glare. "A thin band around your wrist to represent your betrothal."

The heir of Clan Moray gave a grunt as he traded currycomb for brush to scrub the dried mud from Talarf's coat.

Tattoos, he grumbled to himself, though he took care not to let his mood interfere with his horse's comfort and went lightly over Talarf's tender spots. Of all the Picts' idiotic customs, this had to take the prize. Worse

even than keeping enemies' heads. Nothing in the
Brytoni arsenal of traditions could possibly compare
with this. It was one thing to marry a Pict. Now it
seemed the savages wanted to make him look like one
of them.

Dumarec said to Dafydd, "Please tell Chieftain Ogryvan that Lord Urien will be honored to comply." He
dismissed Dafydd with a word of thanks. The man
bowed to both of them and left.

"I have no other choice, then?"

Dumarec answered, "Not if you wish to fully demonstrate your—our—good faith in this alliance." His
countenance darkened.

"Arthur's alliance." Both words left a bad taste in
Urien's mouth.

"Brydein's alliance." Dumarec waved a finger. "In
case you haven't figured it out yet, Son, Moray lands
will double with the addition of Argyll's. Good farmlands, too."

"Yes, Father, I know." Another thought occurred,
and the irony made Urien grin. "The Moray power base
will double, too. Then I'll be able to challenge Arthur
for the Pendragonship—"

"You will do no such thing." Even though Dumarec
kept his voice low, the intensity of his words caused
Talarf to snort and stamp. Urien couldn't remember the
last time he'd seen his father so angry, and it took him
aback. "Your destiny, Urien map Dumarec, is to take my
place. Not Arthur's. And your destiny begins tonight,
when you present yourself to your future wife to receive
the betrothal tattoo and demonstrate your acceptance
of her people's ways, strange as they may seem."
Gripping the stall door's ledge, he leaned closer to
Urien. "Understood?"

After holding his father's gaze for a long moment,

Urien nodded, not so much out of obedience to Dumarec as in acknowledgment to himself, for the first time, that he wanted Gyanhumara more than any woman he had ever known. Only now did he feel the full impact. With any other woman, he would have merely walked away. But his passion for Gyanhumara flew far beyond the desire to control her land. He hungered for her body and soul, too. Her proud beauty drove away all thought of her barbaric origins. His loins ached.

So he would play her little game and wear the tattoos. Eventually, she would pay a price for the indignity. Squatting to reach the underside of Talarf's chest, he allowed himself a smile his father couldn't see. Collecting the toll from his wife promised to be quite a pleasure indeed.

And he vowed never to let slip his ambitions to another soul again.

Blessed by the High Priest of Clan Argyll, Gyan and Urien performed the traditional Caledonian betrothal ritual. Under the watchful eyes of both fathers, the Dalriadans, and as many of Clan Argyll as could pack into the feast-hall, another priest inscribed the woad tattoo of the braided band around the couple's left wrists.

They shared wine from a wide-mouthed, ornate pewter cup specially crafted for the occasion. To the jubilant shouts and foot stompings of the witnesses, lips met lips for the first time.

Gyan felt his mouth devouring hers, as if he wanted his teeth to leave their tattoo on her tongue. Blood thundered in her ears. Her heart hammered like the wings of a trapped dove. The wine on his breath mixed with the tang of his leather tunic and the smokiness of the feast-hall to make her stomach churn. Fighting for breath, she struggled to break away. His arms seemed to crush her tighter for an instant, then relaxed.

She took a step backward. The look he wore seemed fiercely triumphant, as though he had just won the hardest-fought contest of his life. As the glitter of his eyes dimmed, embers glowed in the aftermath of the blaze. She was certain those embers could flare to life at any moment. Without warning.

Her instincts screamed that Urien was not the right man. That it wasn't too late to cancel the betrothal, send the Dalriadans away, and choose someone else. She didn't have a definite reason. Only that somehow it felt . . . wrong.

Yet how could she retreat from this now? Based on what? A mere feeling? What if those instincts were misleading her? What if the true mother of her doubts was fear? Could she deny her people their first chance for peace with their Brytoni neighbors and still live with herself afterward?

No.

Urien's mouth softened into a smile. Gone was all trace of arrogant triumph. Perhaps she had imagined it. She fervently hoped so.

Slowly, Gyan returned his smile. His hand reached out. Blue dye on his wrist glistened in the torchlight, a vivid reminder of the bond. Wrong or not, there had to be a way to make this marriage-union work. And the way would have to begin with her.

With her instincts still blaring their warning, she surrendered her hand to him. He did not squeeze it hard, as she had half expected him to, and her inner alarms fell silent. At least for now. Together, Gyan and Urien faced the crowd, and the feast began.

Chapter
6

Though both warriors were clearly feeling the aftereffects of the betrothal feast, Urien and Per met the next morning on the practice field.

Gyan watched the friendly competition amid the dozen or so clansmen and future clansmen awake enough to brave the forenoon sun. She felt fine. Only four cups of wine had found the path to her lips last night. As she observed the faces around her, the occasional grimaces and squinting, red-rimmed eyes told her the others had not been so judicious.

Per, she noted, was not moving well. His timing seemed off. He let too many chances slip by without taking full advantage. Urien's footwork was better, but his attacks lacked the force she knew he could muster. If she were fighting, both men would have felt the point of her blade today. Without question. Since Gyan had retired from the feast early, she had no idea who had issued the challenge. She doubted whether Urien or Per could remember, either.

As the bout progressed, Gyan was the only silent observer. If anyone noticed, they kept it to themselves. Glancing around, she wondered whether others shared her belief that the contest would have been better fought later in the day. Everyone else seemed to be enjoying it, but she was ready to find something more interesting to do. Like counting rocks on the ground.

A shadow loomed beside hers. It wasn't hard to guess the owner. "Good morning, Father." Her gaze did not leave the field, where Urien was pressing an attack—such as it was. "Been up long?"

"Too long." Ogryvan snorted. "I've been discussing details with Dumarec. He plans to leave at first light tomorrow."

That commanded her attention. She tilted her face to meet his eyes and was grieved by the dark fatigue she found. Retiring for the night at a reasonable hour was a suggestion she and Cynda had been making to him for years. This time, she let it rest.

"And?"

"Urien approached him for permission to winter here." Gyan arched both eyebrows but made no comment. Silence seemed the safer course. Ogryvan continued, "Dumarec refused him."

As she again watched the action on the field, Gyan let out a breath. Her private misgivings had not taken flight with the dawn. Yet her destiny was decided. Hers, and Urien's, and the destiny of two clans. Perhaps even two nations. Nothing could stop the wheels of a wagon that size.

The best she could do to keep the doubts at bay was to maintain an air of normalcy. "They are tiring already." She didn't try to hide her disdain.

"After you left the feast, they tried to outdrink each other." Ogryvan's chuckle rumbled like distant thunder. "Don't ask me who won. I didn't stay long enough to find out."

"Well, that's good to hear, Father." She greeted this news with a thin smile. "For a change."

But his report about her brother and her betrothed spawned a generous dose of reproach. Small wonder they were moving like slugs. Men, she thought with disgust, could be such idiots.

On the field, Per was beginning to falter against Urien's advance.

"And did you and Dumarec discuss my journey to Maun?"

"Of course. He offered a ship to take you there from the Seat of Moray, Dunadd." Gyan glanced at Ogryvan, eyes narrowed. "But I thought you would prefer to ride to Caer Lugubalion with Per and the others, and take ship to Maun from there."

A burst of claps and cheers from the Argyll contingent drew Gyan's attention back to the field. Per's counterattack surged with renewed vigor as he drove Urien back across the enclosure. Gyan nodded approvingly, in response to both her father's remark and her brother's improved performance.

"Urien will meet you at Caer Lugubalion," Ogryvan went on, "and ask Arthur's leave to accompany you to Maun."

"Arthur!" Too many decisions were being made behind her back. Gyan's irritation colored her voice. "Ever since Aber-Glein, I've heard entirely too much about this Roman whelp. I will throttle the next person who speaks his name to me."

Ogryvan laughed. "What's this? I thought you were so eager to run off and fight for him."

"I was. Any action is better than none, after all." She expelled the last of her anger with a harsh sigh. "But if I'm not to fight with him, I should at least be able to meet him while I'm there."

"Indeed, lass? Why?" This was punctuated by a broad wink.

"For diplomacy, Father." She read the tease but was in no mood to rise to the bait. "Why else?"

He shrugged. "I'll have Dafydd mention it, then. I'm sure Urien will be pleased to make the arrangements."

Before she could voice a retort, Dafydd emerged from the crowd to join them and bowed. "Please forgive me, my Lord, my Lady, but did I hear—"

"Your name? Yes." With her smile, Gyan tried to convey the great admiration she held for his linguistic abilities. "We have one more task for you to perform as translator." Her smile faded as she considered what reasons might have brought Dafydd to the side of the training ring nearest where she and Ogryvan were standing. "Unless you're planning to leave us already?"

Dafydd shook his head and addressed Ogryvan, hands spread in a gesture of supplication. "Your pardon, my Lord, but I was thinking about the conversation I helped you with this morning, with Chieftain Dumarec." One hand crept up to his neck. Gyan thought he was going to rub the mark left by the slave collar, but instead his forefinger hooked around a leather thong that lay below the neckline of his tunic. Whatever charm it held appeared only as a slight bulge beneath the fabric. "If I might have my Lord's permission—and my Lady's—" Lowering the hand, he directed a nod and a shy smile toward Gyan. "I and my family would like to winter here and accompany my Lady Gyanhumara to Maun in the spring."

"I don't know, Gyan, what do you think?" Ogryvan's lips were set in a grave line, but Gyan saw the sparkle of mirth in his eyes. "Will we have enough room—not to mention supplies—for a family of freemen for the whole winter?"

As Gyan was about to reply, Dafydd said, "Katra and I have already talked it over. We'll be happy to do whatever tasks you require of us, to earn our keep."

Gyan held up both hands, palms open. "We appreciate your offer, Dafydd, but you and your family are free now. My father was only teasing. There's really no need to—"

His expression grew earnest. "Please, my Lady. We don't want to be a burden to you. We see this service as our God-given duty, regardless of the"—this time, his fingers brushed the scar on his neck—"circumstances."

Shrugging, Gyan turned to her father. "Well, I don't see why not, if this is something they want. Katra must be near to birthing her bairn by now." This was confirmed by a nod from Dafydd. "But I'm sure Cynda can think of something suitable for her to do. Mending, perhaps."

"Aye." Ogryvan studied the former slave, slowly stroking his beard. "But fetching and carrying for me hardly seems appropriate now for our master interpreter here."

A flush rose in Dafydd's cheeks. "It's all right, my Lord. I don't mind—"

"Wait, Dafydd. You may not have to." What Ogryvan said inspired an idea. Gyan put fists to hips, grinning. "That is, if you think you're up to the challenge of teaching me that tongue of yours?"

"Brytonic, Gyan? That's a splendid idea!" Ogryvan beamed first at his daughter, then at his interpreter. "What say you, Dafydd?"

The flash of Dafydd's grin was eclipsed by his deep bow. "Chieftain Ogryvan, Chieftainess Gyanhumara, it would be my greatest honor. And my pleasure."

"Good." This was the best piece of news Gyan had received this morning. Now she could scarcely wait for the day she could speak with Urien privately. Perhaps then she would find the answers she craved. "When do we start, Dafydd?"

Dafydd gave a short laugh. "As soon as I can decide how best to go about doing this. If my Lord and Lady will excuse me?"

"Of course, Dafydd, of course." Ogryvan thumped Dafydd's back. "Take all the time you need, lad."

"But before you do one more thing, Dafydd," Gyan said as he began to leave, "I want you to gather up your family's possessions in the slave quarters and speak to Cynda." She nodded toward the Clan Moray contingent across the field. "I happen to know of some fine guest chambers that will be vacant on the morrow."

"My Lady, you are most gracious." Gyan couldn't begin to measure the depth of his gratitude. Besides being in closer proximity for Dafydd to conduct her lessons, the guest quarters would be a much more comfortable place for Katra to have their bairn. She wondered if Dafydd was thinking of that as well. "How can I—we—ever repay your kindness?"

"Teach me well, Dafydd," Gyan said with as much sincerity as she could muster, "and I'll consider that payment enough."

As she watched him stride off, whistling, toward the slave quarters, groans of disappointment issued from the crowd around her. She faced the field to see Per and Urien, both still standing, their weapons sheathed. The contest, she guessed, must have ended in a draw. Per approached her, staggering and panting heavily. Urien, slowly making his way toward his clansmen, didn't appear to be in much better shape.

"Too much last night." Per looked sheepish as he wiped sweat from his forehead with the back of a hand. "Finish later. Almost had him, though."

This won shouts of encouragement from his clansmen.

Urien, it seemed, was making a similar speech to the Dalriadans, who had split to surround their future chieftain as he crossed the field toward Gyan.

He emerged from the knot of Moray warriors to join the Argyll group. Per and Urien clasped forearms, then faced Gyan. Urien's look echoed the triumph she'd seen on his face the night before. Her instincts renewed their silent tirade. Yet she managed the expected smile. Urien took the cue and folded her into a bone-crushing embrace. Like a falcon stooping to the prey.

Brytonic came easily to Gyan. She was amazed at the similarities to the ancient tongue of her people. And the words with no Caledonian equivalent were not difficult to memorize. In weeks, she and Dafydd were conversing freely in Brytonic. The other inhabitants of the Seat of Argyll grew accustomed to the sight of their chieftainess with the shorter, slighter, darker man as the pair spent hour upon hour in animated, incomprehensible conversation.

Gyan was pleased with the speed of her progress but was not satisfied with learning only the speech. As the snows deepened and the sun grew ever more reluctant to stay aloft in the sky, she began to hunger for the written word as well.

One bitterly cold afternoon found Gyan arranging hide scraps on her worktable in the antechamber beside the pile of charcoal salvaged from the ashes of the previous night's fire. Chafing her hands, she began to pace. Her wool-lined rabbit-fur cloak couldn't repel all of the breath-stealing chill.

Not for the first time, she began imagining the conversations she and Urien would share. There was so much to ask him: about his family, his battles, his education, his likes and dislikes, his desires and dreams. About his responsibilities as a Brytoni chieftain's son and the customs of his people. His opinions about marriage and children and about having a wife who could wield weapons and ride horses as well as she could.

As she mulled the questions, each spawned a dozen more. Enough to fill a lifetime!

A soft knock on the outer door nudged her thoughts. At her command, the door swung open. In the corridor stood Dafydd.

He was not late, she reminded herself. But boredom had driven her from her fireside seat. She strode to the table. "Here, Dafydd." She dumped an aromatic load of hides and cold charred wood into his arms. "Let's have our lesson in the Common. Today you will begin teaching me how to write your speech."

Gyan scooped up the remaining scraps and headed out the door before Dafydd could even acknowledge the change of plans. She smiled to hear him break into a trot to catch her.

The Common was a large, circular room at one end of the clan rulers' private living quarters. The domed stone structure had been built soon after the clan's occupation of the Roman fortress. Its arm-thick walls had no windows and only one door. In this it was akin to the buildings constructed at settlements farther north, many generations earlier, to serve as easily defended refuges during raids.

There all similarity ended. At Arbroch, this building and its granite brethren were used year-round. The Common featured a central raised firepit, vented through a tin chimney tube disappearing into the hole in the dome. The door opened onto the narrow corridor that ran the length of the wing of living quarters. The room was a popular gathering place for Gyan and her family, especially during the hottest and coldest days of the year.

Today the room was packed. Near the firepit, Ogryvan and Per were discussing the journey to Caer Lugubalion. Some of the warriors chosen to join the Brytoni ranks sat in attendance. On the far side of the room clustered Cynda and Mardha and many of the other female servants. The clack of the loom and the whir of the spinning wheels sang through the occasional lulls in the various conversations. Gyan recognized the pine-colored fabric on the loom as the cloth for her new tunic. The male servants, she guessed, were seeing to the safety of the livestock.

Nods and smiles greeted Gyan's entrance. Her armload of hides and blackened wood won a few quizzical looks. To these folk, she murmured a promise to explain later. The lure of learning was tugging too strongly.

At the firepit, the warriors made room for Gyan and Dafydd. She dropped her burden and removed cloak and boots, for the room was comfortably warm. She folded her cloak to use as a cushion on the dirt floor.

As Dafydd sat, something slipped from the neck of his tunic. A pair of crossed oak sticks dangled from a leather thong. The wood around the brass pin fastening the sticks was dark and shiny with age. The longest stick was no bigger than a finger. It seemed an odd adornment for a man. For anyone.

Pointing to his chest, Gyan gave voice, in Brytonic, to her curiosity. "What sort of charm is that, Dafydd?"

"This?" His fingers curled around the trinket. "It's not a charm, exactly." A gentle smile suffused his face. "It's called a cross. A symbol of my Lord, Jesu the Christ. In Caledonian, His name is Iesseu."

Although the word *Christ* held no special meaning, and she had never heard of this Iesseu, she guessed Dafydd was talking about a god. But two crossed sticks? When most gods chose powerful animals or the wild forces of nature itself?

"What does it mean?"

Head bowed, his eyes fluttered shut for a moment. When he opened them again, they seemed to burn with a calm intensity at odds with the Dafydd she knew—more like a lion on a leash.

"My Lady, it's a reminder of how He died."

"Died? But the gods don't die. They can't!" She felt her eyebrows lower. "Else they're not gods at all."

"Mine did." There was no shame in the admission, only quiet pride. "And conquered death to live again."

To die and return to life? Impossible! How could anyone believe such obvious nonsense?

Her smile was not unkind, and not without a hint of pity. Poor, deluded Dafydd . . . perhaps she ought to share her beliefs. Of gods who ruled the lightning and summoned the seas, whose chariots were drawn by the winds. Of goddesses whose fingers lay upon the pulse of mortal events. Deities truly worthy of worship.

But there would be plenty of time for these stories later.

"Dafydd, I think we ought to begin the lesson now." Gyan gestured at the smelly, sooty heap between them.

"As you wish, my Lady." The fire in his eyes dimmed but did not die. He tucked the cross into the neck opening of his tunic. Selecting a hide scrap measuring perhaps two handbreadths by three and a slim piece of charcoal, Dafydd bid her to do the same. He said, "True parchment is more refined. But these hides and charred wood pieces will do nicely for practice, my Lady. How did you know?"

She grinned at the approval in his tone. "Cold ash leaves a mark on your skin." She passed over one blackened lump for one that fit more comfortably in her hand. "And what are hides, after all, but animal skins?"

Caledonians left their marks in nothing less durable than stone. And even then, only for such important monuments as grave and battle markers. The memorization skills of the *seannachaidhs*, preservers of clan lore, called *bards* in Brytonic, left no reason to do otherwise. But Dafydd had taught her that Brytons and other folk who had fallen under Rome's sway used different methods.

"Excellent, my Lady. Now, the letters."

By the time for the evening meal, she could write her name in the manner of the Brytons. Her letters seemed wobbly and uncertain compared with Dafydd's skilled strokes. This, he assured her, would improve with practice. Yet the accomplishment was heady: to see her name peering back at her, disguised in another tongue. A name that, paradoxically, meant "white shadow."

Gwenhwyfar.

Chapter

7

When Dafydd arrived for Gyan's usual morning lesson, he found she had already donned her rabbit-fur cloak and fur-lined boots.

"My Lady! Surely you don't wish to have your lesson outside today—why, the snow has to be knee-deep."

She laughed lightly. "Of course not, Dafydd. Come." She could barely contain her excitement as she strode toward the door. "Before we begin, I have something to show you."

After stopping at his quarters so he could retrieve his outer gear, they stepped from the relative warmth of the building and into a world of frozen white, where children and dogs romped and adults trudged as they performed their appointed tasks. About the snow's depth, Dafydd hadn't been exaggerating. But the main courtyard had been trampled to a more navigable level, and shoveled paths led between the buildings to the other areas around the fortress.

Off to their left, near the gate, clustered most of the slaves, carrying picks, shovels, food, and water. Several priests surrounded the group, talking and gesturing. There was no mystery about what they were doing; this event occurred each year. For today was the eve of Imbolc, the great festival of winter's end, and the way to the Nemeton up in the hills overlooking Arbroch had to be cleared. Studying the activity, Gyan picked out the forms of her father and brother, standing near the priests. She wondered which of them would satisfy the Law by accompanying the workers this year. Her answer came soon enough as Ogryvan clapped Per on the shoulder, and her brother moved off with the group, at the rear of the procession beside one of the priests. Ogryvan headed toward the feast-hall and his waiting breakfast, Gyan presumed.

She felt a twinge of envy as she watched Per pass through Arbroch's gates. The four seasonal rituals were held at night. The only time she had visited the Nemeton in daylight was the day of her confirmation as *ard-banoigin,* which had occurred in midsummer almost two years past. She lifted her gaze past Arbroch's walls to the hills beyond, trying to conjure an image of how the double ring of sentinel stones would look in their snowy shroud, surrounded by whitened oaks and pines. In truth, she could have asserted her right to escort the work party, had she wished. But today more important concerns commanded her attention.

Beside her, Dafydd sighed. His gaze was also directed toward the group, now barely visible beyond the gate and shrinking quickly as they made good progress across Arbroch's vast meadows, scattering snow to either side of the path they were digging. Dafydd's expression was thoughtful. Then Gyan realized this was the first year he and his wife were not required to perform this duty.

"You wish you'd joined them?" Gyan tried to keep

the incredulity out of her tone, but some managed to slip past her control. Of all the slaves' tasks, clearing the path to the Nemeton had to be one of the most tiring and tedious.

He gave her a startled look. "My Lady, I'm sorry, I—no." Into the silence spilled the faint sound of singing, ethereal and hauntingly beautiful. The slaves, Gyan realized, had broken into song to lend rhythm to their work. It was a strangely compelling yet comforting sound. Dafydd's look grew wistful. "Well, maybe I do, a little."

She could scarcely blame him; those people were his friends, and his duties as Gyan's mentor didn't allow him much time to see them beyond perhaps once a sennight, on their day of rest. At her gesture, they began walking toward the area of the settlement reserved for craftsmen and their families. She hoped that the surprise she was planning for him and his family would lift his spirits.

"My Lady," Dafydd said as the smithy came into view beyond the craftsmen's quarters. It seemed to vibrate with industrious-sounding clanks and hisses, as well as the occasional ill-tempered word, and he pitched his voice to carry over the din. "If you don't mind, there's a small matter I'd like to speak with you about, on behalf of my people."

"Ah, yes." His mention of the other Brytons, along with the divine singing they'd just heard, reminded her of something she had been meaning to ask Dafydd for quite some time. "How do you—that is, your people—worship your god?" In response to his confused look, she went on, "We have our temple and, of course, the Nemeton." This was accompanied by a nod, tossed over her shoulder in the direction they had just come.

"The carvings on the Nemeton's standing stones—is it true, my Lady, that each one is the likeness of one of your gods?"

Gyan shook her head. It wasn't like him to evade a question, but she let it pass without comment. Perhaps the customs of his religion were just too personal to share. She resolved to be as open to him about her beliefs as she knew how. "Not a likeness, but a—" Frowning, she tried to think of the right Brytonic phrase to express the concept. None presented itself. So she reverted to Caledonian. "A familiar spirit. A symbol, if you will. Mare of Epona, Bull of Lugh, Stag of Cernunnos, Salmon of Clota . . ." She searched Dafydd's face for signs of disbelief or ridicule and found none. "You believe the Old Ones exist?"

He spread his hands in a gesture that seemed half shrug and half acquiescence. "Many Brytons hold similar beliefs to yours, and the ancient texts of my God do mention other gods." His gaze did not waver as he pointed skyward. "But they describe the Lord God Almighty as the Supreme Ruler of all. That I do believe."

This only fired her curiosity and brought her back to her original question. "You talk about your god often enough, but I've never seen you or the others actually worship him." A thought occurred, and she halted to regard her mentor. "How can you, if you have no images of this god?" She felt her brow furrow as another possibility came to mind. "Or do you have carvings or drawings that we don't know anything about?"

"No, my Lady, it's not like that." Smiling slightly, he tapped his head and his chest. "He dwells here." Dafydd stretched out his hand, palm up. "And everywhere. It doesn't matter where or when you worship Him. In fact, the workers' singing—"

"Was a form of worship?" She had suspected as much. As they resumed their walk, she mulled this bit of information. Although she had been too far away to make out its words, the song had borne a distinctly reverent quality. In her mind, she could still hear the music, rich and full, as though it were resonating within her soul. It was not an unpleasant sensation. No ritual honoring the Old Ones had ever evoked this reaction in her. "Interesting. But surely singing isn't the only thing you do?"

"It isn't." This, from a third voice, behind them.

Startled, Gyan and Dafydd stopped and turned. One of the newest priests, Vergul, was rapidly closing the distance. When he came near enough to stop, he put fists to hips, his expression grim. She wondered how Vergul could have understood her conversation with Dafydd, until she realized that they had failed to switch back to Brytonic. Inwardly, she chided herself for her stupidity.

"Chieftainess, as a spiritual leader of our people, I am duty-bound to tell you that you tread a dangerous path, inquiring about others' gods."

What went without saying was that as a spiritual leader of the clan, a priest could advocate the removal of a clan ruler if the ruler was thought to be unfit for the task. So a priest was never a good enemy to make. But occasionally they needed a reminder of exactly who was in charge.

"Last time I checked, Priest"—despite her ire, she tried to keep her tone as sweet as possible—"I was free to pursue any line of study I wished."

"Indeed." Vergul's lips twisted into a parody of a

grin. He nodded at Dafydd. "Then tell her, Master Interpreter. Tell her about the drownings."

Gyan felt her eyebrows shoot up, but she remained silent.

"A symbol only, my Lady," Dafydd explained. "A new believer is briefly immersed in water, to represent unity with the Lord Iesseu's death and rebirth." His gaze adopted a hard edge as he regarded Vergul. "The only form of death that occurs is death to the old, corrupt way of life."

But Vergul would not be put off. He jabbed a finger at Dafydd's chest. "Now, explain how you eat this Iesseu's flesh and blood."

"Another symbol?" Gyan guessed.

Discomfiture crossed Dafydd's face. "A divine mystery . . ."

"Ha. You see, Chieftainess, these . . . folk"—Vergul made the word sound like an epithet—"actually believe that when they eat bread and drink wine, they consume the flesh and blood of their god. Can you deny it?" This question was directed at Dafydd, who shook his head, gazing at the ground. Vergul glared at Gyan. "Did you enjoy your lesson today, Chieftainess?"

"Enough, Priest." It was not an answer to his question but a command. Vergul recoiled as though she had struck him. "In all these months—years, even— Dafydd has never reviled our beliefs or customs. It would be to your credit, Vergul, to grant him the same courtesy." She was gratified to see the smugness disappear from the priest's countenance. "I thank you for your concern, but as I'm sure you can see, it's unfounded." And as strange as Dafydd's beliefs seemed to Gyan, especially the ones she had just heard about, this knowledge didn't deter her from her original purpose. "Dafydd and I have some unfinished business awaiting us. Good day to you, Vergul."

The priest gave her a bow that seemed vaguely mocking. Under other circumstances, she might have tried to puzzle out its meaning, but such irritating men—whether clad in holy robes or not—were scarcely worth the trouble.

After they had gone several paces, Dafydd asked, "None of what you heard bothers you?" His tone was low and urgent, and this time he spoke in Brytonic.

She shrugged. "Why should it? Your beliefs are your beliefs."

What she didn't say was that sacrifice, human as well as animal, was not unknown to her people, although the practice was reserved for special occasions. To ensure divine aid in times of famine or drought or plague, petitions for victory in battle, and the like. But even in ancient times, the people didn't partake of the sacrificial flesh, mostly because there wasn't much left after the Sacred Flame had had its fill. Gyan wasn't at all sure what to make of the practice Dafydd had mentioned, this supposed transformation of bread and wine into divine flesh and blood. To each his own, she decided.

"My Lady, I appreciate that." Dafydd's relief was obvious. "Which brings me to that matter I mentioned earlier. Since, in honor of your sacred festival tomorrow, the Brytons will be excused from their duties for the day—and I presume I and my family are still included in this?"

"Of course, Dafydd. What is it you need?"

"A jar of good wine. Enough so that everyone who wishes to . . . partake can have a taste."

In a flash of clarity, Gyan understood. The slaves'

wine ration came from the dregs of the barrel—when it wasn't commandeered by the physicians to clean wounds. Evidently, Dafydd and the other followers of this strange god were planning a sacred celebration of their own while Clan Argyll was to be occupied with the Imbolc festivities.

What, Gyan asked herself, would it hurt to spare a bit of wine so these people could honor their god, however odd this ritual might seem? Vergul and the other priests doubtless wouldn't approve, but they had no need to find out. "Tell the steward when we return that you have my permission to take as much as you require."

As Dafydd opened his mouth to speak, Gyan raised a hand, and stopped. Beyond the smithy stood her destination: the wagoner's workshop. She felt a grin form; her surprise seemed to be ready. The wagoner himself, a mountain of a man with a balding pate and a friendly manner, was sitting atop his newest creation, inspecting the wood of the bench.

In Caledonian, Gyan greeted him.

He looked up from his work. "Ho, Chieftainess, well met! Well met, indeed. I am finished, as you can see." With that, he jumped down from the wagon and launched into a description of its features, everything from the whip holder to the rear panel that was hinged for more convenient loading and unloading.

"Well done, Master Wagoner. This will suit my purposes nicely." Gyan gave the craftsman a wink.

"And what say you, Dafydd?" he asked.

Dafydd stepped toward the rig to run his fingers over the expertly dovetailed joints and the carefully planed and sanded planking. So intent was his examination that he missed the wagoner's answering wink to Gyan. She, in turn, signaled to a stable boy who was loitering near the building. The lad nodded and ran toward the stables. Dafydd said, "A fine piece of work, sir. The finest wagon I've ever seen." He looked up at the wagoner, clearly puzzled. "But why ask me?"

"Because, Dafydd," Gyan replied, moving to stand beside him, "it's yours. For your excellent service to me these last several months, teaching me to speak and write Brytonic."

Dafydd seemed pleased for a moment, before a more somber expression descended. He shook his head. "This gift is too lavish, my Lady. I mean, it's wonderful, but I—I'm sorry, but I can't accept it."

"Nonsense, Dafydd, I insist." She turned to look at the approaching horse, being led by the stable boy. She took the halter, expressed her thanks to the lad, and dismissed him to his regular duties. Grinning at the now gaping Dafydd, she pressed the lead rope into his palm. "Besides, as good an animal as this is, you and your family still wouldn't be able to make it to Maun piled onto his back." She gave the drayhorse's neck a pat, and he seemed to lean into her touch.

"I—my Lady, I—" Again, Dafydd shook his head, slower this time, and stroked the horse's muzzle. "I don't know what to say."

"How about 'thank you'?" She felt her delight flow into her smile.

"All right, then. Thank you, my Lady." His soft chuckle enhanced the gratitude she saw in his eyes. "For everything."

On the day of Imbolc, no cloud obscured the weak sun. The priests pronounced this a good omen, for the purpose of the ceremony was to greet the spring and bolster the sun's return. Inclement weather during Imbolc was never welcome.

Custom decreed a suspension of duties for all, slave and master alike. The Brytons enjoyed their day of rest—and some ceremony of their own, as Dafydd had implied—in their quarters. The Caledonians were content to spend most of the day crammed with their kinfolk in the feast-hall.

The center of the hall had been cleared of tables and benches to make room for the Dance. Symbolic of the Nemeton, men and women formed two nested rings to whirl and clap and shout in a frenzied blur. Only the man and woman at the Dance's center, each holding a candle lit from the Sacred Flame, stood immobile.

From first light to last, the Dance did not stop. Any adult could enter the rings, and the rested replaced the wearied in steady succession. But each couple to serve a turn at the hub of the living wheel did so in preparation for marriage, to be formalized at the Nemeton during the evening ritual.

Those not dancing were drinking, eating, telling stories, arm-wrestling, singing. Often trying two or three at once. Sometimes with success, sometimes not. A few had already collapsed from the heather beer and fatigue and were carefully removed to their quarters for the safety of all.

Mishaps on feast days were ill omens to be avoided at any cost.

Gyan sank onto a bench along the wall, dashing sweat from her forehead and fighting for breath after spending her third turn in the Dance. Her dove-feathered ceremonial robe was oven-hot. She tugged at the high neckline, wishing she could yank the accursed thing off. Silently, she thanked the gods that she didn't have to wear a winged headdress, like the priests. She reached for the pewter cup.

Across the hall, her father was boisterously challeng-

ing all comers to arm-wrestling. The sleeve of his
ceremonial robe was hitched up over the elbow of his
sword arm, the twilight-gray feathers shaking and
shimmering under the force of his effort. A triumphant
laugh burst from his lips as his opponent's arm thud-
ded to the tabletop beneath his. The challenger
grinned in amicable admission of defeat, and another
stepped forward to try his luck.

It was futile, of course. At this game, Ogryvan the
Ogre never lost.

The couple now entering the center ring, the fifth
since the Dance had begun, could have been herself
and Urien. And later, in the privacy of their chambers,
the union with Clan Moray of Dalriada would have been
made complete. Relief washed over Gyan at the thought
of this temporary reprieve.

As the cool heather beer soothed her parched
throat, Gyan recalled for the hundredth time the night
of her betrothal. Urien had seemed to accept the
betrothal tattoo willingly enough. She wondered how
he would have reacted today.

Gyan gazed at the blue-robed couple standing back-
to-back with their candles at the center of the Dance, a
secret voice scoffing at her foolish fears. Marriage to
Urien would bring peace, not problems. Yet she remained unconvinced. Why, she had no idea. Perhaps
this odd reluctance truly was born of foolishness. She
tried to wash it away with another gulp of beer.

Sunset signaled the end of the Dance. The wheel
halted. An expectant hush fell over the gathering as the
feast-hall emptied.

Outside, the priests arranged the procession according to ancient custom. The High Priest and his attend-
ants formed the head. Behind the priests walked
Ogryvan, Gyan, and Per, followed by the five couples to

be wed, then the warriors, farmers, craftsmen, and servants, with their families.

The High Priest led the procession to the temple, where each adult lit a torch from the Sacred Flame. With the lighting of the final torch, the droning chant began.

A chill night wind enticed the smoke and flames into the sky as the procession snaked its way up the path to the Nemeton. The chanting swelled as the procession approached the clearing. The priests clustered around the brush-covered altar. The five couples stepped between the outer and inner stone rings, and each man faced his bride across the gap. Ogryvan, Gyan, Per, and the rest of the clan circled the outer ring in ranks that spread through the clearing like waves around a rock dropped into a still pond.

At the High Priest's hand signal, the first couple entered the Most Sacred Ground. Together they thrust their torches into the brush, and the Sacred Flame devoured the twigs. Cheers drowned the chanting as the newly married couple kissed. The High Priest intoned his blessing and delivered a prophecy, doubtless, Gyan mused, about the number and sexes of their children. The Sacred Flame danced ever higher as the four remaining couples were wed.

Upon completion of the joinings, the High Priest called for the sunderings. Weddings performed on Imbolc night could be broken the following year with no shame clinging to either person. This year, no pair stepped forward for the sundering. More cheers raced skyward.

The congregation lined up to receive personal blessings and prophecies. As Gyan watched her father cross the Most Sacred Ground to dip his torch to the Sacred Flame, she tried to guess what the High Priest's words to her would be. A year ago, he had spoken of betrothal to a foreigner. She recalled the depth of her disbelief, for there had been no alliance with the Brytons then, just seemingly unquenchable hatred.

Yet the impossible had occurred.

A gust wrestled with the flames as she approached the priests. Their faces were impassive in the wild light, as secretive as the stones. Gyan gave her torch to an attendant and knelt, head bowed, in ritual submission before the High Priest. The feathers of her robe whispered their own prophecies in the wind. Gnarled hands settled lightly upon her head.

The High Priest's voice sounded subdued and sad: "A powerful chieftain of Brydein is fated to bring you great joy and great sorrow." His voice dropped to a rasping whisper Gyan had to strain to hear. "And death."

Chapter 8

Stifling another cough lest Cynda overhear and scold her for being out of bed, Gyan braced against the window ledge. Cold seeped from the stone into her hands, but she paid it little heed. She had more important worries than mere illness, even though this bout had kept her abed for a sennight already.

Outside, the pines were staggering at the mercy of the leonine winds. There was no snow yet, though the clouds' sullen threats grew more ominous by the moment.

Another day, another year, she would have smiled at the bleak beauty of the battling pines. Like valiant warriors, their refusal to break under the ruthless attacks had always won her admiration. Not today. Today, her heart felt heavier than the leaden skies.

She turned her back on the annual skirmish and reached for the poker. The flames hissed like angry serpents as she prodded them into action. She set the poker aside, hugged arms to chest, and began to pace the bedchamber. Her frown deepened as a cough tickled her throat. Now the eighth day of her confinement, she could be free if not for this blasted cough.

She snatched the mug from the small bedside table to drown it with a swallow of Cynda's herbal tea. The warm, honeyed concoction soothed the scratchiness well enough.

Too bad it couldn't do the same for her spirits. But, she admitted to herself, this illness-imposed imprisonment was not the true cause of her melancholy.

She sat cross-legged on the floor before the hearth, chin resting on one fist and cup clenched in the other, and stared into the flames, but they failed to sear away the picture of the High Priest's face on Imbolc night. Wreathed by fitful torchlight, dire words spilling from the age-cracked lips, it was a picture she would never forget.

Every sword stroke and javelin cast was a pointed reminder that she might die at the hands of the enemy one day. She had long ago accepted that fact, so contemplation of her death didn't bother her. No greater glory could a warrior hope to win than death in honorable combat. These were the lucky ones, who joined the Otherworldly ranks of fallen comrades to fight eternal battles in the realm of the gods.

Death was inevitable. Its reminders lurked everywhere: in the lambing shed and cow byre, the sickroom, the feast-hall, the forests and meadows and streams, in the great dance of the sun and seasons. Death was the mother of life.

What disturbed Gyan was that Urien would somehow cause hers.

It had to be Urien, she reasoned. He was a Bryton. One day, he would become chieftain of a strong clan. No enemy could bring joy as well as sorrow; only a husband wielded that sort of power. Did this mean her husband would betray her? Become her enemy and strike her down in battle? Or, worse yet, would she be denied a warrior's final honor? Perhaps to die in childbed, like her mother?

Maybe the augury was wrong. No, priests' predictions were never wrong. The impossible betrothal to a foreigner had come to pass as foretold. To doubt the power of prophecy was to doubt the Old Ones themselves. Not a wise path to travel.

Hoping the herbs had the strength to clear her reeling brain, Gyan inhaled deeply of the tea's pungent aroma. It seemed to help. With the last swallow sliding down her ravaged throat, she again reflected upon her options.

She could select another consort. By Law, it was her right. But did this also grant her the right to risk starting a war with Dalriada, perhaps all Brydein, too, if the Pendragon got involved?

For the first time in clan memory, Caledonians and Brytons were learning to trust each other. Trust was the mortar to build a rock-solid alliance against the marauding Scots and Saxons. And, Gyan had to admit, her marriage to Urien was a keystone. Breaking the betrothal might destroy any chance of lasting peace between Caledonia and Brydein.

This was not a deed for which she wished to be remembered.

Another possibility presented itself. She could ask the High Priest to intercede with the gods on her behalf. For a modest fee, of course. While this didn't guarantee success, any action was better than blithely accepting the whims of fate. Yet what could she tell the High Priest to pray for? Not to escape her destiny; that was the coward's solution. Gyan would play the dice as they fell, and woe to him who falsely accused her of doing otherwise!

Besides, if the tales were true, the Old Ones usually

didn't take much interest in mortal affairs. There were stories aplenty of Nemetona blessing a favorite warrior with extra strength for an important battle, Clota influencing the selection of a clan ruler, and the like, events worthy of divine attention. Nothing as mundane as helping a woman survive a doomed marriage.

How much would the gods be willing—or able—to do for her?

More to the point, how could she admit to the High Priest that she needed his help? In all her previous dealings with him, he'd seemed kind enough. But as chieftainess, her relationship with the spiritual leader of Clan Argyll was crucial, and she suspected an admission of this nature would diminish his respect for her ability to handle the other facets of clan rule. The Law empowered the High Priest to remove any man or woman deemed unfit for leadership. Such cases were rare but not without precedent. Could this, she asked herself with trepidation, happen to her?

The lump in her stomach was the only answer she needed.

Recognizing Cynda's cheerful humming in the anteroom, Gyan rose and faced the door. In moments, Cynda bustled into the bedchamber.

"Gyan! What are you doing out of bed?" Cynda deposited the tray on the table to plant her hands on ample hips.

"I'm feeling fine now." Her voice croaked the betrayal. "Really, Cynda, if I don't see something other than this room soon, I'll go mad!" It wasn't far from the truth.

"Hmph." She viewed Gyan suspiciously. "You still sound terrible. But your color is much better, I'll grant." With a short nod, she retrieved the tray, which held a fresh mug of tea and a piece of parchment. "Tea

first," Cynda insisted as Gyan set down the empty cup
to reach for the message.

After drinking enough to satisfy her self-appointed
physician, Gyan examined the parchment. It was folded
twice, and the edges were sealed with a sea-blue
dragon.

How odd, Gyan thought. No Caledonian used this
mark. Messages between members of different clans
were always delivered orally. It had to be from a
Bryton. But who? The Pendragon's symbol was a
dragon, but the wax on his treaty was scarlet.

She smacked her palm against her thigh. "Curse this
sickness! I should have been there to greet the messenger—" This touched off a coughing fit that left her
doubled over and wheezing.

"Easy, Gyan, or it's back to bed with you." With one
arm, Cynda steadied the trembling shoulders and lifted
the mug to Gyan's lips.

The coltsfoot and honey did their work, and the
coughing subsided. Gyan broke the blue dragon to read
the message. And crumpled it into a ball and flung it at
the flames.

"Gyan, what's wrong? The message—"

"Was from the commander of the Pendragon's war-
fleet." Gyan watched in satisfaction as the parchment
blackened, ignited, and collapsed into a heap of smoking ash. "Bedwyr map Bann, of Caerglas." When Cynda
looked at her blankly, she explained, "That's where
we'll be spending one night of our journey to Caer
Lugubalion. According to this Bedwyr, not all of us will
have the benefit of shelter inside the fort."

"Now, Gyan, I'm sure he didn't intend offense."

"Indeed! Then do guests have such little honor in a
Bryton's home?" Cynda recoiled as though she'd been

slapped, but Gyan's ire burned too hotly for her to stop. "Or do they think we are no better than dogs?"

"Of course not. Think on what you're saying, Gyan. You will be marrying a Bryton. Would they treat you with anything less than the highest honor?"

"A slight to even one of my clansmen is a slight to me."

"I don't think Bedwyr meant this as a slight to anyone. Did he explain?"

"Oh, yes." Eyes closed, she visualized the Brytoni words and hunted for Caledonian substitutes. "He said that the crews of the ships haven't yet left Port Caerglas for their spring patrolling runs."

A frigid blast spewed snow into the room. Cynda scuttled to the window to refasten the leather window coverings.

"With this wretched weather, I'm not surprised. Caerglas must be too crowded to handle five hundred extra warriors and their horses and supply wagons." She wagged a finger at Gyan. "You can't blame the man for something beyond his control."

"I suppose not . . ." A glance at the flames caused another matter to clamor for attention. As Cynda turned to leave, Gyan caught her hand. "Cynda?" So far, no one knew about the prophecy. Not even Cynda, who'd been privy to all Gyan's secrets.

"Aye, my dove?"

The woman's advice had helped Gyan more times than she could count. Yet what could Cynda say this time? No words could change the one fact that was the hardest to bear: Gyan was a captive of destiny. Words might ease the torment, but comfort was not what she sought. She wanted no pity, only freedom.

No one owned the key to her prison.

Gyan swallowed thickly and cleared her throat. "I'd like some more tea." Cynda hesitated, as though attempting to read Gyan's thoughts. But this was one burden Gyan would have to shoulder alone. "Please, Cynda."

Cynda left the room. The secret remained locked within Gyan's heart.

The following morning dawned as bright and calm as its forebear had been dismal and wild. A mantle of snow was proof, despite the tradition that declared Imbolc as the first day of spring, that winter remained unbroken. But the sun's radiant promises streamed from the heavens. Like the cycle of death and birth, the advent of spring was inevitable, and just as jubilantly celebrated.

Gyan's cough was gone. Her announcement won a critical stare from Cynda, followed by a flurry of motion as she felt Gyan's forehead, cheeks, and neck.

"Bad tidings, Gyan." As Gyan began to protest, Cynda grinned. "I'm afraid I'm going to have to send you back to your duties. Can't have you lounging around here with so much to be done."

Laughing, Gyan flung a pillow at her would-be tormentor, who deftly caught it and tossed it back. Feet draped over the side of the bed, Gyan flexed her arms. "Does this mean everything? Sword practice, too?"

"Aye, sword practice, too." Cynda expelled a noisy sigh. "Mind you don't overdo, though, or you'll just end up back here again."

Gratefully, Gyan donned her battle-gear for the first time in more than a sennight. Small wonder she hadn't forgotten how. Hefting her practice sword, she was dismayed at how heavy it seemed.

"Don't worry, dear. Your full strength will return

soon." Cynda patted the doves on Gyan's arm. "Just give it time."

So this illness was determined to leave its legacy. Gyan knew only one sure remedy: weapons practice. And taking this medicine would be a pleasure. She bid Cynda a cheery farewell and left her chambers.

In the corridor, Per favored her with a warm hug, although for an instant he seemed strangely hesitant, as if he feared she might break.

"Gyan! I'm so glad to see you're feeling better." His practice sword bounced against his leather-clad thigh as they resumed their pace. "Are you well enough for a bout?"

Against Per, who always managed to win, even on her very best days? No, it would be much wiser to recover her strength against the practice posts. Per would have to wait for another day.

They reached the main entrance and stepped outside. Snow was beginning to retreat before the sun's steady advance, leaving glistening mud like the track of a monstrous worm. Already, the yard was a slushy mess from wagons and animals and people passing through. The practice fields didn't appear to be any better. Yet several pairs of warriors were engrossed in mock combat, doubtless glad not to be penned inside the feast-hall.

She was about to tell Per of her decision to practice alone when an unusual sight caught her eye.

"Well, Gyan? Are we going—"

"Shh, look."

Across the compound, a knot of slaves rethatching a building had climbed down to rest. But this was no ordinary rest period. Rather than trying to devour as much food and water as possible, the men seemed more interested in someone standing in their midst.

Finally, the slaves' overseer ordered them back to work. Four Brytons remained: Dafydd, his wife, Katra, and their two oldest children. They crossed the yard slowly, heads bowed. Their third child, the infant born a few days after Samhain, was nowhere to be seen.

Dafydd, Gyan realized as the family approached, was singing. More like chanting, actually, so low that the words were difficult to make out. But even when he drew close enough that she thought she should be able to understand him, she could not. The chant was not Brytonic, but it still evoked that same sense of the divine that Gyan had discerned in the slaves' song.

In Dafydd's arms rested a short, rough-hewn oak coffin.

Gyan gasped. She turned to her brother. "Per, do you know anything about this? When did the bairn die?" Although Dafydd and his family were well out of earshot on their way to Arbroch's main gate, Gyan didn't raise her voice above a whisper. "And why didn't anyone tell me?"

Per took her hand. "It happened three—no, four days ago. You were so ill, Cynda thought it best not to upset you."

She pulled her hand away and gazed at the mourners in tortured silence. The bairn, conceived in slavery yet born in freedom, would never know the delights of this world. Or the next. The Old Ones had no use for children in their realm.

Caledonians believed the spirits of children walked the earth. Their bodiless voices wove special music: the chuckle of the brook, the sigh of the willow, the wail of the wind. A bleak eternity indeed.

For this reason, the death of a child was beheld as a tragedy, like the late spring frost that kills the flower before it can bear fruit. A Caledonian child was never mourned quietly. And the family never mourned alone.

Not so with Dafydd's wee son.

Feeling tears well in her eyes, Gyan wiped them away. She couldn't fathom the calmness of Dafydd and his family in the face of their loss. Didn't they realize the bairn's spirit would never know rest? Or did they believe in a kinder fate, one that offered eternal peace even to children?

Could this god of Dafydd's grant such a wish? For the sake of the child and his family, Gyan hoped so.

Dafydd, Katra, Mari, and young Dafydd disappeared through the gates. Gyan watched even after they were well beyond sight. The bairn's death triggered the memory of the night of the prophecy in all its brutal detail. For the first time, Gyan appreciated just how much power the memory—and the prophecy itself—held over her. It was not a welcome feeling.

She shook her head to banish the scene. Letting a handful of mere words control her life was absurd. The High Priest didn't say when she would die. Each day, then, deserved to be lived to the fullest. Beginning now, with that swordfight Per wanted.

But before she could move, a sharp crack and a startled outcry caught her attention. She traced the sounds to the building the slaves had been rethatching. A man atop one of the ladders had evidently lost his footing when the rung he'd been standing on broke. Now that ladder lay on the ground, useless, while the man clung to the thatch and his comrades scrambled to bring another ladder to bear. Too late; he lost his grip and fell. The ground cut off his scream.

Without realizing where the command had come from, Gyan found herself sprinting, not toward the accident as Per had done, but to the infirmary. At the first physician she saw, she stopped only long enough to blurt out what had happened, then took off again. Only by the sound of an extra pair of pounding feet did she know the physician was following her. But, as Cynda had predicted, Gyan's accursed sickness spawned an overwhelming urge to cough. When she halted, hands to knees and gasping, the physician also stopped, but between coughs she waved him on. The spasm passed, and she continued at a walk as brisk as she dared.

By the time she reached the scene, her cough was back under control—but the crowd wasn't. Gyan couldn't believe the number that had gathered in such a short time, children and animals included, and they were leaning forward and writhing and wriggling and standing on tiptoe and shoving and yapping and anything else they could think of to improve the view. Even many of the priests had come to investigate. Of the physician there was no sign; presumably, the people had had sense enough to let him through. Seeing the fallen slave from Gyan's position behind the mass of bodies was impossible. But if he were still alive, he wouldn't remain that way much longer if the crowd didn't back off to give him air.

She cleared her throat and, in the best command voice she could muster, ordered everyone not directly involved to return to his or her duties. Obedience was not swift at first, but as people realized who had spoken, they began, reluctantly but respectfully, peeling away like layers from an onion. Gyan stood her ground, arms crossed and expression stern, until the only folk to remain were Ogryvan and Per, the priest Vergul, the slaves of the original work party, their

Caledonian overseer, a woman slave with three children, and, of course, the physician and his patient.

Gyan recognized the slave as Rudd, one of the most skilled of the slaves at Arbroch. Small wonder he'd been up on that ladder. He was lying on the ground, presumably where he had fallen, and very much alive. His head was thrashing, and groans escaped from between gritted teeth as he flailed both fists against the ground in obvious pain. The physician was massaging his legs, which were curiously still. More than once, he asked Rudd to try moving them, but despite the slave's exertion, nothing happened. Rudd's wife, Gweneth, knelt at his head, stroking his temples as tears coursed down her cheeks. The children, none older than ten, stood quietly behind their mother, their faces displaying a mixture of sadness, confusion, and fear.

Gyan approached her father and gave him a questioning look.

Fingers to chin and frowning, he slowly shook his head. "It's bad, lass. His back—he'll never walk again." He laid a hand on Gyan's shoulder and Per's. "Come. There's nothing more we can do here." Sorrow dominated his tone. His hands fell away as he turned to leave. Per fell into step beside him, but when Gyan didn't, Ogryvan glanced back. "Gyan?"

As with the impulse to fetch the physician, she felt a distinct urge to stay. But what more could she do? The children. The sight of the poor waifs, with their father lying in crippled agony before them, wrenched her heart. Fist in mouth and eyes wide, the youngest shrank from her to cling to her mother's tunic, but the older two didn't seem to mind when Gyan knelt to wrap an arm around each of them. Blinking away tears and afraid her voice might betray her, Gyan gazed up at

Ogryvan with a look she hoped would convey the idea that she would leave only after she had given what comfort she could. With a nod of apparent understanding, he motioned for Per to follow him to the training area.

The physician rose and ordered the construction of a litter. The movement from the work party in response to their overseer's commands seemed obscene when weighed against the fact that one of their number would never again be able to do even the simplest tasks.

"You're not giving up already?" Gyan asked the physician.

"I might be able to help his pain, but—" Sighing, he ran a hand through his graying hair. With a glance at the grieving family, he beckoned Gyan to join him. She gave the children another hug, stood, and walked to where he had moved, a few paces away from the man's feet. He whispered, "My Lady, I've seen this sort of injury before. Too many times. Different variants but all with the same result." Helplessness and frustration invaded his gaze. "The best physician alive couldn't heal an injury like this."

Though Gyan wanted to deny it, for the sake of Rudd and his family, her heart confirmed the stark truth of the physician's statement. She glanced at the stern-faced Vergul, then back at Rudd. There was no use asking for divine intervention. No Caledonian priest would pray for a Bryton. And even if the gods consented to listen to Gyan, she could pray all day and half the night to no avail. As a slave—and a Bryton, at that—Rudd was so far beneath the Old Ones' notice, he might as well have been born a sparrow.

And yet, Gyan realized with growing incredulity as she peered past the physician's shoulder, praying was exactly what Gweneth seemed to be doing. To the One God, Gyan guessed. Gweneth had shifted to cradle Rudd's head in her lap, palms pressed flat to his cheeks. Her head was bowed so far that her chin rested on her chest. Her lips were moving, but if any sound was emerging, Gyan couldn't hear it. Even the children, now kneeling around their father, had struck similar poses.

Didn't they realize the futility of their actions?

The sound of running drew Gyan's attention. Dafydd, fresh dirt caked to his hands and fresh grief marring his face, was approaching. His family—what was left of it—wasn't far behind him. Apparently, they'd just returned from burying their bairn to learn of the accident; with as many people as Gyan had had to chase from the scene, she wouldn't have been surprised if all Caledonia found out within the sennight.

But what did surprise her was to see Dafydd drop to his knees, clasp Rudd's hand without taking the time to wipe the dirt from his own, and begin to chant. Soft and reedy at first, the sound gradually swelled until his voice seemed to pulse with confidence. Katra and Gweneth blended their higher voices with his, to stunning effect. It didn't matter to Gyan that the words were unknown to her. If this divine-sounding music couldn't charm the One God into doing something for this unfortunate man, then nothing could.

Without giving any outward indication of what she was doing, Gyan silently added her own prayers for the man's recovery. To whom she was praying, she wasn't sure. The Old Ones couldn't be bothered with the plight of a foreign slave, and the One God certainly had no reason to heed her, either. But that didn't prevent her from hoping some good would come from her supplication.

A bizarre thought crossed her mind to ask Rudd to move his feet. Skepticism wrinkling her brow, Gyan glanced around. The physician was directing the placement of the completed litter, the slaves were doing his bidding, Dafydd and the women were still singing, Vergul was regarding the singers with patent disgust, and the work party's overseer was standing several paces off, looking increasingly impatient to get his men back to their roofing work. Where, Gyan wondered, had that thought come from?

But when it repeated, more insistently, she acted upon it. Two slaves stooped to move Rudd to the litter, but she ordered them to wait, knelt beside him, and gave voice to her strange mental command. Rudd winced and clenched his fists again. When no movement occurred, Gyan was disappointed for him but not surprised. Then a look slowly spread across his face—not of pain but of consummate joy.

One foot twitched, then the other.

Gweneth gasped and burst into tears. Faces and palms turned skyward, Dafydd and Katra began singing one word, over and over: "Alleluia." As the rest of the onlookers watched in stunned silence, Gyan included, Rudd pushed himself to a sitting position to embrace his wife. With her help, he gritted his teeth and proceeded, slowly and shakily, to gather his feet underneath him and stand.

The physician was the first to shed his astonishment. He poked and prodded every handspan of Rudd's back and legs. What he was looking for, Gyan had no idea. Since Rudd admitted he was still in pain, though clearly not as much as before, the physician advised him to go to the infirmary as originally planned. The overseer reluctantly agreed. With the physician supporting one arm and Gweneth the other, Rudd started his journey on uncertain feet. But at least they were moving, which was a whole lot more than Gyan had expected five minutes before.

The overseer told two men to carry the unused litter to the infirmary and ordered the rest back to work. As they cheerfully obeyed, he approached Gyan. Vergul was not far behind him. "It seems our Rudd wasn't as badly injured as we all thought, Chieftainess."

Dafydd, swiping at his eyes with the back of a hand, rose and joined them. "I believe he was. And that he was made whole again," he said in Caledonian, not so much to the overseer as to the priest, "by the power of Almighty God."

The overseer gave Dafydd a contemptuous grunt, bowed to Gyan, and returned to his duties.

Arms crossed and eyes narrowed to slits, Vergul asked, "And what do you believe, Chieftainess?"

Gyan wasn't sure, but this priest was seriously starting to irritate her. She strove to keep her tone even. "I believe that whatever the reason, Priest, we should all be thankful Rudd will be all right."

Without waiting for a reply, she turned and stalked off. Her mind was reeling with the events of the day—the death of Dafydd's bairn, the injured slave, and, behind it all like a low but persistent drumbeat, the prophecy. Soon she could think of nothing else. She decided that what she needed above all was some hearty physical exertion to clear the confusion. She strode toward the nearest practice field.

Her brother, standing at the rail while Ogryvan was sparring with another warrior, gave her a questioning glance. "Rudd?"

"Will recover. Completely."

Per's jaw dropped. "But how? He—his back—"

"Whatever happened, he's walking now." Shrugging,

she clapped hand to hilt. "I thought you wanted a match, Per."

"If you think you're ready, dear sister." His grin was pure impish delight. "Then I'm ready to give you a mud bath!"

"I hope you enjoy eating those words," she retorted with a lilt that sounded at odds with how she felt.

If Per noticed the hollowness of her challenge, he made no comment. On the training ground, their banter ceased. Combat, even for practice, was serious business. Only a fool made light of it. In battle, fools rarely lived long enough to learn from this mistake.

Like a pair of charging bucks, Gyan and Per crossed weapons with a fearsome clatter.

There had been other days when her body was slow to obey her commands but nothing like this. Reflex and instinct did little to lighten the leadlike weight of her sword. With each step, she felt as though she were wading hip-high through a river of mud. Only raw determination kept her arms and feet moving.

With grim effort, she summoned reserves for a rapid series of feints and slashes.

Everyone knew that battle-madness drove a warrior to perform feats far beyond mortal expectations. Innocent of real battle, she had no idea how the madness felt. Surely, this was close enough not to make much difference. Some remote part of her hoped this could strike the High Priest's words from her mind. Yet even as the thought formed, she knew it would be impossible. The prophecy might as well have been etched in granite.

Per retreated before her onslaught but refused to quit, although she had him on the defensive. As she tried to press the advantage, the well of her strength ran dry. In an eyeblink, their positions reversed. She struggled to defend against her brother's merciless advance.

"Enough, Per!" Point buried in the ooze at her feet, she leaned on her hilt and gasped for breath. "I concede."

An arm came to rest across her shoulders. She slumped against Per's chest.

"I say it's a draw, Gyan." Quiet pride rang from each syllable. "Illness or no, this is the best you've ever done against me."

Gyan did not feel like celebrating.

Chapter
9

Nothing compared to the first ride through the countryside after spring flung off winter's dreary cloak. The wind shed its icy claws to caress face and hair and hands with a lover's touch. Colors gleamed brighter: the crisp blue of the sky, the vivid white and yellow and purple of the crocuses, the light green of infant leaves. Cheerier temperaments seemed to thrive in the greetings of folk tilling the fields as their chieftainess flashed by.

For the sake of appearances, a smiling Gyan returned their waves. But inwardly her emotions churned like the snow-swollen stream beside which Brin now raced.

In less than a fortnight, she would depart from Arbroch. She was running out of time—and options.

Beyond the meadows, she steered Brin onto the track that would lead them into the foothills. Yet this was no pleasure ride. Today would find her where no one outside the priesthood dared to tread. Were the priests to find out, the Nemeton's altar might soon be bathed in human blood—her own.

But she had to take that risk. The alternatives were

sure to bring heartbreak and ruin to more people than she could possibly imagine. There was no turning back.

Time and again, the winding track tested the mettle of horse and rider. Budding boughs tried to bar the way. Rocks and roots seemed to appear at will around Brin's hooves, and his footing grew less sure with each stride. Still, Gyan urged him on, drawing comfort from his faithful obedience.

She almost missed the rock, hidden by a clump of holly, that was engraved with a tiny pair of Argyll Doves. The marker's placement within the evergreen thicket was no accident. Strangers were not meant to stumble upon the clan's spiritual heart.

Gyan dismounted to lead Brin off the main track, tethered him where the trees would screen him from view, and slipped through the deer-sized break in the wall of trees.

As she picked her way toward the site, she recalled the only other time she had made this journey with the sun as witness: the morning she had received the Mark of Argyll, a memory she was glad to relive. At dawn, the priests had taken her to the temple for the rite of purification. While the clan-mark was taking shape on her sword arm beneath the eternal glow of the Sacred Flame, the rest of the clan assembled at the Nemeton to witness her confirmation as *ard-banoigin.* How proud her father and brother had sounded as they raised their voices with the clan to greet her. On that day, she could have conquered the world!

She rounded the final turn in the path. Cold and forbidding, the Nemeton's granite sentinels reared before her. The memories fled. Into the void rushed a feeling of utter vulnerability.

The clearing was tomb-silent. No breeze stirred the

boughs. No bird flew overhead. No creature rustled through the brush. No insect hummed in the grass. It was as if the Old Ones had banished every mortal thing from their holy place.

Gyan approached the stones. The sound of her boots against the gravely ground crashed in her ears. Anyone within a half day's ride ought to hear it, too. But even the thought of unwanted visitors failed to halt her progress. She located the stone she sought, careful not to step inside the Sacred Ground, for to do so without the permission of a priest would spell certain death.

"E-Epona?" She pressed fingertips to the lichen-crusted stone and stroked the engraving of the prancing mare. Her affinity for Brin made her feel especially close to the patroness of equestrians.

Silence.

She cleared her throat and tried again, louder. "Epona?"

Still no response.

What was she expecting? A disembodied voice? A thunderclap?

"Maybe you and the other gods only speak to priests." Gyan drew a swift breath to summon an extra measure of courage. "But you can still listen to me, can't you?" She heard nothing, saw nothing to discourage her from continuing. "You—I guess you know I'm betrothed to this Bryton, Urien map Dumarec, in fulfillment of last year's Imbolc prophecy. But this year's—" She swallowed hard as a new thought occurred. "I chose to marry Urien because it seemed our union would be good for the clan. And his. I take this year's prophecy to mean that he will somehow cause my death. But does this mean harm will befall Clan Argyll, too?" Her throat went dry.

A breeze stirred the tops of the pines. Whether this

was a divine answer to her question, Gyan couldn't begin to guess. An image of Arbroch, defenses breached and buildings smoldering, assaulted her brain. She tried to will it away, and failed. Her own fate she could accept; the fate of her people was another matter altogether.

"Please, Epona, I—I don't know what to do." It was the hardest confession she'd ever made. The rest of the words tumbled out in fervent haste to be heard. "I need your help!"

A pair of crows blundered into the clearing. Their cackling seemed to mock her prayer. She studied the graven horse before her. Perhaps the birds were not far from the truth. After all, what was she doing? Talking to a rock. An unmoving, unthinking, uncaring hunk of granite.

Doubt twisted her heart. What if the gods were no better than these weatherworn stones? Did they care so very little about the course of mortal lives?

An idea formed. Normally, it would have been the farthest thing from her mind; two months ago, she would have been shocked speechless by the suggestion. The part of her that remained loyal to tradition blared its alarm; the plan involved a terrible risk. But her craving for answers outweighed all else.

Gyan squared her shoulders, thrust out her chin, stepped past the sentinel stones, and strode resolutely into the innermost ring.

"Epona, I am here! Here, on your Most Sacred Ground. Without a priest to intercede." Eyes squeezed shut so tightly that she felt tears begin to form, she raised face and arms skyward. "If what the priests say is true, then I am committing the greatest of blasphemies. I must be punished. Epona, hear me! Strike me now!"

If this didn't draw divine attention, nothing would. Every muscle tensed for the blow.

It never fell.

The crows flapped away, chuckling.

In dejected misery, she sank to the ground at the foot of the altar. "Epona, where are you?" Her voice was a croaking whisper. "Why don't you hear me? Now, of all times . . . when I need you most?"

A musical chant drifted on the breeze. Though she didn't recognize the words, she recognized the effect the chant had upon her. Gyan looked around, relieved to discover she was still alone. Quickly, she rose to follow the sound past the Nemeton's outer circle to the far side of the clearing.

She peered over the precipice. Not far from the base of the cliff was a place she had never visited, although she knew its purpose: the hillock where the slaves buried their dead.

The solitary singer was too far away to name by sight. But she could have identified his voice even in the dark. The last time she'd heard his prayerful singing, she had witnessed its awesome result: the healing of the injured slave. It was still a favorite topic of speculation for many, and the consensus—at least among the Caledonians—was that Rudd had faked the severity of his injury to win a reprieve from work. Though Gyan refused to engage in the debate, she knew what she had seen. Rudd's agony had been real. So had the power that had made him whole. And to invoke that power, Dafydd had prayed to the One God and the Christ. That much she had been able to discern from the jumble of foreign words.

So, Gyan reasoned, maybe this Christ, having tasted death, too, would care enough to help her face her predicament. And maybe, just maybe, the One God might consent to cancel the prophecy altogether. He had the power to do so, Gyan knew beyond a doubt.

Strengthened by her resolution, she strode from the Nemeton.

As she sighted her horse, Brin greeted her with a friendly nicker. She released the tether, mounted, and spurred him down the path.

They emerged from the pines to the distant whinny of another horse. Brin answered. Gyan nudged him into a canter to the top of the burial place, slid from his back, and turned him loose to graze. There they found the other horse hitched to a wagon amid the rippling mounds. The graves were unmarked save the crowns of new grass spring had bestowed. All except one, which bore a crudely carved stone replica of the symbol of Dafydd's god. The cross stood no taller than a forearm's length.

It was beside this marked grave that Dafydd knelt, chin to chest, hands pressed together. The chanting had stopped sometime during Gyan's ride from the Nemeton. Now his lips moved slightly but birthed no sound.

Certainly a strange way to talk to a god.

Yet this would seem to be no ordinary god. If Dafydd had spoken truly, he followed a god who died to live again. A god whose symbol was a pair of crossed sticks. Who heard prayer without speech.

Moon madness! Pity welled in her heart for Dafydd, who professed to believe this nonsense, and for herself, for thinking this god could help her. But that didn't deter her from trying to offer Dafydd comfort.

He glanced up and stood as Gyan neared.

"Forgive me, Dafydd. I didn't mean to disturb you."

He dipped his head in greeting. "I was just leaving, my Lady."

By turning toward his horse, he hid his face, but the slope of his shoulders betrayed his sorrow. She stretched out a hand. "Dafydd." He straightened under her touch, and she let her hand fall away. "Is there anything I can do?"

"Thank you, my Lady." His thin smile seemed tinted with sadness. "But no. You've already done enough for my family and me. More than enough." As he patted the chestnut's flank, she knew he was referring to her gift of the horse and wagon.

"But your child, surely he needs a proper lament—"

"Samsen is with God." He passed a hand over his eyes and took a deep breath. "If you want to do something, my Lady, help me put aside my grief by rejoicing with me to know that he will be safe and happy forever."

"Will he, Dafydd?" With a frown, she surveyed the cerulean sky. "If children lived in the Otherworld, there wouldn't be enough room for anyone else." Or so her priests had always taught. Then again, they were also quick to preach the power of the Old Ones, about which she was having serious doubts.

"God's dwelling place has many, many rooms, my Lady. More numerous than the stars. He has prepared a place for all who follow the light of His eternal lamp."

"Wee bairns, too?"

"Yes. The Lord Iesseu has issued a special invitation for them."

There was no trace of doubt in Dafydd's steady blue eyes that Gyan could discern, or madness. He was twice her age, but those eyes seemed to reflect an ageless wisdom. Her gods would not—or could not—stir a finger to alter mortals' destinies. Rudd was given back the use of his legs through the power of fervent prayer. Obviously, Dafydd's god would intervene, if necessary, even in the life of a slave. He surely ought to be able to help her.

What was she thinking? This was blasphemy! Even to consider abandoning the Old Ones . . . she wondered if moon madness had smitten her, too.

Perhaps. But she couldn't ignore what had just happened to her in the Nemeton. The Old Ones, it seemed, had already abandoned her. Her faith in them felt as empty as that stone circle. And just as cold.

Slowly, she said, "Tell me about your god."

"You're terribly quiet this morning, Gyan." Ogryvan snaked an arm across the table, past the cheese wheel and dark bread and pitcher of frothy milk, to pat her hand. "Anything wrong?"

Without looking up, she shook her head. "Just thinking, Father." First batch of the day, the bread was wonderfully warm and fragrant. She finished a thick slice and chased it with a long swallow of milk. "About my journey." A journey of sorts, but not the one now the subject of everyone else's discussions.

"Ah." Both hands on the tabletop, he pushed to his feet. "Then perhaps some sword practice will help clear your mind."

Once that might have worked for her. Not today.

As Ogryvan headed toward the door leading from the kitchens to the outer courtyard, another figure entered. The chieftain paused to accept a word of greeting from Dafydd and glanced back at his daughter. "Coming, Gyan?"

"In a while, Father." Nodding, Ogryvan left. She beckoned Dafydd to join her and switched to Brytonic. "I have some questions, Dafydd. About the One God."

"That's perfectly natural, my Lady." He cut a slab of cheese, took a bite, swallowed. "Lord willing, I shall try to answer them for you."

Nearby at the hearth, a slave was basting the boar fated to be the main attraction of the evening feast. Others were busy scouring pots, kneading dough, plucking partridges, skinning hares, slicing vegetables—all under the careful scrutiny of their Caledonian masters. The kitchens were entirely too crowded for Gyan's taste.

She motioned for Dafydd to accompany her outside. When they were well beyond the kitchens, she went on, "I understand that a god may take on different forms. Our Life-Goddess cloaks herself in the shape of Maiden, Mother, or Crone as the need arises." She locked her gaze with Dafydd's. "But not all at once. How can the One God be Father, Son, and Spirit at the same time?" Dafydd hesitated, and she plunged ahead. "How can a mortal woman be both maiden and mother? How can a man born of this woman walk the earth—sometimes the sea—as a man and be a god, too? How can the death of this one man atone for the wrongdoings of all people, even those not yet born?"

They resumed their walk past the feast-hall, along Arbroch's inner perimeter wall. Gyan's clansmen had become so accustomed to the presence of Dafydd at her side that they no longer paid him heed. She answered their waves and words with feigned cheerfulness.

Dafydd displayed a rueful smile. "Those are good questions, my Lady. Wiser men than I have pondered them through the centuries."

"What? Either the One God is all he claims to be, or he is not." She felt her eyes narrow. "And if not, then he must be a fraud."

Dafydd's intensity ignited. "He most certainly is not a fraud."

"Indeed. Then kindly explain all these impossible feats."

"God is all-powerful. He knows and sees everything." Dafydd shrugged. "A better answer than that, my Lady, I cannot give you."

All-powerful? Surely this couldn't be true. The Old Ones each possessed special skills. Only by working together could they keep the world in balance. Such a burden was too great for a single god. Wasn't it?

She gave voice to her doubts.

"My Lady, God can do anything, no matter how big. Or small."

Gyan searched his face, looking for deception and finding acceptance that seemed childlike in its simplicity. "You truly believe this, don't you?" Dafydd nodded. "If this god is so powerful, why didn't he cause us to free all our Brytoni slaves at once?"

"To be sure, He could have, if He'd willed it. No army can withstand Him. The army of Egypt drowned in the Sea of Reeds while trying to pursue the children of Israel. God caused the sea to dry up just long enough for His people to cross safely, and when the Egyptian charioteers drove onto the seabed, God sent the water back."

Egypt? Sea of Reeds? Children of Israel? Gyan had no idea what Dafydd was talking about, other than the fact that he seemed to be describing some sort of miraculous retreat. Resolving to ask him more about it later, she kept to a subject with which she was quite familiar. "Then why didn't this god do something dramatic like that to make us free all our slaves?"

"I don't know, my Lady. No man can know the mind of God." Head bowed, his voice drifted into a reverent whisper. "I only thank the blessed Lord Jesu for our release and pray that freedom for the others will be granted soon." He looked at her and smiled. "But I do know from experience that God seems to delight in working through the ordinary events just as much as the extraordinary."

Whether he knew it or not, Dafydd was raising more questions than he answered. Gyan lapsed into uneasy silence as she wrestled with her doubts.

Ahead loomed the steeply pitched roof of the open-air temple, perching atop four carved stone pillars like a giant timber falcon. Beneath its peak sat the great bronze dish that cradled the Sacred Flame. Vergul was pacing around the dish, chanting the words that would keep the Flame burning ever brighter. He acknowledged Gyan's approach with a nod and resumed his prayer.

Recalling their earlier confrontation with this priest, Gyan made sure she and Dafydd were out of sight from the temple before she stopped and faced him. "As chieftainess, I would still be expected to attend all the high rituals—Samhain, Imbolc, Beltain, Lugnasadh. Do you think the One God would mind?"

"The ancient texts tell us he is a jealous God. He commands that we worship no other—"

"But I wouldn't be worshipping the Old Ones, exactly," she protested. "Just watching the ceremonies."

"Then that would be between you and God, my Lady. I cannot speak for Him." Dafydd spread his hands. "I know my answers haven't been much help to you. But I am sure of this: anything you ask in the holy name of His Son Jesu, He will do for you." His steady gaze captured hers and would not let go. "Anything."

"But Dafydd, didn't you plead for the life of your bairn?"

At once, she regretted the remark. He jerked his head as though she'd slapped him and looked down. "I did. God knows how I—" His voice caught. When he regarded her again, determination creased his brow. "Please forgive me, my Lady. I don't mean to mislead you. Sometimes—" He sighed. "Sometimes the answer to a prayer is no. But whatever the answer, you can be sure it will be rendered according to God's perfect will. He does have our best interests at heart, despite how it may appear."

She couldn't imagine how it could be in everyone's "best interests" for a free child to sicken and die while a slave had his health restored. But for Dafydd's sake, she kept it to herself. Instead, she asked, "How can you be so sure?"

"He has given us His Word." Dafydd's lips twitched in a slight smile.

Word—honor—was a concept Gyan knew well. A warrior whose word couldn't be trusted was a warrior who died alone. And, Gyan realized, the word of a god could not be lightly dismissed.

"And all I have to do is ask?" Dafydd nodded. Gyan didn't bother to hide her disbelief. "That sounds too easy. Surely there's more to it than that. A payment? Or a task to perform?"

"The only payment God requires has already been made, in full, for all time." Her confusion must have been apparent, for he continued, "The blood of His Son."

That again. Blood sacrifice Gyan could understand. But that the blood of a single man could suffice as payment for all she still found difficult to believe, and told Dafydd so.

"That's where faith takes over, my Lady. You need only believe that God's promises are true and present your petitions to Him based on that belief." Dafydd's gaze seemed to unfocus briefly. "Please be assured that He knows what's best for us and delights in giving us what we need—though not necessarily what we want." He regarded the cloud-laced sky. "His ways are far above our ways . . . mysterious but wonderful to behold."

Mysterious and full of wonder, most certainly. Gyan got a reminder of that every time she caught a glimpse of Rudd in a work party.

Hope pulsed anew within her. What she needed more than anything was help—divine help—to face a doomed marriage and do whatever was necessary to keep that doom from spilling over onto her clan. She felt certain that the One God wouldn't deny this heart-felt request.

But what of the Old Ones and the only religion she had ever known? Her experience at the Nemeton had shown her the futility of that set of beliefs. Presuming the Old Ones even existed, if they wouldn't bestir themselves to punish her for profaning their holy ground, why should they care what she did now?

She signaled Dafydd to follow her toward Arbroch's gates. The walls would offer shelter from the curious eyes of her clansmen. Outside the settlement, they found a deserted spot out of sight from the gates, shaded by an oak branch that cascaded over the wall. Gyan seated herself in the grass and gazed up at her mentor. "I need the One God's help, Dafydd. But—" A memory intruded, and she frowned. "There's no stream here, and we have no bread or wine . . ."

"Trappings only, my Lady. Reminders. What God cares about most is what's in here." He tapped his chest.

Not unlike the Oath of Fealty ritual between warriors,

she mused, but without the sword or its accompanying mark. Just a different type of surrender. And a very different type of allegiance. "Very well. Show me what I must do."

From his angle in the temple, Vergul saw the chieftainess passing through Arbroch's gates, accompanied by Dafydd. He didn't need to hear them to know what they were discussing. Again.

He shed his vestment. Naked to the waist and caring nothing for what others might think of his behavior, he stepped over to the trunk of the oak growing near the wall. On his way up, he prayed that he might be able to gather more evidence to support his suspicion that Gyanhumara had abandoned the faith. The trunk's rough bark hid his smirk as he imagined the uproar his discovery would cause. Not to mention his certain advancement among the brethren.

Upon climbing as high as he dared, he was rewarded with the sound of voices. Whispering voices, a man's and a woman's. Close. Vergul inched forward, licking his lips, to peer over the wall. What he saw almost made him lose his grip on the bough.

Chieftainess Gyanhumara was kneeling next to the Bryton. Both heads were bowed, both sets of hands were folded as he had seen the slaves do many times. Though he could not make out their words, his heart screamed the truth.

Unlike any other crime, proving religious treason required having at least two other priests as witnesses. The Law was absolutely clear on this point. But as his mind raced to recall the locations of his brethren, Gyanhumara and the Bryton rose to leave.

Vergul pounded the branch. The rattling leaves seemed to mock his failure. A priest could be stripped of rank for even suggesting something like this without solid proof. Disappointed beyond measure, he started the downward climb.

His only option was to keep his eyes open and his mouth shut, and bide his time. The Old Ones were patient, their memories eternal. Sooner or later, the traitor would pay for abandoning them.

He retrieved his vestment, slipped it over his head, and resumed his role as guardian of the Sacred Flame. The gods in their abundant generosity would reward their faithful servant Vergul.

The only reward he desired was the honor of wielding the ceremonial dagger.

Chapter
10

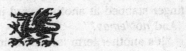

The disarray revealed by the flickering oil lamps might have startled a visitor to Gyan's workroom. Parchment covered the tabletop. Ink pots and unused goose quills fought for their share of space. Broken quills poked from between the floor rushes.

Hunched over the documents, Gyan steadily scratched her quill across the parchment. At intervals, she glanced up to reach for fresh ink or for her dagger to sharpen the quill's point. Time and again, she paused, fist to chin, while trying to puzzle out the meaning of the treaty's obscure Brytonic words. It wasn't easy.

A knock broke her concentration. She bade the person to enter, unsure whether to treat the interruption as a blessing or a curse.

The door opened to reveal Dafydd, cradling a small cloth-wrapped package. She was pleased to count his arrival as a twofold blessing.

"Here is your extra parchment, my Lady." He crossed the room to set the bundle on the table. "How is the work coming?"

"Slowly. I'm finding many words I don't know." She frowned. "Too many."

"Don't be discouraged, my Lady. Treaties are like that. Show me which ones." She pointed to the first, and Dafydd bent to squint at the page. "Ah, *engagement*. You would say 'betrothal.'"

She nodded curtly; he'd affirmed her guess. This piece of the puzzle was beginning to take shape. Her finger stabbed at another word in the same sentence. "And *nobleman?*"

"It's another term for 'chieftain.'"

The meaning of the passage crystallized. And she did not like its implications one bit. "Or 'chieftain's son'?" The words grated out between clenched jaws.

"That's right, my Lady." Dafydd seemed as quietly unperturbed as ever. "Do you need help with any other words?"

Brave man.

"Not now." Her tone teetered on the border of civility as she slapped the quill onto the tabletop and stood. "I must find my father. Have you seen him?"

"In the Common, my Lady." He stepped aside, bowing, to let her pass.

Gyan heard the shuffling of parchment behind her as she strode to the door. Evidently, Dafydd was satisfying his curiosity about the reason for her questions. Behind the fickle candle shadows flirting with the ivory page lurked the first Brytonic word he had taught her to write. But whether he discovered it or not, she didn't care.

Gyan's white-knuckled hand on the handle of the Common's door trembled with her effort to retain self-control. It was no use. With a savage shove, she burst into the room.

Ogryvan was there, as Dafydd had said, palming a whetstone across his sword. He was alone. But even if the room had been overflowing, it wouldn't have mattered.

"Father!" she howled. "Why didn't you tell me?"

"Calm yourself, Gyan." The sword whined as it disappeared into its scabbard. "Sit down. What didn't I tell you?"

She ignored the command. "The treaty! I am named—in Brytonic, but it's there in the treaty. Gwenhwyfar." The translation of her name sounded alien to her ears. "Gwenhwyfar ferch Gogfran—'daughter of Ogryvan,' in that wretchedly backward way of theirs! For all the world to see. And you never breathed a word of it. I knew marrying a Bryton would be politically sensible, Father, but this—this treaty clause! Why did you keep it from me?" Fists on hips, she shot the words at him like steel-barbed arrows. "You didn't think I needed to know?"

"No, lass." Ogryvan set the whetstone on the ledge, rose from his firepit seat, and lumbered over to his daughter to lay a hand on each shoulder. "I didn't want the knowledge to taint the process of selecting your consort."

"Indeed! I'm not a child anymore!"

"I know."

Sorrow creased his face. This was the man who had authored her life, gifted her with strength and knowledge and courage and skill. Through the years, he had given of himself selflessly and without reservation. Soon she would be going where he could not follow. And what was she doing, ungrateful wretch that she was? Trying to salve her wounded pride at his expense.

"I'm sorry, Father." She stepped into the comforting circle of his arms. "But why? Why the marriage?"

Staring at the firepit's dead ashes, she rested her cheek against his chest. "And why only me?"

"Because, Gyan, Argyll is the strongest clan of the Confederacy. Arthur needed a way to ensure that we would not attack the Brytons."

"By marrying me off to one of his allies." The ire resurfaced. "I am Chieftainess! By what right did he—"

Ogryvan cupped her face in his hands and forced her to meet his stern gaze. "By right of the strongest sword, of course." When she made no comment, he added, "Arthur recognized your right under Caledonian Law to choose your consort. He didn't have to."

As if there'd been any choice from the start. "Remind me to thank him sometime."

"Would you rather have been surrendered as hostage, like Alayna's son?"

Up sprang images of what the unfortunate lad must be going through: separated from home and family, thrust among uncaring strangers, the slender thread of his existence controlled by the whims of a single man. A Roman.

Gyan shuddered. "No. I suppose it's better for me this way. And for the clan." She pulled away from her father to lean against the lip of the firepit. "But what happens if I decide to marry someone else?"

"Having second thoughts already, Gyan?"

How could he possibly know? But a swift survey of his face revealed the tease. She drowned her surprise with a splash of feigned indifference.

"I want to know what my options are. I must marry a Brytoni chieftain or chieftain's son, then?"

Now it was her turn to bear scrutiny. As she battled to maintain a neutral expression, she prayed her hammering heart wouldn't betray her.

After what seemed like half an eon, Ogryvan nodded.

"Aye. If he isn't, he would have to be strong enough to defeat the Pendragon. Breaking the treaty would be an open declaration of war." His face crinkled with mischief. "Or you could marry the Pendragon himself."

"The Roman? Ha! Be serious, Father!" Her bonds of tension dissolved with a burst of laughter that seemed forced, shrill with relief.

If her laughter sounded odd to him, Ogryvan didn't appear to notice. Chuckling, he returned to his seat. He drew his blade, reached for the whetstone, and motioned Gyan into the other chair. This time, she was glad to comply.

"The last of the warriors from the outlying villages are due later today. What about you, Gyan? Are you ready for this journey?"

"Of course." The prospect filled her with more excitement than ever, making it easier to ward off the lingering doubts about Urien. "Don't worry, Father. Per and I have everything arranged."

"Worrying is a parent's privilege," Ogryvan retorted. "Let's go over the plans again."

She ticked off the points on her fingers. "The wagons are loaded. We don't have to take a lot of foodstuffs. The Pendragon's writ will get us whatever provisions we need along the way."

"You have the document? Somewhere safe, I hope?"

"It's in my chambers, along with my copy of the treaty, which is almost finished. I will carry both documents with me when we ride."

"And the route?"

"Couldn't be easier. South past Senaudon to the Antonine Wall, then southwest to Caerglas. We should make Caerglas by nightfall on the second day. And from there—"

"I know all that, aye. But have you sent word to the Brytoni forts you'll be passing along the way?"

"Just Senaudon and Caerglas," Gyan replied. "I sent information on the company's size in warriors, number of wagons and extra horses, and when we expect to depart. The Pendragon's scouts can track our progress from Caerglas—if they haven't sighted us before then." There was nothing forced about her mirth this time. "We'll be about as easy to miss as a blizzard on Beltain!"

Ogryvan's answering smile was brief. "You wrote the messages yourself? I thought you wanted to keep your knowledge of their tongue secret for a while."

"Tell me, Father. Who would believe that I mastered the written Brytoni language in less than half a year? Speech, perhaps. But reading and writing? No, I think my surprise is quite safe. Whoever reads the messages will surely think I had help. Now, have I forgotten anything?"

The hand upon the whetstone stilled. He squinted at the sword gleaming in his lap as though searching for the tiniest imperfections in its deadly edge. Stroking his sable beard, Ogryvan asked finally, "Who are you taking with you?"

"Personally? Well, Cynda, for one—"

"No, Gyan. It's out of the question."

"What? But Father—"

"I said no, young lady." He shoved the chair back, sword in one hand and whetstone in the other, to rise to his full height. "I will not let you rob me of the one woman who knows best the running of my household."

Not to be intimidated, Gyan also stood. It did not bother her to tilt her head to meet Ogryvan's dark glare. The very thing Cynda had predicted all those months ago was now coming to pass. She stilled the giggle that gathered in her throat.

"Not even if a suitable replacement can be found?"

His short bark of laughter seemed laced with disbelief. "You can't train someone overnight what it took Cynda years to perfect."

"It's already done. Cynda's been working with her replacement all winter." More disbelief gamboled across Ogryvan's face, chased by a mote of curiosity. Gyan took that as a signal to continue. "Mardha. You've seen her, I'm sure. The pretty raven-haired one?"

A sly smile vanquished the disbelief. "I have indeed. Gyan, you really have thought of everything, haven't you?"

The sparkle in her father's eyes told Gyan all she needed to know.

By means not divulged to the uninitiated, the High Priest of Clan Argyll had long ago set the date for the departure of the five hundred Argyll warriors and their retainers. And he had chosen well. No mist shrouded the mountains. The air was redolent with the promise of renewed life. Helmets and spearheads and shield bosses winked in the warm spring sun.

Gyan mounted Brin, grateful to be in the saddle at last. The rest of the company followed her lead. Ogryvan stepped toward her. Gyan looped the reins over her shield arm, threw her other arm around his neck, and pressed her cheek to his. As she straightened, she saw that although his face wore a proud smile, his dark eyes glistened in the early-morning light. The reason hit her like a hard slap.

Per and the other warriors would be home before the harvest, but not Gyan. She fought back the tears to return her father's smile.

Ogryvan took his place among the onlookers as Per guided Rukh to her side. In Per's right hand was the spear bearing the Argyll standard: a pair of silver turtledoves winging across a midnight-blue field. Fluttering whitely from the shaft below the clan's banner was the universally recognized symbol of peaceful intent.

The journey to Caer Lugubalion began to the encouraging shouts of the rest of the clan. Like the first dove of dawn, surging on pearly wings to embrace the sun, Gyan was eager to be away. And when she flew, she spared not a single backward glance.

The Argyll company thundered to the gaping ditch on the northern side of the Wall of Antonius. Behind the ditch stood the wall, a turf embankment twice man-height. A pile of bramble-choked rubble was all that remained of an abandoned Roman fort. Gyan noticed ribbons of smoke rising above the Antonine Wall, presumably curling from the chimneys of a nearby Brytoni village.

Dozens of field-workers appeared on top of the wall. At the sight of the Argyll host, they screamed in terror as they dropped their tools and sprinted away, amid the frantic bleating of sheep. In moments, the muted clanging of a bell flowed over the wall. The Caledonians paid little heed except to exchange hoots of laughter as they streamed past. Staying north of the wall, as planned, the line of Argyll horsemen bent southwest toward Caerglas.

It was the farthest Gyan had ever ridden from Arbroch, and she was enjoying herself immensely. She wished her father could share it with her. The hills bearing the Antonine Wall on their backs seemed wild and open compared with the intimacy of the mist-shod, pine-cloaked, snow-crowned mountains cradling the Seat of Argyll. She tried to memorize every detail of this new place, but there was little to relieve the eye of the endless stretch of undulating, heather-dotted, tree-less terrain.

As the westering sun blazed to its evening rest on their second day from Arbroch, Gyan gave the command to halt. From the ridge, she could make out the walls of Caerglas, bathed in the sun's fiery glow. And in the River Clyd beyond the garrison, like a birch stand in a winter storm, swayed the masts of the Pendragon's war-fleet.

The ships clustered along the docks were swarming with men. The bustling activity led Gyan to believe that Caerglas was indeed as crowded as the Brytoni fleet commander had claimed. She imagined how Cynda would have reacted to the sight and suppressed a grin. Riding near the end of the procession on a supply wagon deprived the woman of an opportunity to tease Gyan about how she had dealt with Bedwyr map Bann's message. Just as well.

Although the parchment remains had long since been swept away, she easily visualized the message. She selected twoscore warriors to accompany her, as the son of Bann had requested, and ordered the rest to make camp. Her band was soon met by a mounted Caerglas patrol.

The two groups approached warily. As the Argyll commander, Gyan rode alone ahead of her clansmen. Per followed closely as her second. Behind him on Rukh rode Dafydd, borrowed from his wagon to participate in Gyan's little conspiracy by serving as translator to further the fiction of her ignorance of the Brytoni tongue. The remaining warriors followed their commanders, riding four abreast.

Gyan reined Brin to a halt. The charcoal gelding tried to rear, but she held him firmly in check. Dafydd dismounted and positioned himself between the two parties.

"They're led by a woman," came the muttered comment from the rear of the Brytoni troop.

"Sure can handle a horse," was the hushed reply.

The patrol commander irritably barked the order for silence.

Gyan heard the exchange and smiled inwardly. Her plan was already beginning to bear fruit.

She took a moment to study the Brytoni patrol, searching for weaknesses and not finding many. These were not green boys who had trouble finding the bridle end of a horse, but seasoned warriors. The myriad scars had etched proof on legs, hands, arms, and faces. Though little more than half the number of Gyan's contingent, those grim faces promised a courageous effort.

As much as she craved combat, now was not the time to put that courage to the test.

The commander's cloak was scarlet, like the one worn by Urien on the day of his departure from Arbroch. Unlike Urien, whose cloak-pin was bronze, this man sported an iron dragon. His men wore metal-studded leather armor under short brown cloaks. A large blue oval shield was strapped to each rod-straight back. A double-edged Roman cavalry short sword gleamed from every belt.

The old revulsion toward Romans rose like bile in her throat. Remembering her mission, she swallowed it, straightened in the saddle, and spoke in Caledonian to the opposing commander. "I am Gyanhumara nic Hymar, Chieftainess of Clan Argyll of Caledonia. We come at the request of the Pendragon to join his army at Caer Lugubalion."

After Dafydd translated her words, the patrol commander extended a hand. "Let me see your orders."

She curbed the impulse to honor the request until Dafydd had repeated the words in her birth tongue. To support the illusion, she removed both documents from the pouch at her saddlebow and permitted Dafydd to select the correct one.

The commander scanned the document and its red dragon seal. With a curt nod, he returned it to Dafydd, who in turn gave it back to Gyan.

"Everything is in order, Chieftainess. In the name of Fleet Commander Bedwyr, welcome to Caerglas, home of the Bear Cohort and headquarters of the Fleet of Brydein." He thumped fist to chest in what appeared to be a type of salute. "I am Decurion Catullus, and I am instructed to aid you in any possible way." Dafydd translated *decurion* as "commander of tens."

When Dafydd had finished, she instructed him to reply, "Many thanks, Catullus. The rest of my clansmen have made camp for the night." She waved an arm in the general direction. "We plan to be on the road by dawn, but for now my men are spoiling for their promised supper. I would be grateful for your assistance in this matter."

"Of course, my Lady." Catullus passed the word to his second, and the horseman spurred his mount toward the garrison's gates. "Now, if you will follow me, Chieftainess, Commander Bedwyr is looking forward to meeting you before you retire for the evening."

Dafydd relayed this comment, and Gyan, struggling to remain neutral toward the prospect of meeting yet another Roman, nodded her assent. At her word,

Dafydd scrambled back onto Rukh behind Per. Escorted by the twenty-one riders of the Second *Turma* of the Bear Cohort, the Argyll company cantered to the docks on the River Clyd.

A pair of long, tall wooden buildings loomed over the river, arousing Gyan's curiosity. As she watched, crewmen rowed a listing warship toward the first building, and it disappeared inside. After a few minutes, muffled shouts and splashes and the groan of timber drifted to her ears. A score of vessels were moored at docks near the buildings. Half again as many ships rested on supports along the riverbank in various stages of readiness. Stacks of smooth oak planks and stout pine posts squatted among the ships, beside mountains of treenails, rope coils, and piles of thinly worked sheets of deep blue leather. Activity dwindled as the shipwrights collected their tools and migrated toward Caerglas and, presumably, their evening meal.

Catullus dismounted and beckoned to Gyan. With Dafydd at her side, she followed the patrol commander to a beached vessel, where a man of medium height and build was inspecting the hull while a trio of shipwrights looked on in silence. His straight brown hair was pulled back and bound with a sky-blue leather thong at the nape of his neck. Unlike the cavalry patrol, to Gyan's surprise there was nothing obviously Roman about this man. He might have been another of the workmen, to judge by his simple gray linen tunic and trews. He ran slow, sure hands over the patch, where new oak paled beside the salt-soaked planking. Frequently, his fingers paused to test the fit of treenails along the seam of the repair.

Catullus waited until the inspection was finished before stepping forward to make the introduction.

The fleet commander turned from the warship and

beheld Gyan and her clansmen. The smile that lit the darkly tanned face was deep, and genuine, and contagious. After wiping wood dust on a trouser leg, Bedwyr map Bann offered his hand to her in greeting. Gyan was delighted to accept.

She instantly liked this Brytoni shipbuilder and sailor, with his open, honest face and easy manner. Inwardly, she warred with the temptation to betray her knowledge of his tongue, to learn more about him and his fleet without the pretense of having to direct her questions through Dafydd.

Her desire to surprise Urien won, barely.

Yet, despite the linguistically awkward conversation that followed, Gyan was glad for this brief respite in her horseback journey and the rare opportunity it afforded to meet one of the Pendragon's highest-ranking, and obviously non-Roman, officers. Judging by the enthusiasm of Bedwyr's replies, even to her most mundane questions about the size and duties of the fleet, it seemed he was enjoying the exchange as much as she.

Dafydd bid farewell on Gyan's behalf. As she and her party followed Catullus to the Caerglas guest quarters, Gyan found herself hoping for the chance one day soon to renew her acquaintance with Fleet Commander Bedwyr, the first Bryton she truly felt pleased to consider an ally.

The Roman road slicing through the Lowlands to connect Caerglas and Caer Lugubalion with points farther south was well trodden but in good repair, and Gyan's troop made excellent progress. Early in the afternoon on the fourth day from Caerglas, while the main column was walking their mounts, the Argyll scouting party returned at a hard gallop. Gyan halted the column to hear the scouts' report.

"Chieftainess, a mounted Brytoni unit approaches, just over the next line of hills." This from the scout leader, a burly man named Rhys, one of the clan's most revered warriors. He twisted in the saddle to point the way. "Fivescore, my Lady. Their leader is a man of your"—though his lips stayed set in a solemn line, Rhys winked—"acquaintance."

Urien map Dumarec. Her stomach knotted.

At Gyan's command, the warriors mounted and started forward. No sense in postponing the inevitable, she told herself. Silently, she called upon the One God to grant her the strength and wisdom to face the man who would one day become her husband. And her death.

The gray cloud smeared against the tree-darkened horizon marked the presence of the Brytons. Soon the thunder of four hundred iron-shod hooves hammering the paving stones rumbled across the plain. As the distance narrowed, the front ranks of the Argyll company watched a lone rider separate from the Brytoni unit and spur his mount into a gallop. The knot in Gyan's stomach tightened.

Like raindrops driven by a gale, questions battered her brain. Questions not only of Urien but also of herself. Still chief among them was whether this betrothal was the right thing to do.

It had to be. By the Pendragon's treaty, she was honor-bound to marry a Brytoni lord. Argyll and Moray were neighbors. No other Brytoni lands touched hers. Prophecy or no, Urien was the only logical choice.

Wasn't he?

With the questions whirled stinging doubts. Preventing the emotional storm from exploding across her face took every ounce of will.

Per was speaking to her, she realized with a start. She tore her gaze from the approaching figure of Urien and turned in the saddle to regard her brother. "Forgive me, Per. I wasn't paying attention."

"That much, dear sister"—an entire war-host could have ridden through his grin—"is obvious. I said, aren't you going to greet Urien?"

"Greet him? But—" Then it occurred to her what Per meant. As her lips rounded into an *O*, he chuckled.

"I can manage the column, Gyan. You go on ahead." For just the two of them, he added, "I think you need to."

He was absolutely right. A few moments alone with Urien might make a world of difference. Go on ahead? Per made it sound so easy. What was holding her back?

A warrior's worst enemy. Fear.

There was only one remedy.

She kicked Brin's flanks. Startled yet more than willing, he leaped to obey. In minutes, she was close enough to read Urien's face. Joy bubbled in the depths of his laughing brown eyes. No deceit or death lurked there. Only simple love.

Surely the High Priest had been wrong!

They pulled their mounts to a halt. Urien jumped to the ground, strode to Gyan, snatched her hand, and tugged. She wobbled in the saddle, caught herself, and dismounted in a more orderly fashion. Laughing, they embraced.

She was smitten by the urge to show off her newfound knowledge of his native language. But before she could utter a word, his mouth descended upon hers—though not like the last time. Then she had felt like a caged creature, struggling for freedom. No trace of that sensation lingered now. Briefly, she wondered why but became too busy enjoying herself to pay heed to her more skeptical self. His kiss ignited fires she never knew she had. If this was the passion the servant lasses were forever babbling about, perhaps it wasn't such a bad thing after all.

Talking could wait until later. Much later.

Their lips had not parted when the first members of both bands arrived.

Riding at Urien's side, Gyan observed that Hadrian's Wall was nothing at all like its northern counterpart. A determined war-host could overrun the Antonine Wall with little trouble, since enough of the ditch could be filled overnight to get horses and wagons across.

Not so with the southern Wall of Hadrian.

The ditch on the north side of this wall was deeper than the Antonine and twice as wide across the top. Near Caer Lugubalion, Hadrian's Wall was an earthen mound as tall as three men. Unlike the Antonine Wall, Hadrian's Wall was crowned with a parapet of dressed granite blocks. Here Roman-garbed Brytoni soldiers patrolled on foot between the gate towers that controlled access at various points. Gyan saw so many of those despised uniforms that she was actually beginning to get accustomed to the sight.

The afternoon was flying toward evening as Urien and his men led the warriors of Clan Argyll to the massive, iron-bound timber gates closest to one of the few remaining operational Roman forts, Camboglanna. From the slotted window in the gate tower, the guardsman called out the sign. Urien responded with the countersign. Gyan did not recognize the words, although they sounded a wee bit like Dafydd's chants. Another question to ask Urien when the chance arose.

The gates swung open to admit both companies. On the road paralleling the south side of the wall, the combined force turned west toward nearby Caer Lugubalion.

Built on the southern bank of the River Eden at the junction of seven Roman roads, the port of Caer Lugubalion presented an impressive sight. Its gleaming stone walls soared even higher than Hadrian's did. Watchtowers flanked each gate and appeared at regular intervals between. A dense forest guarded the approach to the western and southern walls, but not close enough to conceal a sneak attack. Assault from the east would be extremely difficult, Gyan realized, because of the rugged terrain. Grudgingly, she conceded that the man who had chosen this site for his headquarters had made a wise decision indeed.

At the northern gate, Urien again exchanged sign for countersign with the sentry. Led by the Brytons, the Argyll warriors nudged their mounts inside the fortress. Urien halted his troop in front of an equestrian training pen. After a word with his second, he sent the others ahead and beckoned the Argyll warriors to follow. But he motioned Gyan to stay.

With a silent nod of understanding—for she had yet to find the proper moment to boast her prowess with the Brytoni tongue—Gyan signaled the equivalent Caledonian command. As the column started forward, she called Per over. Side-by-side, they followed the line of Urien's gaze.

In the center of the ring, a scarlet-mantled rider spurred his mount through a series of complicated combat maneuvers. As the white stallion curvetted, sidestepped, reared, and plunged, the man slashed at imaginary foes. The sword, no blunted practice weapon, glinted bright and deadly in the sun's last rays. From the pommel flashed a ruby the size of a child's fist. Surprisingly, the scabbard strapped to the saddlebow was plain leather. The way the warrior and stallion seemed to flow together into a single being was magnificent, as though they spoke not leg to flank but mind to mind.

Gyan watched in silence, oblivious to the clamor behind her. Brin pawed the ground and tugged at the bit in his eagerness to show off. She steadied him with a firm hand. And she tried to keep a tight rein on the admiration and awe threatening to dominate her expression.

She felt her mouth curve into a faint smile as she realized she had better command of her horse.

The man reined his charger to a halt, sheathed the sword, and dismounted. He surveyed the line of Caledonian warriors parading past the enclosure before acknowledging Urien's salute. His eyes rested briefly, but intently, upon Gyan.

It was a look she knew she would never forget.

He called to the waiting stable boy to take the foam-flecked mount and watched for a moment as the unlikely pair—one whistling and the other snorting—slowly trod the perimeter of the ring. Tucking leather riding gloves into his belt, the man strode toward Urien, Gyan, and Per.

Gyan sent her brother to summon Dafydd from his wagon, which had not yet reached the training ring. Following Urien's example, she dismounted to meet the approaching warrior. Instinct warned her this could be only one man. The victor of Aber-Glein and author of the treaty that had changed her life.

Arthur the Pendragon.

Chapter

11

By his wiry slimness and lack of beard, Gyan marked the Pendragon as a young man. Older than herself, perhaps, but certainly younger than Urien. Yet his youth was not the last of his surprises. In height, he topped her by half a head. Blond locks, darkened with strands of red, escaped from under the bronze helmet. Vivid blue eyes regarded her beneath thick golden brows. And if the power radiating from him had been touchable, it surely would have burned her hand.

Through Dafydd, Urien said, "Lord Pendragon, I present my betrothed, Chieftainess Gyanhumara of Clan Argyll." His tone throbbed with exultation. "Gyanhumara, this is Pendragon Arturus Aurelius Vetarus, *Dux Britanniarum.*"

Dafydd rendered the Pendragon's second title into Caledonian as "Duke of Brydein."

Gyan clasped the Pendragon's forearm in warrior fashion. There was no hesitation as his hand curled around the Argyll Doves.

She relaxed her hand and drew back, ignoring the compelling desire to rub her arm. But there was no escaping the eyes that plumbed the depths of her soul.

This man, she realized, would never tolerate information to be withheld from him.

In perfect Brytonic, with an accent hinting of the mist-bound lochs and spear-sharp mountains of her birthplace, she asked, "Well, Lord Pendragon, would you care to examine my feet now? Or would you rather see my teeth?"

Gyan flashed a dazzling smile. She thought Urien might faint.

The Pendragon threw back his head and roared with laughter. Heartily, he clapped his subordinate on the back. Urien shook his head in an apparent fight to dispel his shock and embarrassment. "That's a fine, spirited mare you've got here, Tribune Urien. You sure you can handle her?"

"Oh, yes, my Lord." The glance Urien shot Gyan was savage, like a wild boar ready to charge. "She just needs to learn who the master is."

Gyan's eyebrows climbed her forehead in surprise. Master, indeed! "I already know that, Urien."

She turned from the heir of Clan Moray to watch the stable boy leading the stallion. "That's a magnificent war-horse, Lord Pendragon." The prospect of just touching such a fine animal sent shivers of delight down her spine. "May I ride him?"

As the Pendragon started to speak, Urien broke in, "Surely not, my Lord. Geldings and mares are fit mounts for a lady. But a stallion is a man's horse."

"We shall see." The Pendragon killed the argument with a sharp glance. To Gyan, he continued, "Certainly, you may ride him, Chieftainess. His name is Macsen."

Gyan nodded her thanks. Murmuring the stallion's name, she reached for the creamy nose. Ears back and nostrils flared, he tried to jerk away, only to be checked by the stable boy. Persistence with her greeting paid off, and he yielded to her touch. Slowly, she worked her way around to his side, tracing gentle fingertips over the sleek muscles.

She withdrew her hand and vaulted into the saddle. With the reins in one hand, she drew her sword and nudged Macsen's flanks. He needed little encouragement.

If sitting astride Brin made her feel taller, on Macsen she was on top of the world! As she and the stallion flew around the ring, she felt as if she could rip open the sky itself. She loosed a peal of laughter for sheer joy.

But such pleasures, unfortunately, must end. Still smiling, Gyan sheathed her sword and reined Macsen to a halt in front of the men. She patted the proud neck and was rewarded with a pleased-sounding snort.

The wagon carrying Gyan's personal effects, guarded by Cynda and a pair of menservants, had reached the ring. Cynda seemed to be bursting with pride. If Per's grin had been any wider, his face would have split in two. Though his mouth didn't show it, the Pendragon's admiration shone from his eyes.

Urien displayed nothing but disapproval.

She cocked a glance at her betrothed, wondering how he could fail to be moved by her performance. He did not see her silent question. At that moment, his attention belonged to his second, who had ridden back to the ring.

"Tribune Urien, I'm having trouble making the Argyll men understand where to stow their gear."

"It can't be that difficult, Accolon," Urien growled at the soldier.

"Perhaps I can help." Gyan dismounted and handed Macsen's reins to the stable boy.

"No." Breaking into an indulgent smile, Urien reached for her hand. "You get some rest, my dear. I'm sure you must be tired after so long in the saddle." He gave the hand a pat and released it. "I'll just take Dafydd with me, and we'll have this little problem set to rights in no time."

Rest? She was a warrior! Not a child's doll to crumble in a careless fist!

But before she could voice the thought, the Pendragon spoke. "See that you do, Tribune. I will not tolerate chaos in my fort."

Urien saluted—a bit sullenly, Gyan thought—and remounted. After barking a command to Accolon to bring Dafydd, he kicked his horse into a trot without waiting for the other two.

Gyan tried to decipher Urien's reactions, while Accolon helped Dafydd mount up behind him, and the men rode off. Urien appeared reluctant to accept the Pendragon's authority. But why?

"May I escort you to the *mansio,* Chieftainess?"

She wrenched her gaze from the road and Urien's shrinking form to find the Pendragon's attention directed squarely upon her. Though the sternness he had shown Urien seemed to be gone, his eyes had not lost their intensity. Her heart gave an odd flutter as she fought to maintain composure.

"The—dignitaries' inn?" Grateful for the chance to retreat from those piercing eyes, she glanced up the thoroughfare. The last of the Argyll wagons were pulling away. From what she could see, Caer Lugubalion was laid out much like Caerglas. She pointed at a building across the road and a fair distance from her position. The building was large by any standard but dwarfed by its neighbor. "Isn't that it over there?"

"Next to the *praetorium.*" In response to her puzzled look, he amended, "The garrison commander's quarters. Yes."

She switched to Caledonian to address her brother. "Per, you'd better go with Urien and get settled into your new quarters." With a brief smile, she laid a hand on his forearm. "Don't worry, I'll see you again before I sail."

"And if you don't, Gyan, I'll have your head!"

"My head, indeed!" She playfully slapped Rukh's rump. "Go on, before Urien leaves you behind and you get into trouble with your"—she slid a glance at the Pendragon—"new commander."

Urien, having already caught the lead riders of the Argyll contingent, had stopped the procession near the *mansio* and was apparently using Dafydd's services to carry out the Pendragon's orders. Per kicked Rukh into a canter. Vaulting onto Brin, Gyan realized she had forgotten to make arrangements to dine with Urien later that evening. With a word to the wagoneer to drive on to the *mansio,* she spurred her mount past the rest of the wagons in pursuit of the other men.

The Pendragon, astride his stallion, joined her.

"Really, Lord Pendragon, you don't have to trouble yourself." Straight and tall in the saddle, he looked more the Roman conqueror than ever. Her inborn aversion to Romans resurfaced. Civility swung on a slender thread. "I can find my way."

"No trouble, Chieftainess. My business takes me in your direction." Again, she was smitten by that soul-searching gaze. "You handle horses very well."

She wondered what sort of hidden power this man wielded to make her feel so uneasy. No one had ever done this to her before. And it was most disturbing. To hide her discomfiture, she raised a shield of words. "Ha. For a woman, you mean."

"For anyone. Not many can boast of being able to stay astride this brute." He stroked the stallion's neck. The mane shimmered like liquid silver as Macsen tossed his head. "Chieftainess Gyanhumara, your demonstration was quite impressive." The Pendragon's smile enhanced the sincerity of his statement.

Gyan meant to return his compliment. She thought his exhibition was far more impressive. But her verbal shield was beginning to buckle. All she could manage was a modest word of thanks and a slim smile, which vanished as she riveted her gaze to the road. What in the name of the One God was coming over her? This man was Roman, a son of her people's deadliest enemies.

Yet here was a Roman she might learn to like. Could this be possible?

So it would seem. But it was scarcely appropriate to reveal that emotion, either. Perhaps silence would serve where words had failed. She retreated behind the invisible barrier. Mercifully, the Pendragon made no further attempt to draw her out.

They were close behind the others when Urien leaned over to whisper something to Accolon. Both men burst into laughter.

"Babies," Urien chortled. "She won't have time for swords and horses once the babies start coming along."

Jabbing Brin's flanks, Gyan raced for Urien's side. Her searing glare withered his smile. "If you think you can tie me down with children, Urien of Dalriada," she snapped, "you are sadly mistaken!"

Arthur watched the chieftainess wheel her black gelding around with expert grace and fly toward the *mansio*. Her fleeting glance announced that she needed to be alone. When Urien turned to follow her, Arthur drove Macsen into his path.

"See to the quartering of the Caledonians first, Tribune." He knew there could be no mistaking the authority in his tone. Or the disgust.

Urien's eyes narrowed in defiance. But to his credit, he did not have to be told twice. Urien gave his horse a savage kick to send it leaping toward the barracks. Centurion Accolon accompanied him.

Gyanhumara's brother also tried to follow her. Arthur could hardly blame the man. Had it been Arthur's younger sister, he would have felt the same way. But a breach of discipline was not to be tolerated for any reason. He directed his stallion to bar the way.

The Caledonian regarded him with upraised eyebrows. Arthur signaled Peredur to follow Urien. Rebellion clouded across Peredur's face, but he did not disobey.

Sparing a glance for the archway where Gyanhumara had disappeared into the courtyard of the *mansio,* Arthur felt his chest tighten, as though his heart were trying to break bonds that had somehow grown too small. It was a strange sensation, quite unlike that which any other woman had evoked within him.

And not at all unpleasant.

He tried to destroy the feeling with a shake of the head. To covet the woman promised to one of his strongest allies was sheer lunacy. Yet the desire refused to die.

To fight this unseen foe, he needed advice. If any man could help him now, his cousin could. Arthur urged Macsen toward the *praetorium.*

Merlinus Dubricius Ambrosius, Bishop and Garrison Commander of Caer Lugubalion, stood in the council hall of the *praetorium.* The tall window offered an excellent view of the street two stories below. Arthur, Urien, the Caledonian chieftainess, and her party appeared no bigger than puppets. But this was no children's show. The tense faces and harsh movements belied that notion.

With his fist, he thumped the thick-paned glass. An outrageously expensive luxury, invaluable for sealing out winter's chill, it also blocked most sounds. An accursed nuisance at a time like this. Yet Merlin did not need to hear the words to marry a theory to his observations.

Chieftainess Gyanhumara, speaking in anger to her betrothed. Arthur guarding her escape, even against her clansman. Urien and the Argyll warrior both treading the dangerous line of insubordination.

An awful foreboding gripped Merlin's gut.

The scene ended, and the players went their separate ways without further incident. But the foreboding did not go away.

One sound that rendered the glass powerless was the bell of nearby St. John's. Merlin withdrew from the window to obey the bell's summons to vespers meditations. Upon leaving the council hall, he descended the wide, black-veined marble steps and headed toward his private study.

He never made it.

Arthur was standing in the atrium with Centurion Marcus, his scarlet-crested helmet nestled under one arm. Slapping gloves to palm, the Pendragon ordered his chief aide to check on the progress of the Argyll contingent. With a smart salute, Marcus left the building. Glancing up the staircase, Arthur met Merlin's gaze. Beneath that cool control lay smoldering ire. Unless Merlin missed his guess—which did not happen often—Arthur would be wanting to talk.

"In my workroom, Merlin, if you have a moment."

Vespers prayers could wait.

Most men did not own courage enough to look beyond the azure fire of Arthur's glare. The years of their close association, first as priest and tutor and later as military adviser and friend, had gifted Merlin with this ability. Even so, it was never easy to read his young cousin's moods.

Merlin ordered a passing servant to fetch a pitcher of *uisge* as he fell into step beside Arthur. A nagging voice told him he was going to need all the help he could get, however improbable the source.

They entered the antechamber. Arthur dropped gloves and helmet on the table, strode through the inner doorway, and started stalking the floor of his private workroom like a hound on the scent. Merlin dragged a chair over to a wall, well out of the way. The servant arrived with the *uisge*, filled both cups, set down the pitcher, and left with a bow.

Without prompting, Arthur's tale of the afternoon's events unfolded.

"Sit down, Arthur, before you wear out the tiles. Have you any idea how expensive replacements are these days?" He spoke in Latin, a habit that had lingered even after his time as Arthur's tutor had passed.

Merlin was the only man Arthur would tolerate that tone from—in any language—and both knew it. But he ignored Merlin's injunction. Finally, Merlin closed his eyes to the distraction of Arthur's pacing.

"And then she said, not missing a beat, 'But I already know that, Urien.' There was no doubt what she meant." The sound of footsteps stopped. Merlin opened his eyes to find Arthur's gaze upon him. "I honestly thought he was going to throttle her. But before he could do anything, she asked to ride Macsen. She had him behaving like a kitten in no time. Her clansmen loved it. God, what a woman!"

Cradling the small pewter cup, Merlin pondered the amber depths of his distilled barley *uisge*. "Urien will have his hands full." He took a sip. The potent liquor sketched a fiery trail all the way down.

Arthur shoved aside an unrolled scroll and some loose parchment to make room for his drink on the large worktable. He abandoned it beside the quills and inkwell, untouched, and the pacing resumed. "Urien doesn't have a clue what his hands will be full of, other than flesh. I'll lay odds all he can think about is what fine sons she will bear him. How beautifully she will ornament his hall." He stopped at the table, reached for the cup, and stared at it before finally taking a swallow. "And, no doubt, how much land he will control through her."

Merlin scrutinized his prodigy, trying to divine the young man's thoughts. That Arthur was attracted to the chieftainess was obvious. Exactly how much damage had been done was anyone's guess.

"Well?"

"I think she deserves better, Merlin."

"And I think it's none of your business."

In two strides, Arthur crossed the gap to Merlin's chair. Eyes glittering, he bent to grip the carved oaken armrests. "It is, if I make it so."

The damage was worse than Merlin had feared. He hoped a dose of cold logic would seal this breach.

"Use your head, lad. You can't afford to lose Moray's support. Not with Cuchullain and his pirating Scots swarming the Hibernian Sea like flies on cow dung." Arthur did not disagree, and Merlin forged ahead while he believed the balance still tipped in his favor. "And if the West Saxons' buildup leads to their capture of Anderida, what do you think their next step will be?"

Arthur released his hold on Merlin's chair and straightened. His eyes flicked over the map of Britannia and Hibernia draped across one end of the table. A finger stabbed the inkblot in the center of the Hibernian Sea.

"Maun."

"Precisely. You need a strong commander on Maun, at Dhoo-Glass." Merlin gestured with his cup. "Urien is your man."

"I know, Merlin. But I need her, too." The words were quiet but no less certain. "And not on Maun."

The most surprising aspect of Arthur's admission was that he had volunteered it at all. And they weren't even in confessional. That alone betrayed the severity of this problem. Yet Arthur could have forsaken talk for action, like his father before him. Perhaps the son of Uther could still be diverted from this path to self-destruction. Time for a switch in tactics.

"What about Chieftainess Alayna of Clan Alban?"

Arthur shook his head. "I already have all I want from Alban."

"Senaudon? The cavalry troops?"

"And Alayna's son. We'll see what kind of warrior he makes. If he's anything like his mother—" He gave Merlin a hard stare. "Nice try, Merlin. You almost dragged me off the subject. And don't give me that innocent-as-a-babe look. You know what I mean."

Merlin shrugged. "Well, it almost worked."

"Almost isn't good enough. I want Chieftainess Gyan-humara at my side. Not Urien's." Arthur retrieved his cup but did not drink. Instead, he turned to the window and the graying twilight beyond. "The more I think about a Moray-Argyll union, the less I like it."

"You think Urien's house might grow too strong?"

"Allied with Argyll and backed by the rest of Dal-riada? I know it will." He drained the cup and set it down with a heavy *thunk*. "I was a fool to have allowed this to come to pass!"

"It came to pass," Merlin patiently reminded him, "because Dumarec and the other Brytoni lords were anxious for solid assurances that another Aber-Glein would not occur anytime soon. Don't be too hard on yourself, lad. You can't be expected to foresee every-thing."

"No. But I can correct the situation." The azure fire returned to his eyes, even brighter than before. "I must."

"For God's sake, Arthur, don't do anything rash! For my sake, too. I cannot repeat for you what I had to do for your father." Ugly memories assaulted him, and he fought them off. In fact, the event had been instrumental in Merlin's decision to take vows—not in the hopes that the decision would excuse him from his responsibility but to ensure his being forgiven for it. But with forgiveness came the cost of service. Service, he thought with irony, in ways he had never imagined. He gave a wry smile. "You have no idea the trouble that caused."

"Oh, yes. I do." Arthur strode to the wall of shelves. Amid the stacked scrolls stood Uther's games-helm. Arthur lifted it down to trace the intricate gold embossing. "His lust cost me the chieftainship of my clan." He returned the helm to its shelf.

"If it hadn't been for his lust, you wouldn't be here now. And Britannia would be torn apart by her enemies like a doe in a pack of winter-starved wolves." Not for the first time, Merlin was amazed at how God could bring forth good from an evil event. Arthur made no reply but continued to stare at his father's helm. "Listen to me, Arthur!" Arthur whirled. In that instant, Merlin knew no words would sway the son of Uther. So he surrendered. "At least, let her come to you of her own accord."

"She won't. Not if she honors the treaty." Poignant disappointment paraded across his handsome face. "I do not qualify under the terms." A harsh laugh escaped. "My terms."

Cup in one hand, Merlin stood and laid the other on Arthur's shoulder. "Take heart, lad." The war might be lost, but this battle was his. And he wanted to celebrate. "If it is God's will, it will happen eventually."

Arthur shrugged the hand away. "I want it to happen now!"

Of all the foolish, mule-headed . . . how very like Uther, Merlin realized. But he reminded himself that Arthur had made the initial effort to seek advice, something his father had not done until it had been far too late.

"Haven't you heard a word of what I've said, Arthur? Don't force the matter! That's the surest way to stir up trouble." Merlin brushed his knuckles across the part of the map that represented Dalriada. "Trouble you can ill afford right now."

"You worry too much, Merlin." A world of confidence lived in his grin. "You taught me well enough to handle anything."

"I hope so." Merlin sighed.

And he hoped his fledgling dragon would not try testing newfound wings against this emotional storm. Such a test could prove fatal—for Merlin's nerves, if nothing else. He tossed back the rest of the *uisge*. Its fiery taste failed to sear away the doubts.

"For the sake of Britannia, Arthur, I do hope so."

Chapter
12

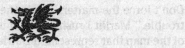

Gyan led Brin into the stables behind the *mansio*, ordered a brush from the waiting stable hand, but refused his help and began attacking the day's accumulation of road dirt marring her horse's hide. Weighted by exasperation, her hand was much heavier than usual. Brin stamped and snorted in protest. She called the stable hand back to Brin's stall and left him in the older man's care.

Storming away from the stables on her way to the main tile-roofed stone building, she passed two small structures. The aromas of beef and bread wafting through the open door of one marked it as the kitchen. As she passed, two men emerged from the other, laughing and shaking droplets from their hair like a pair of waterlogged hounds. This building's function posed a mystery she was in no mood to solve.

She found Cynda and the menservants waiting beside the wagon in the outer courtyard. By Cynda's black glare, it appeared she had already endured a bout of frustration from trying to make the Brytoni innkeeper understand her wishes. Though it took only a few minutes to set matters straight, the delay did not improve Gyan's humor.

The innkeeper assigned her quarters on the top floor of the two-story *mansio*, overlooking the rectangular inner courtyard. The chambers consisted of a reception room, where Cynda was to sleep, a dining room, and a bedchamber. While not lacking for basic comfort, the rooms did not display an overabundance of luxury. The linens and pillows and window coverings and wall hangings and other furnishings were adequate but plain. Cynda lost no time in pointing this out.

"Don't worry, Gyan. When the men get here with your things from the wagon, I'll have this place looking like home in a thrice."

Gyan made no comment. In her present state of mind, the spartan chambers suited her perfectly.

As soon as everything was toted to the chambers, she dismissed the men for the evening. She could contain her anger no longer.

"Cù-puc!" She hefted a pewter goblet and flung it into a corner of the bedchamber. It hit the timbers with a satisfying clang. "I have consented to marry a *cù-puc!"* She didn't care that likening Urien to the unlikely offspring of a hound and a pig was an insult to both creatures.

Unperturbed, Cynda put down the pillow she was fluffing. She filled another goblet with wine from the pitcher and pressed it into Gyan's hand. "Have some of this, dear. It'll make you feel better." Gyan downed the wine in four swallows and thrust the goblet back at Cynda. "Now, tell me what happened."

Gyan paced to the window to grip the ledge with whitening knuckles as she repeated Urien's remarks about knowing who was master and what types of horses a lady should ride. And the comment about children.

"Perhaps he didn't mean those things the way they sounded, Gyan."

"Oh, he meant them, all right." She came away from the window to drop onto the bed.

"So what are you going to do?"

Gyan's laugh was mirthless. "You think I have a choice?"

"Aye. Break your betrothal, and marry someone else."

With all her heart, Gyan wished her course could be that simple. "And have Urien lead his clansmen to war against us? Or have you forgotten that Moray is our neighbor?" She shook her head. "No. I won't expose the clan to that threat. Not because of someone who cannot consult his head before opening his mouth."

"Those kinds of men are the easiest to handle, anyway, once you learn to ignore what they say." That coaxed a faint smile to Gyan's lips. Cynda patted the dove-tattooed arm. "Are you all right now? Shall I try to find us something to eat?"

"Good idea. But I'd better come with you to prevent any more misunderstandings."

Together, they went from the bedchamber, through the dining area into the antechamber. Cynda tugged open the outer door. In the corridor, fist poised to knock, stood the scion of Clan Moray.

The mere sight of Urien rekindled Gyan's rage. She fought to contain the blaze. It wasn't easy.

"Cynda, let him enter. And leave us, please." Though she was still speaking in Caledonian to Cynda, she glared at Urien. "It's time for some answers."

Cynda looked first at Gyan, then at Urien, and back to Gyan. "Are you sure you want me to go?"

The days of clinging to her nursemaid's skirts were long past. This man would soon be her husband. If she could not confront him now, unaided, her marriage truly would be doomed.

"Yes."

Muttering and wagging her head, Cynda pulled the door shut behind her.

Gyan retreated to the window, whirled, and crossed her arms. "Well. Would you care to explain yourself, Urien?" Her eyes narrowed to slits. "Or have you come to deliver more insults?"

"I did not intend to insult you, my dear." As Urien strode across the room, the smiling arrogance dimmed. "I'm sorry if my words were so upsetting." He reached for her hand.

She could practically hear Cynda crowing, "See, what did I tell you?" Indeed, it was tempting to hope in the sincerity of his apology. To shrug the matter off and take refuge in stoic acceptance, to convince herself that he wasn't such a thoughtless boor after all . . . how easy it sounded. She was fated to spend her life with this man. What good would it do to remain angry with him?

Yet there was something she had to know.

"Then why did you make those remarks?"

The smile vanished. He yanked on her hand, pulled her to his chest, wrapped his other arm around her, and crushed her against the wall. She struggled to break his hold. And failed.

"You will learn, Gyanhumara"—she did not like his emphasis on the word *will*—"that the wife of a Bryton never questions her husband's actions."

Another woman would have surrendered to the futility of the situation. Gyan did not.

"It is you who have much to learn, Urien map Dumarec," she growled. "I question things as I see fit."

"Good. Then question this."

He fastened his lips to hers. When she clenched her teeth to deny passage, his mouth attacked her bare throat. Her heart thrashed against her chest.

Enough was enough! Gyan planted a foot against the wall and shoved with all her strength. Startled, Urien loosened his grip. She broke free, dashed past him, flung open the door, and reached toward her boots. As she turned to face him, a dagger gleamed in each fist.

"Get out." Deliberately, she kept her voice low. "Now."

"As you wish, my dear. We will have time aplenty to engage in these . . . games." Thumbs hooked in his belt, he sauntered to the door. She wanted to carve that leer from his face. "A word of advice, Gyanhumara: no one ever denies me what is rightfully mine." The leer twisted into a snarl. "Least of all a woman."

Gyan slammed the door on his churlish laughter. The thick wood muffled it; distance diminished it even more as Urien strode down the corridor. Eventually, the laughter disappeared altogether. But silence could not erase the memory of that dreadful sound. It echoed through the chambers of her brain like a demonic chorus.

What in heaven's name had she done? More to the point, what was she going to do now?

She returned the daggers to her boots. No telling when they might be needed again. Head in hands, she sank to the couch, her mind racing to formulate options.

She could refuse Urien and marry a Caledonian of a strong clan, one that could provide many warriors to help fight Clan Moray. Alban, perhaps. No. That plan would never work. The Pendragon's treaty had sapped the clans' strength, especially Alban's. Besides, she was bound by that treaty to marry a Brytoni lord.

And Arthur the Pendragon was not a man to be crossed. Their meeting, brief as it was, had taught Gyan that much.

The door creaked. She glanced up. Cynda stood in the open doorway with a boy in tow.

"Gyan? Is anything wrong?"

Donning a smile that she knew would never fool Cynda, Gyan rose. "Who is this boy?"

"I don't know." Cynda nudged the Brytoni youth forward. "I caught him dawdling outside your chambers."

Gyan studied the lad, who couldn't have been much older than eight summers. The neatness of his straight blond hair and white tunic suggested that his presence at her door was no accident. Lowering his eyes, he dug a sandaled toe in a crack between the tiles.

"Yes, boy?" Gyan prompted softly in Brytonic. "Have you a message for me?"

"Aye, my Lady." His bow was well practiced. "His Grace, Bishop Dubricius, requests the honor of your company for dinner. In the *praetorium.*"

"Bishop . . . Dubricius, did you say?"

"Aye. He commands the garrison, my Lady." Pride seemed to swell the small chest. "His Grace is the Pendragon's right-hand man."

"I see. Thank you, lad." This was exactly the kind of diversion she needed to take her mind off Urien for a while. "Please tell his Grace that I shall be delighted to accept."

As the boy scampered away to fulfill her directive, Cynda marched into the room. "Well?"

"I've been invited to dine with the garrison commander this evening." Gyan suspected Cynda was not referring to the message, but she was in no mood to wrestle with explanations. "I'll need your help with my hair."

"That's not what I meant, young lady." Cynda waved an accusing finger. "And you know it. Did you get your answers?"

"From Urien? Oh, yes." Gyan paused at the threshold of the dining chamber. All her years of combat training combined couldn't leave her feeling so utterly weary. To steady herself, she laid a hand on the heavy, wine-dark fabric. "More than I ever bargained for."

Cynda sighed with exasperation when Gyan refused to elaborate. Grumbling, she collected brush, mirror, and combs and followed Gyan into the bedchamber.

For her meeting with the Bishop of Caer Lugubalion, Gyan selected an azure gown of the same hue as the clan-mark and betrothal tattoos on her forearms. A torc of twisted gold encircled her throat; matching armbands adorned both upper arms. All three torcs bore the dove motif of Clan Argyll. Her hair tumbled, unbraided, in flaming waves over the saffron-and-scarlet-banded midnight blue of her woolen clan mantle. Ankle-high calfskin boots protected her feet from the evening chill.

The only drawback: no place to conceal a weapon. She fervently hoped the need would not arise in the house of a holy man.

Cynda pinned the sapphire-eyed gold dove brooch to a fold of Gyan's mantle.

"Epona herself would be jealous, Gyan."

Epona, indeed. As though a stone carving could be jealous of anything. Yet Gyan appreciated the spirit in which the compliment was offered. She gave Cynda a

quick hug and strode off to keep her appointment with
Bishop Dubricius.

Earlier, the Pendragon had pointed out the *praetorium*, with its unusual square, tiled pond in front, so
Gyan knew where to go.

Outside, Gyan took a moment to survey her surroundings. The main thoroughfare of the fortress was
all but deserted. Only a small unit of foot and a handful
of mounted soldiers traveled the road. Most inhabitants, she surmised, were already enjoying their evening meal. Across the street, she recognized the long,
low building of officers' quarters. Many chambers were
lighted against the advancing dark. One had to be
Urien's, although she did not know which. Nor did she
have any desire to find out.

During those fateful days of his visit to Arbroch half
a year ago, how could she have failed to discern his
true character? The language barrier was no excuse.
Other signs, she realized miserably, had been present.
His actions on the practice fields and in the feast-hall
had shouted volumes. How could she have been so
deaf, so blind?

That wasn't true, she reminded herself. Her instincts
had given ample warning. She had chosen not to heed
them. Now her choice trapped her in an emotional bog.
Why?

Duty—the same concept that now prevented her
from seeking escape. Duty to the Pendragon and his
treaty. Duty to her people and Urien's, who stood the
most to gain from their marriage and the most to lose
from a broken betrothal. Duty to her father, who had
been the first to recommend the match and whose
counsel she had always held in the highest regard.
She'd have traded her sword arm for some of that

counsel now. Because her burden left no room for duty to self.

So be it; she vowed to survive as best she could with the tools at her disposal. Wits, skill, and courage would have to suffice. They were all she had.

A cool breeze toyed with the ends of her hair, and her thoughts winged back to the task at hand. If Bishop Dubricius was as closely associated with the Pendragon as the messenger boy had implied, Gyan couldn't give Dubricius cause to suspect that anything was amiss between Urien and herself. No sense in alerting the Pendragon to the possibility of trouble. Doubtless, he would ally his forces with a fellow Bryton.

Time to see how well she could pretend. Drawing a deep breath, she walked briskly toward the *praetorium*.

Gyan paused at the edge of its manmade pond. A statue of a woman stood in the center. Light from the rising moon danced across the contours of her smooth face and bare arms and flowing gown, and dark shapes glided through the water around the statue's feet. In her arms rested a large jar, poised to pour. Its mouth spewed a steady stream of water that fell with a musical tinkle into the pond.

Cupping her hand under the trickle, she found the water refreshingly cool. She lifted it to her lips and was surprised by the faintly metallic taste. Flicking the rest away, she wished for more time to study this strange pond.

Two soldiers approached and saluted. They introduced themselves as officers of the bishop's personal guard ordered to be her escorts. Nodding once, Gyan followed them across the court, up the steps, past the smartly saluting guards at the entrance, and on into the building.

The private quarters of the commander of Caer

Lugubalion were the most lavish of anything Gyan had yet seen since entering Brytoni territory. On the way to the dining area, she took note of the lovely mosaic floor tiles and shiny white stone sculptures. Most of the sculptures were busts, perched atop fluted pillars. A few depicted the full body, like the woman in the pond. All were carved with amazingly lifelike detail, so lifelike that she found it difficult to dispel the impression of being watched.

Arched doorways and columns bore intricately carved flowers and animals and curls. Furnishings were sparse yet gracefully elegant, in what she suspected was typical Roman style.

The building was quite warm. This aroused her curiosity, for she had seen neither open fire nor brazier. The oil-burning lamps bracketed to the walls were too few in number to be the source of this much heat. Since she had accepted the invitation to forget her troubles for an evening, Gyan resolved to ask Bishop Dubricius about the mystery.

Her escorts halted at the doorway into the dining room. One stepped into the chamber to announce her arrival, withdrew with a salute, and took up a position outside. The other stood guard on the opposite side of the doorway. A servant appeared from an adjoining corridor to take her mantle, which she gladly surrendered. Feeling much more comfortable, she strode into the room.

The dining chamber was furnished much like the one in her set of rooms in the *mansio*. A large, low table crouched over the mosaic dolphins frolicking across the center of the floor. The table was corralled by three long, high-backed, cushioned couches. Here the similarity ended, for more of these odd couches lined the walls. The bishop certainly seemed accustomed to entertaining many guests.

To her surprise, two men stood as she entered the room.

The older man stepped forward to greet her. He wore a long white robe edged in scarlet, bound at the waist by a matching cord. An elaborate gold cross hung from a chain around his neck.

"Good evening, Chieftainess Gyanhumara. I am Bishop Dubricius, called Merlin."

Gyan studied the face with its deep creases, hawklike nose, and sharp dark eyes. Now they regarded her with kindly warmth, although she was sure they could instantly seem as hard as steel beneath the black brows. The hair on his head, what was left of it, was iron gray.

She inclined her head. "I am honored to make your acquaintance, your Grace."

"Please, just Merlin. Only the help calls me 'your Grace.' To tell the truth, I'm not quite used to even that yet," he whispered. Louder, he said, "It's been barely four months since I took the cope and miter."

That won her smile. "I understand, my Lord— Merlin."

"Good. Now, I believe you've already met my cousin." With a graceful sweep of the arm, he gestured toward the room's only other occupant.

When the Pendragon had been wearing a plain leather tunic stained with sweat and grime from his ride, she had not been able to appreciate completely how handsome he was. Now, bathed and dressed in the Roman military regalia of his rank, she was struck by the full impact of his appearance.

Sandaled feet gave rise to bronzed, well-muscled calves. The rippling thighs disappeared into the gold-

and-white-fringed linen kilt. Hands and forearms were obscured by the proud back. Over the burnished gold breastplate dipped a fold of the gold-trimmed knee-length scarlet cloak. A ruby-eyed gold dragon, ringed by a braided band of red, blue, and green, rode the right shoulder. The firm, square jaw; the full, sensuous mouth; the fine, straight nose; the prominent cheek-bones, intense blue eyes, high forehead, red-gold hair—his every aspect made her pulse race.

Her hatred of Romans evaporated. Urien map Dumarec might never have existed at all.

Gazing only at Arthur, she answered, "Yes. I have."

Arthur raised his right fist to his chest. "Chieftainess Gyanhumara." As his hand fell to his side, the smile that dawned upon his face made her knees feel like liquid wax.

Inwardly, she rebuked herself. Control! She had to exercise control. She was no tavern wench to drool over the first handsome face to notice her, but chieftainess of the most powerful clan of the Caledonian Confederacy. And here stood the man responsible for defeating the clans and thrusting her into a betrothal that had been all but prearranged from the start—a betrothal that promised to make her life miserable.

That ugly reminder, coupled with the memory of her most recent encounter with Urien, helped her rein in her runaway emotions. But she couldn't prevent herself from returning Arthur's smile, however briefly. She inclined her head. "Lord Pendragon." Using his title seemed the safest course.

Did she hear the bishop sigh? She glanced at him, but he had already begun to move toward the center couch. "Chieftainess, if you please?" Merlin pointed to the bench on his left. Arthur had already claimed the other, lying on his side, facing the table, propped on one elbow. The bishop adopted a similar pose. Gyan must have looked as flabbergasted as she felt, for Merlin gave a low chuckle. "This is our custom for dining. Welcome to Little Rome."

Rome, indeed. The men looked so bizarre, she decided this was one custom of which she wanted no part. "Thank you, Merlin, but if you don't mind, I think I'd rather sit."

"As you wish, Chieftainess." If Merlin was perturbed by her choice, he didn't show it.

She settled to the floor, legs tucked beneath her as best she could within the confines of her gown—and was surprised to discover that the tiles were warm. "This floor is heated! How?"

"Hot air," said Merlin, "forced through a series of pipes connected to a furnace below the building. Each pipe serves an area of dead air beneath the floor of a given room. The system is called a *hypocaustum*. In Brytonic, it literally means 'under-burning,' which is exactly what the furnace does."

"Well, Merlin, it's obvious to me that you've"—Gyan allowed herself a small smile—"warmed to this topic." She was rewarded by the sound of both men's laughter.

Still chuckling, Arthur said, "Don't mind him, Chieftainess. He misses being a teacher."

"That does explain much. And the warm floor heats the entire room?" Heat without open fire and the annoying smoke that accompanied it was one Roman innovation Gyan could become accustomed to very quickly, she decided.

"Exactly." Arthur grinned unabashedly at Merlin. "It's one of my cousin's favorite luxuries."

"Ah, you may spare the chieftainess a list of my vices, Arthur. I'm sure she will discern them on her own soon enough." He looked at Gyan, his smile dimming. "It is also our custom—and this has nothing to do with Rome, though many folk practice it there as well—to invoke God's blessing upon the meal. With your permission?"

"A blessing? Of course." It took her a moment to realize what he was talking about, and that he'd asked her leave to proceed rather than simply plowing ahead as a certain member of her clan's priesthood would have done under similar circumstances. Dafydd had mentioned this type of prayer to her, but because her meals at Arbroch had been spent with her clansmen, she'd never had the opportunity to put it into practice. She held out a hand toward the bishop, palm up. "Please, sir, go right ahead."

Both men bowed their heads, and Merlin began speaking in the language of Dafydd's chants. Gyan tried to follow their example. But this fortress, this building, this chamber, these people, their mannerisms, their language—and especially the man who wasn't speaking, who was starting to coax from her feelings she had never dreamed she could possess—everything seemed so alien, she couldn't concentrate on her own silent prayer.

While the bishop droned on, she opened her eyes and found her gaze drawn to Arthur. Even with neck bent and eyes closed, he seemed to radiate power, as though a portion of him refused to submit to anyone.

Without warning, his eyes opened. Their gazes met, and a hint of that captivating smile formed on his lips. Horrified that he had caught her staring at him, and even more horrified to show her embarrassment, she choked down a gasp and studied her hands, which lay folded demurely in her lap. To slow her careening heart, she closed her eyes and focused on each breath. And on what his smile might mean. Just about anything or, she realized glumly, nothing at all. Mentally cursing her foolishness, she decided on the latter.

The prayer ended, and the thump of a fist on wood dragged her from her thoughts. As she looked up, servants began parading in with an array of pitchers and platters, even a tureen of lentil soup. Everything, down to the smallest slotted serving spoon, was made of polished silver embossed with gold designs. Gyan had never seen such a hoard in her life. In moments, there wasn't enough room on the table to set a pair of dice. The meats and cheeses had already been cut into finger-sized pieces, and there wasn't a knife anywhere. It was indeed an eyeful: roast venison and onions, poached salmon with carrots, ham smothered in a creamy herb sauce, light and dark breads, several different cheeses, stewed spiced winter apples, nut-meats, even a platter of small steaming towels. And, of course, plenty of wine. The mingling aromas were enough to tempt the fussiest eater.

Gyan regarded her host. "And whose army were you planning to feed this evening, my Lord Bishop?" She felt her lips stretch into a grin.

Merlin chuckled, waving an arm over the spread. "My apologies, Chieftainess, if the *cena* seems a bit overwhelming. We normally have it served by courses." He ladled soup into two of the empty bowls and passed them to Arthur, who in turn gave one to Gyan. "But I must confess, I didn't invite you here purely for a social visit. We have some serious business to discuss, and I didn't want us to be interrupted by a constant stream of servants. I do recommend the salmon, Chieftainess." When Merlin selected a piece from the platter, popped it into his mouth, and swallowed, his face transformed into an expression of bliss. "It's always superb, but tonight I'd call it heavenly."

Merlin was right. In fact, everything she tasted was delicious—and not, she suspected, because she'd survived most of the past sennight on dry travel rations.

Despite his announcement, the conversation remained light throughout most of the meal: Gyan's journey and what subjects she'd be studying with the monks on Maun, what scrolls she could expect to find in their collection, what life was like for a Caledonian woman who ruled a clan. Not to be outdone, Gyan asked about Arthur's background and training and got enough answers—surprising ones, even—to last to the stewed apples. Arthur offered her the bowl.

"Really, Lord Pendragon, I couldn't possibly . . ."

Again, she was smitten by his insistent gaze and found it impossible to resist. She reached for the bowl, wondering what manner of man could command without speaking. And what manner of fool she was, for allowing herself to be swayed by this power.

Their fingers touched. Quite by accident, but Gyan felt a tingling in her hand and heat in her cheeks. She all but wrenched the bowl from him in her haste to escape. What in the name of heaven was coming over her? She gave him an apologetic smile and busied herself with ladling a portion into her bowl. The irony made her want to laugh out loud: according to one of the stories Dafydd had told her, this fruit had gotten the first woman on earth into trouble, too.

She cleared her throat and regarded the bishop, grateful for the respite from Arthur's scrutiny. "And this important business you mentioned? I can't believe the plans for my time on Maun were what you meant."

"In a sense, yes." Merlin dabbed at his lips with a cloth. "But there's more. Arthur?"

A change overcame the Pendragon's features, as though he had raised a mask. Gyan realized she had seen that mask earlier, when he had been dealing with Urien and his other subordinates. Was that how he regarded her, too, as just another subordinate? But she had no time to explore that thought as Arthur began to speak. "Our scouts report an escalation in hostilities on Hibernia. The Attacots are slowly but surely pushing the Scots off the island. Laird Cuchullain has nowhere to take his people but—"

"Maun," Gyan finished for him. "And Brydein after that, I presume. Unless there's a chance of negotiating with this Cuchullain, maybe offer to help him fight his battle?"

Arthur shook his head. "My envoy to Cuchullain returned"—his jaw clenched, and Gyan could practically feel his fury kindle—"in pieces."

She curled her lip as a gruesome image leaped to mind. "You didn't attack the Scots for that outrage?"

There was no mirth in Arthur's laugh. "Though some would dub me the savior of Brydein, at present I can fight only one war at a time. Your people, Chieftainess Gyanhumara, were keeping me too busy."

"Ha." Folding her arms, she glared at Arthur. "If you'd secured Cuchullain's aid against us, it would be his daughter sitting here now, in my place." It made a great deal of sense, and she didn't like the implications at all. She began gathering her skirts to stand. If she'd had her daggers with her, she'd have been greatly tempted to use them. "My Lord Bishop, I do thank you for the fine meal, but I've heard all I can stomach for one evening."

Arthur's hand gripped her forearm. Gyan whipped her head around and was surprised to find not anger blazing from his eyes but an earnest appeal. Determined to resist the unspoken command, she jerked her arm free and shot to her feet.

"Please, Chieftainess, hear us out." This from Merlin, who had risen to a sitting position. Arthur, too, was now sitting upright, gripping the edge of the wood so hard his knuckles were whitening. With outspread hands, Merlin went on, "I won't deny the truth of your words. In fact—" He glanced at Arthur, who returned his look with a curt nod. "Yes. That was our original plan. But for whatever reason, the Lord God in His infinite wisdom decreed otherwise. Of course, we never expected Cuchullain to be so blatantly unwilling to negotiate. But we were pleased to discover that your people saw the wisdom of making peace with us."

"Ha. Wisdom at swordpoint—"

"Is still wisdom," Merlin insisted. "So here we are, Chieftainess, not as adversaries but as allies." He rose and made his way to where Gyan was standing, his hand outstretched. "And, I hope, as friends."

Merlin's smile was so uncannily similar to her father's that it disarmed her ire. What did it matter, after all, what their original intentions had been? As he had said, the One God had decreed otherwise. She uncrossed her arms to grasp his hand. "Friends, Merlin."

He patted her hand before releasing it, sat on the bench across from Arthur, who had visibly relaxed, and motioned for Gyan to join him, which she did. "I'm glad you feel that way, because we"—he tossed a nod in Arthur's direction—"consider our alliance with Caledonia to be of great importance. And you, Chieftainess, are the key."

"I am?" Gyan's laughter faded before Merlin's somber gaze. "You're serious about this. But why me? Because of my . . . association"—she couldn't bring herself to say "betrothal"—"with Urien?"

"In part, yes," said Merlin.

"Because of the increased threat of a Scotti invasion," Arthur said, "I'm assigning two squads of Caledonian horsemen to the Manx Cohort."

"Why not just attack him now that you have the Caledonian cavalry on your side?" Gyan asked.

"I will demonstrate." Arthur selected four apple slices. As he transferred the fruit to his bowl, sauce dripped between the spoon's slots. "Transporting forty horses over water is difficult enough." He thrust the spoon deep into the remaining apples to lift up a heaping mound. Most of the slices slipped off, splattering the sauce. "A thousand is quite another matter. I believe you met my fleet commander?" When she nodded, he continued, "Bedwyr designed the vessel you will be taking to Maun specifically for shipping horses in safety and comfort. Right now, it's the only one of its kind in the fleet." He dumped the rest of the apples, with the spoon, back into the bowl.

Gyan couldn't believe what she was hearing. "You won't avenge the death of your ambassador because it's too much trouble?"

"Believe me, Chieftainess. If the situation were any different, I'd be at Cuchullain's throat faster than he could draw his next breath. But after the Scots, I'd have the Attacots to contend with. Or both at once, if they decided to bury their differences to unite against me. The island of Hibernia is not worth that kind of effort—or loss of life. But let them come to us, and I will defend Brydein with my final heartbeat." Arthur saluted her with his goblet before taking a swallow. "And everyone who lives here."

As she studied the Pendragon this time, she tried to tell herself that the heat rising in her cheeks was purely from excitement at the prospect of battle. "So an invasion is likely. When? Sometime this summer, perhaps?"

"Hard to say. I don't think Cuchullain can afford to mount an invasion this year." Arthur's expression turned grim. "But he could be sailing to Maun now, for all I know." He gave Gyan an appraising look. "The idea of being involved in a Scotti war doesn't disturb you?"

"Ha, no! It's what I was born for." Though not necessarily what she would die for, depending on how that accursed prophecy came to pass. But, of course, she couldn't tell them that.

Arthur nodded. "Then I'll need your help, Chieftainess, to resolve difficulties that might arise among the Caledonians."

"Urien will need your help, too." Merlin exchanged an unreadable glance with Arthur.

"Of course. I'll do what I—what?" She stared at Merlin, at Arthur, and at Merlin again. "Urien?"

"Has been assigned to command the Manx Cohort." Arthur's tone seemed oddly subdued. "On my orders."

"The Manx troops? Well." To mask her plummeting spirits, she devised what she hoped was an appropriate response. "This should give us a chance to become better acquainted. But I thought—" What she thought, but couldn't voice, was that she would rather spend the time becoming better acquainted with Arthur. "Wasn't he just promoted to head the new Horse Cohort?"

"Yes, Chieftainess," Merlin said. "But since we're almost certain the next threat to Brydein—and ultimately Caledonia, though Lord forbid that should happen—will come by way of Maun—"

"Then you need your ablest men on Maun." What else could she say? Certainly not the truth, that she wanted as little to do with her betrothed as possible. And most certainly not the idea that flitted through her head, as hard as she tried to dismiss it as utter nonsense: that Arthur might come to Maun in Urien's place.

"All our ablest warriors," Merlin amended with a smile.

He stood and offered Gyan his hand. As she rose, so did Arthur—and so did her pulse, making her thankful that the visit seemed to be over. But she had one last shot in her arsenal. She wrenched her gaze from the Pendragon to grin at Merlin. "My Lord Bishop, could shameless flattery possibly be another of your vices?"

"You see, Arthur, I told you she'd find me out." Merlin's chuckle trailed away, but the twinkle in his eyes did not disappear. "But my dear lady, I believe I was telling the truth. I also believe that all Brydein will one day be blessed by the gifts you have to offer."

That, Gyan mused as she murmured her thanks and farewells, was a prophecy she could certainly live with.

Chapter
13

The more Arthur learned about Chieftainess Gyan-humara, the more fascinating she seemed. His mind raced to devise ways—sensible ways that couldn't be misconstrued by anyone, especially Urien—that he might see her again. If she would consent. He was still mentally kicking himself for the twist in the conversation that had led her to discern his original plan for conquering her people. When the messenger's remains had returned from Hibernia, and Merlin had tried to calm Arthur's rage with the platitude that "God works all things together for good," Arthur had seriously questioned Merlin's sanity. Now, Arthur had his answer—at least in part. Without doubt, Gyanhumara was the woman with whom he wanted to spend the rest of his life, the woman who could help him forge a united Brydein. The fact remained that she was betrothed to Urien, a fact that she didn't seem anxious to change. But if he could see her again, he reasoned, perhaps he could convince her otherwise. The problem was, no appropriate activities came to mind.

As he watched Gyanhumara retreat to the dining chamber's doorway and the servant who waited there with her cloak, an idea hit. "Chieftainess, wait." Facing him, she displayed a smile that could have ignited every oil lamp in the room. Again, he felt that strange tightness in his chest, a feeling he was learning to welcome. "Your ship doesn't sail for two days yet. Would you care to join me for sword practice, perhaps tomorrow afternoon?" Merlin glared at Arthur, but he ignored him.

"Lord Pendragon, I would be honored." Mischief invaded her smile. "But mornings are when I'm at my best. Shall we meet at the training enclosure you were using earlier?"

He nodded, pursing his lips to keep his smile under control. "After breaking fast, then."

She returned his salute with a graceful dip of her head, turned to allow the servant to drape her cloak about her shoulders, and strode from the room. Once he was sure she was out of earshot, he sighed. God, what a woman!

"Oh, to be twenty years younger." Arthur turned to find Merlin regarding him, fists on hips. "But you, lad, owe me ten Our Fathers."

"For what?" Arthur was reasonably sure Merlin was referring to his less-than-stellar self-discipline but decided to claim innocence. "I didn't do anything."

"Ha. Not too overtly, at least, or I'd have you doing a lot more penance than simply reciting prayers." Up came the accusatory finger with which Arthur was all too familiar. "But I see you stepping onto a dangerous path with this woman, Arturus Aurelius Vetarus." Not since Arthur had dodged his lessons to join a week-long hunt when he was ten had Merlin used Arthur's full Latin name in that tone of voice. "I don't like it. Not one iota."

Merlin did have a point, Arthur realized. But he wasn't ready to concede to his spiritual adviser just yet. "Would you believe me if I said I only want to evaluate her swordsmanship?" Crossing his arms, Merlin emphatically shook his head. Arthur switched tactics. "What if this is all part of God's will? Wouldn't it be worse for me"—*for her?*—"for all of us if I tried to resist?"

"The Almighty is not a God of chaos." Arthur couldn't remember when he had ever seen his mentor scowl so fiercely. "But if you insist on pursuing this woman—who, permit me to remind you, is a vow away from being married to your primary rival—then chaos is exactly what will result." The scowl lightened, and Merlin advanced to grip Arthur's shoulder. "I'm not trying to make your life miserable, lad. I hope you can understand that." His fingers tightened briefly and withdrew. "God help me, Arthur, I just don't want you to go through what your father did."

"'The sins of the fathers shall be visited on the children.' Yes, I do recall that lesson." Arthur also recalled—though he bloody well would never admit it to Merlin—wondering if such a thing would ever apply to him. Now he knew better. "I will keep it uppermost in my thoughts. I promise you that, Merlin." He bared his teeth in what he hoped was a convincing grin. "And if you catch me acting like a besotted fool again, I will gladly perform any penance you assign."

"Well?" demanded Cynda. "Then what happened?"

Gyan fingered the plush wool of her clan mantle. How could she describe the most wonderful evening of her life? An evening that witnessed—yes, she had to admit it, if only to herself—the birth of emotions of a depth she never thought possible. Mere words could not suffice. No point in even trying. She draped the mantle across a chair.

"Then we ate."

"Honestly!" Cynda threw up her hands in mock disgust. "You have got to be the worst storyteller of all time."

"So I'm not a *seannachaidh.*" Gyan shrugged, stepped out of the azure gown, and accepted the nightgown. "Find me one, and I'll bring him along next time." She slipped the nightgown over her head.

"Next time, I will," threatened Cynda, and Gyan had to laugh. "So what did you do?"

"Do?" Settling the nightgown across her shoulders, Gyan grinned. "I tell you, Cynda, these Romans have the strangest customs. They actually lie down to eat."

"No!"

"Yes. They looked so funny, it was all I could do to keep my composure."

"Did you try eating like that, too?"

"Are you serious? The table was too low to reach without being all hunched over, so I just sat on the floor. They seemed a wee bit surprised, but it suited me just fine. I'm sure the food tasted the same, anyway. We had salmon and—"

"Never mind the food. What did you talk about?"

Well did Gyan know what sorts of things Cynda wanted to hear, but she couldn't resist baiting her. "Their heating system."

"Their what?"

"How they keep their rooms warm without fire. It's really quite fascinating."

"Ach, to be sure. And with the most gorgeous man in this entire place beside you, all you could think to talk about was how he warms his feet?"

"Well, not exactly, no. We also discussed what I'll be doing on Maun." Fist clenched, Gyan jabbed the air with an imaginary sword. "They think I might get my first taste of battle there!"

"Wonderful." Cynda rolled her eyes. "Just when I thought I was done with patching you up for a while." Hands on hips, she asked, "And what about Urien, Gyan?"

A lump formed in Gyan's throat. The words barely squeezed out: "He—he is to command the force . . . on Maun."

Gyan sighed and sat on the bed, drawing knees to chin. What about Urien, indeed. She had an answer. Whether it was the best one, she had no earthly idea. Nor had she any idea how to usher it into reality.

And if Cynda couldn't help her, no one could.

"Six months ago, I told my father that if I ever saw the right man, I would know." As she recalled this and later conversations with Ogryvan, hindsight told her that he had admired Arthur from the start. Missing her father more than ever, she wondered how he might advise her now. But craving the impossible never helped anyone. She sucked in a breath. "Today, I met the right man."

"Arthur? The Roman?" Cynda's incredulity was plain.

Gyan nodded. "Brytoni, too, by his mother . . ." She took a moment to decide how best to translate Ygraine's name into Caledonian. "Ygrayna. She is chieftainess of his clan, Cwrnwyll of Rheged. Although there was apparently some complication regarding Arthur's birth, which prevents him from ever becoming chieftain."

She closed her eyes, overwhelmed by the jumble of conflicting emotions clawing at her heart, a brambly thicket the sharpest sword couldn't part. Arthur was so Roman, it was hard to imagine him as part of any clan. As though he belonged to none—and all. The afternoon memory sprang up of the ruby-headed sword, the milk-white stallion, the scarlet-cloaked warlord. And at dinner, arrayed in that magnificent uniform . . . her throat went dry.

Gyan swallowed thickly and tried to adopt a candid tone. "He's stronger, militarily, beyond question. Argyll would gain a lot from our union."

"And you're falling in love with him. No, don't deny it, Gyan. It's etched as plain on your face as those tattoos on your arms."

"The tattoos." She chafed the betrothal-mark on her left wrist. It galled like a slave collar. "Cynda, I don't know what to do. I want Arthur as my consort. But I am afraid."

"Of breaking the treaty?"

"No." She shrugged. "It's Arthur's treaty, after all. He could grant an exception if he wanted to. If—if he wants me."

"Ach, what kind of talk is this? You have wealth, beauty, intelligence, strength. How could he not be honored to be your consort?"

"I couldn't read him," Gyan confessed. "His smile was . . ." His smile was so indefinable, she had trouble finding words for it. So she opted for a different angle. "It was nothing like Urien's. It wasn't proud or arrogant or triumphant." Or, Gyan realized with a sigh, affectionate. "Arthur could've simply been acting polite toward me."

Cynda grinned. "Dear Gyan, I suspect there's a lot more happening with this Arthur than you might think."

"Oh, Cynda, I hope you're right."

Cynda's eyes narrowed. "But there's something else troubling you, I can tell. What is it? Come on, Gyan, my dove. Tell your old Cynda."

A host of nightmarish visions sprang to life. Central to each was the scion of Clan Moray.

"Urien," Gyan said at last. "If I break our betrothal, it's not just what he might do to me or Argyll that worries me. There seems to be some friction between him and Arthur already. I don't know why, but I sensed it earlier today. If I choose Arthur, and Urien turns against him, then Arthur would lose the Isle of Maun. As we discussed at dinner this evening, control of Maun is vital. A civil war with Urien and Dalriada would be disastrous." Her voice dropped to a ragged whisper. "The Scots would move in and make beds from our bones."

Gyan stared blindly at the floor tiles. All too vividly, she could imagine the death screams, the rivers of blood, the acrid stink of destruction. And afterward, the inconsolable tears of the innocents: for food, for shelter, for their fathers and brothers and husbands and sons . . .

No! She could not bring such evil upon her people. Or upon the man who had sparked the embers of her love. The most logical course would be for Arthur to defeat Urien in the *dubh-lann*, the duel prescribed by Caledonian Law to settle challenges to the consort—or future consort—of the *ard-banoigin*. But, to be legal and fair, the challenge had to be issued by the challenger without overt counsel by the *ard-banoigin* herself. In his treaty, Arthur had demonstrated some knowledge of her people's Law, but his education surely could not have covered this obscure clause. And there was the very real danger that Arthur could be killed, a thought Gyan couldn't bear. There had to be another way. But it refused to reveal itself.

She shivered, but not from cold. Sitting next to her, Cynda wrapped an arm around her shoulders. Gyan did not lift her gaze from the floor.

Gyan knew every detail of her battle-gear was perfect, from her helmet down to her knee-high boots. Cynda had done a fine job of braiding and pinning her hair, and her sword and shield were in top condition. Her blunted practice sword also swung from her belt. She had even taken care to eat only a light meal of bread and tea.

Then why, she asked herself as she strode toward the training ring in the brisk, clean-scented morning, did her stomach feel as though it were trying to turn somersaults?

Arthur the Pendragon.

She banished the nervousness with a toss of her head. The object of this morning's match, as far as she was concerned, was to show off her fighting skills to their best advantage. Which would never happen if she couldn't detach herself from her budding feelings toward this man. And if she didn't beat him to the practice area to give herself a few minutes alone to prepare, her task would be that much more difficult. She quickened her pace.

In contrast to the previous evening, the thoroughfare was already bustling with traffic: wagons and carts of every description, marching units and mounted squads, herders driving their livestock, couriers, soldiers walking alone or in small groups. There wasn't one Caledonian in the lot, which, though a bit disappointing, didn't come as a surprise. Gyan supposed they were too busy learning their new duties. No one paid her any heed; everyone seemed bent on his own mission. She'd wondered whether her duel with the army's war-chieftain would attract attention, but now it didn't seem likely.

At last, the enclosure came into view. To her relief, it was empty. She presumed it was used primarily for equestrian training, since it contained no freestanding practice posts. For what she had in mind, a section of the fence would have to suffice.

Gyan left her battle sword sheathed and gripped the hilt of the practice sword. Closing her eyes, she focused on the balance of the sword and the weight of the shield. When she flicked her eyes open, the sights and sounds of the drilling troops and rumbling wagons, the prickle of the breeze on her bare forearms, and the scent of dew-dampened dirt retreated into a corner of her consciousness. And the dance began: slashes and spins and kicks and thrusts, to the rhythm of her sword and boots thumping the wood.

Finally, Gyan stopped, panting, and leaned her shield and practice sword against the fence. She dashed the sweat from her brow with the back of a hand. The clamminess of her linen undertunic she would have to live with. While in the grip of this drill, the passage of time lost meaning, and she hoped she hadn't overtired herself for the real challenge to come.

The sound of a pair of hands clapping caught her attention. She turned to behold the Pendragon striding toward her, helmet tucked under one arm, looking every inch as handsome in this bronze and boiled-leather version of the uniform he had worn the night before. The ruby of his sword's pommel sparkled above the sheath as he moved. As near as she could tell, it was the only weapon he had brought. To her surprise, he had no shield.

Her stomach began its gymnastic routine anew. Resolutely, she ignored it.

"A marvelous display, Chieftainess." He offered his sword hand. As she gripped his forearm, a tingle spread from her arm beneath his fingertips, straight to her heart. He let go to point at the section of fence bearing the scars of Gyan's practice session. Some of them, she realized with a flush of embarrassment, were quite deep. He arched an eyebrow. "But if you insist on chopping down one of my fences, I think you'll have better luck if you use an ax next time." As their laughter faded, his gaze intensified. "Joking aside, Chieftainess, I would like to know: was that drill something you developed yourself? Is it the same each time you practice it, or do you change it? Do all warriors of your clan use some variant—"

Grinning, she held up both hands in mock surrender. "To answer your first question, no. It's a drill my father taught me, that he learned from his mother, and so on. Originally, there was only one form of the routine, but over time most clans have developed variants to incorporate moves to symbolize the clan's patron creature." She chewed her lip as she cast about for an appropriate example. "Clan Alban's routine, for instance, contains a stylized leap, to represent their lion."

"And Argyll's variant?"

"None, actually. But since our symbol is the dove, we strive to perfect the grace and speed of the moves."

"I could tell." His smile was but an echo of what he had displayed the night before. By the time he donned his helmet and drew his sword, the smile was gone. She wondered if she'd seen it at all. "Ready?"

Her brow creased. "Don't you need to prepare first?" Arthur had seen at least part of her exercise and doubtless had already noted some of her strengths and weaknesses. She was glad she hadn't made any mistakes in the routine this morning, but she had hoped to have a similar opportunity to observe the Pendragon.

Shaking his head, he raised the flat of the blade before his face in salute.

So be it, she thought. She imitated his gesture. Swords at the ready, they began stalking each other. Gyan had lost count of how often Ogryvan had preached what to do at this point in the fight: evaluate the adversary. And that is exactly what Arthur became to her, not a potential consort but a potentially dangerous adversary, as the litany of her father's lessons marched through her mind.

The first thing to note was the body armor, style and material, and the apparent vulnerable places. Since this was practice, to end when one warrior knocked the other down, finding the spots where the deathblow could be struck was not the object. Still, drawing first blood was a vital first step toward victory, and locating more unprotected areas increased chances dramatically.

His torso and shoulders were covered with a muscled bronze breastplate. A fringe of thick, metal-studded leather protected his groin and thighs. The gold-tipped scarlet horsehair crest of his helmet shimmered in the sunlight. It all added up to formidable protection, even without a shield. To draw first blood, she would somehow have to get past his guard to nick a forearm or strike with a low lunge to the legs.

Of equal importance was the shield: how much of the body it could protect and how the opponent held it. A skilled warrior used it for offense as well as defense.

Arthur was not using his shield, Gyan reasoned, because his sword was probably easier to control with both hands. In battle, she never would have forgone the protection her shield could offer. But she suspected she'd have the advantage of speed and agility with her lighter weapon, so she let the shield stay beside the fence.

The final and most important part of the evaluation involved the body itself: the stance, the gait, the limbs, and the face.

In a solid stance, the warrior's balance was centered perfectly, front to back and side to side. Fighting on the balls of the feet was a grave weakness. Those who fell prey to this habit often found themselves struggling to regain balance after taking a hard blow. If they were lucky enough to maintain footing at all. Another weakness was stiff joints—knees, shoulders, elbows, wrists—all easily exploited by an aggressive attack.

Arthur's stance was as good as that of any warrior Gyan had ever seen. Winning this match was not going to be easy.

Body movements usually betrayed how much tension the opponent was feeling. A certain amount was to be expected. Too much could be fatal. Hunched shoulders, a too-tight grip on the sword, and an uneven gait were more weaknesses to shorten the fight.

Many swordsmen swore the key to victory lay in watching the enemy's eyes. Sparring with Ogryvan had made Gyan adept at keeping others from reading her actions in this manner. He had taught her to focus on the opponent's chest and the elbow of the sword arm, and to let her peripheral vision absorb what the shield and feet were doing.

Eyes could deceive. The true secret was the elbow. The elbow controlled the sword's basic movement, modified to a lesser extent by the wrist. By watching the elbow, an experienced swordsman could accurately anticipate the enemy's moves. Gyan had often seen Ogryvan unnerve opponents by seeming to know their next move even before they did. This *lann-seolta*, "blade-cunning," was a skill won only through years of relentless practice. She knew she was a long way from claiming mastery, but today her limited experience would have to suffice.

They circled for what felt like half an eon. He appeared to be inviting her to attack first. She noticed him favoring his left leg a wee bit, as though troubled by an old wound. Bearing full weight seemed to be a problem reflected not only in his gait but occasionally in his eyes, too. A clever warrior might feign such a weakness to trick his opponent into doing something foolish.

There was only one way to find out.

She lunged toward that side. He parried the blow with ease and answered with a counterattack so forceful, it was all she could do to block the bone-jarring blows. Injury or no, the Pendragon knew his craft. And she was half dismayed yet half pleased to recognize that, unlike in her matches with Urien, Arthur was holding nothing back. But as the ache in her arms and shoulders mounted, she knew she had to devise some other tactic, else this would soon become the shortest bout on record.

After parrying one of his lighter blows, she spun away to disengage, catch her breath, and collect her thoughts. Sword raised, she again started circling him, relieved that he didn't seem anxious to reengage. Briefly, she noticed that a crowd was forming along the rail; soldiers, mostly, gesturing and shouting words she couldn't understand—nor did she wish to. She blotted them out to open all her senses to her opponent, even down to the huskiness of his breathing and the tangy odor of his sweat, trying to think of anything that might work to tip the balance in her favor.

An image flashed to mind of a bout with her father, fought on the eve of Urien's arrival at Arbroch. Inspired by the outcome of that fight, she swiftly formed a plan. It carried high risk and no guarantee of success. She never would have attempted such a move in combat. Here, the only danger if she lost would be to her pride. But if she won . . . she bit her lower lip to keep her face from betraying her intent.

This time, she let Arthur initiate the attack. While advancing to meet the blow, she feigned a stumble, fell, and rolled to her stomach. As expected, he quickly moved in to claim the victory. The crowd cheered. But before she could feel the prickle of his sword on her neck, she twisted aside and hooked his legs with hers. Luck favored her; with a startled yelp, and equally startled noises from their audience, he went down. She scrambled to her feet and pinned him under the point of her sword. Amid the overall roar of disappointment, she could pick out phrases like "Trickery!" and "Not fair!" But the taunts didn't bother her one bit; victory had never tasted sweeter! Her only regret was that Ogryvan and Per and the rest of her clan couldn't savor it with her.

Studying Arthur for a reaction, her grin soured. For several seconds, he stared at the sky as though stunned; whether physically or mentally, she couldn't tell. Her concern rose as she wondered if she had actually injured him. Finally, he shook his head and attempted to sit up, but her sword still barred his way.

"I concede the match, Chieftainess." He released his

sword and waved his open hand. "I won't try anything—unique. You have my word. Thank God my
enemies aren't half as devious as you are." His grin
could have stopped the sun in its course . . . and it was
having an arresting effect on Gyan's heart as well. "But
I wouldn't advise using that move in battle. Much too
risky."

"Oh. Yes, I—I know." Chiding herself for how silly
she must sound, she sheathed her sword and thrust
out her hand. He accepted her unspoken offer, gripped
her forearm, and hauled himself up.

Pain stabbing her arm forced a strangled gasp from
her throat. He shifted his grip to her hand and gently
turned her arm to expose the underside. A long cut lay
perilously close to one of the veins, seeping blood. He
traced the vein lightly with a fingertip.

"When did I do . . . this?" His voice was a hoarse
whisper.

Staring at the cut, she wondered the same thing.
Probably during their initial clash, though she really
had no idea. She shrugged. Now that fatigue was
making itself felt in earnest, even that motion made her
wince.

"Chieftainess, I didn't mean to—" A stricken look
shattered his bearing. He squeezed her hand. "God in
heaven, Gyanhumara, I am so sorry."

She wanted to reassure him that she'd be all right;
the wound looked clean and wasn't much deeper than a
scratch. In fact, it was the least of her concerns.
Enchanted by the sound of her name on his lips and
mesmerized by his gaze, she felt the world seem to
collapse to just the two of them. His face hovered over
hers, his lips a handspan away. The warmth of his
nearness had an intoxicating effect. She was acutely

conscious of the tugging of her heart, as though it was trying to pull her even closer to him. It wasn't an unwelcome idea.

But breathing became an effort as dizziness overcame her. Not now, she silently pleaded to the One God, no! She could only stare down in disbelief as her traitor knees started to buckle. Before she could fall, his arm wrapped around her waist. The back of his fingers felt cold against her cheek.

"You're burning up, Gyanhumara. I've got to get you to the infirmary."

Arthur tried to take a step with her, but she refused to move. "No, please, I—I don't need—"

"You must allow me. My Lord."

She and Arthur glanced up to see Urien crossing the ring, a displeased set to his features. Why hadn't she realized he could have been watching? Rebuking herself for the idiot she was, Gyan pushed away from Arthur to stand, unassisted, as Urien drew near.

Urien offered her his hand, which she readily accepted; it seemed the wisest course. He gave her an appraising look. "My dear, are you all right?" She nodded, and he regarded the Pendragon. If his eyes could have shot daggers, Arthur would have died on the spot. "You weren't trying to kill my bride-to-be, were you, Lord Pendragon?"

Up went that mask of Arthur's again. "Far from it, Tribune. If you had watched our match, you'd have seen her best me."

"I saw enough." Expression softening, Urien caressed her cheek. "Come, my dear. Arthur is right; you really do feel too warm."

She shook her head. "It's the exertion." That was mostly true, she told herself. She wasn't about to admit the rest of it, to either of them. "I'll be fine after I rest awhile." And after she left the presence of the man who was stealing her heart. She hoped.

"That may be so." Urien gestured at her wound. "But you must have that seen to. I insist. The fort's physicians are excellent." Gyan sighed; Cynda had dressed far worse wounds than this. But she was too exhausted to argue. Obviously pleased with her acquiescence, Urien moved to her left side and placed her uninjured arm on top of his. "And I also insist," he said, leveling another hard stare at Arthur, "that there be no more of these matches between you two."

Fists on hips, Arthur said, "An order, Tribune?"

Urien shook his head. "I was merely expressing concern for my beloved." The kiss he planted on her lips was surprisingly gentle.

Panic seized her with the thought that she had to act as though she were enjoying Urien's attentions, else he might suspect something was happening between her and Arthur. So she did the only thing that came to mind: she closed her eyes to imagine that her lips were pressed to Arthur's, that she was clasping his body to hers, running her fingers through his red-gold hair . . .

The kiss ended. To savor the moment, she kept her eyes closed.

"Get her to the infirmary, Tribune." The harsh sound of Arthur's voice startled her, and she opened her eyes to see him whirl and bend to snatch up his sword, slam it into its sheath, and stalk from the field, his cloak a scarlet billow behind him.

She glanced at Urien, who seemed decidedly smug as he watched Arthur's retreat. With a start, she realized how her response must have appeared to Arthur. To Urien, too, for that matter. It was without doubt the stupidest thing she could have done! Desperately, she wanted to call out to Arthur, to explain what had really happened, despite what Urien might think. Or do. But it was too late. Arthur was gone, taking a piece of her heart with him—although he'd never know it, she admitted miserably.

Urien again took her uninjured arm, smiling broadly at her. "Come, my dear Gyanhumara. The infirmary is this way."

Gyan felt numb to the core, devoid of strength and will. There seemed to be nothing left but to do Urien's bidding. And to get accustomed to the idea that she'd be doing his bidding for the rest of her life.

Chapter
14

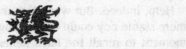

Propelled by rage and frustration, Arthur strode from the field as fast as dignity allowed. He should have held his ground and waited for Urien to leave first, but having to watch him walk off with Gyanhumara would have been a worse torture than anything Arthur could have devised.

Most of the crowd had already dispersed, probably to start spreading the tale of what they'd seen. Let them talk, he thought grimly. If it damaged his reputation, then so be it. He deserved every bloody word. For losing the match by failing to discern the trick, and for losing her.

He ignored the remaining onlookers as he cut through their ranks. Along the way, he was stopped by four of his staff centurions. Unit readiness reports, promotion recommendations, intelligence briefs, supply requisitions—none of it mattered to him right now. What mattered was fulfilling his urgent need to get away, to reclaim a remnant of self-control, and to think. God, how he needed to think! He ordered the men to deliver their reports to Marcus and dismissed them with a wave.

Upon resuming his punishing pace, he didn't let up until he'd reached the stables, snatched Macsen's bridle from its peg in the tack room, and whirled to find one of the stable boys staring up at him, blocking his way.

"Need help, my Lord?" The lad's gaze looked hopeful.

Help, indeed. But what Arthur needed help with, a mere stable boy could do nothing about. It took him a moment to recall the lad's name: Wat, who for some odd reason preferred the less flattering nickname of Wart. Arthur felt stupid for his lapse. Aside from himself, Wart handled Macsen better than anyone else on earth.

Except, maybe, her.

Arthur blinked to erase Gyanhumara's face from his mind. That only strengthened the image. He suppressed a sigh. The tierce bell hadn't yet rung, and already this day was nothing but a series of losing battles.

Arthur thrust the bridle into the lad's outstretched hand. "Thank you, Wart." As preoccupied as he was, he probably would have tried to saddle Macsen backward. The rumor mongers had enough grist for the mill already.

Wart looped the bridle over his shoulder and lifted the saddle and pad from its rail. Breaking into a cheerful whistle, he scampered from the tack room and disappeared around the bend toward the stalls.

For once, Arthur took his time, using the pretense of inspecting the horses along the way to ponder what had happened in the ring.

The match was easy to analyze. He had but one word to describe Gyanhumara the warrior: astounding.

Form, speed, skill, agility, even her strength had far exceeded his expectations. True, she took the bait he'd offered in the guise of a feigned limp, but not in a way that overcommitted her, as an opponent eager for a quick victory would have done. Arthur knew then that he'd have to wear her down by sheer force. He'd been within a few strokes of succeeding, in fact; he had seen fatigue flare in her eyes, dimming the fiery determination. But he should have realized that he had not seen a hint of surrender. She had duped him, with that perfectly timed and executed fall, into thinking he'd won and promptly threw his arrogance back into his face.

And, God help him, he had loved her all the more for it. Sprawled on the ground with her sword poking his chest, he had tried to deny that simple truth, and failed.

After she had helped him rise and discovered her wound, she had seemed so vulnerable, so precious . . . and so ready to accept the kiss he had been about to bestow—audience or no audience—had she not picked that precise moment to collapse. Perhaps, he thought in disgust, that had been a ploy, too.

He reached Macsen's stall to find his horse already saddled and bridled. Currycomb in hand, Wart was easing tangles from the stallion's mane. Macsen whickered a greeting. Wart flattened himself against the wall as the stallion stepped forward to thrust his head over the stall's waist-high door. Absently stroking Macsen's cheek, Arthur bade the lad to finish. Wart saluted with the comb and went to work on the tail.

Why, he asked himself for the hundredth time, why on earth did Gyanhumara fling herself into Urien's arms with such passionate abandon? Until that moment, he'd have wagered his horse that she had been less than thrilled at Urien's arrival. Could he, Arthur, have been fooled by her earlier signals? Had she devised those signals only to make Urien jealous and therefore more attentive toward her?

It was entirely possible. The tactic had certainly seemed to work. And she may as well have taken her sword and run him through, instead of kissing Urien. It would have hurt a whole bloody lot less.

Heartily, he wished he had heeded Merlin's advice to break off pursuit of this maddening woman. Maddening, deceptive, manipulating . . . clever . . . intelligent, intuitive, powerful, confident, witty . . . glorious . . . Arthur belayed the wish. Helen of Troy may have had the face that launched a thousand ships, but Gyanhumara of Caledonia could easily capture a thousand hearts. Including his.

And by God's holy wounds, he would gladly fight the other nine hundred and ninety-nine men for the privilege to stand alone at her side. He could no sooner stop loving her, no matter how much she hurt him, than he could stop the dawn.

The trouble was, she would be sailing for Maun on the equally unstoppable morning tide. Not to mention the fact that Urien, acting well within his rights as her betrothed, had made his wants all too clear. In more ways than one.

"He's ready for you, my Lord."

With a start, Arthur focused on the stable boy, who was smoothing a patch on Macsen's withers with his palm. Of course, Arthur realized, Wart had been referring to his horse, not his rival. A smile forced its way to his lips. "Excellent job, Wart."

In fact, Arthur's stallion had seldom looked better.

The same could be said of the lad, too; it was amazing what good could be wrought with a word of praise. It gave him an idea. He moved aside and swung open the door to let Wart and Macsen leave the stall. Arthur paced them while Wart led the horse out from under the stable roof's overhang. But when the lad paused to hand over the reins, Arthur shook his head.

"You take him out for his exercise today, Wart. I've just remembered I have some work to do."

"Oh, sir! May I, really? You mean it?"

By way of an answer, Arthur boosted the grinning lad into the saddle. Wart's whistling began anew as he double-wound the reins around one hand, nudged the stallion's sides, and they trotted away. Again, it brought to mind Arthur's initial encounter with Gyanhumara, when she had mastered Macsen so quickly—and when the most Arthur had felt toward her was admiration. God, how simple life had been! Simple but, he was forced to admit, empty. Wars and rumors of wars were one thing. Discovering his soul's mate was quite another. And she was worth every loss and every ounce of pain she or Urien or anyone else could inflict upon him.

He said to no one in particular, "Yes. I mean it."

Head bowed like a prisoner being led to the gallows, Gyan mounted the wide steps. The blue-veined white stone brought to mind what she had seen in the *praetorium* the night before, and she looked up. And stopped to stare in awe at the edifice looming in her path. Sprouting from the top of the steps were several tall pillars, supporting an elaborately carved roof crowned with rounded crimson tiles. On top of the roof, as if an afterthought, sat a huge bell, surrounded by its private shelter. The entire building shimmered in the sunlight as though touched by the One God Himself.

"What's wrong, Gyanhumara? We're here."

"This?" She didn't hide her astonishment as she pointed at the structure. "This is the infirmary?"

Urien gave her an indulgent smile. "No, my dear. This was built as a temple for the Roman god Jupiter, but it's now called the Church of Saint John the Evangelist." Gyan mentally translated the latter phrase into Caledonian as "Ian the Holy Messenger"—one of the Christ's closest followers, she recalled from Dafydd's stories. Glancing sunward, Urien tugged her elbow. "The infirmary is in a back wing of the church. But if we don't hurry, you'll have to wait to be seen until after the third-hour office is done."

By "third-hour office," she could only assume he meant something that was about to happen inside the church, although she couldn't imagine what it might be. As the bell began to toll, she got the distinct impression she was about to find out. Its mellow tone seemed to beckon to her. Gladly, she obeyed and continued up the stairs, feeling more of her fatigue drain away with each step she took.

This time, Urien lagged behind. "Where are you going?"

"Inside, of course." Gyan gestured at the folk, a mixture of soldiers and civilians, who were quietly passing them on either side to enter the building singly or in pairs. "I can, can't I? Or is this third-hour office only for residents?"

Urien shook his head. "All are welcome." He stepped up to reach her side. "But disturbances aren't. Once we're inside, you'll have to be quiet."

As if she were a child! She rolled her eyes. "I do know how to be discreet, Urien."

Arms crossed, he said, "And that swordfight with Arthur was your idea of discretion?" He leaned closer, eyes glittering. "Or his?"

Up came her left hand, fingers knotted into a fist, to wave the accursed betrothal-mark before his face. It was all she could do to restrain herself from ramming it where it most needed to go. "This is here by *my* choice." She jabbed her finger toward the twin mark on his wrist. "So is yours. Don't forget it."

He caught her hand in his. She braced herself, physically as well as mentally, for his angry retort. To her immense surprise, it never came.

"Believe me, Gyanhumara, I don't forget. I can't. My tattoo won't let me." He kissed her betrothal-mark. "But what it reminds me of most is the mark you've carved"—he placed her left hand on his breastplate, over his heart—"here."

"Indeed." Cocking an eyebrow, Gyan pulled her hand free to rest it on her hip. "Forgive me, Urien, but you seem to have a strange way of showing it." She tried to curb her cynicism by keeping her voice soft but wasn't sure how well she was succeeding.

Bowing his head, he sighed. "I know." As he lifted his gaze to meet hers, earnestness dominated his expression. "I want this marriage to work, Gyanhumara. More than anything I've ever wanted in my entire life. Not just for our clans, or for Brydein, but for us. But we—you and me and the cultures that bred us—we're so—so—"

A list of words popped to mind, and she selected what she thought was the most innocuous. "Different?"

"Exactly." Again, he captured her hand and raised it

to his lips. "Help me, Gyanhumara. Help me learn to overcome these differences."

Gyan battled a new wave of surprise. Help Urien, when Arthur was the only man she wanted? But since she had hopelessly alienated Arthur with her ill-considered behavior, she no longer had a choice to make.

Or rather, she corrected herself sadly, the choice she had most wanted to make was no longer an option.

"Very well. Ready for your first lesson?" When Urien nodded, she said, "I am not an object to possess, nor merely a means for producing heirs, but a warrior and a chieftainess. And neither is symbolic. If for whatever reason you have trouble accepting me in the former role, then I strongly suggest you try respecting the latter. Because if you don't, you will never win the support of my clan."

A strange look crossed his face, as though he'd never considered that point before. He stroked his chin. "Our cultures really are different, then. For a Brytoni woman to rule a clan is rare."

She thought of Arthur's mother, while struggling not to think of the woman's son. "But not unheard of. Am I right?"

"You are absolutely right, my dear." His smile could have charmed a squirrel out of its winter hoard. "And I see now that I've been acting like a—"

"A *cù-puc?*" she offered, grinning.

"Is that Caledonian for 'selfish oaf'?"

"Roughly." Sunlight glinted off his dragon cloak-pin, turning the bronze golden. Her heart lurched, jolting the grin from her face. The image of Arthur's face seared through her mental defenses. Not as she had seen it last, but earlier, just before Urien had entered the ring, when Arthur had almost kissed her—a kiss that, despite the probable consequences, she would have welcomed with every fiber of her being. "Lesson two: if I say I need to be alone for a while, I mean it."

"Now?" He looked disappointed.

She nodded. "Meet me back here after . . ." Something occurred to her, for which Ogryvan would have chastised her soundly had he been present. With a rueful laugh, she pointed toward the training ground, where some of her gear was still leaning against the fence. "After you do me the favor of taking my shield and practice sword back to the *mansio*. Please?"

"I'll do better than that, Gyanhumara." Urien spread his hands. "Give me your battle sword, and I'll arrange to have all your gear cleaned and polished." When she hesitated, he said, "Weapons aren't permitted inside the church anyway."

Despite his argument's validity, misgiving chilled her soul. For a Caledonian warrior, the surrender of the sword implied the surrender of self. She knew Urien wasn't asking this of her; he was merely trying to be helpful, and a part of her appreciated the unexpected offer. But this was one custom she vowed never to teach him.

Murmuring her thanks, she unhooked the sheath from her belt and laid it across his upturned palms. Since the Caledonian Oath of Fealty ritual was performed with the naked blade, giving Urien the sheathed sword dispelled all but her most stubborn qualms. She watched his progress down the steps and back the way they'd come, until she was certain he was indeed going to fulfill her request.

Her heart churning in turmoil, Gyan turned and raced up the remaining steps two at a time, slipped between the columns, and headed toward the church's arched entryway. She stopped to regard the pair of dark oak doors before her, standing open as though inviting her to enter. Out spilled strains of musical chanting that reminded her of Dafydd's songs, magnified a hundredfold. And a hundred times more compelling. As she crossed the threshold, the sound grew, resonating throughout the huge vaulted stone chamber and deep into her soul.

Urien needn't have worried about her creating a disturbance. As though in the grip of an invisible power, she stood motionless except for her head as she marveled at the details of her surroundings.

A spicy aroma permeated the air. Gyan looked up to study the ceiling's gilt mosaics. It didn't matter that she had no clue what people and scenes they depicted; they were still magnificent to behold. The vast floor was overlaid with black slate, interrupted at intervals by white columns. Beside each column sat a table holding a score of lit candles. Engravings and statues adorned the many recesses along the walls, where some people knelt or stood with bowed heads and clasped hands. The rest were kneeling before the cloth-draped altar, where a robed priest was standing with his back to the sanctuary, doing something with his hands that she couldn't see.

He turned, and Gyan gasped. In the next breath, she decided she shouldn't have been surprised. The priest was Merlin, called Bishop Dubricius in this setting, she reminded herself. She met the bishop's gaze and noted his flicker of surprise.

In one hand, he held a dish with a loaf; in the other, a cup. Both arms were raised aloft as he chanted. With the choir singing a response, he slowly lowered his arms, and the people began making their way to him to share the meal he was offering.

This, Gyan realized, was the rite she and Dafydd had spoken of but, because of the need to preserve the secrecy of her conversion, could never conduct in her presence at Arbroch. Just the sight of the loaf and cup in Merlin's hands filled her with a hunger that far surpassed mere physical need. That hunger warred with profound sorrow: she could not accept the bishop's invitation to dine at this sacred table without running the risk of her clansmen—and ultimately Argyll's priests—finding out.

Fighting the trembling of her chin, she tore her gaze from the bishop. As if the inability to partake of the loaf and cup weren't difficult enough, what she saw next pierced her heart. Suspended by drawn gold wire from the ceiling over the altar was a life-sized oak carving of the tortured Christ, arms outstretched as though to embrace the entire world. Sunlight streaming from the side windows illuminated the face's details. The sculptor had given his subject ragged hair circled by a band of thorns that seemed so realistic, Gyan could easily visualize blood streaking the scratched forehead. Hands and feet were pinned to the beams by thick nails. He looked anguished and vulnerable, this Christ, yet imbued with the calm strength born of the certainty that, even through the vale of death, a glorious future awaited beyond.

Gyan had no such certainty. In fact, she had never felt more uncertain in her whole life. The only thing that seemed clear was the stark reality of the Christ's sacrifice. A flash of insight told her that while on earth, He had been, in a sense, His Father's sword incarnate, and He had offered Himself to His enemies in the ultimate act of surrender and love. And as proof, He bore not one mark but many. The enormity of this selfless act threatened to overwhelm Gyan. But it was heartening, too; death truly had no power over Him, as evidenced by the empty tomb. Like a true leader, the Christ had entered first into the abyss so that His people could follow in safety, under His guidance. When Dafydd had helped her through that first faltering prayer and even in the days afterward, Gyan had not fully comprehended what it meant to follow this Christ, this Leader of leaders and Lord of Lords. Now she did.

As she sank to her knees, tears washing her cheeks even as her spirit felt buoyed by the voices of the unseen choristers, she begged Iesseu the Christ to guide her steps and share a wee bit of His strength with her.

Back at her chambers in the *mansio* at last, Gyan lay on her stomach across the bed, slowly stroking the neatly applied bandage that hid the clan-mark as well as the cut on her sword arm. Urien had been right; the physician who had dressed her wound was excellent. Even Cynda hadn't been able to find fault with the job.

What a day this had turned out to be, she mused. After the service, Merlin had approached her to offer his assistance. She'd regained her composure and footing—and her wits—by then and dismissed her emotional response as a product of exhaustion and awe. It was the only portion of the truth she dared confess to Arthur's adviser, kinsman, and friend.

Urien had caught up with her shortly after that and displayed more of his newfound kindness while escorting her to the infirmary and later, while giving her a tour of the fortress. To fill the time, she'd asked about his home and upbringing, which seemed to please him immensely. In a few short hours, she learned more about Urien map Dumarec, Clan Moray, and the clan seat at Dunadd than she had ever bargained for. Including a practical reason for uniting her clan with his: with the exception of Maun, Clan Moray possessed mountainous islands that were fit for pastures but not much else. The bulk of Argyll's wealth came from its excellent farmlands, but suitable pastures were in short supply. The combination of these lands through Gyan's marriage to Urien would bring prosperity to both clans.

But signs of the Dragon were everywhere they went: banners, carvings, and the badge on the cloak of every soldier they met. Not to mention the one Urien wore. Each sigil was an agonizing reminder of the one man on earth she wanted but could never have. Unable to bear it any longer, she had excused herself on the pretense of wanting to rest. The kiss Urien had given her at their parting was as tender a kiss as she could ever desire . . . had Arthur the Pendragon never invaded her heart.

Maybe Urien really did believe she loved him. Which was probably all for the best anyway. Sighing, she laid her cheek against her crossed arms. The rough bandage provoked memories of the morning's encounter. She knew the bandage would come off and the cut would heal in time. But with the inevitable scar as an ever-present reminder of Arthur, she doubted that her heart ever would.

Someone knocked. Gyan ignored it. Another knock rattled the door, longer and more urgent-sounding. "Go away."

"Gyan, my dove." Cynda's muffled voice filtered through. "There's someone here to see you."

"I don't want to see anyone!" That was almost true.

But the possibility that Arthur was waiting in her antechamber was laughably remote.

"But he's a"—Gyan heard a giggle—"a messenger."

Annoyed, Gyan got up, stalked to the door, released the bolt, and yanked the door open. "I said—" She gasped. "Per!"

She couldn't get through the door fast enough and all but flew into her brother's arms. As he completed the embrace, she was assaulted by countless memories of their childhood escapades, memories of a time when no thought of marriage had ever entered her head. A time before . . . him. The man she loved; the only man she would ever love.

Sobs welled from the depths of her soul. Desperately, she tried to choke them down. If Per saw her crying now, he would naturally ask why, and the wound Arthur had wrought on her heart was the last thing she wanted to confess to her brother. But as raw and frayed as she felt, this was one fight she knew she was destined to lose.

Not since the death of a favorite hound puppy when she'd been about eight had Peredur mac Hymar seen his sister so distraught. "Gyan? Gyan, what's wrong?" She only clung tighter to him and cried harder. Concerned, he glanced at Cynda, who was standing nearby with folded arms and a look on her face that seemed to say this was exactly the sort of behavior she'd expected. Which was no help to him at all. "What do you know about this, Cynda?"

"If she wants to tell you, she will. It's not my place, Per." Her tone was unusually gentle, but before he could question her further, she turned to busy herself with some towels near the wash stand.

He wasn't surprised by Cynda's answer, but it had

been worth a try. So he silently held Gyan, stroking her hair and back until her tears seemed to subside. Then he reverted to the tactic he used whenever his sister needed cheering: he tugged her braid.

The look she gave him was a strange mixture of sorrow, gratitude, and affection. But despite the reddened eyes and tear-stained cheeks, her grin was genuine, and Per was glad to see it. "Beast!"

She released her hold and stepped back, scrubbing her eyes. Cynda proffered a wet towel, followed by a dry one, both of which Gyan put to good use. Cynda collected the towels, favored him and his sister with one of her typical knowing glances, and left the room. Now Gyan looked much more like the sister Per knew. Only—and this puzzled him because the idea seemed so bizarre—older, somehow.

But he knew better than to ask her directly, so he tried a different approach. "Miss me already, dear sister?"

"Ha. Among other things." Her eyes seemed to focus on something he was wearing. She drew close enough to tap his new Dragon Legion cloak-pin. "Why are you wearing that?"

"Ah, my rank badge." In his best imitation of what he'd seen the Brytoni soldiers doing countless times over the past two days, he took a pace backward and thumped his chest. *"Centurio Equuo* Peredur mac Hymar, Seventh *Ala,* reporting." He couldn't keep down the grin. "Gods, what a mouthful! I'm not even sure of what it all means yet."

"That you're in charge, I think." Her laugh was too brief, and sadness again dominated her gaze. "Your badge, it—" Determination chased away the sorrow, and she ventured a thin smile. "It becomes you, Per."

Why would a simple cloak-pin elicit a reaction like

that? It was nothing special, just a copper dragon inside a red enamel ring, with a sapphire chip set in the dragon's eye . . . the dragon's eye—the Pendragon! Whatever was bothering her had to do with him, Per was certain. If that Roman *cù-puc* had hurt her . . .

Casting about for more clues, since it was obvious she wasn't going to start volunteering answers, his gaze fell upon her bandaged forearm. "The Pendragon did this to you." Per felt his anger mount. "Didn't he?"

She gave him a startled look, as if she hadn't heard him. He stabbed a finger toward the bandage, and she raised her arm as though to study it more closely. "Oh, this? Yes." She sighed.

"I thought as much." He'd heard about their match, of course—the men had been talking about little else all day—but not about her getting wounded. His fingers curled into fists. Like a torch, his battle-fury ignited. "I have some business to attend to." He spun toward the door.

She caught his hand to pull him back. "Per, please, no!" He faced her. Her eyes were wide with fear and . . . beseeching?

"Give me one good reason why I shouldn't kill him."

Horror crossed her face, followed by exasperation and, finally, resignation. "I'll give you two good reasons. First, this wound is nothing. A scratch." She enunciated each word as though speaking to a simpleton, which was exactly how Per was starting to feel for overreacting. "The attending physician got too zealous with the bandage roll, that's all." She cocked the injured arm and punched him in the shoulder, hard.

"Hey! That hurt!" He massaged the spot, but it continued to throb.

She grinned. "You deserve it, you big idiot." Circling her arm about his waist, she laid her head against his chest. "But I appreciate you wanting to protect me. I really do." She looked at him plaintively. "I wish you could come with me to Maun."

"For protection?" Certainly not from the Pendragon; Arthur would be remaining at legion headquarters. Per felt his eyes narrow as he regarded his sister. "From whom?"

"Myself." She shook her head and pushed away from him, expelling a noisy sigh. "Never mind. I've said too much already." She wandered to the table, braced both arms against its surface, and bowed her head.

Her defeated posture—from the lass who despised losing anything to anyone—wrenched his heart. He walked around to the front of the table, bent over, and lifted her chin so he could see her face. Again, it was clouded with sadness. "Gyan, you haven't said nearly enough. At least, you owe me that second reason of yours."

"The second reason"—she jerked her chin free and dropped her gaze to the tabletop—"is a lost cause."

Gods! Briefly, Per studied the rafters. Gyan hadn't been this reluctant to divulge information since the day she'd hidden his first helmet down a well, furious that Ogryvan had declared her to be too young, at age six, to start training. Only after her father had relented did she consent to reveal the helmet's location. And then, Per recalled with a slim smile, her first lesson with her new practice sword occurred when Ogryvan had applied the flat of its wooden blade to her bottom. She didn't sit for days afterward, but even now Per couldn't decide whether that had been from the pain of Ogryvan's "lesson" or because she'd been too busy fighting mock battles with the sword to engage in more sedate activities.

Wrestling his mind back to the present, he tried to

piece together the hints to divine her problem. But Arthur and "lost cause" didn't make any sense. If she now preferred Arthur to Urien, well, the remedy for that was simple enough. Per wasn't entirely ready to accept the idea of his little sister taking any man into her bed, no matter how worthy. But above all else, Argyll's line of succession had to remain secure, and that was Gyan's most important duty.

Quietly, he ventured a guess: "You love the Pendragon, don't you, Gyan?" After a moment, she nodded but did not look up. Why, then, would she consider Arthur to be a lost cause, unless . . . "But he has refused to become your consort because he doesn't love you." He smashed his fist to the tabletop and straightened. That got her attention. Wounding his sister in the heat of combat was one thing; wounding her heart was quite another. "Now I *am* going to kill him!"

The fiery intensity of her glare rooted him to the spot. "You do that, Peredur mac Hymar, and I'll have your head so fast, I guarantee you will never know what happened." And by all the gods, he believed her. The glare dimmed as she moved from behind the table to face him. "Arthur didn't refuse me. I haven't—" She took in a breath and let it out slowly. "I can't choose him. Ever." Her upraised hand prevented him from voicing the question forming on his lips. "Please don't ask me to explain, Per. It's too . . . complicated."

Painful, too, if he didn't miss his guess. And the last thing she needed was more pain, especially from her kin. Per caught her hand. "Is there anything I can do to help you, anything at all?"

Not unexpectedly, she shook her head. "You're already helping me, Per, more than you might realize. Your support, your love, your concern—" A hint of the old Gyan returned in the mischievous grin, and she gave his hand a squeeze. "Even your thick-witted overprotectiveness." As their laughter faded, she adopted a pensive look.

"You've thought of something, Gyan?" She could have asked him to die for her, and he'd do it a hundred times over if the gods would consent.

"Something to help me, yes." Hands on hips, she regarded him levelly. "Serve Arthur the Pendragon of Brydein to the very best of your ability, you and all of Argyll with you."

An odd request, but . . . "It shall be done as you command, Chieftainess." He bent double in a bow, careful not to grin until he was sure his face was hidden from her view.

"Beast!" She clapped her hands to his shoulders and pushed him straight so quickly, he couldn't suppress the grin in time. "I meant what I said, Per. Treaty or no treaty, he deserves at least that much from . . . us."

"I know, Gyan." Thinking about Arthur in a more rational fashion forced to mind Per's mission. He slapped his forehead in disgust. She gave him a questioning look. "Just call me six kinds of fool, dear sister. I was supposed to deliver you a message." Now knowing what he did, he wasn't at all sure how Gyan would react to his next statement: "From the Pendragon."

Chapter

15

Crossing her arms, Gyan regarded her brother and mentally girded herself for the worst.

"You needn't look so worried, Gyan," Per said. "It's just a dinner invitation."

"Just a dinner invitation. Ha." She'd plunged unwittingly into her emotional quagmire the night before by accepting "just a dinner invitation." But her innate curiosity conquered her gut reaction to deliver an outright refusal. "Do you know any details?"

"Aye. It's a sendoff for the officers traveling to Maun." Which meant Urien would be invited, too. Wonderful, she thought as Per gestured at her with his upturned hand. "And, of course, yourself."

Of course. Vividly, the image of Arthur's barely leashed fury as he left the training field coursed through her mind. Had she alienated him so badly that he was willing to go to all the trouble of hosting a farewell dinner just to prove that the sight of her and Urien together no longer bothered him? She dearly hoped that wasn't the case, but no better explanation presented itself.

Again, she opened her mouth to refuse the invitation, but curiosity took control: "Where?"

"The garrison commander's quarters. What's that Roman word of theirs? The pra-pray—"

"The *praetorium.*" Of course. "I'm somewhat familiar with the place." In response to the question in his eyes, she said, "Please don't ask, Per." But when she saw his hurt, she relented a little. "All right, maybe later." If she could find a time when they both had an hour or four to spare, which didn't seem likely before the following morning, when her ship was to depart. "When is this dinner to take place?"

He twisted to glance out the window and gave a rueful laugh. Gyan followed the line of his gaze. The vibrant red-gold of the sky—the color of Arthur's hair, she noticed dismally—announced the sun's retreat. "Now. I'm sorry, Gyan. We started talking, and I forgot, and I—I'm sorry." Gone was all trace of his usual teasing mirth.

"Don't be, Per. It's my fault." As she jabbed her chest with her thumb, an idea occurred. "Have you eaten yet?"

"No. But I'm not—"

"But nothing. You're coming with me."

If her tunic and leggings didn't constitute the expected attire for this event, so be it. Never mind that there wasn't time to change; she couldn't be sure what Arthur was planning to accomplish with this dinner ploy, so above all she wanted to feel comfortable. Including having one true ally at her side. She gathered her clan mantle from the chair, flung it across her shoulders, and deftly fastened the dove brooch in place.

"As your . . . protection?" Per's impish grin returned in full force.

"Beast!" She playfully slapped the spot on his shoulder that she had punched earlier and was rewarded by his exaggerated wince. "As my escort." Since there was no time to find Cynda, she smoothed her hair as best she could. Unlike the day before, though, she wasn't concerned with trying to impress anyone.

"Just do me one favor, dear brother." As Per held the door open for her, he raised an eyebrow. "Let me be the diplomat."

"Gladly, dear sister." Echoing in the corridor, his hearty laugh was a joy to hear. "Gladly!"

In the courtyard of the *praetorium*, Gyan and Per were approached by the same guardsmen who had escorted her the night before. Although the men's salutes were no less sharp, their demeanors seemed cooler. Probably, Gyan mused, because they didn't like anyone who could dump their war-chieftain on his backside. A chill crawled up her spine with the recollection of Urien's words: "Least of all a woman." Did they all feel that way, including Arthur?

"Are you all right, Gyan?" The concern in Per's hushed tone was clear.

Nodding once with an air of finality, she quickened her stride.

Although she never would have believed it possible, releasing her sorrow into her brother's arms had done wonders toward reasserting her grip on reality. Proof came when she discovered she could now regard the soldiers' dragon cloak-pins with only the slightest twinge. Which was just as well. If reality decreed Arthur the Pendragon to be forever lost to her, there was no sense in mooning about him for the rest of her life.

"I could get accustomed to this," Per murmured as they passed the set of saluting guardsmen at the building's entrance.

She surmised that he was referring to the much stricter form of discipline enforced in the Pendragon's army, which seemed to manifest in an almost godlike veneration of the officer corps. "They don't know you from Lugh, Per." Since they were already speaking in Caledonian, she saw no need to keep her voice low. "They're saluting your badge."

He snorted. "That's my dear sister," he said to a guard, who probably didn't comprehend a word and kept his gaze focused on a point across the corridor. "She really knows how to cheer a lad."

The austere Roman formality of the surroundings restrained her to a verbal retort rather than a physical one. "You wouldn't like me to lie to you, would you?"

Per's expression was frank. "I don't like partial truths, either."

"Point taken." She raised a hand to forestall further comment as they neared the closed doors of the dining chamber. As before, the escorts opened the doors, stepped inside to announce the visitors, and retreated to their posts. "Prepare yourself," she said with a smile to her brother, "for the way these Romans like to—"

A gasp caught in her throat. The strange Roman dining furniture was gone. Instead, the room was filled with long trestle tables and backless benches that might have graced any Caledonian feast-hall. Even the sculptures had been removed. Only the floor mosaic reminded Gyan that she hadn't been magically transported back to Arbroch.

But the feeling was so eerily strong, she half expected to see Ogryvan in the group that had risen from their seats upon the announcement of her arrival. He wasn't, of course; Arbroch was days away even with a daily change of mounts. That didn't stop her from wishing for her father's presence—for more reasons than simply having another staunch ally beside her.

Gyan didn't recognize most of the men, including the two Caledonian warriors who had been chosen to command the cavalry squads Arthur was sending to Maun. Like Per, they had replaced their clan brooches with the Pendragon's badge. Only by their cloak patterns could she identify one man as being of Clan Tarsuinn and the other Clan Rioghail. Even so, they greeted Gyan with looks of unfettered admiration and fists upraised in the Caledonian warrior's salute. Evidently, the results of her match with Arthur had spread faster than she'd expected. Perhaps if she, Gyan-humara nic Hymar, had led the Caledonian host to victory at Aber-Glein, she wouldn't be faced with an unwanted marriage while having to bid farewell to . . .

No. Such a fantasy was worse than useless. What was done was done. An ocean of wishes could never change it.

And there he stood, too, the invader of her heart, flanked by Merlin and a Brytoni soldier she didn't know—apparently a high-ranking one, if the silver of his badge was any sign. Conspicuous by his absence was Urien, which Gyan found odd.

Every man in the room seemed to be watching her, Arthur more intensely than the others, as though expecting her to make the first move. So she obliged them: she returned the Caledonians' salutes with a flourish, brandishing her bandaged arm like a mark of honor. Perhaps, in a sense, it was. She doubted whether anyone could survive an encounter with Arthur the Pendragon unscathed . . . or unchanged.

As she lowered her arm, she couldn't prevent her gaze from locking to Arthur's. A tingling rush flooded her body. If her cheeks were as red as they felt, she hoped he wouldn't notice—and in the same breath realized it was likely a vain wish. While she struggled to maintain a neutral demeanor, regret and longing assailed her heart with redoubled force.

Arthur grasped a goblet from the table before him and raised it level with his eyes. "Well met, Chieftainess Gyanhumara." The sound of his voice speaking her name made her throat so dry, all she could do was incline her head in response. "Men, I present to you the first person in a long time—of either gender—to outmaneuver me in single combat."

"Foolery is what I heard," muttered the soldier beside him.

The glare Arthur turned on the man could have liquefied a snowdrift. "It was a fair fight, Cai." Again, Arthur regarded Gyan, that maddeningly enigmatic smile bending his lips. "An excellent fight." His eyes narrowed as he seemed to shift his gaze to something behind her, and she battled the impulse to turn and look. "I challenge any man to say otherwise." He gestured at Gyan with the goblet, lifted it to his lips, and drank.

"What did he say?" whispered Per beside her.

"A commendation for my fighting skills."

The question uppermost in Gyan's mind, though, was not what Arthur said but what he meant. Did he seriously think that a little flattery would send her flying into his arms? She was a chieftainess! With people and lands to consider, not just the whims of her heart, no matter how alluring those whims might be. If only her life—her choices—could be so simple. But Argyll could lose everything if she chose Arthur over Urien, and Urien chose to retaliate. Arthur, too, could lose much, and so could everyone who looked to him for protection. Didn't he recognize that? Or even care?

Apparently not. Perhaps she'd been wrong about him after all.

"Lord Pendragon, I do thank you for this . . . unique reception." Her gesture indicated the room and its contents. "But it appears you've neglected to invite someone."

"No, he didn't."

Hand to hilt, Per spun. Gyan didn't bother; she knew that voice all too well. Flashing Gyan a sheepish grin, Per relaxed and faced forward again as Urien claimed his now-familiar place on Gyan's other side.

Urien rendered the customary, if somewhat less than enthusiastic, salute, which Arthur acknowledged with a terse nod. "Forgive my delay, Lord Pendragon. I stopped at the *mansio* to escort Gyanhumara over here, but—" Disappointment reigned on Urien's face as he glanced at Gyan. "You'd already left, my dear. Escorted by your brother."

Gyan thought she heard a note of jealousy but chose to ignore it, instead expressing her appreciation for Urien's thoughtfulness. On impulse, she reached up to pull his face to hers and closed her eyes. From somewhere in the room came a muffled "alleluia."

But as their lips met, she couldn't purge Arthur from her mind. Or her heart.

Arthur stared into the dregs of his goblet—not that he was looking for anything in particular, and he certainly knew not to hunt for solutions there. But it was better than being ignored by the one person in the room he had hoped, by his special dinner arrangements, to please.

"Arthur?" He felt an elbow jab his side. "You awake?" The look Cai was giving him was not unlike the mouse that had stolen past the napping cat to feast upon fallen crumbs. Arthur arched an eyebrow. "I asked if you had anything to add to the training drills for the Manx Cohort."

He shook his head in answer to Cai—and in disbelief of what he, Arthur, had done by ordering Urien to command that unit. At the time, it had seemed an eminently sensible decision. Militarily, it remained a sensible decision. But for Arthur personally, it had become a disaster.

Again, he played out the likeliest scenario in his mind. Gyanhumara, who seemed to be sinking further under Urien's influence each time Arthur saw her, would irrevocably come to love her betrothed while with him on Maun. Urien might be too ambitious for his own good, and rash on occasion, but he was no imbecile. The heir of Clan Moray had repeatedly demonstrated the cunning necessary to achieve an objective on the battlefield; the flawless execution of his *ala's* flanking maneuver at Aber-Glein was a prime example. Now, as he watched Urien and Gyanhumara converse—Arthur was too far away to hear the words, but he saw her laugh lightly at something Urien said— it was apparent that Urien knew how to achieve objectives off the battlefield, as well. And once they stepped onto that vessel in the morning, there would be nothing Arthur could do to stop him. He couldn't even accompany them to Maun, in good conscience. As tempting as the idea was, four thousand men depended upon him, not just the eight hundred of the Manx Cohort. Forget the eyebrows it would raise on Merlin and Cai and Urien and everyone else if without warning Arthur were to announce the relocation of headquarters to Maun. Effectively commanding the legion from that tiny island would be so bloody difficult, it wasn't a viable option.

Merlin leaned over to whisper, "What's wrong, Arthur?"

Arthur followed the line of Merlin's gaze down to his own hand, which was curled so tightly around the goblet's bowl that the silver had begun to distort. He gave a short laugh. "Nothing." In confessional later, he might concede the truth. He set the goblet down. "I think it's time to put an end to this"—inwardly, he grimaced at his choice of the next word and the double meaning it engendered—"mess. If you would do the honors?"

Nodding, Merlin rose and bade everyone else to do the same. As the bishop intoned the benediction, Arthur stole a final glance, past all the bowed heads, at the woman who had enslaved his heart. To his surprise, she was looking at him, her expression a jumble of emotions Arthur couldn't begin to fathom. But when he offered her a smile, he saw in her eyes a brief but unmistakable flash of love. Hope rekindled. Another time, another place, he would have crossed the gap in an instant to crush her body to his, to revel in the feel of her sensuous lips, and the devil take anyone who disagreed with his choice of actions. And yet, despite the inappropriateness of the setting and the company, his battle for self-restraint had never been harder fought.

The officers began taking their leave. Gyanhumara lagged behind, flanked by her brother and, naturally, Urien. She seemed to be having trouble with the clasp of her brooch but refused all offers of assistance. As the last of the Manx Cohort centurions left the room, she got it fastened to her liking and looked up. She seemed hesitant, as though unwilling to leave.

"Are you ready, my dear?" Urien asked her. "I'll be happy to escort you back to the *mansio*."

She glanced at her brother and then, imploringly, at Arthur. That she didn't want Urien to accompany her was obvious; the question was why.

Arthur had a guess. "I'm sure you would be, Tribune," he said dryly. "But I suspect the chieftainess would like to spend some time with her brother before she leaves. Am I right, Chieftainess?"

For a moment, she looked as though she might say something else. Finally, she nodded.

Urien said, "But Centurion Peredur is—"

"Her escort for the rest of the evening. By my command." Arthur said to Gyanhumara, "You will relay this to him, Chieftainess?"

"Of course, Lord Pendragon." Despite the formality of her tone, Arthur thought he detected a note of gratitude.

As she translated the order, Peredur grinned at her, then did his best to adopt the expected somber expression as he saluted Arthur. He didn't entirely succeed, but he looked so much like his sister that it was impossible for Arthur not to like him anyway.

It was also impossible for Arthur not to feel jealousy as Urien kissed Gyanhumara and promised to see her in the morning. She murmured her acquiescence. Apparently satisfied by her answer, Urien saluted Arthur and left the room. After giving Arthur one of his I'll-talk-to-you-later grins, Cai followed Urien. Only Merlin and Peredur remained, which was still too big of an audience for Arthur's taste, with no good way to change that. So be it.

With her brother a pace behind her, Gyanhumara approached Arthur. "Lord Pendragon, I truly appreciate the trouble you went through tonight. All of it. I'm sorry I wasn't a better dinner guest." She looked down;

at what, Arthur couldn't be sure. When again she gazed at him, her intense longing smote his heart. "I—Arthur, I'm sorry for—for everything."

Arthur was sorry, too: sorry that she was leaving so soon, sorry that he'd run out of chances to see her again, sorry that he had ordered her betrothed to be posted to Maun with her, sorry for writing that bloody marriage clause into the treaty at all. And supremely sorry that he couldn't tell her any of this. Or change it.

She extended her right hand. Instead of clasping her wounded forearm—the wound he had given her, which was something else he was sorry for—he took her hand, raised it to his lips, and released it quickly, before Merlin or Peredur could even think of voicing an objection. Her soft intake of breath, the slight flush in her cheeks, and her sad but gentle smile provided the only clues to how she felt. Yet they were enough, and he was grateful for them.

"God be with you, Gyanhumara." As Arthur took a step backward in preparation for the salute, he felt the tightness in his chest that signaled a surge of love for this gorgeous, remarkable woman. His fist hit his chest over the source of that feeling, but it didn't abate. He was grateful for that, too.

Slowly, she nodded. "And you, Arthur."

She murmured something to her brother, and together they turned and left the chamber.

"Our Father," whispered Arthur, "which art in heaven . . ."

Beside him, Arthur heard a chuckle. "Thy will be done." Merlin's hand came to rest on his shoulder. "Indeed."

Arthur cast him a sidelong glance. "God's will—or mine?"

"God's, of course." Merlin clapped Arthur's shoulder

before removing his hand. "But for your sake, lad, I hope it will be both."

So did Arthur, to the core of his soul.

With her pulse thundering in her ears and her throat so dry she could barely swallow, Gyan couldn't retreat from Arthur's presence fast enough. She tried to tell herself her body was responding to the swift pace she had set. But even as the thought formed, she knew it was a lie.

Beyond the *praetorium's* gates, Per caught her shield arm and pulled her to a halt. "Gyanhumara nic Hymar, what in the name of all the gods is going on with you?" He glanced at the *praetorium*, then back at her. "With both of you?"

By "both," Gyan suspected Per wasn't referring to her and Urien. She laughed mirthlessly, twisted free, and resumed her pace. "I wish I knew." At the entrance to the *mansio*, she stopped and turned toward him. "Per, I'm really going to miss you—"

"Oh, no, Gyan. Don't go changing the subject on me. You're either going to tell me the whole story right now, or—or—" His expression grew thoughtful, before transforming into the biggest grin Gyan had ever seen. "Or I'll just have to repeat the first sword lesson Father gave you!"

His good-natured bluff made her smile briefly. Glancing down, she cradled the hand Arthur had kissed against her chest. The skin was still tingling faintly where his lips had touched. With a sigh, she released the hand and regarded her brother. "This isn't the type of farewell I'd expected to bid you, Per." Then again, nothing that had happened to her over the last pair of days could have been expected. "But I think it's the one we both need."

Resolving to share with her brother every frustration, fear, doubt, and, yes, desire that besieged her heart whenever she thought of Arthur the Pendragon of Brydein, Gyan beckoned Per to follow her into the building.

Cuchullain, Laird of the Scots, woke with a start. Sweat soaked his hair and chilled his brow. His heart was hammering like the hooves of a runaway horse.

By Lugh Longarm, he'd never been plagued by such a dream! The final scene bothered him the most: hundreds of corpses strewn across a blood-soaked plain, while overhead amassed a flock of ravens so vast, their writhing bodies blotted out the sun as they descended to the feast. Cuchullain rolled to the edge of the bed and spat out the bitter taste of troubled sleep. It didn't help. The grisly image still burned his brain.

Beside him, Dierda groaned. As he watched with growing alarm, her lovely head turned this way and that on the pillows as though she were locked within her own nightmarish prison. Gently, he touched her hand and was grateful to see her thrashing cease. But the peaceful expression he loved so well didn't return.

As he considered initiating an activity they both enjoyed, the light seeping into their bedchamber revealed that he wouldn't have enough time. Mentally cursing the dawn, the dream, the Attacots, the Brytons, and every other infuriating thing that came to mind, he sat up, eased himself from the bed, padded to the window, and pulled aside the covering. The pale sky was already starting to pinken. He was grateful to observe that the myriad gray streaks marring the emerald hills were only from cooking fires, not Attacotti atrocities. Even so, all too soon would Cuchullain become immersed in the day's war preparations. Just like the day before. And just, he thought with another silent oath, like the next would be.

The swish of fabric alerted him that his wife was awake. She stole up behind him to trace the scars on his back. He fought the impulse to flinch under her touch. She was only demonstrating her love, he told himself. Though he had war-wounds aplenty, the scars she had chosen to caress reminded him not so much of a battle that had been but of a battle to come.

No living soul, not even Dierda, knew that Cuchullain had borne those scars since he was a boy of eleven, the day he had hidden in one of the ships of his father's war-fleet in the hope of winning his first taste of glory at Conchobar's side. That day had ended not in glory but in disaster: Laird Conchobar and most of his warriors dead, others captured, bodies plundered and desecrated, ships burned. And one small boy was driven screaming from a flaming ship into the arms of the waiting Brytoni soldiers. Uther's men. Sons of tavern whores, the son of Conchobar amended.

Two decades later, Cuchullain could still feel the blinding agony and hear their brutal laughter as they scourged him, sluiced the stripes with seawater, and set him, sobbing and shivering, in the one remaining vessel able to take him anywhere but straight to the bottom of the sea. But, oh, how he'd prayed for that fate anyway.

By either a miracle or a curse of the gods, Cuchullain finally made it home, only a few weeks older but a lifetime wiser. And bearing three lifetimes' more hatred toward Uther the Pendragon of Brydein.

No longer able to restrain himself, Cuchullain turned and seized Dierda's hands. Her gasp of surprise gave way to a grin as she pressed her body to his. "Oh, I beg ye, my Lord, donna be hurting me!" Her upturned chin flashed the white of her neck in a bewitching invitation.

Even in this game they sometimes played, hurting Dierda was the last thing he ever wanted to do. She was his one pure rainbow in the unending storm his life had become ever since . . . that day. He brushed his lips across her throat, and she breathed a pleased-sounding sigh.

Reluctantly, Cuchullain released his wife's hands to face the window, gripping the stone ledge.

"The war, my love?"

He snorted. "Wars. Aye."

In addition to the ever-present, thrice-cursed Atta-cotti threat, Cuchullain's inner storm had intensified two years ago, upon learning that he would be forever denied the chance of avenging himself upon Uther. Now a new Pendragon patrolled Brydein's shores: bastard Uther's bastard son. Venting his rage on Ar-thur's messenger last year hadn't been satisfying enough, not by half. But he was pleased with the progress of his plans. Central to those plans was the capture of Maun. A base there would give his people a much-needed respite from the Attacots, a place to rest and regroup. And if the gods were still with him, Cuchullain og Conchobar would meet Arthur map Uther on Maun's shores and carve up the Pendragon himself.

He felt Dierda nod against his cheek as she wrapped an arm around his waist. "I dreamed something." Her grip tightened.

"Something pleasant?" As the words formed, the pit in his stomach told him what the answer would be.

She shuddered, and he pulled her close. " 'Twas evil, Cuchullain. Evil! I fear for ye, my love." Tears glistened in her eyes. "For us all. I—" She studied him for a long moment. "Please forgive me, husband, but killing the Pendragon's emissary may have been—"

"A mistake? Nonsense, Dierda. Arthur hasna retaliated." Not yet, his inner voice reminded him, and he silently swore at the seed of doubt it planted. "That be proof enough for me." For Dierda's sake, Cuchullain hoped he sounded more confident than he felt. What if this Arthur, like himself, was a man who did not forget? A man with a spider's cunning and patience, willing to spin an elaborate trap and wait for the fly to blunder into it?

He pounded the window ledge to banish that womanish line of thought. If Arthur remembered the insult, what of it? Cuchullain had beaten such men before, and by Lugh Longarm he would again! His twenty-year memory had governed his life thus far, and he doubted that it would fail him any time soon.

It couldn't fail him. His beloved wife and the people on this fair Isle of Eireann who called him laird were depending on it.

"I, too, had a dream, my love." Her eyebrows quirked upward, and he smiled, hoping the interpretation he devised would reassure her as much as it did him. "I dreamed I was laird of the ravens, leading my flock to feast upon Brytoni bones!"

Chapter
16

"And from Mount Snaefell, you can see the lands touching the Hibernian Sea: the cliffs of Brydein to the north and south and east, and Hibernia to the west. In case of attack, Mount Snaefell serves as the main signal beacon site . . ."

As Urien rambled about the Dalriadan island of Maun, Gyan listened with only half an ear. She had every intention to explore the island as thoroughly as time permitted in the coming weeks. For now, the tangy wet breeze and snapping sails and creaking oars and wheeling gulls were far more interesting. But nothing could make her forget the man she had come to love in two short days but was now forced to leave behind.

Still her betrothed droned on. During the slender pauses, she nodded or mouthed a word of agreement. Only a few hours separated the ship from Caer Lugubalion, and the captain announced the ship would be pulling into Port Dhoo-Glass in a short while. To Gyan, it already seemed like the longest day of her life.

Part of the reason was simple fatigue; she and Per had talked long into the night. Although Per helped her realize she could no sooner stop loving Arthur than stop breathing, he had no solutions on how to break her betrothal without courting disaster. But what her brother did offer at their parting meant just as much to Gyan: a sincere reiteration of his pledge, for her sake, to serve Arthur to the best of his ability.

She suspected that as one of many cavalry officers, Per would likely experience no more than incidental contact with the Pendragon. Yet it seemed so natural to envision him and Arthur training together, perhaps joking, or charging side-by-side into battle.

A wave sloshed over the rail. Before Gyan could move her arm, seawater seeped through the bandage, making her gasp from the sting.

"My dear, are you all right?" Genuine concern flooded Urien's tone.

"I will be." She shook off the excess water as best she could. The sting gradually dulled to an ache. "Please continue."

With a nod, he launched into a dissertation about the various merchants who regularly plied their trade on the island.

Massaging her arm, Gyan recalled the swordfight and everything that had happened as a result. She was surprised to discover how much it hurt to have two of the most important men in her life now inhabit some of the same thoughts—men whom, along with her father, she would not see again for a long time.

Shadows glided beneath the water's surface, pacing the ship. Gyan leaned over to catch a better glimpse. As though sensing an audience, the seals began to leap and dive in a playful display. Their capers coaxed a laugh from her throat.

"You're not paying attention, my dear," scolded Urien mildly.

"Forgive me." Reluctantly, she turned her back on the sea clowns. "You were saying?"

"I was saying that Port Dhoo-Glass controls Maun's shipping activities. Its fort is the largest of the four coastal stations, which is why the headquarters of the Manx Cohort is there."

And there Gyan would be dining with Urien at every meal, training with him, exercising their horses together, and the One God alone knew how many other times she'd see him during the normal course of her day. What a thought. She closed her eyes to ward it off.

Taking the unintentional cue, Urien covered her mouth with his. The tender, moist heat of his lips was crueler than any torture she could imagine. Yet, to keep peace, she had to give him a taste of what he desired. But not while envisioning Arthur in Urien's place. That tactic had wrought far more harm than good—to herself as well as to Arthur—and she wasn't anxious to rely on it anymore.

When at last she could bear Urien's touch no longer, she squirmed away. "No, Urien. We mustn't."

He seemed genuinely surprised. "Why not?"

For one wanton moment, she fancied how he might react if she broke the betrothal now. Fortunately, good sense prevailed.

"Not here. It isn't—proper." She gestured at the deck, awash with crewmen performing their appointed tasks. More than one showed the couple a gap-toothed grin in passing. "Can we not wait until we get to port?"

He frowned. "We won't have time, Gyanhumara. My cousin Elian will be expecting you at Tanroc."

"Fort Tanroc? On the western coast?" She could

scarcely believe this stroke of luck. But to preserve the secrecy of her true feelings, she molded raw relief into refined disappointment. "I'll be living at Tanroc?"

"Didn't anyone tell you?" Urien scanned the heaving horizon. "No, I suppose there wasn't time. Fort Tanroc is closest to the monastery where your tutors live." As he clasped her hand, sadness flashed across his face. "As soon as we put in at Port Dhoo-Glass, you're to join the troops bound for Tanroc."

"I see." With no small effort, she smothered the elation in her tone. "Then we won't be seeing as much of each other as—as I'd—"

"As you'd hoped? Don't worry, my dear." He lifted her hand to his lips to bestow a lavish kiss and did not see her wince. "Tanroc is but a short ride from Dhoo-Glass."

Even so, this was far better than having to endure Urien's presence daily. At Tanroc, she would have the benefit of Dafydd's company, too, and that of his family, since Dafydd had decided to resume his studies at the Brytoni school. Perhaps, Gyan mused, her stay on Maun might not be as arduous as she had come to expect.

For inventory and placement of furnishings, Fort Tanroc's eastern guardroom was no different from its kin. A rack of spears lined one wall. A glittering array of swords, axes, bows, and full quivers faced them from across the room. Every edge was honed razor-perfect, every shaft stout and sure. The wall opposite the door featured the chamber's only window. Four stools surrounded a large, rough-planked table in the center of the floor. An oil lamp perched on each corner of the table.

Though the soldiers were out on patrol, the lamps were not dark but shed their glow upon the pair of scrolls spread across the tabletop. The two students who had borrowed the haven for the afternoon attacked their work with energetic silence.

Until the rumbling began.

"Horses!" Angusel mac Alayna of Clan Alban of Caledonia dashed from his stool to the window.

His companion didn't appreciate the interruption. The Latin medical treatise she was studying was difficult at best. But Morghe ferch Uther of Clan Cwrnwyll of Brydein had known Angusel long enough to realize that if she didn't respond in some way, he'd keep chattering at her until she did.

"Can you see them yet, Angus?" Morghe continued to stare at the scroll, hoping to retain a shred of concentration.

"Aye! The reinforcements are here—Chieftainess Gyanhumara, too!"

Reinforcements, Morghe thought with mild interest, ought to provide a refreshing change of scene. Languidly, she pushed away from the table to join Angusel at the window.

His finger bobbed to count the ranks. "Looks to be a cavalry *turma* and a century of foot. Maybe more!"

Morghe regarded Angusel with tolerant amusement. "A hundred and thirty, Angus. According to Arthur." As she returned her gaze to the scene outside, she felt a tug on her hand.

"Come on, let's go." Angusel started for the door.

"Go?"

"To meet them, of course."

"You go ahead." Disappointment seemed to cloud Angusel's eyes. Morghe smiled an apology. "I'm not up to matching your pace today, and I don't want to slow you down." The harmless lie served to get him out of the room.

His pounding footsteps faded on the timbers of the outer corridor as he raced for the stairway. She pictured how he must look as he took the stairs three at a time. Moments later, he popped into view beneath her window, pelting down the road leading to the wooden palisade's gates. Many of the fort's resident children had also seen the troops. Angusel's following grew into a dusty, laughing parade.

The truth of the matter was that as the youngest daughter of Chieftainess Ygraine, Morghe felt no obligation to run to meet anyone. Including a Picti chieftainess.

Morghe brought to mind Arthur's message that had come by way of a merchant ship the day before. Her brother had mentioned Gyanhumara of Caledonia only briefly. Apparently, this woman was betrothed to the Manx Cohort's newly appointed commander, Urien, and would be living at Tanroc while studying with the monks at the monastery on St. Padraic's Island. Morghe wondered why Arthur had not foisted his opinions about this Gyanhumara upon her. He never spared her about anything else.

So much thinking about Arthur poisoned Morghe's mood. She had yet to forgive him for her unjust exile to this bee-infested island in the center of a sea boiling with enemy ships.

Upon the death of Uther, their father, Arthur had wrenched her from her place as one of Merlin's pupils. He needed their cousin's military expertise. So he said.

Morghe knew better. Snippets of overheard conversation confirmed that Merlin himself had recommended the move because of her flowering interest in non-Christian lore. Living at Rushen Priory under the watchful eye of Prioress Niniane—isolated from the rest of the world, with the sea to enforce the sentence—was supposed to have killed Morghe's lust for things unholy.

The thought sparked a snort of derision. If anything, she craved the arcane knowledge all the more. But it was one of many cravings she had yet to find a way to satisfy.

Now beginning her third year on Maun, she liked it less with each passing season. Yet this year promised to be different, now that she had won free of the priory and its oppressive mistress.

Life at Rushen Priory had been agonizingly dull. Morghe still missed Caer Lugubalion and the constant excitement of the comings and goings of merchants and craftsmen and soldiers and ships and horsemen. Visitors at the priory were more rare than snow on Lugnasadh. The worst of it was having to beg permission to ride to Dhoo-Glass on market days, such as they were in that backwater port. Yet riding to Port Dhoo-Glass, if only for the day, had offered welcome relief from the constant presence of Niniane, who so admired Arthur that she'd given him that priceless sword, Caleberyllus, to secure his election to the Pendragonship. Why the prioress had done this, Morghe couldn't begin to fathom. Morghe ferch Uther would have sooner given it to her bitterest enemy.

She shattered that line of reasoning with a rueful toss of her auburn braids. The Fates certainly had peculiar ideas about the course of mortal lives.

The highlight—if it could be called that—of most days during her incarceration at the priory had been the lessons in the healing arts and herbal lore. Morghe had to admit that the Lady Niniane was a talented physician and teacher. She'd managed to squelch her dislike of the prioress long enough to soak up all the knowledge she could and set herself along the path to becoming a highly skilled healer. With a smile, she recalled the medical scroll she'd been studying all afternoon. How the body reacted to treatment, and what plants and other tools of nature made up the various remedies still provided a constant source of fascination.

During one of her woefully infrequent furloughs outside the priory walls, Morghe had heard about the library kept by the monks of St. Padraic's. This library was reputed to house scrolls covering the gamut of subjects: from history to mathematics, poetry to philosophy. And, of course, the Christian Scriptures, which didn't rank high on her reading list.

That day, Morghe decided Niniane no longer possessed the right to be her jailer and moved to the western side of the island to live at Tanroc while she studied at the monastery across the strait. No small amount of cajoling and wheedling and threatening had broken Niniane's grip. Being accepted as the only female pupil of the monastic school had presented another challenge. But her determination had won out on both accounts in the end.

Actually, it didn't take long to charm the monks into accepting a woman in their midst. A glance usually sufficed to keep her tutors from becoming too charmed. Like sheep, they were easy to handle and useful. And for company, they were about as stimulating.

The friendship of Angusel helped more than Morghe would have guessed. They'd met soon after her arrival at Tanroc, and his unquenchable cheerfulness and exuberance provided a pleasant contrast to the solemnity of the monks. And she identified with the Picti lad. He'd been sent to Maun after the Battle of Aber-Glein as hostage against the continued good behavior of his mother, Chieftainess Alayna of Clan Alban. Although Morghe now lived in a place more to her liking—which could be said of any place that was not Rushen Priory—Arthur's refusal to let her come home meant only one thing. She, too, was a noble hostage.

As the troops marched through the palisade gates, Morghe noticed that Angusel had already befriended Gyanhumara. Although she was too far away to hear the words, she could tell they were speaking in their native Picti tongue, which Morghe was learning from Angusel. But the lad's animated face and the chieftainess's laughter told the story. Vines of jealousy twined around Morghe's heart. Angusel was the one person on this entire rock fit to call friend, and a stranger was already usurping his attention.

Her nails drummed the ledge as she regarded this Picti stranger. She was beautiful, regal, and . . . armed? Wounded, too? A warrior, then, like Angusel's mother. And probably just as likely to stir up trouble against Brydein—which explained why she was betrothed to a Brytoni nobleman. Another hostage for Arthur's growing collection. And, Morghe observed with a derisive laugh, the Picti woman was acting as though she didn't recognize her captive status.

Then it occurred to her that Arthur had made no mention in his letter of Gyanhumara being a warrior. How odd, Morghe thought. Maybe he wasn't aware— no. If Arthur had caught even a glimpse of this exotic-looking woman, he would have made it a top priority to find out as much about her as he could. And since the chieftainess had come to Maun by way of Caer Lugubalion, there was no way on this side of the River Styx that Arthur could have missed seeing her.

Morghe slowly licked her lips. Not everything about this Gyanhumara of Caledonia, she decided, was as it seemed. And she resolved to find out why.

"Well now, and here comes our welcome, if I'm not mistaken." Cynda pointed at the giggling flood of children gushing over the crest of the hill.

Gyan raised her freshly salved and bandaged arm to shield her eyes from the afternoon glare. "I wonder who the lead boy is. He's dressed like the others, but I don't think he's a Bryton." A vague recollection nagged. "I feel I should know him."

"Aye, you should." Leaving Gyan to puzzle out the mystery, Cynda busied herself with the task of driving the supply wagon.

Gyan fixed her with a commanding stare. And was placidly ignored. That woman could be so infuriating! Still no closer to an answer, Gyan at last admitted defeat.

Smug satisfaction lit Cynda's face. "Chieftainess Alayna's son."

"Angusel of Clan Alban?" Gyan didn't hide her surprise. "Are you certain?"

Cynda had no time for more than a single nod as the children eddied around the company in gleeful confusion. Well did they know not to get in the way of marching men and prancing horses and lumbering wagons. Their leader fell into step beside Gyan and Brin.

"Chieftainess Gyanhumara, well met!" His use of

Caledonian erased all doubt of his identity. "You don't know how glad I am to see other Caledonians again!" The sentiment shone plainly in the golden-brown eyes.

Gyan couldn't begin to imagine what life had been like for him these past several turnings of the moon, but she was not immune to the stirrings of sympathy. "Well met, Angusel." Gyan's smile was gentle.

"My Lady, you—you remembered!"

Angusel was four when Alayna had come to Arbroch to visit Ogryvan shortly after the death of Angusel's father, during Gyan's eighth summer. Gyan had not seen much of him then, for he'd spent most of the time with the younger children. The strong resemblance to his mother was her only key to recognizing him now.

If it made him happy to think she'd remembered him from an encounter several years ago, she wasn't about to dispel the notion. A quick warning glance at the supply wagon's pesky driver forestalled trouble from that quarter, too.

"My Lady, you're wounded! How did—"

She waved her hand in a dismissive gesture. "A sword practice that got a little too intense." Before another round of memories could assail her, she changed the subject. "How goes it with you, Angusel? Have they treated you well?"

"Well enough, my Lady. Everyone is kind to me. And I'm learning all sorts of things." As he studied the rocky path at his feet, his voice dropped to a whisper. "But it's just not the same as being home . . ."

"I know." Up rose an image of Arbroch, cloaked in the emerald majesty of spring. She saw the meadows resplendent with wildflowers, the barley fields neatly furrowed with rich brown earth, the pastures dotted with mares and cows and she-goats and ewes and their nursing young. Amidst this blessed bounty rode her father to oversee their domain. And she wasn't there to help him this time. She wondered if Angusel's sorrow was even half as heavy as hers.

She got an idea that she hoped would cheer them both. "Angusel, in the next day or two, as our duties permit, why don't you set aside some time to take me around the island?"

"May I?" He gave her a lopsided and thoroughly endearing grin. "I'd be honored, my Lady!"

Angusel's enthusiasm made her laugh, the first real laughter she'd enjoyed in weeks. No, that wasn't true. Someone else had made her laugh like that yesterday morning—which seemed like weeks ago. Someone she vowed to think about as little as possible.

On the hilltop stood their destination. And it was quite unlike anything Gyan had ever seen.

"You may begin by telling me about that." She pointed at the massive living thorn wall guarding Fort Tanroc.

"The hawthorn hedge? Beautiful, isn't it?"

Magnificent was the word Gyan would have chosen. It was taller than two men, and its snowy buds hid the deadly brambles behind a delicate shield. While passing through the main double-gated pine portal, Gyan observed that the hedge was even thicker than it was tall.

"And see those dead brambles over there, my Lady?" Angusel gestured toward the thorny bundles stacked neatly inside the hedge beside the gates. "Some are used to hide the gates. The rest can be packed into the portals as a little surprise for an invading army."

Within easy bowshot of the hedge stood the fort's thrice-man-height wooden palisade. The gate guards admitted the company with cheerful waves. As most of the children scampered to their homes and evening meals, the troops halted inside the palisade. Those on horseback dismounted. Ready to greet the newcomers, flanked by a small detachment, stood the garrison commander.

And it seemed every pair of eyes was turned solely upon Gyan.

She was smitten by the resemblance between Elian and Urien in face and build and coloring. The major difference was age, for Elian was of Dumarec's generation. And he had the gray hair, creased brow, and wealth of battle scars to show for it. To Gyan, it was like peering a score of years into the future—a future she had no desire to attain but no hope to avoid.

"Centurion Elian, I am honored to present Chieftainess Gyanhumara nic Hymar of Clan Argyll." Through Angusel's excellent Brytonic, his excitement bubbled like a pot on the boil.

After saluting, Elian started to extend his hand in greeting, appeared to notice Gyan's bandaged arm, and swept her a deep bow instead. "My Lady, permit me to say that the Pendragon's description does not do you justice. Urien is a lucky man, indeed." Murmuring her thanks, she wondered how she was ever going to be able to live in close association with the kinsman of the man she didn't want to marry. "Please permit me, also, to offer my congratulations. Both for your betrothal and your victory." She gave Elian a questioning glance, and he smiled. "The Pendragon is a difficult adversary to defeat."

Gyan felt her eyes widen. "How did you—"

Angusel was quicker. "Chieftainess! You defeated the Pendragon?" Something akin to goddess veneration sprang to life in his eyes. "Does this mean I can go home now?"

Sighing, she patted his shoulder, hating what she would have to say next but knowing she had no other choice. "I wish it did, Angusel. I truly do." In more ways than one, she mused ruefully. She withdrew her hand. "But, no. I'm sorry. It was only a practice bout." As Angusel dropped his gaze to the ground, Gyan banished her reticence. "If you like, Angusel, I'll tell you about the fight sometime."

He looked at her, disappointment chased away by that same worshipful expression, only stronger. "Oh, yes, my Lady, I'd like that very much!" His grin returned in full measure.

Elian gave Gyan a grateful glance and favored Angusel with a teasing smile. "Dodging your lessons again, lad? Or are your tutors not giving you enough work to do?"

"Oh, no, sir! Nothing like that. I'd heard the reinforcements were due today, so I asked to be excused."

Nodding, the garrison commander glanced around the courtyard. "And where is Lady Morghe?"

"East guardroom, sir." Angusel jerked his chin over his shoulder in the general direction. "Sounded like she wasn't feeling well."

"It's not like her to miss meeting someone," Elian murmured, apparently to no one in particular. He returned his attention to Gyan. "No matter. I'm sure you will be meeting the Pendragon's sister soon enough, Chieftainess."

Gyan swallowed her surprise—and dismay. Arthur had a sister? Here? Just what she needed, she thought with a mental sigh: a living reminder of him.

Before she could voice her questions about this Morghe, Elian was already barking orders to the guard. There were horses to stable and soldiers to house, and food and drink to supply for everyone. Gyan gave

Brin's reins to one of the Caledonian warriors. Elian's men split into two groups, one to lead the cavalrymen and their mounts to the stables and the other to show the foot soldiers the barracks. As the troops marched away, the remaining group dwindled to Elian, Angusel, Gyan, Cynda, Dafydd, and his family.

Addressing Dafydd, Elian said, "Your quarters are ready, sir. Angusel will show you. The wagon can be kept with the others, near the stables."

Angusel jumped up beside Dafydd, pointing the way. As the wagon lurched away, the lad twisted around to honor Gyan with the Caledonian warrior's salute. Heartily, she returned it, to his obvious delight.

"I will escort you to your chambers, my Lady." Elian gave Gyan an apologetic smile. "Normally, I would offer my arm to such a lovely young lady as yourself. But since you're a warrior, too, I suppose it wouldn't be appropriate."

"It's all right, Elian," she assured him. "I do appreciate the thought."

As she and Elian strode toward the officers' wing, with Cynda scurrying behind them, a young woman emerged from the guard tower across the courtyard. She was short of stature, and her dark auburn hair cascaded over her figure-flattering violet gown. Although she wasn't hurrying, she had clearly set herself on a course to intercept them.

"Lady Morghe, well met." Elian inclined his head as she stopped before them. "Well met, indeed. This is Chieftainess—"

"Gyanhumara. Of Caledonia." To Elian, she said, "Gwenhwyfar, in our tongue." She directed her attention back at Gyan. "Or Gulnevere, if you prefer the guttural noise the Saxons call a language." Despite their physical differences, Morghe's slim smile was so like Arthur's, Gyan found herself wrestling with her composure. Morghe turned her alluring violet gaze on the centurion. "Elian, be a dear, and let me show the chieftainess her chambers, will you? Please?"

He chuckled. "An excellent idea, Lady Morghe." Saluting Gyan, he said, "If you need anything, Chieftainess, I am at your service."

"Thank you, Centurion Elian. You are very kind." And Gyan meant it.

Elian spun and headed for the barracks, while Gyan and Cynda followed Morghe toward a cluster of low buildings in the opposite direction.

"Well, Gyanhumara—may I call you Gyanhumara? We'll be studying together, and using titles all the time can be so"—Morghe casually flicked her hand—"tiresome."

Gyan pondered the sister of the man who owned her heart. Kin and close friends she permitted to use the shortened form of her name. Morghe, so far, was neither, and Gyan wasn't at all sure she wanted that to change. Something about her made Gyan uneasy, though she was hard pressed to define it. Strange as the thought seemed, it was as if Morghe was Arthur's antithesis, and not simply in physical appearance. "You may forgo using my title, Morghe," she said cautiously.

At the entrance to one of the buildings, Morghe stopped to give Gyan a long appraisal. Finally, she mounted the steps, beckoning Gyan and Cynda to follow. "Our quarters are in here, Gyanhumara." She turned to point at Gyan's bandaged arm. "I have several salves that may help, depending on what sort of injury that is."

Inside the building, Gyan took a moment for her eyes

to adjust before moving to catch Morghe. "It's a cut. From a sword." Instinct warned her not to mention that Morghe's brother was responsible.

"Does it still trouble you?" Morghe asked.

"The salt spray hasn't helped it any."

"Ah." Again, Morghe's smile looked so much like Arthur's that Gyan bit off a gasp. "I have just the thing for it, then."

She selected a door—her own chambers, Gyan surmised—and pushed it open. Out wafted a heady aroma of herbs too numerous to identify. Gyan and Cynda followed Morghe inside. Every shelf, tabletop, and spot of floor was overflowing with parchment, quills, ink pots, piles of bark and berries and roots, several smooth stone mortars and pestles, and an army of tiny earthen jars and their stoppers. Some were empty, and some weren't. Bunches of herbs were drying suspended from the rafters. A cauldron containing a thick white mixture was bubbling slowly over the fire.

Morghe went to a group of sealed jars, opened one, smeared a trace on her finger, took a sniff, and nodded with apparent satisfaction. "This is the one." She rubbed the salve between her fingers until it disappeared and brought the open jar to Gyan. The salve, Gyan noticed, had a faint bluish tint.

"What's she doing?" Cynda whispered to Gyan.

"Being hospitable, I think," Gyan murmured as she began to unwrap the bandage.

Cynda stayed Gyan's hand. "I want to know what's in that salve first." Gyan cocked an eyebrow. "Go ahead, Gyan. Ask her."

Morghe grinned. "Elder and valerian, mostly. In a lard base, of course." Her Caledonian was quite good, and Gyan felt her other eyebrow shoot up. Cynda's surprised expression was downright comical. "And one or two"—Morghe's grin widened—"secret ingredients." With the jar cradled in the palm of her hand, she thrust it toward Gyan, who got the distinct impression Morghe was challenging Gyan's trust.

Gyan wasn't at all sure she should trust this young woman. Then again, she was Arthur's sister. No good could come from deliberately offending her. She reached for the salve.

Cynda snatched the jar from Morghe's palm.

"Cynda! I was just going to—"

"I know what you were going to do." Cynda's frosty stare was directed solely at Morghe. She said to Gyan, "I won't have anything foreign touch you until I've had a look first."

Apparently, the double meaning wasn't lost on Morghe. She adopted a look that was somewhere between annoyance and disgust. Still speaking in Caledonian, she said, "Your guard dog needn't be so vigilant around me, Gyanhumara."

Cynda, busy with her examination of the salve—which included tasting it—either didn't hear or chose not to react to the insult.

Gyan, however, wasn't in a tolerant mood. "Cynda is not my 'guard dog.' She is the only mother I have ever known." Gyan's fingers found the pommel of her sword. "If you wish to remain on good terms with me, Lady Morghe"—Gyan stressed the title to communicate her displeasure—"then I suggest you treat her with the same respect you would your own mother."

Morghe loosed a peal of laughter and dropped Cynda a deep curtsey. "As you command, Chieftainess." Gyan couldn't tell whether Morghe was mocking only Cynda or both of them.

It didn't matter. Gyan had to get out of there before she yielded to the temptation to run this insolent upstart through, Arthur's sister or not. "If you would kindly tell us where our quarters are, Lady Morghe, we won't take up another moment of your precious time." She turned toward the door, and Cynda, still holding the salve pot, did the same.

Grinning, Morghe sidled past them. "Oh, no, Chieftainess. I promised Elian that I would take you there, and so I shall."

Before either Gyan or Cynda could react, she slipped out of the room. As Gyan stepped into the corridor, she saw Morghe standing beside the next door in line, resting a hand on her hip.

Morghe said, in Brytonic this time, "Here are your quarters, Chieftainess Captive."

Gyan couldn't believe what she'd heard. "Excuse me. My Brytonic must not be as good as I thought it was. Did you say—"

"That your quarters are in here? Yes." Humming, she bustled inside. For Cynda's benefit, she switched to Caledonian. "Keep the salve. Use it or not, as you see fit. It should be quite safe." She splayed the fingers she'd used to sample the salve. "See? These haven't fallen off—yet." This was followed by another burst of laughter.

Gyan laid hold of Morghe's arm and spoke in Brytonic. This was one discussion she didn't want Cynda listening to. "That's not what I meant, Morghe." Scowling, she folded her arms. "And I think you know it. You said something about me being a captive?"

"Ah, that. As a matter of fact, I did." She laughed again. "Why, Chieftainess, you look positively astonished. Didn't you know? Arthur has quite a distinguished collection of us here. Angusel, me . . . now you. Welcome to Tanroc Prison, my Lady." Still laughing, she tugged the door shut as she left the chamber.

Gyan, a captive? Morghe must have been joking. And yet it made a certain amount of sense. If not a political prisoner, like Angusel, Gyan was still a captive of her own destiny, forced into an unwanted marriage—a marriage that was fated to be her doom—while the one man she did want to marry remained agonizingly out of reach. In stunned silence, she sank into the nearest chair.

"Gyan? What's wrong? You look like someone just stepped on your grave." Gyan snorted but didn't reply. "Your arm, my dove?"

Gyan glanced down to see that she was absently stroking the bandage. In fact, her arm had begun to ache again, resonating with the ache in her heart. Maybe her ill-conceived love for Arthur was nothing short of folly. Maybe his sister, so like him in a few ways yet so different in most others, had been thrown into Gyan's path to remind her how futile were her hopes. And maybe, she thought glumly, residing at Port Dhoo-Glass with Urien wouldn't have been such a bad idea after all.

Chapter

17

The following day dawned bright and fair. Despite the newness of the surroundings, Gyan had slept like the dead and woke feeling better than she had in many a sennight. A talk with Cynda helped her put her thoughts back into perspective. Gyan's love for Arthur was neither futile nor ill-conceived, Cynda pointed out. Given the proper opportunity, that could all change. Armed with Cynda's optimism, Gyan resolved to be ready for such an opportunity, however long it might take to present itself to her. Meanwhile, on Cynda's suggestion, she set about establishing the pattern of her daily routine, hoping to make it intricate enough to ease the pain of separation—from home, from kin, from clan, and especially from the man she loved.

After breaking fast, Gyan took her sword and spear down to the training ground to practice her drills. Amidst the other warriors, she noticed Angusel, honing his martial skills under Elian's supervision. Gyan soon found herself watching with interest.

Angusel seemed remarkably strong for his age, as he swung his sword as easily as though it were a stick. Yet youthful inexperience was equally evident. With each stroke, his head betrayed his next attack. This common mistake often went unnoticed by the common opponent. Against an uncommon foe, it would be fatal.

Elian did not miss a parry and answered with staggering blows. It didn't take long for the veteran to dump his pupil into the dust.

Gyan's smile sprang to life in remembrance of the countless sessions with her father and brother that had ended with the same result. Although it had been a victory, the memory of her most recent match caused the smile to fade. Determined not to let these feelings overwhelm her, she set a brisk pace toward an unused practice post.

"Ho, Chieftainess!"

Gyan halted and turned. Looking as if he were carrying half the dirt of the training ground with him, Angusel was hurtling toward her, sheathed practice sword jouncing against his leg. Elian was following at a more dignified pace, some distance behind him. As Angusel arrived, panting and beaming, she greeted him with a clap on the shoulder. "And good day to you, Angusel."

She didn't think it was possible, but his grin widened. "Well, Chieftainess, what did you think?"

"Of your match with Centurion Elian?" By this time, his mentor had caught up. She gave him a nod and returned her attention to Angusel. "You have strength and agility. I think you show a lot of promise. But no *lann-seolta*—" For Elian's benefit, she amended, "no blade-cunning, yet. You need to concentrate on your opponent's elbow, not where you plan to strike next with your sword." As disappointment began to cloud his features, she said, "Look, I'll demonstrate." She drew her sword. "If you don't mind, Centurion?"

"My pleasure, Chieftainess." Elian glanced at Angusel, then back at Gyan. "It's something I've been trying to teach him for weeks. If you can pound it into his skull, my Lady"—he gave Angusel's head a good-natured scrubbing, to the lad's laughing protest—"then more power to you."

She explained to them both the drill Ogryvan had used with her, which started with a short, simple series of prearranged thrusts and parries, to accustom the student to the idea of watching the opponent's elbow and relying on peripheral vision for the rest. As the student's aptitude increased, so, naturally, did the length and complexity of the routine. Gyan and Elian performed the novice series, then she invited Angusel to try it against her. Though the drill was obviously awkward for him at first, she was pleased to see that he was a quick study. Before long, his head was scarcely moving at all, save to the rhythm of her sword arm's movements.

"Very good, Angusel," she declared. "Keep this up, and you'll be besting the centurion here before you know it." And one day, she predicted to herself with a smile, nigh unto everyone else to dare crossing swords with this young warrior.

"You really think so, my Lady?" Angusel gazed at Gyan with undisguised admiration. "I can hardly wait. Let's go another round!"

Elian laughed. "My demise can wait for another day, lad. It's time to get ready for your lessons."

"Aye, sir." Angusel turned to Gyan. "My Lady, may I escort you to the monastery? Show you around and introduce you to the brothers?"

"Excellent idea, Angusel," Elian said. "After putting up your weapons, you can meet down at the boats."

"And I can paddle us both over," Angusel offered. "The tides can be tricky at this time of day."

Gyan began to voice disagreement. After all, how

would she ever learn the tides if someone else always managed the boat? Yet Angusel's concern was charmingly sincere. She smiled her acceptance.

As she moved to follow Angusel to the living area, Elian drew her aside. "I'm glad you're here, Chieftainess. It's not easy for him, being alone among strangers."

"I'm not exactly what you would call an old friend, either."

"No? Well, I've never seen him happier. It was beginning to affect his studies, here"—his gesture encompassed the training ground—"and at St. Padraic's."

"I'll be pleased to help any way I can, Elian." Morghe's comment came to mind, and she gave a rueful laugh. "If not for the betrothal clause in the treaty, I'd probably be in the same position right now." That she really did consider herself to be in the same position—forced into a situation against her wishes— was something she would never admit to Urien's kin.

After returning to her quarters to put away her weapons and shield, she found her way down to the small inlet where the currachs were kept. Angusel, paddle in hand, was standing next to the two-person craft he'd selected for the short trip.

He floated the boat into the shallows and motioned her aboard. "You need to sit with a foot in each corner, my Lady, for balance."

When she was settled, he climbed in, facing her with his back against the opposite side. Runnels of seawater that had stowed away on their boots collected around their legs. While the water itself could not penetrate the tough leather leggings, the coldness did. She could not suppress a shiver.

"You did this all winter, Angusel? Wasn't it too cold?"

"Maybe a little, at first. I don't feel it so much

anymore." He pushed the boat through the choppy waves with short, powerful strokes. "You'll get used to it soon, my Lady."

Upon reaching the islet, they disembarked, and Angusel carried the craft across the finger-sized beach to a popular stowing area, well above the tidemark. Several similar boats lay there, wicker-framed cowhide bottoms turned skyward like a convention of sea turtles.

Angusel led Gyan up the path through the rocks toward the monastery.

Inside the perimeter of the earthen enclosure sat dozens of beehive-shaped, mud-daubed wattle huts. Now empty, they apparently served as the monks' sleeping quarters. The huts bore a striking similarity to the Commons at Arbroch. She paused at the closest hut to run reverent fingertips over the rough red-brown wall. Everything on this tiny isle seemed destined to remind her of what she'd left behind. A sigh escaped.

"Something wrong, my Lady?" Angusel's brow furrowed.

"I was just thinking." As her hand fell away from the building, the smile she showed her companion hinted at her sadness. "About home."

"I know how you feel," he said quietly. "I think about it a lot, too." Turning his head, Angusel's gaze grew distant, and Gyan realized he was looking to the northeast. Toward Caledonia.

She murmured, "Do you ever think about . . . him?" And could have bitten off her tongue for making such a stupid remark. Many more slips like that, she chided herself, and soon all Brydein would know how she felt.

Angusel was clearly puzzled. "My Lady?"

Since the damage was already done, she had no choice but to continue. Trying to make her voice sound as brisk as possible, she said, "The man responsible for you being held captive here: the Pendragon."

"Oh, him. Aye." The fingers of his sword hand curled into a fist. "Do you think Caledonia could've won at Aber-Glein if we'd done anything differently?"

What a question! And only the One God knew the answer. Privately, she didn't think the Caledonian host had had much of a chance, based on what her father and brother had told her afterward. But for Angusel's benefit, she said, truthfully, "I don't know, Angusel. I wasn't there."

His fist clenched tighter. "Neither was I. Do you think if we—you and I—had fought—"

"Ha. Battles don't hinge on the performance of individual warriors, despite what the *seannachaidhs* would have us believe."

Angusel stated quietly but firmly, "Someday, mine will." Gyan had no doubts about what he meant, and to her surprise she found herself believing him. His intensity died as he relaxed his fist and sighed. "But I suppose if I'd been in the Pendragon's position, I'd have done the same thing. Taken hostages, I mean." His expression grew thoughtful. "My Lady, I know you had a practice match with him, but you did speak to him, too, didn't you? Did you ask him how much longer I have to stay here?"

"We spoke, yes." Ruthlessly, she suppressed the memories of those conversations and the feelings those memories elicited. "But the subject of your captivity never came up. I'm sorry, Angusel." In truth, it might have, if she hadn't been so tightly focused upon her dilemma about Arthur and Urien, but she couldn't admit that to Angusel. Instead, she said, "Arthur the Pendragon seems like a reasonable man."

Angusel snorted in obvious disbelief, but Gyan refused to let that put her off. "I'm sure that if we—you, me, and all Caledonia—prove that we can work with him rather than against him, he'll set you free soon." She harbored no illusions that her own "captivity" could end so easily, but for the lad's sake, she hoped she was right. "Angusel mac Alayna, are you willing to try?"

Angusel's grin flashed as bright as the morning sun. "If you are, Chieftainess, then so am I!"

Gyan nodded her satisfaction with his answer. It was all she—or Arthur, for that matter—could ask of him.

Resuming their pace, they twisted through the unruly semicircle of huts toward the compound's center. Once clear of the closely spaced sleeping quarters, they stopped beside a tall, intricately carved stone cross, one of many scattered throughout the compound. Angusel wrapped an arm around its tapered shaft, his ebony hair brushing the bottom of the cross's nimbus as he began to point out the other buildings.

Beyond the last hut on their far left stood the flower-framed, whitewashed, thatched cottage where the abbot lived. The cottage's nearest neighbors were the guesthouse and the square refectory where the brethren met for every meal. The livestock pens were hidden behind the refectory's kitchen. Lowings and bleatings and squeals and squawks announced the presence of at least a pair of cows and more than a few sheep, pigs, and chickens. Around the far side of the enclosure ranged storage sheds of various sizes.

Set against the earthen embankment, well apart from the other buildings, was what appeared to be a second guesthouse. In reality, this was the library and main study hall. To the right of the library stood a small apple orchard. The boughs were smothered with blossoms, delicately tinted like clouds at dawn. Their scent floated on the light breeze. It wasn't difficult to imagine the popularity of the place when the temptation of being outside on a fine summer afternoon became too great to resist.

At the center of the monastery, dwarfing every other structure by its commanding presence, was the church. Shaped like a cross, its timber-topped, ivy-clothed stone arms seemed to reach out to embrace Gyan and Angusel as they drew near.

Wisps of smoke curling from the kitchen's chimneys and the faint sound of chants drifting through the church's walls were the only signs of human habitation in the compound.

"The monks are all inside?"

"In their temple, aye, my Lady. It's midmorning prayer time for them." They paused near the church's rounded oaken doors. "I'd hoped they would be done by the time we got here."

The chanting stopped, and the doors swung open. Like a dark wave, the black-robed monks poured quietly forth into the sunlight. Most of the monks greeted Angusel with friendly warmth, but the reaction to Gyan did not seem nearly as favorable.

"It's because you're a woman," Angusel explained in a whisper after one particularly chilly reception. "Some of them still aren't used to having women students. My friend Morghe studies here, too. She's probably in the library. Shall we go look?"

Gyan found it hard to believe Morghe could befriend anyone. Then again, it was equally hard to believe Angusel's disposition could fail to sway even the toughest cynic. But rather than raise those issues with Angusel, she said, "I ought to meet the abbot first." After the outcome of yesterday's meeting, Morghe ferch Uther was the last person Gyan wanted to see. Urien included.

"Oh. Of course."

He waited until the exodus had ended before motioning her to follow him into the church.

That this was another dwelling-place of the One God there was no doubt. In comparison with the church of St. John at Caer Lugubalion, this sanctuary was much smaller, lending it a more intimate feel. Holiness pulsed in the myriad candle flames, drifted on the sweet wings of incense, whispered in the air, nestled among the stones.

Reluctant to shatter the sanctity of the chamber, Gyan stopped. Angusel obediently followed her example.

Her gaze traveled to the pair of statues flanking the altar. One she recognized from her talks with Dafydd: Moira cradling the infant Iesseu. The other statue, a man wrestling a great, dagger-fanged serpent, was unfamiliar to her. Both were crafted of unblemished snow-white stone with the same remarkably lifelike detail she had seen at Caer Lugubalion. Candlelight shimmered at each statue's base. The man's sandaled feet and the hem of Moira's mantle seemed smoother and shinier than the upper portions of the statues— why, Gyan couldn't begin to guess.

Before the altar knelt an age-bent man. Two boys knelt to either side. Heads bowed, the figures were almost as still as their stone companions. And behind the altar loomed the wooden cross with its mortally wounded Prisoner, captured forever in dying agony.

The altar was draped with undyed, unadorned linen. On a gilt platform in the center, encircled by glowing tapers, stood a small, reddish clay cup. Whether empty or full, Gyan couldn't tell. Either way, it seemed odd for the humble-looking vessel to occupy such an exalted position.

As she contemplated the mystery, the priest lifted his frosty head. The boys rose as one to help him to his feet. With a trembling hand resting upon each young shoulder, the man turned.

Gyan stepped forward to greet the abbot. Assuming a pace that pushed the upper limits of decorum, Angusel moved to catch her.

"Ah, Angusel, my son." His ancient voice crackled like autumn leaves. "And—Morghe?" He squinted at Gyan, wagging his head. "No, you're not Morghe. You're much too tall. That much I can see. Who are you, my child?"

Gyan began to speak, but Angusel broke in. "This is your new student, Father Lir. Chieftainess Gyanhumara."

"Ah, yes. Of course. Now I remember. Welcome, my daughter. Welcome. I am Abbot Lir. But the students call me Father, as you may have noticed. Pilgrims call me the Keeper of the Chalice."

"The cup on the altar?" She tried to curb the incredulity, without success.

His lips stretched into a ghost of a smile. "It's not just any cup, my daughter, however it may look. Come. Let me show you."

Assisted by his acolytes, the Keeper of the Chalice stepped up to the altar to retrieve the relic. The aged hands, amazingly, did not tremble as he lifted the cup from its golden shrine. Sheltering it against his black-robed breast, he returned to Gyan and Angusel. He carefully placed it in her hands.

The rough clay vessel was no taller than the length of her hand from heel to middle fingertip. Its base fit on one palm with room to spare. A host of strange symbols was etched around the bowl. If they represented a language, it was unlike any she had ever seen. The cup was empty. At the bottom, the clay was much darker, as though it had once held wine. Or blood.

Gyan voiced her speculation.

"Both, my child. That cup," whispered Abbot Lir, "was the last earthly thing ever used by our Lord Jesu when He was a man."

Gazing into the Chalice, Gyan was smitten by the intense desire to partake of the miracle that transformed bread and wine into the Christ's flesh and blood. She regarded the abbot, the question sitting on the tip of her tongue. But she stopped herself from asking it. Angusel's presence was not the issue. What changed her mind was a feeling, as she held the cup that had been sanctified by the touch of the Lord's hand, of utter unworthiness.

She returned the Chalice to its Keeper.

But just the sight of the Chalice filled her soul with unparalleled joy.

Complaining of stomach pains, Brother Ian, Morghe's tutor, had not risen from his bed this day. Dutifully, Morghe had seen to the preparation of his healing tisane, but there was no word yet on his recovery. Lucan, the only other monk who might have taken her under his wing in the interim, was occupied with his new pupil, the Picti chieftainess.

Actually, that suited Morghe just fine. She sat in a small study room on the upper floor of the library, a copy of Horace's *Odes* spread across the table before her. Ian preferred to combine Latin grammar lessons with history, subjecting her to such tortures as Livy's *A History of Rome*. Worse yet, Suetonius's *The Twelve Caesars*. Knowledge was knowledge, true. But Morghe had serious doubts about the usefulness of studying the lives of men whose bones had long ago fattened the worms.

Horace—now, there was a man who knew how to entertain his readers. Morghe smiled as she ran reverent fingertips across the yellowed scroll. How pleasant it would be to meet a man like him. World-wise and witty, unlike the monks, who were pious to a fault, and the soldiers, who together couldn't boast of enough brains to amount to a hill of horse dung.

She sighed, gazing at the clouds scuttling past her window. The sea, driven by the same winds that herded the clouds, beat upon the rocks with relentless fury. The air was thick with salt spray and the sound of fleeing dreams—dreams Arthur had chased away by sending her here. The most laughable part was that he thought he was doing this for her own good, when in truth he could no sooner recognize what was good for her than fly to the moon. Morghe's idea of "good" was to find a man with considerable power to share with her—one who didn't question her preferred avenues of study, including the arcane arts—and get on with her life.

Morghe's thoughts returned to her meeting the day before with the Picti chieftainess. Gyanhumara had acted so aloof and evasive, and so damnably superior, it had been impossible for Morghe not to dislike the woman. Especially after her servant had profaned Morghe's initial attempt at kindness. Baiting the two of them after that had been sheer pleasure, although it had denied Morghe the chance to find out anything more about Gyanhumara. Like why, for instance, an odd expression flashed across the woman's face whenever Morghe smiled a certain way. No matter; this was a small island, with opportunities aplenty to solve this mystery.

Yet, despite how she felt about Gyanhumara, Morghe had to admit the Picti woman had all the luck. Already a leader of her clan, the strongest of the Caledonian Confederacy, and betrothed to the heir of another, the most powerful clan of Dalriada . . . the potential of that union was staggering. Morghe's lips twitched into a malicious grin as she imagined what would happen if

Gyanhumara and Urien ever decided to turn their combined forces against Arthur.

What a pretty picture that would make, and so easy to paint.

Painting herself into Gyanhumara's place was just as easy. But Urien barely knew that Morghe existed. Perhaps she ought to devise an excuse to visit Port Dhoo-Glass more often, to start fixing that problem. But Gyanhumara, surely she would never give up a prize that meant the doubling of her power. What sane woman would?

With another sigh, she returned her attention to the Horace scroll and found something she had not noticed before. She reread the passage slowly to be sure. Yes, there it was. Some careless copyist had omitted a phrase. Anyone with half a brain could discern the meaning despite the omission—which probably explained why Morghe had missed it the first time. Still, an error was an error and had to be reported. She giggled with delight over her discovery.

After rolling up the scroll with special care, she tucked it under one arm and all but danced from the room.

As Gyan and Angusel walked from the church to the library, they passed several small knots of monks. The shave-pated men sat on the benches under the apple trees or strolled the grounds, arms waving to punctuate their discussions. Their language seemed vaguely familiar.

"Latin, my Lady," Angusel responded, in Caledonian, to Gyan's query. "It's the first thing you'll learn."

She nodded, remembering a similar remark Ogryvan had made to her six months ago. Six months! The passage of time seemed more like six days, although the few days she'd spent at Caer Lugubalion seemed like years.

The library's double doors swung open, and a pair of monks emerged to begin a slow descent down the wide stone steps. The elder of the two leaned heavily on a cane, while his companion helped to support his opposite side.

"The one with the cane, that's Brother Stefan," Angusel whispered. "He's in charge of the library and the students."

"The students? But I thought Father Lir did that."

"He's the abbot, so of course everyone looks to him. But Brother Stefan actually does most of the work. Keeps records of everyone's progress, and who's studying what, and all that."

"And the other monk?"

"Brother Lucan? He's one of the tutors—" Angusel broke off as the men neared and switched to another language to greet them. From the sounds, Gyan presumed it was this tongue called Latin.

The monk Stefan regarded Angusel from under stern black brows, wagging a crooked finger, and asked Angusel something. When Angusel opened his mouth to answer, Stefan fired another querulous-sounding question. Angusel spoke a few words in protest, which were promptly rewarded by an apparent reprimand.

Stefan gestured with his cane toward the library doors and spoke again.

Nodding, Angusel murmured what seemed to be an agreement. In Brytonic, he said to Gyan, "I'm sorry, my Lady. I must go now."

"I understand. Thank you for your help this morning, Angusel."

After grinning briefly, he scampered up the steps. His slim form soon was swallowed by the gaping doorway.

Brother Stefan turned his critical glare upon Gyan. "Good," he said, in Brytonic. "At least we won't have to start with teaching you the Brytoni tongue, as we did with Angusel. Chieftainess . . . Gyanhumara, is it?" He glanced at Lucan. "That will be a challenge to translate into Latin, eh, Lucan?"

Lucan's dark brown eyes took on a faraway look. "I— I will have to think on it, Brother Stefan. It's an unusual name. And a pretty one." His lips curved into a shy smile not directed at the other monk.

Stefan delivered Lucan some sort of warning before returning to Brytonic to address Gyan. "I crave your pardon for Brother Lucan, my Lady. He has not been long among us and still suffers occasional . . . lapses."

Lucan became engrossed in a line of red ants parading through the dust past his sandaled feet.

Too late; Gyan had already seen the glow of his embarrassment. To spare him further discomfort, she suppressed her amusement. "I take it, Brother Lucan, that you are to be my tutor?" He nodded, hesitant to meet her gaze. "Then, may we begin? I should like to see the library."

"An excellent idea, Chieftainess," said Stefan. "Please permit me the honor of conducting the tour. If I may borrow your shoulder again, Lucan, to get me up these blessed steps."

Lucan positioned himself on Stefan's right side. As Stefan reached for Lucan's shoulder, the sleeve of his robe fell back to the elbow, revealing a sinewy forearm crossed with deep scars. Gyan moved to Stefan's other side, and the ascent began.

"Please forgive a warrior's curiosity, Brother Stefan,

but how did you injure your leg? What battle were you in?"

"How do you know I wasn't born like this, young lady? Or that a disease didn't leave me this way?"

"I've yet to see a cripple born with scars like yours."

Stefan nodded slowly. At the landing outside the doors, the trio paused. He lifted the hem of his robe with the cane's tip to display a foot twisted at an unnatural angle, the legacy of a badly set break.

"You're right, Chieftainess. I've lived with this condition by the grace of God for more than forty years. Fought under Germanus of Auxerre and got this wound during the Alleluia Victory."

"The what?"

"Alleluia Victory—*alleluia* means 'praise be to God.'" Stefan peered into the distance. "It was the Brytoni battle cry that day, and"—he grinned at Gyan—"praise be to God, it worked."

And *alleluia,* she realized with a jolt of recollection, was a word someone—Merlin, probably—had used when she had kissed Urien during that farewell dinner. Gyan got another jolt when it occurred to her what Brother Stefan was talking about.

During the incident now known to the Caledonians as the Great Disaster, some clans had drafted a tenuous alliance with the Scots and Saxons in an attempt to seize lands from the Brytons south of Hadrian's Wall. But the thunderous Brytoni battle cry had so terrorized the Scots and Saxons that they had dropped their weapons and fled the battlefield without striking so much as a single blow. The Caledonians made a valiant stand, but without the supporting numbers of their would-be allies, it was doomed.

The defeat led to a redistribution of power in the Confederacy. Since the leaders of Argyll and Alban had scented trouble from the beginning and had kept their clans out of the ill-fated operation—bearing the scornful derision of the other Confederates—they benefited the most in the aftermath. When the survivors crawled home to lick their wounds, no one was jeering.

But it ensured that no Caledonian would ever trust another Saxon or Scot.

Brother Stefan's robe whispered to the ground. As Lucan held open the door, he and Gyan stepped into the library.

The large chamber glowed with light cascading from the many tall windows. Reading tables and scribes' easels were positioned to take advantage of the sunlight, where monks bent silently over their work. Between the tables stood row upon row of shelves, piled with scrolls of various sizes. Willow baskets stood everywhere. Carved wooden knobs of more scrolls peered over each basket's rim.

Although Gyan counted at least a score of monks in the room, it was nearly as quiet as the Sanctuary of the Chalice had been. Except for the occasional crinkling of parchment, or a muffled cough, or the soft slap of sandals on the tile floor as a monk went to retrieve or replace a document, the silence was complete.

If outside Brother Stefan had seemed infirm, in his element he was a different man. As he walked unassisted around the room, quietly revealing the order of the manuscripts, his limp all but disappeared. It was easy for Gyan to forget there was any reason for the cane other than to point out documents of interest residing on the highest shelves.

At the far end of the chamber, a staircase led to the upper floor, where Morghe was descending. She carried a scroll tucked under one arm. Her gaze met Gyan's, and a look of surprise crossed her face. Surprise quickly yielded to determination as she approached Gyan and her escorts.

She grasped the scroll in both hands and began to pull it open. "Brother Stefan, look what I've found."

"Later, lass," said the master of the library. "Can't you see I'm busy?"

"There's a mistake in this manuscript. You said to report mistakes as quickly as possible, so they can be fixed."

"It can wait this time, Morghe. Just go and set it in my workroom, and I'll attend to it later."

Gyan saw the sparks gathering in that violet glare of hers. "Brother Stefan, you've shown me enough for now. I'm ready to begin my lessons—"

"I don't need your help, Chieftainess," Morghe hissed. She clamped her arm over the scroll and stalked toward the stairs.

As the sounds of her sandals slapping the flagstones echoed into silence, Brother Stefan shook his head. "That Morghe. Quite a handful, she is. The man she marries will need divine help to keep her under control, I fear."

Silently, Gyan agreed and offered a quick prayer for him, whoever he might be.

Chapter

18

Angusel flipped the dripping currach belly-up onto the stack, stowed the paddle, and clambered up the rock-lined path to the fort. His head was throbbing. Images whirled in frenetic confusion: circles and triangles and squares and angles and weird symbols he only halfway understood. To escape, he sought his favorite refuge.

Sweet hay and the richness of oiled leather mingled with the pervasive scent of the horses to concoct an aura of welcome that embraced him like an old friend. The resident mouser, a huge ginger tom, lounged in a patch of sun. He acknowledged Angusel's presence by opening one golden eye the merest fraction. The striped tail thumped once. As Angusel stooped to scratch the cat's ears, he was rewarded with a loud purr.

Straightening, he gazed down the line of stalls.

Most of the horses were gone. Since the afternoon sky carried no hint of rain, the horsemen of the Second Manx *Turma* were out drilling with their mounts. The draft animals were toiling in the fields. Too late for planting and too early for haymaking, their work at this time of year involved hauling logs and rocks for the construction of buildings and fences. The drayhorses, including Dafydd's, were out on errands with their masters. Even Morghe's black-footed white mare was absent, probably at Dhoo-Glass, since that was where Morghe seemed to be spending much of her free time lately. Only two horses now dozed in their stalls.

One was Chieftainess Gyanhumara's Brin. Angusel half expected to find her in Brin's stall, brushing the big gelding's coat until it gleamed like polished jet. Other than the horse, though, the stall was empty, and it made him think. Yes, his lessons had finished early. What a mercy that had been.

He reached in to stroke the glossy neck. "She'll be here soon, Brin." Snorting, the horse tossed his head as though in agreement.

Several stalls away, a dappled gray nose thrust into the straw-strewn walkway. With a final pat to Brin's cheek, Angusel grabbed a boar-bristle brush from a nearby ledge and hurried to join his horse.

Hefting the brush, he lifted the latch and stepped into the stall. Stonn greeted him with an enthusiastic nicker and began his customary quest for treats.

"Sorry, boy." Angusel set down the brush to display empty hands. "No carrots today."

Stonn answered with a loud *whuff* that sounded very much like a sigh. Ears back, he swung around to tug wisps from his hay crib.

"I said I was sorry," Angusel muttered as he began applying the brush to the stallion's flanks.

Stonn was an unusual Highland horse. Even at a distance, his black-accented gray coat marked him as a breed apart. He stood taller than his kin by at least two handbreadths. The birthing of the leggy colt, two springs before, had nearly killed his dam. Angusel wondered whether Alayna regretted giving Stonn to him, now that Clan Alban's breedmasters were denied the stallion's valuable stud services.

He was beginning to wonder why she had given him the horse at all. A guilt offering, maybe? Because she wouldn't let him fight in the Aber-Glein campaign?

A memory threatened to destroy his mood. He pushed it away.

Stonn was all that mattered now. As he drew the stiff bristles over Stonn's coat, he imagined those magnificent muscles rippling and bunching between his thighs.

Angusel sighed. For though Stonn was his in name, other men knew the feel of those muscles. Other men, usually one of the cavalry warriors, took the stallion out for his daily exercise. Angusel had never been on Stonn's back. And no one at the fort knew.

Sustaining the fiction was easy enough. Tanroc's Brytoni inhabitants didn't concern themselves with the comings and goings of a foreigner. Prevailing upon someone to exercise Stonn was easy, coupled with the excuse that his studies kept him too busy. The only person who might have noticed that things weren't quite as they seemed was the chieftainess, but she usually stayed later at the monastery. Angusel was confident that his secret was safe. But that didn't make it any easier to live with.

Today would be different! It was early. The stable hands still sat at their midday meal. Chieftainess Gyanhumara was not due for some time yet.

Angusel left the stall, replaced the brush, and headed into the tack room. Lifting Stonn's bridle off its peg, he briefly considered taking the saddle as well. But no, that would only complicate things.

Stonn perked his ears forward as Angusel approached, bridle in hand. Putting it on posed no problem, since he'd seen it done often enough. His hands trembled with excitement as he gathered the reins to lead his horse into the shimmering afternoon.

The stables were situated well away from the living areas. Behind the stables, butting up against the south-western palisade wall, was a small training enclosure. It was seldom used, since most riders preferred to exercise their mounts across the hills and valleys beyond Tanroc's gates. For Angusel's purposes, it would be perfect.

He was just leading Stonn around the end of the building when a shout drew his attention. His heart plummeted.

"Angusel!" Smiling brightly, Gyanhumara strode toward him, clad in her riding leathers. Evidently, her lessons had also finished early. "I'm taking Brin out, too. I wouldn't mind the company, if you don't mind waiting a few minutes."

His brain raced through a list of excuses while she fixed her steady sea-green gaze upon him. Even before reaching the end of the list, he knew he was trapped. "No, my Lady, I don't mind." He tried his best to sound more cheerful than he felt. "I don't mind at all."

"Good." She glanced at Stonn. "Bareback riding today?"

"Aye, my Lady. I—" Angusel broke into a crooked grin. "I've never tried it before."

"Well, it's a bit different. Your backside may be complaining tomorrow."

No doubt about that, whether he used a saddle or not. But he put on what he hoped was a brave face. "I was going to take Stonn to the ring to—to get used to the feel of it."

"Good idea. I'll meet you there when I'm ready."

As Gyanhumara disappeared into the stables, Angusel hurried Stonn over to the training ring. With any luck, they'd have several minutes to themselves before she and Brin appeared.

He stopped his stallion next to the rail fence and climbed it. Having grown up around horsemen, he knew the proper way to mount. But it seemed best to go slowly at first.

Stonn stood amazingly still as Angusel eased onto his back from the fence. Heart hammering, he wanted to shout for pure joy.

Imitating a motion he'd seen every other rider use, he touched the stallion's sides with his heels. As Stonn obediently moved forward, Angusel straightened. The reins went taut. The horse stopped. Then Angusel remembered what pulling back meant.

"All right, Stonn," he whispered into one black-edged gray ear. "Let's try again. I think I've got the way of it now."

He kicked Stonn into a walk. After a couple of turns around the ring, getting used to controlling the horse's direction, he dared a trot. And immediately regretted it. Never mind the jolts to his backside. He thought his teeth would bounce out of his head. Worse yet, his knees were losing their grip. Wrestling to maintain balance, he accidentally touched Stonn's sides with his heels. The stallion leaped into a canter. With a startled cry, Angusel fell.

As he rolled onto his back, Stonn walked over and nuzzled his face. Nothing really hurt except his pride. He put up a hand to caress the soft nose.

A chuckle greeted him. He scrambled to his feet. Outside the dusty enclosure near the gate stood Brin. Gyanhumara straddled his back with a casual, confident, and thoroughly enviable grace.

"Angusel mac Alayna! Where on earth did you learn to ride like that?" Her tone carried more surprise than reproach.

Angusel gathered Stonn's reins and shuffled toward the gate, trying to give himself enough time to think. But there was no other way around the question except the truth.

"I taught myself, my Lady." He looked her square in the eyes. "Today."

"You mean you've never—but your mother—" She drew a breath. "Clan Alban has some of the finest horse-warriors of the Confederacy. Why did no one teach you? At your age, I was already a good rider, and learning to break and train horses."

It was true about his clan's horsemen. Caledonians were practically born in the saddle. They lived and fought and died in the saddle. And Clan Alban boasted the best. Angusel shrugged.

"It was the Aber-Glein campaign, my Lady. Everyone was too busy training and making weapons and armor and gathering supplies. No one had time to spare for someone who wouldn't be fighting." He studied the hoofprints around his feet as the memory invaded. The argument he'd had with his mother about going to battle rang as loudly in his mind now as it had the first time. She had even refused to let him participate in the defense of Senaudon; not that another spear would have made a difference . . .

"Not even the son of the *ard-banoigin?*" Gyanhumara asked softly.

Still staring at the ground, Angusel shook his head. "And afterward, when I was sent here, there wasn't anyone I wanted to ask to teach me." He looked up. "Except you."

"Me? Oh, no, Angusel. You want someone with

combat experience. Urien, perhaps. He commanded a cavalry wing at Aber-Glein."

"But I need the basics, first," he argued. "You could teach me that. Please, my Lady?"

She looked at him for a long, stern moment. Finally, she smiled. "Let's go find someplace outside the fort where we can practice without being disturbed." She held up a hand to cut off any reply he might have made. "But first, let's make an agreement: no more of this 'my Lady' nonsense. My friends call me Gyan."

Angusel beamed. "And mine call me Angus."

Thus began a custom that continued as spring blossomed into the crystal days that heralded the advent of summer. Gyan was immensely pleased with her decision to help Angusel learn to ride. Those afternoons afforded excellent opportunities to explore the Isle of Maun, with its sparkling beaches, stark cliffs, rolling pastures, warm lowlands, and apple-shaded river valleys. And over all loomed the gray-green Mount Snaefell. That such diversity existed on so small an island was a constant source of delight.

In truth, Maun offered Gyan everything she could possibly ever want. Except her father and brother, her clan, her home—and Arthur.

"Gyan, it's market day at Dhoo-Glass," announced Angusel one day as they saddled their mounts. "Can we go there this afternoon? Please?"

"Why? What do you need?"

"Need? I just want to look!" He smacked fist to palm. "I'm tired of all this practice, practice, practice!"

"Boy, it's practice that will make you into a better warrior. Not gawking at the merchants' stalls." Gyan chuckled at Angusel's tragic face. "All right, we'll go. I could use a new sword belt. You can practice jumping obstacles with Stonn on the way."

Angusel groaned. "More practice!" He spied Morghe approaching them and waved. "Morghe, we're going to the market at Port Dhoo-Glass. Want to come?"

Regarding the pair with a neutral expression, Morghe shook her head. "Perhaps some other time, Angus." She raised her empty basket. "I must gather herbs for the infirmary's stores."

Angusel turned to watch Morghe disappear into her mare's stall. After a moment, he whispered to Gyan, "I'd sure like to know what's wrong with her these days. She just isn't much fun anymore."

As the recipient of Morghe's frosty attitude many times already, Gyan had a fair idea of what was bothering her. But in response to Angusel's comment, she merely shrugged.

True to her word, Gyan made Angusel jump his mount over shrubs, rocks, fallen trees, and anything else she could find to stretch his skill. At times, their path wound back and forth across the rivers Neb and Dhoo. Angusel whooped with obvious pleasure at each new challenge he conquered. Gyan noted his improved attitude and skill with a smile of approval. When the port finally came into sight, her pride was soaring with the gulls. For the first time since his equestrian training had begun, Angusel had not fallen once.

To cool their sweating horses, they dismounted outside the city gates and led them to the stables. Gyan left instructions with the stable hand to feed and water the animals, then she and Angusel set off for the market square.

Angusel clearly yearned to stop at every stall, but

Gyan made a beeline for the armorers. To take care of her business first, she explained. With the promise of plenty of time to browse afterward, Angusel tagged along.

An entire line of stalls and tents boasted the furnishings of war. As everywhere else in the market maze, the folk visiting this section were an odd mixture of clients and the merely curious, with one marked difference. Here the true customers were easy to identify. Without fail, they bore evidence of their work, if not by the overt presence of battle-gear, then by an abundance of scars or the swaggering manner that seemed the special province of the warrior caste.

Gyan was the only woman. Nor did this go unnoticed.

She paid no heed to the whispered remarks and sidelong glances that kept pace with her from stall to stall. Men too ill-mannered to shutter their rude thoughts were hardly worth the effort of a response.

Instead, she concentrated on the task at hand. And what a task it was! Every armorer offered belts by the score, segmented rectangles to encircle the waist and metal-studded baldrics that looped across the chest. Gold and silver and enamel and jewels decorated the ceremonial belts. Their working cousins displayed sterner faces of iron or bronze.

None came close to what Gyan sought. She wanted something to guard her middle as well.

The word at every stall was the same. If Adim Al-Iskandar of Constantinopolis did not sell it, such a thing simply did not exist. Bypassing the remaining armorers, she threaded her way to Al-Iskandar's stall.

"Ah, my Lady, I believe I can be of service to you," crooned the fat, dark merchant in response to Gyan's query. "I have been saving this piece for just the right

owner." Grinning broadly, he bowed and ducked into
the tent behind his stall.

He reemerged a few moments later, carrying in both
hands the finest piece of armor Gyan had ever seen.
More than a sword belt, it was a work of art. What
caught her eye was the dragon cleverly worked in relief
across the front—and not only for the excellence of its
craftsmanship.

Al-Iskandar let her scrutinize the armored belt while
he spoke in an odd, lilting accent about its origins and
features.

"Bronze, for maximum durability." He gave it a
resounding thump with bejeweled knuckles. "Based on
a design favored by the Ostrogoths, only better. The
middle part rides higher, here, to protect more of your
vitals. And you can see there is a place in front where
you can attach a short-sword or dagger sheath."

Sparing a glance for the crowd swelling around his
stall, he asked, "Would my Lady care to try it on?"

In reply, Gyan unbuckled her belt. With deft fingers,
the merchant fitted the bronze piece around her waist,
over her leather tunic, and cinched the fastening
thongs across the small of her back. He removed the
scabbard from her old belt and attached it to the new
one. The onlookers breathed a collective gasp of admiration.

Gyan's hand dropped to her sword hilt as if to draw
the weapon; in reality, she was judging the scabbard's
placement. It was perfectly comfortable. In fact, everything about the piece was perfect. Yet to haggle the
price down, she had to discover some flaw. It simply
would not do to take it at asking price. Folk might
wonder. Specifically, Urien.

"I would need someone to help me put it on," she
said. "Not very convenient in a surprise attack."

"A small price to pay, my Lady, for the vastly superior protection it offers you." Al-Iskandar's teeth, bared in a wide grin, glistened like pearls against the natural darkness of his skin. "Besides, I daresay a warrior of your obvious eminence should have the way of it mastered in no time."

In response to the shameless flattery, she suppressed her own grin. Some merchants would go to any length to make a sale. Doubtless, this man could outdistance the best.

"Gyan, it's fabulous!" Angusel exclaimed.

"Indeed," said a new voice. The crowd parted to make way for Urien.

"Gyan—Chieftainess Gyanhumara? This lovely lady is your betrothed, my Lord Urien?" Gyan could have sworn the merchant's surprise was an act.

Urien didn't seem to notice. Nodding, he reached Gyan's side and pushed Angusel away, none too gently. Angusel stumbled back against a one-eyed herdsman. Laughing coarsely, the man planted a hairy paw between Angusel's shoulders and shoved. Angusel whirled and drew his dagger against the offender.

"C'mon, laddie." The herdsman beckoned, grinning. "Lessee what yer made of."

The spectators cheerfully pulled back to give the combatants more room, and a chorus of encouragement began.

"Angusel, stop!" shouted Urien.

Angusel turned. The herdsman landed a clout to the back of his head. The startled warrior fell to hands and knees in the dust, dropping his dagger. The townsfolk roared in appreciation. Loudest among them was the herdsman.

Looking to Urien for help in gaining control of the

situation, Gyan found him to be enjoying the scene as much as everyone else, if not more so. The fires of anger roared to life. Now was not the time to play the simpering female! Not with a comrade's honor at stake.

The sight of an arm's length of naked steel commanded silence, even from Urien. But the herdsman, doubled over with his good eye closed, kept chortling.

"You, man! Get out of here. Now," Gyan growled. "And if I catch you making trouble again, I'll be seeing what you're made of." As she stalked toward the man, the others seemed more than happy to scramble out of her way. "From the inside out!"

The herdsman opened his eye to find the point of Gyan's sword half a handspan away. His glee disappeared. Bobbing his head in a parody of a bow, he stepped back into the crowd.

Gyan's sword screeched as she slammed it into its sheath. She offered a hand to Angusel, and he hauled himself up, rubbing his head. After retrieving his dagger, he scowled at Urien, whose mouth was still bent in amusement.

"Peace, Angus," Gyan hissed, in Caledonian. No longer in a mood to barter, she began tugging at the sword belt's fastenings.

Scurrying up to Gyan, Al-Iskandar touched fingertips to forehead and chest in a dramatic bow.

"Please, my Lady Gyanhumara, I am grievously sorry for what has happened. I would be deeply honored if you would accept the belt as a gift. A token of my sincerest good wishes. All I ask"—and with clasped hands, he displayed an expression that reminded Gyan of a begging dog—"is that you do not forget your humble servant Adim Al-Iskandar when you have need of arms or armor in the future."

"Thank you, Adim Al-Iskandar." She smiled despite her irritation. "I certainly shall not forget your kindness this day."

Al-Iskandar smugly watched Gyanhumara and Urien pass through the crowd, trailed by the glowering young warrior. The arms merchant knew that he, Adim Al-Iskandar, would not forget this day, either. He had known from the start with whom he had been dealing, of course. In all the lands touching the seven seas, Al-Iskandar had never seen the aura of power melded to such an exquisite female form. And he made it his business to learn as much about his clients—and potential clients—as possible.

And when word of his generosity and the subsequent pledged patronage of the Picti chieftainess became common knowledge, he expected his business on this island would increase threefold at least. Already, several men were stepping forward to examine his wares. He had no doubt his investment in goodwill would be well worth the price.

"Hai, Adim," came a harsh whisper from behind him.

He craned his head around and cursed. To attend the customers, he rousted his apprentice from the tent and motioned impatiently to the one-eyed herdsman. The man followed Al-Iskandar into the empty tent.

"Idiot! The embarrassment you caused me—" Al-Iskandar did not shrink from the judicious use of guilt to achieve the desired effect. "Not to mention the loss of an important sale!"

"This'll take care o'yer whinin', to be sure." The herdsman drew a smelly scrap of cowhide from the neck of his tunic. Al-Iskandar snatched it out of his hand. "Y'know where this goes, Adim. Collect when y'get there, as usual." With his uncovered eye, he winked. "Now then, what do y'know 'bout that woman?"

"Oho, that will cost you, my friend." The merchant's lips pulled back in a grin. "Up front." Casually leaning one hand on the worktable, he extended the other, palm up.

The herdsman reached into his boot. With a practiced flick of the wrist, the silver-hilted knife lodged in the wood at Al-Iskandar's fingertips. The merchant jerked back his hand with a gasp of alarm.

"There, thief. Take this an' be done." He glared at Al-Iskandar. "But if I don't like what I be hearin', ye'll find me other knife in yer gut."

Chapter

19

Fingering his sword's pommel, Urien rounded on Angusel. "I would like to speak to Gyanhumara. Alone."

"You could apologize first, Urien." Gyan suspected he would ignore her suggestion, but it was worth a try. "That fight was your fault."

"How was I supposed to know the man was going to react that way?"

"Ha! You think a commoner is going to play by the rules?" She left the disdain in her tone undisguised. "They know none." She spun and strode away, with Angusel close behind her.

"Gyanhumara, wait." Urien pitched his voice over the throng. "Please!"

The Caledonian warriors stopped.

After catching up, Urien thrust out a hand. "I apologize, Angusel."

Angusel clasped the proffered arm.

Neither warrior saw Gyan's eyebrows twitch. Her surprise was twofold: at the apparent sincerity of Urien's gesture and at Angusel's acceptance of the apology.

"Thank you, Urien," she said. "Now, you wish to speak to me?"

"Yes, my dear." Urien turned his attention upon Angusel again. "Can I trust you to stay out of trouble for a while?"

Angusel's scowl slowly faded. As Arthur's ranking officer on the island, Urien had the authority to curtail his freedom. Gyan was glad to see that Angusel had the sense to remember this and abandon any further attempts to jeopardize his position.

"Aye, sir," he replied, eyes lowered.

In Caledonian, Gyan said, "Don't worry about him, Angus. He barks more than he bites."

Looking up, Angusel smiled briefly. She gave his shoulder an affectionate pat.

For Urien's benefit, she switched back to Brytonic. "Go ahead and explore the rest of the market. I'll meet you later this afternoon."

"Gyanhumara, surely you're not thinking of riding back to Tanroc so soon? We haven't seen each other in a week," Urien said.

And what a blissfully uneventful sennight it had been. Ever since their arrival on the island, Urien seemed to be slipping back into his old arrogant ways; today's incident with Angusel was just the latest of many. Gyan had no idea why. But she didn't like it. So today she had hoped to escape back to Tanroc without Urien being any wiser. His appearance in the market had destroyed that plan. Now that he had found her, there was no sense in fabricating an excuse to leave. Best to fuel the fiction, not the suspicions, especially since he had chosen to act in a halfway civil manner.

"Why, you're absolutely right, Urien." To Angusel, she said, "Meet me after dinner in the stables. Now, off with you."

Gyan followed Angusel's progress until he disappeared into the crowd. Urien took her hand. Forcing her lips to curve into a smile, inwardly she steeled herself against his touch. She ached for the caress of a different hand, one forbidden to her by distance and duty. Desperately, she fought to will the pain away. And failed.

"Was that really necessary?" Urien was asking.

With heartrending effort, she exiled Arthur's face to glance at her betrothed. "What?"

"Speaking to Angusel in your tongue."

Gyan shrugged. "Certain ideas don't translate well."

"I've missed you," Urien said as they resumed their course between the market stalls.

To avoid an awkward response, she dodged behind the question that was uppermost in her mind. "How did you know I was here?"

"My dear, you are not exactly the type of woman who can blend into her surroundings very well." His chuckle grated in her ears. "Once the gate guards reported your arrival to me, all I had to do was ask around." The mirth gave way to a harder look. "Why didn't you let me know you were here? I hope you weren't going to try to slip away without paying me a visit."

"Oh, no, Urien. I would never do that." The lie left a vile taste in her mouth, and she hated herself for it. Yet, to keep peace, she could think of nothing else to do.

They neared a wharfside tavern, which was overflowing with patrons of questionable origin. Sailors, presumably. Sea-stained clothes and rolling gaits and coarse mannerisms and even coarser speech were shared by most of the men. A few merchants graced this group, notable by their rich robes and expansive smiles. Every face wore a look of veiled danger.

"Shall we stop here for refreshment, Gyanhumara?" Without bothering to wait for a reply, Urien strode through the salt-eaten doors.

Given a choice, Gyan never would have selected this establishment. The rough patronage she could handle by letting her sword do her talking. The tavern itself gave her chills. Smoky gloom bred shifting shadows. The One God alone knew what was creeping through the stale straw underfoot. Her first instinct was to keep walking and deal with Urien's reaction later. But roasting beef and baking bread competed with the ale and cheap wine to send temptingly fragrant arrows aimed straight at the vitals. Her stomach demanded to stay. Hand casually resting on her sword's hilt, she followed Urien.

He claimed a table in the far corner of the room, beckoning curtly to the tavernkeeper in passing as though the man were a personal servant. For all Gyan knew, he might have been, by the way he rushed to await Urien's pleasure. The man seemed to know Urien's preference without asking. Each fist clutched an ale flagon.

"I hate ale," Gyan informed the tavernkeeper, smiling pleasantly. Per's advice about guarding her back sprang to mind as she settled into a chair against the wall. In this place, there was no question about the strategy's necessity. "You may bring me some wine instead. Your best, of course."

Bowing, the tavernkeeper snatched up the unwanted flagon and melted into the shadows.

To Urien's questioning look, she stated, "I see no point in accepting something I don't want."

"Ah." He claimed the chair beside the adjacent wall, took a pull from his flagon, and dragged the back of a hand across his lips. "Yet you accepted the sword belt."

"Yes." She didn't add that she had been prepared to trade anything for it, short of her life.

"You know my clan's sign is the boar," Urien said. "I'm sure the merchant must have had others—"

"I didn't think to ask." Gyan's annoyance began to rise. "This was the first piece Al-Iskandar showed me. The dragon is magnificent." Her fingernail made a dull *thunk* against the bronze.

"The dragon"—Urien's eyes became slits—"is Arthur's symbol."

As if she didn't know it! "Then it is all the more appropriate. I am one of his warriors now. Or will be," she amended with frustration, "if I ever see any action other than town brawls."

Urien's right hand closed over her left forearm, and he bent her arm up. His left arm shot across to grasp her hand. Their betrothal-bands fused. Gyan's stomach lurched at the thought of how easily the illusion could become reality.

"See these, my dear? First and foremost, you are mine."

More than once, she had wondered just how much of his high-handed arrogance she could swallow before making herself sick. Now she had her answer. She wrenched free of his grip and stood. The chair smacked into the wall.

"Not necessarily, Urien of Dalriada!"

Gyanhumara brushed past the startled tavernkeeper, who had returned with her wine.

"Just set it down, man," Urien ordered. "It won't go to waste."

The proprietor obeyed and retreated from the table. Through narrowed eyes, Urien watched his woman stalk away. Gyanhumara paused at a table near the door. At first, Urien couldn't identify the table's occupants in the gloom. Then the door swung open to admit more customers, and the waning afternoon sunlight briefly shone across the face of the man with whom she was conversing. It was the merchant, Al-Iskandar. The other men at the table were strangers to Urien, though he imagined they must be traders. They all wore that same greedy look as they regarded Gyanhumara with undisguised interest. She ignored them.

Urien's anger mounted as he saw Gyanhumara bestow upon Al-Iskandar what appeared to be more gratitude for the gift, to the merchant's obvious pleasure. Finally, without a backward glance, she strode from the tavern. While she was never the easiest of women to understand, sometimes her behavior was downright mystifying to him.

After taking another pull, Urien set the flagon down with a heavy thump. Several drops slopped onto the table. A few heads swiveled toward him and quickly turned away. He drank again, this time finishing it.

"That woman!" he spat into the empty vessel.

But, he reminded himself, eventually that woman would become his wife, whether she welcomed the union or not. She had to marry him if he, Urien map Dumarec of Clan Moray of Dalriada, had any say. Too many of his plans were hinging on it.

Though the sun had already begun to disappear behind a horizon-hugging cloudbank, Gyan was in no mood to stay the night at Port Dhoo-Glass and risk another chance encounter with Urien. Fear didn't drive her decision to leave. She simply could not trust what she might have said—or done—to him.

Angusel was still lingering near the arms merchants'

stalls. She tersely informed him of their imminent departure.

"I thought we were staying for supper. I'm starved!"

"We'll eat when we get to Tanroc. You can thank Urien for that."

Without another word, Gyan retrieved Brin from his stall, slapped the saddle in place, led him from the stables, mounted, and spurred him into a canter through the city gates. She scarcely noticed that Angusel was keeping pace. Her only concern was to put as much ground as possible between herself and her tormentor.

"Urien!" Unwittingly, Angusel uttered the last name she ever wanted to hear. "I still can't believe what he did to me in the market."

"It happened. Believe it." With luck, Angusel would sense her ill humor and leave her in peace.

But luck had fled with her cheer. Angusel went on, "First, he shoves me into that cattle herder. Then he distracts me—"

"I was there," she snapped. Would his mindless prattle never cease? "Save your tale for someone who wasn't."

At last, he seemed to hear the unspoken message. "Gyan, what's wrong?"

"It's none of your concern."

"You're not angry with me, are you? For getting into the fight?"

His earnest expression drove spikes of guilt through her soul. "No." The murmur was nearly lost under the drumming of the horses' hooves.

Angusel lapsed into silence. Gyan retreated into the cave of her thoughts, only to find the company to be much less comforting than she'd hoped. Arthur's image did not help this time. It only served as a blunt reminder that her heart's desire was so miserably far from reach.

A mile later, Angusel ventured another question. "Is it Urien?"

Most topics would have provided a welcome interruption. This one did not. "Angus, I said it's none of your concern."

"But it is! You're my countrywoman and my friend. Never mind what he did to me. Anyone who makes you so unhappy is no friend of mine."

An angry reprimand died in her throat. "I appreciate your support, Angus. I really do." A brief, wan smile was the best she could manage. "But this matter is between Urien and me. I don't want you to get involved. What I said earlier, about his bark and bite, I said to cheer you. Believe me, Angus, if you cross him, he will shackle you so fast, you won't know what happened until it's far too late."

This seemed to satisfy him, at least for a while. Another pair of miles passed before Angusel spoke again: "Gyan, I just don't understand why you ever consented to marry such a mannerless dog of a Bryton."

"Angusel mac Alayna! Guard your tongue."

"Well, it's true, isn't it?"

Who knew better than she did? But truth and diplomacy seldom trod the same path.

"Truth or not, you should never insult your allies. Even if you don't think they can hear you."

"Some ally," he muttered. "If he upsets you so much, why don't you break your betrothal, Gyan? It is your lawful right."

"You don't know how much I wish it could be that simple, Angus." Gyan realized that for a lad of twelve, there was no such thing as middle ground. After transferring the reins to her sword hand, she held up her shield arm. The fingers clotted into a fist. "But duty binds me tighter than this betrothal-mark. And sometimes duty can be a poor companion."

Frowning, Angusel cocked his head. "What do you mean?"

What, indeed? How could she tell him that she was in love with someone else but was powerless to do anything about it? That his face lived in her dreams to torture her with the visions of what she could not possess? And barring that, how could she possibly tell Angusel that the man who imprisoned her heart, mind, and soul was his jailer, too?

Instead, she shook her head with a sigh and studied the darkening western sky, now licked by a forked tongue of lightning. She reined Brin to a halt. Angusel pulled Stonn in beside them.

"Tanroc's gates will be shut for the night at any moment with this storm coming on." The first heavy drops began to batter the ground. "If they're not already. I hope you don't mind sleeping in the mud, Angus."

"What about Rushen Priory? They let travelers in at all hours."

"It's a women's place, though, isn't it? Will they let you stay, too?"

Angusel thoughtfully chewed a gloved knuckle. Finally, he shrugged. "I don't see why not. I could always sleep in the stable."

His crooked grin won a soft chuckle. So this was what having a younger brother might have been like. It was not an unpleasant thought.

"Very well, Angus, let's go!"

She pulled up the hood of her cloak to ward off the

quickening rain as they spurred their horses toward the promise of shelter.

The novice set the mug on the tabletop over the spot indicated by Niniane's gracefully tapered finger. "Will you be needing anything else this evening, Prioress?"

"No, child, thank you. If I do, I can get it myself."

The novice bobbed a curtsey and slipped out of the room, easing the door shut behind her.

Niniane breathed a sigh as she reached for the steaming cup. Chamomile—just the thing for many ailments. Including a throbbing head.

It was not easy, having the Sight.

The images tormented her sleep with relentless clarity. In a natural dream, Niniane was always a detached observer, swept through a parade of bizarre events soon forgotten upon waking. During a visitation of the Sight, she actively participated in the events, invariably as someone else. She had lost count of the number of times she had awakened with the cold, rough flagstones beneath her bare feet, gasping as though she had just dashed across the island and back. And the scenes could never be forgotten.

Before, Niniane's visions had mostly concerned Arthur. Sometimes others. In fact, the Sight hadn't troubled her in months, which had been heavenly bliss.

Three nights ago, it had begun again in earnest, as though trying to make up for its long absence. This time, there were new pairs of dream-eyes to See from. Unfamiliar eyes. And being whirled from one perspective to another in quick succession was particularly exhausting.

Eyes closed, Niniane inhaled deeply of the chamomile tisane's applelike fragrance and took a tentative sip. The herb's characteristic bitterness was masked by the soothing sweetness of mint and honey. Silently blessing Marcia for remembering these additions, she took another sip.

With the ache in her temples beginning to subside, she returned to her work: creating sketches of the medicinal herbs. She knew she was doing her eyes no favor, toiling by lamplight. But she was anxious to finish her latest drawing, the hollyhock, before retiring for the night, so she could begin afresh on the hyssop in the morning.

Or so she tried to make herself believe. In reality, any activity that could postpone her nightly appointment with the future was welcome.

Absorbed with attempting to capture the likeness of the model plant with the greatest possible accuracy, and lulled by the rain pattering against the window's shutters, she did not respond to the frantic tapping right away. At length, she glanced up at the door, wondering who could possibly wish to see her at this late hour.

Niniane straightened from her work, smoothed the wrinkles from her undyed linen robe, and tucked an errant chestnut lock under the wimple. *"Ave."*

The novice Marcia appeared in the doorway. The rainwater sliding off her cloak puddled on the stone floor. Her wringing hands and wide, flaxflower-blue eyes betrayed fear.

"What is it, child?" Niniane crossed the workroom toward the girl, who was shivering like grass in a windstorm. "Why did you go outside on a night like this?"

Marcia, too flustered to remember her curtsey, blurted, "Visitors, Prioress. Two warriors, a young man and a woman, both armed and mounted." She shuddered. "They wish to spend the night."

"Are they Brytons?"

"They speak Brytonic. At least, the woman does. The other didn't say anything. Just . . . looked at me. I think they're foreign, Lady."

Niniane pondered the information, fingering the slim silver cross that hung at her breast. Last night, she had Seen a lady warrior fighting another lady warrior in the midst of what had appeared to be a great battle. The Sight had not revealed the outcome. It rarely did in a single visitation but presented tiny pieces of a vast puzzle in capricious order.

Finally, she declared, "Marcia, this holy house has never turned away anyone in need of help. Nor shall we break tradition now. Show them to the stables, and then—"

"B-but, Prioress, they'll slit our throats while we sleep!" Marcia buried her face in her hands to hide the flood of tears.

Ignoring the distraught girl's sodden mantle, Prioress Niniane drew her into an embrace. "Of course they won't, child." Stroking Marcia's damp head cradled against her shoulder, she wondered what manner of folk could so terrify her. "God's hand protects us, so even if try, well, so much the worse for them."

With firm fingers beneath the novice's chin, Niniane made her look up. "You are a daughter of God, Marcia. You needn't fear anything, or anyone. Do you understand?"

Blinking back the tears, Marcia nodded.

Niniane smiled her approval. "Good. Now, help them see to the comfort of their horses, and bring them here to me. Then you may retire. After I've finished speaking with them, I will show them to the guest chambers myself."

Returning to the table as Marcia left, Niniane gazed mournfully at the now-cold cup. Though temperature did not affect its healing essence, the herbal drink would have been much more enjoyable hot than cold on a raw night like tonight. She drained the mug and again lost herself in her work.

No drug on earth could have prepared her for the warriors who were ushered into her presence.

The lad carried himself with a catlike grace quite at odds with his apparent age of twelve or thirteen summers. There was something hauntingly familiar about the curly black hair and golden-brown eyes. Whether Niniane had Seen him before as an older man, she could not be certain.

But of the woman she had no doubt. Tall and lithe as a maple sapling, crowned with autumn braids, the bronze dragon blazing across her trunk; yes, Niniane had Seen her. And not just through other eyes. The arm wielding the sapphire-headed sword against the enemy woman with such savage strength had been painted with woad doves. Every aspect of the lady warrior was startlingly familiar, except the sword. No gem adorned the pommel of the weapon riding her hip.

So the Sight had left another mystery. As usual. With a soft sigh, Prioress Niniane glided forward to greet her guests.

"Your pardon for the intrusion, Prioress," began the woman. "I am Chieftainess Gyanhumara, and this is my companion, Angusel. We seek only a bite to eat and shelter from the storm, for our mounts and us. Rain or no, we'll leave at first light."

So these were the Caledonians studying with the brethren at St. Padraic's. Niniane had guessed as much.

Though neither looked much like a scholar, she knew looks could deceive. "It's no intrusion, Chieftainess. The priory is honored by your visit." Niniane flashed what she hoped was a reassuring smile. "Our fare and lodgings are humble, but you may have anything within my power to give you. Here we welcome all who are loyal to the Pendragon. Now, if you will please follow me—"

"If you please, Prioress," Angusel broke in, "I'd like to hear about the Pendragon's sword. Caleberyllus."

The chieftainess turned a sharp look upon her comrade. They exchanged words in what Niniane assumed was their native tongue. A reprimand, judging by the woman's tone and the lad's contrite response.

Switching back to Brytonic, Gyanhumara said, "Please forgive him, Prioress. He is young and sometimes forgets his manners. I'm sure you're as anxious to retire for the evening as we are."

"Well, I did promise you anything within my power. And the story of Arthur's sword is certainly that." Niniane extended an open-palmed hand. "Come. Let us make ourselves comfortable by the fire."

It was the first image she had ever Seen, the forging of Caleberyllus, "Burning Jewel," the sword that was said to slice through stone like cheese. She had been a little girl then, terrified by the white-hot fire and incessant ringing in her dreams, and the screaming ache of arm and back upon waking, chestnut curls matted to her forehead by rivers of sweat. Even now, a quarter century later, she could still feel the intense heat and hear the hammer's rhythmic clang. And the furious hissing, like a mighty serpent, as glowing steel violated icy water to beget billowing mist.

The vision had stayed with Niniane as she grew older, but she had shared it with no one for fear of being branded a lunatic—or worse. At last, she was driven to seek counsel secretly from Henna, the village wise-woman. Henna recognized Niniane's gift for what it was, and not the beginnings of madness as Niniane had feared. Eventually, Niniane learned to focus the Sight and to interpret the visions.

It was with Henna's help that Niniane discovered that she must obtain this weapon for the man destined to unite all peoples of Brydein: Arturus Aurelius Vetarus, called Arthur map Uther.

Niniane did not tell her guests how she had come to learn of the sword. Only a trusted few knew of her gift. In truth, it was the primary reason behind her entry into the Church. She had desperately needed reassurance that the power was a gift of the Lord of Light, not the Lord of Lies.

Instead, she spoke of how she had "heard" of the sword, of how she had found it upon the forge of Wyllan, the most famous smith of Brydein, whose smithy lay in the bosom of Mount Snaefell. Of how Wyllan had been instructed in a dream to entrust his finest creation to a holy woman for safekeeping and had given the sword to Prioress Niniane.

Angusel listened with rapt attention. Even Gyanhumara's attitude reflected more than polite interest. Perched on the edge of the low wooden bench, she did not look down as she slowly traced a long, pale scar on the underside of her right forearm.

Then Niniane spoke of the Council of Chieftains, the rulers of the northern Brytoni clans that had assembled shortly after Uther's death to elect a new *Dux Britanniarum,* Duke of Brydein.

The position, reminiscent of the Roman occupation, was not an empty one. As in the days of the legions, the holder of this office, bearing the title of Pendragon,

"Chief Dragon," commanded all forces stationed between the walls of Hadrian and Antonius. This army had disbanded upon the withdrawal of the legions to the Continent. Most of the forts were abandoned when the native Brytoni auxiliaries, such as Niniane's great-grandfather, had gladly returned home to hang up their weapons and turn helmets into cooking pots.

Those pots would have been better left as helmets. Into the vacuum created by the legions' departure rushed enemy peoples from all sides, eager to claim the verdant Isle of Brydein for themselves. Angles, Frisians, Jutes, Saxons, and others from the Continent attacked the south and east. Scots from Hibernia raided the villages along the west coast. And, of course, there was the blue-painted menace from the north.

At the mention of the Caledonian threat, her guests exchanged a glance. Niniane suspected they knew more about the history of that conflict than she and elected to keep her sketchy—and biased—knowledge of it to herself.

She described instead the scheme of the power-drunk tyrant Vortigern, who attempted to keep the Scots and Caledonians at bay using Saxon mercenaries. This plan worked only as long as Vortigern's wealth held more sway over the Saxons than their desire to snatch land for themselves. One night, his Saxon wife stabbed him in his sleep in an attempt to aid her people's cause. Vortigern's death went unlamented by his countrymen.

Shortly thereafter, two Brydein-born Roman brothers, having grown to manhood in Armorica, just across the Narrow Sea on the Continent, returned to Brydein with an army at their backs to assert their claim over the Island of the Mighty.

The brothers, Ambrosius, called Emrys, and Vetarus,

called Uther, plunged into the chaos and attempted to restore order using disciplined Roman ways. This was effective enough against their foreign-tongued enemies. But it only served to alienate the chieftains of the southern and western Brytons. These men had no desire to bear again the yoke of Rome, however remote the possibility. Once the immediate threat to their lands was removed, they summarily withdrew their allegiance.

Emrys and Uther relocated their force in the north, between the walls, where the fighting was long from finished. The chieftains of the northern Brytoni clans were more appreciative of the brothers' efforts, if not overly thrilled at having Roman neighbors again. Emrys revived the position of *Dux Britanniarum* to ease relations with his allies by underscoring the fact that his authority was more military than political. But he did not bear the title of Pendragon for long. Illness claimed his life, leaving Uther to finish the work.

This work had yet to be completed when, a score of years later, Uther's last earthly sight was that of an Angli spear sprouting from his chest, with his men falling in panic-stricken confusion around him. If he watched his son transform the rout into an orderly retreat to save as many lives as possible, it was not with the eyes of this world.

Uther's death served as a brutal reminder to the chieftains that their lands were by no means safe. They could not hope to stand against their enemies unassisted. Thus, after interring Uther beside his brother with due honor, the Council convened.

What a wild week that had been! In three days, the initial field of candidates dwindled to just two. The Council became deadlocked. The Dalriadans stood unswervingly behind their choice, Urien. Most Low-

land clans backed Arthur. But with several chieftains
unwilling to commit, neither candidate owned a clear
majority. Bribes flowed as freely as ale, producing
similar, and sometimes disastrous, effects.

Niniane with her Sight-aided knowledge sought out
the young Arthur. The army, what was left of it, was
desperate for a sign of new hope after Uther's devastating defeat and did not care how the Council would
vote. With one thunderous voice, they acclaimed Arthur as their Pendragon at first sight of the peerless
Caleberyllus in his fist. The army's support swayed the
undecided chieftains to Arthur's side.

As she finished her tale, Niniane watched a smile
grow upon Chieftainess Gyanhumara's lips, mirrored in
the summer-green eyes.

Chapter
20

Cuchullain og Conchobar, Laird of the Scots, stood in his war-chariot at the Doann Dealghan waterfront. His matched pair of jet-black mares fretted in their silver traces, pawing the ground and tossing their heads and causing the laird's charioteer a great deal of trouble. At last, they quieted under the man's canny touch, and the silver-and-green-enameled chariot ceased its boat-like rocking.

Around them eddied the clamor of commands and the clattering of equipment as warriors piled by the score into the wolf-prowed warships. Cuchullain's smile, as he rested one hand on his sword's hilt, hid his disappointment. He sympathized with his fiery beauties. More than life itself, he wanted to go with the men, to wreak havoc on Brytoni flesh in retribution for what Uther the Pendragon's men had done long ago to him. Unfortunately—or fortunately, as far as his beloved Dierda was concerned—the renewed Attacotti threat bound him to these shores.

It was a risk for him to be even this far—a full day's ride—from his Seat at Tarabrogh. At the height of the war-season, practically anything could happen on his way home. Yet the operation his warriors were embarking upon was of the utmost importance, and the presence of their laird clearly meant a great deal to them.

Not for the first time, Cuchullain swelled with pride as a ship was shoved into the water to join its kin bobbing in the harbor. The ruby sails remained furled to their masts. No overcurious trader or fisherman was going to betray this secret. Even the Silver Wolf banner at each mast's tip was lashed down. If this endeavor was to open the door to Maun, surprise was the key.

Across the droning waves lay the prize. A white veil of mist demurely hid its emerald-crowned cliffs and diamond-bright beaches, but Cuchullain didn't have to see it to know it was there. Nor did he have to see the island's defenders, a pox on their black hearts!

Having to spare half his fleet to transport more than a thousand of his best warriors was a bitter tonic. Yet those fatherless Brytons, who only this season had doubled the number of troops there, left Cuchullain with no choice. He would have preferred to wait until another year, long after the Brytons deemed themselves safe enough to recall most of their men back to the larger island. But it was either strike at the lands toward the rising sun now, or else perpetuate the war against the blood-lusting Attacotti until no living creature remained upon this fair Isle of Eireann except the wolves and the ravens.

Perhaps he could yet hold back a boatload or two, depending upon the latest report. If the courier arrived in time. For, confirmation or no, the fleet would sail tonight. And as the sun sent Cuchullain's shadow creeping toward the shoreline, his hopes of seeing a final message from his contact on Maun sank with it.

As though sensing his thoughts, the short, stocky

warrior at his elbow bellowed, "Where be that blasted merchant? He should have been here days ago."

Cuchullain turned full attention upon his battle-leader. "Calm yourself, Niall." He tried to make his grin display naught but confidence. A confidence he hoped was not misdirected. "Your yelling willna be putting wind in his sails."

As the two longtime friends shared the laugh, they scanned the dimming horizon.

Niall pointed. "There!"

Following the invisible line drawn by Niall's finger, Cuchullain squinted into the distance. All he could make out was a flash of white; a sail, perhaps, or a gull's wing. "Can ye be sure?"

"Nay," said Niall. "But there be time yet."

General Niall strode toward the last of the beached warships, his thin auburn braids bouncing against the bright red, green, and gold plaid cloak. While he talked with his men, the white patch with the dark blot beneath resolved itself into a trading ship, bearing for Doann Dealghan Harbor.

Cuchullain stepped down from the chariot and paused to stroke each velvety muzzle before joining Niall. He hoped the news would be encouraging.

It was not. The fat foreign merchant waited in respectful yet expectant silence as Cuchullain studied the figures on the curled cowhide scrap. Scratched with a hunk of charred wood and smudged in places, the crude message disclosed the precise layout of foot and horse on the island. The unwritten message was just as clear: every man now committed to this invasion would be essential.

In sheer numbers, his warriors would have a slight advantage, though the enemy's cavalry units would remove that edge in a pitched battle. But the Brytons were dispersed among four coastal stations. Such a pity.

The plan just might work. Would work. Had to.

Flushed with the anticipation of success, Cuchullain tugged off an emerald-studded silver ring and pressed it into the merchant's palm. The man grinned his thanks and slipped it into a pouch hanging by a thong at his neck. Touching fingers to forehead, he bent in an elaborate bow. Without a word, he stepped into the small craft that would take him back to the tall vessel anchored in the harbor's deeper water. Nodding to the oarsman, he departed.

Cuchullain thrust the message into Niall's hand. They gripped forearms in farewell, and Cuchullain gave the broad shoulder a hearty thump. Whistling the tune of a favorite drinking song, Niall headed for his ship.

As the last of the warships began to fill, Cuchullain bounded to his chariot. At his word, the charioteer snapped the reins across the twin ebony backs to send the gleaming chariot lurching toward higher ground.

The charioteer halted the team at the top of the rise. The mares snorted and quivered with fierce excitement. Cuchullain's pale gray and green cloak fell away from his shoulders as he raised his arms to address the men.

A shrill, throbbing squeal pierced the dusky air. He whipped his head around to see a thick column of smoke erupting from the hills. No, not smoke. Night hunters.

Below, the men were pointing and shouting. A portent, they were calling it. Many warriors folded fingers into the sign against strong evil.

The eerie shrieks lingered among the hills long after the bats had vanished into the fading twilight.

"My brothers!" Laird Cuchullain called to the men

on the beach. He knew his speech would travel to the others quickly once they reassembled on the opposite shore. "My brave brothers, listen!" And most did. "This be a portent, aye, a portent of victory! For those cries"—every eye was upon him now—"they be the cries of the Brytoni warriors fated to die by your mighty swords as ye make their island ours!"

The drumming of spearshafts on timber hulls, the bleating of war-horns, the hoarse shouting, sweet music all. It made Cuchullain wish he had learned the harp, so he could make this hour be remembered in heroic song forever.

In the ashen light of dawn, Angusel slipped into the Tanroc stables. Stonn whickered softly at Angusel's approach and nosed the saddle pack looped over one of his arms. In the other hand, Angusel carried his bow. A full quiver bounced against his back.

Beaming with affection, he produced the expected treat. As Stonn greedily destroyed the carrot, Angusel set down his burdens to retrieve saddle and bridle from the tack room.

The guardsmen at the palisade gate tower gave him no trouble after he explained that the chief cook had asked him to go bird hunting for the evening meal. It wasn't exactly a lie: he was going to hunt birds and planned to give the game over when he returned. But the idea was entirely his own.

Within moments, Angusel and Stonn became the first ones of the day to pass through the palisade and hedge gates.

After the fort had disappeared behind the first line of hills, Angusel nudged Stonn into a canter. Soon they were flying along the coastal path toward Maun's northwestern cliffs, which boasted the best rookeries on the island.

It felt delightfully wicked to miss arms practice. If hunting were good, perhaps he would even escape his mathematics lesson. He already considered himself skillful at plain figuring. What use had a warrior for geometry and trigonometry? Those topics were best left to the men who designed buildings and catapults and boats and the like. Their ranks he had no desire to join.

Angusel closed upon his chosen destination. Nearby lay the deep, pine-sheltered hollow that was his favorite blind. But something was wrong this morning. A feathered cloud of screaming, diving bodies was fighting over food on the beach. Or, he realized with quickening pulse, sounding an alarm.

Topping the rise, Angusel saw the cause of the birds' excitement. A fleet! He swallowed thickly. From each mast bulged the crimson Scotti war sail.

He urged Stonn into the hollow, dismounted, and cast the reins over the nearest limb. Bow in hand, he crawled to the lip of the sandy depression. He parted clumps of grass and spine-collared dusty blue sea holly for a clearer view.

At least thirty vessels swarmed the cove south of his position. As he watched in shocked disbelief, some were just scraping onto the beach in groups of three and four. Others were already disgorging their heavily armed occupants. Several men remained with each ship, probably as guards. With much swearing and sweating, their comrades pushed the boats back into the water to rejoin the swiftly growing number anchored offshore, safely out of bowshot range from the land.

Angusel was sundered by indecision: fight or fetch help? His first instinct was to rush back to warn Tanroc. The enemy troops' movements as they hit the beach convinced him that Tanroc—and maybe St. Padraic's monastery—would be their first targets.

As strong as it was, Tanroc could not hope to stand long against a force that outnumbered the defenders by four to one. Tanroc would need reinforcements. Desperately.

Angusel added up distances and times. And hated the answer. Divine intervention was the only way Urien's relief force could arrive fast enough to save Tanroc—or Gyan.

Tears stung his eyes as he pounded his fist into the sand. He had to get back to the fort, to fight at her side. To kill as many Scots as he could before they killed him.

As he rose to mount, he heard footsteps nearby. He ducked and flattened himself against the side of the hollow. Heart thudding like the surf on the beach below, he prayed to every god in the Caledonian pantheon that the person would not discover him. He gripped Stonn's bridle with whitening knuckles to prevent the stallion from tossing his head.

Someone must have heard his prayer. The man passed just a few paces from the hollow but looked only toward the beach now seething with Scots. It was the Dalriadan herdsman of the black eyepatch, without his cattle. To Angusel's growing astonishment, the man strode boldly down to meet the enemy troops.

Angusel drew an arrow from his quiver and nocked it. He had no doubt that the herdsman had sold the island to the Scotti invaders. Some detached portion of Angusel's brain wondered what the man was now saying to the small conclave of Scots who were the apparent leaders of the force. He ruthlessly shoved curiosity aside. Smiling grimly, Angusel aimed the bow and waited for the traitor to move back into range.

The commanders' meeting ended when the last of the troops landed on the beach. Something flashed golden-bright in the morning sun as it arced through the air from the hand of one of the leaders. The herdsman snatched it with greedy dexterity and stashed it in a pouch hidden beneath his hide-patched tunic. The Scot clapped him on the back. The whiplike auburn braids flanking the war-leader's face swung to the rhythm of his laughter. He moved off to join his men, a unit of the most elitely armed warriors Angusel had seen all morning.

The one-eyed man bowed and turned back toward the path leading from the beach.

An arrow in the throat seemed too good a death for the traitor. And Angusel saw a way to avenge the blow the herdsman had dealt to his pride a few days earlier.

He released the tension on the bowstring and laid the bow in the sand. The quiver joined it. As he unsheathed his long hunting knife, he was overwhelmed by the desire to carve out the man's guts, deprive him of his manhood, and then slit his throat.

Tracking the cattle herder's slow progress up the sandy bluff, Angusel considered letting his prey go. A glance at the departing Scotti troops reminded him that time was not his ally. Yet the man's betrayal had earned death, if only for Gyan's sake. It was the least Angusel could do for her. And the last.

He tightened his fingers around the knife handle, gathered himself into a crouch, and waited.

Stonn's impatient snort betrayed Angusel's position. The man jerked his head toward the hollow. Propelled by burning anger, Angusel sprang.

The herdsman's lone eye rounded in surprise and narrowed as recognition set in.

As Angusel watched the broken-nailed fingers claw toward his face, he realized this would not be the kind of fight for which he had been trained. Against each other, warriors followed certain rules of engagement. Not many, granted, but they were religiously observed. Commoners, as Gyan had remarked, knew none.

Still, this was not unlike the scrapes he had gotten into with the other lads back home at Senaudon. But in those fights, the only things at stake were pride and honor, the only risks scratches and bruises.

Now he fought for his life. To survive this game, he threw away the rules.

Angusel ducked the blow, whirled, and connected a booted foot with the man's groin to send him sprawling, groaning, to the ground. Knife poised, Angusel pounced. But the herder had recovered enough to heave Angusel away like a bundle of cattle fodder. Angusel rolled to his feet in time to see his foe bearing down upon him, bellowing rage. A rust-flecked iron dagger sprouted like a talon from one hairy fist. The good eye gleamed with malice.

The combatants locked arms in a deadly dance, each writhing to free his weapon hand from the other's grip. Angusel dug his fingers into the spy's tendons with brutal ferocity. Reluctantly, the hand opened. The dagger slipped to the ground.

Before Angusel could press the advantage, the herdsman landed a savage kick to his knee. Searing pain tore up and down the leg. He stumbled backward. His knife was jarred from his grasp as he fell.

He rolled clear as the heavier man tried to leap on top of him, but he couldn't get to his feet in time. A hard blow to the jaw drove his head into the sand.

Reflexively, Angusel brought up his hands to grip his foe's arms as the thick fingers tightened around his throat.

Like a beacon, Gyan's image flashed into the spreading blackness. With a surge of strength, Angusel broke the stranglehold, punched at the glaring eye, and twisted free. As he lay gasping on his back, his outflung hand landed on cold metal.

Gratefully, Angusel retrieved his knife. The herdsman leaped. The blade bit into the unprotected belly. Angusel shoved the wounded man off.

Still panting, he withdrew the knife and stood. A crimson flood burst from the wound. Yet the man lived, feebly flailing at his torn, bloody tunic. Angusel took no chances. He drove the knife through the spy's throat.

"That is what I'm made of, you stinking traitor," Angusel spat at the dead man.

He cleaned his knife on the grass, sheathed it, faced Tanroc . . . and swore. During the fight, the first ranks of the Scotti army had covered more than half the distance to the fort. There was no way to skirt the column unseen and still arrive ahead of it.

With bow and quiver, he limped to where Stonn was patiently cropping the salty grass. Climbing into the saddle was painful, but he managed. He sat astride his stallion and massaged the injured knee, thinking.

Now his only option was to ride to Port Dhoo-Glass, for whatever good it would accomplish. As Angusel reined Stonn around, he groaned. A group of Scots had split from the larger column, heading southeast. Toward Dhoo-Glass.

Why had the gods spared his life only to rob him of this one slender chance to save Gyan? What had he ever done to displease them so much?

His gaze fell upon the Scotti fleet serenely riding the

waves in the bay. It reminded him of yet another possibility: the signal relay. Raising the alarm would bring the wrath of Arthur the Pendragon down upon the Scots' heads.

Pointing Stonn to the northeast, he kicked him into a gallop, but not toward the main signal beacon. Light from Mount Snaefell would be seen by friend and foe alike. Angusel raced for the small outpost at the northern tip of the island, Ayr Point.

On the bluff overlooking the Scotti beachhead, the first ravens had noticed the patch-eyed corpse. A stiffening hand clutched the pouch containing a Scotti bauble the herdsman had not lived long enough to enjoy.

Gyan was midway through her Latin lesson in the monastery when the church bells started pealing wildly. As one, she and Brother Lucan ran to the window, which overlooked Tanroc across the strait.

Scots! Lying, cowardly, heathen Scots were pouring over the hills in a raucous flood. She could practically smell their lice-ridden hides already. And there wasn't enough time to return to the fort before the portals were sealed. Her first chance to prove herself in battle, and she was trapped at the monastery like a caged rabbit!

A detachment broke away from the main column. To her horrified surprise, the smaller unit began heading toward the strait. What could these animals possibly want with the peaceful servants of the One God? Or was wanton destruction their evil game?

She would not let that happen—not while she still had breath in her lungs. Bracing palms against the window ledge, she racked her brains to devise a plan.

At high tide, the only approach to St. Padraic's Island

was by boat. But the tide was now at its lowest ebb, and the channel would not be difficult to wade. Without archers to defend the strait, the monastery was totally vulnerable.

There just had to be another way to thwart the Scots!

She addressed her tutor, who was twisting and untwisting a fold of his robe as he watched the advancing troops. "Do you have weapons?"

Lucan stuttered in momentary confusion. "Do I? Oh, you mean the monastery."

"Yes, yes. Swords, knives, pitchforks—anything!"

"A few things, my Lady. Hidden in the church's side chapels. Some of us even know how to use them. I do," the monk said proudly.

"Good." She caught his hand and pulled him into a run. "I'll need all the help I can get."

As they dashed outside, heading toward the church, she noticed that the other monks were also converging upon the same destination. "You meet here to make your stand?"

"If we have to," Lucan replied between breaths. "Mostly to pray. And to hide the valuable things."

They stopped outside the building. Gyan surveyed the timber roof of the Sanctuary of the Chalice and shook her head. "If they torch the roof and we're inside, we're dead. No, Brother Lucan. That's not a chance I'm willing to take. Distribute the weapons to those who can use them. Hide the Chalice and the other valuables, if you must. But bring everyone out here to me. Quickly!"

As the monk ran into the church, Gyan circled its perimeter. She formed a silent prayer of thanksgiving for the long-dead architect who had designed the cruciform structure. Two stone walls afforded much better protection than one.

She selected the corner facing away from the monastery's entrance for the greatest surprise factor and awaited the monks.

Of the hundred-member monastic community, fewer than thirty carried weapons of any sort. Gyan counted a handful of swords and a few more daggers and warknives. The remaining armed monks clutched staffs. Only Gyan wore any sort of armor, and only because she hadn't bothered to change after weapons practice.

Dafydd and Morghe had also been trapped at the monastery. Dafydd she wasn't overly worried about. But Morghe's presence created a special problem.

"Morghe, I want you against the wall. Try to stay hidden." When she began to protest, Gyan stated coldly, "Do it. The Scots have quite an appetite for beautiful slave women."

"But Arthur would never let—"

"But Arthur is not here. Now, move!" As Morghe rather sullenly obeyed, Gyan looked around. To no one in particular, she said, "Where's Angusel?"

One of the monks shrugged. "He never came for his lesson with me this morning, my Lady. I don't know where he could be."

In Caledonian, Gyan thoroughly cursed her ill fortune. Not only could she have used the warrior at her side, but his presence there meant not having to worry about where he was. Protecting Morghe and the monks single-handedly was a burden great enough for the hardiest veteran.

Ogryvan's lessons had never prepared her for what surely must be the worst aspect of combat: the waiting. Hearing the enemy's shouts and the monks' frantic whispers grow louder. Feeling the blood-lust boil in her veins. Fighting the urge to break rank and vent her rage on the closest Scotti target. Time crawled.

When she thought she was about to die of anticipation, the first soldiers rounded the corner of the church.

"Brethren, attack!" Without turning to see who followed her, Gyan lunged into the enemy's midst.

Killing was easier than she had expected. Though vastly superior in numbers, these men fought little better than straw targets. But they looked and sounded and smelled far worse when she was through with them. She had often wondered whether she would feel sorrow toward the victims of her sword.

How could she feel anything but contempt for these filthy dogs, who had invaded without provocation? They had the audacity to threaten her life and the lives of those she had come to love. And they paid for the outrage in this world's most precious coinage.

The death of a comrade was another matter entirely. When the first monk fell, screaming and clutching his middle in a hopeless attempt to prevent the spread of the scarlet stain, she wanted to stop in mid-swing and rush to his side. Grief ached like a gaping wound in her chest, made more acute by the apparent futility of her plan.

The menace of slashing Scotti swords rekindled her battle-frenzy. More invaders tasted death served by her voracious blade. Yet, despite her efforts, she could not turn the brunt of that menace upon herself. The Scots seemed strangely reluctant to cross swords with her except in self-defense. The rare offensive blow was struck not with the weapon's edge but with the flat.

The enormity of the insult drove her hand even harder. "Leave them alone, you murdering *cù-pucs!*" she howled. "It's me you want!"

All too soon, she learned the terrible truth of those words.

Chapter

21

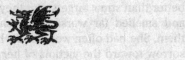

"Angusel, this is absurd." Centurion Bohort fingered the stout applewood rod that was the symbol of his authority as commander of Ayr Point. "My lookouts would've spotted the fleet as it crossed over from Hibernia."

They had been discussing the matter for some minutes already. Actually, *arguing* fell closer to the mark in Angusel's estimation. No, that wasn't accurate, either. Angusel was arguing. The centurion was stubbornly refusing to believe him.

He made an effort to steady his voice. Perhaps quiet reason would serve him where loud urgency had failed. "Not if they crossed by night, without lights, sir."

"Impossible. The Scots are good seamen, I'll grant you, but they don't use that tactic in their raids."

"With all due respect, Centurion, I don't think a fleet of thirty warships is a mere raid." Angusel shook his head in frustration. "Besides, they had to have sailed last night. The ships were already anchored offshore when I saw them this morning."

"A fine story, my lad, but I've more important matters to attend to." Something approaching a tolerant smile crept across Bohort's rugged face. "You've had your sport for the day. Go on back to Tanroc now"—returning to his worktable, he flicked his hand in a casual wave of dismissal—"before I really get angry with you."

Caution be hanged! There just had to be a way of getting this man's attention. "I can't go back to Tanroc, sir. It's probably under attack by now, and Port Dhoo-Glass is sure to be next!"

It worked. Too well. The centurion rounded on Angusel, tolerance hardening into irritation as he brandished his rod in Angusel's face. "Now, see here—"

"Please, sir, you've got to believe me! Just send someone to look. If there's no fleet, then you can send me to Tribune Urien and—" Squaring his shoulders, Angusel summoned his last drop of sincerity. "And have him throw me into the viper pit!"

Centurion Bohort's eyebrows twitched in apparent surprise, but he didn't answer for what seemed like half an eternity.

"Very well, Angusel. I will order the patrol to check out your report. If there is a Scotti fleet, you can light the signal fire yourself. And if not, there will be hell to pay. Not the viper pit." He slapped the rod meaningfully against his palm. "But I think you can guess the punishment for wasting my time, and my patrol's."

The Ayr Point mounted patrol left the outpost shortly after Angusel's interview. The report they brought back confirmed his story. The men had seen the Scotti invasion fleet, which had weighed anchor and was now heading their way. Worse still, a column of black smoke was billowing out to sea from the direction of Tanroc. While the Ayr Point soldiers prepared for the withdrawal to Port Dhoo-Glass, Angusel was permitted to light the signal beacon to bring the Pendragon to the Isle of Maun.

But the patrol had also returned with the still-warm body of a one-eyed Brytoni cattle herder.

A shout pierced the din. The Scotti warriors ceased the attack. Glancing around, Gyan found herself to be the last bulwark of the defenseless brethren. The rest of her erstwhile band lay dead or dying around her. All of this, she realized with stark clarity, had been unnecessary. The Scots didn't want the monastery, its treasures, or the monks. They wanted her. For what purpose, she could only guess. All she knew was that she had just led more than a score of good, brave men to their deaths, needlessly. How could she confess this to the other brethren, and to the One God? How could they ever forgive her? An anguished scream pounded at her teeth. She clenched her jaw to hold it back.

She wanted nothing more than to lend what comfort she could to the wounded and to express her profoundest apologies to them for the grave error she had made. But the warrior who had issued the stop-attack order was striding toward her, the point of his sword leading the way as he stepped over the bodies of Scotti warriors and Brytoni monks. His battle-tunic and sword were streaked with blood, though Gyan could not recall fighting against him. If she had, he would not be moving now.

She stood in flex-kneed wariness, her sword's ruddy point leveled against his approach. Despite her grief for the fallen monks, first and foremost she was a warrior and vowed to conduct herself as one no matter what befell her—or those around her.

"I order ye to surrender, Chieftainess Gyanhumara."

Her eyes narrowed to glaring slits as she buried the

surprise sparked by his knowledge of her name, her rank, and the Brytoni dialect.

"You must be mad," Gyan snarled. "I would rather die than surrender to a Scotti cur!"

The Scotti commander refused to acknowledge her insult. "Chieftainess Gyanhumara, surely ye realize that resisting is pointless. I can kill ye, if ye wish. Then we shall slaughter the rest of the monks and anyone else we find here, and raze every building on the islet. But if ye surrender, the others shall be spared, and we willna break so much as an eggshell." He lifted his sword in a salute. "By Lugh Longarm, I swear it."

With every muscle still tensed for combat, Gyan reflected upon her options. That the Scots wanted her alive was obvious. The question was why. To be made a slave and probably concubine for one of their chieftains seemed the likeliest answer. Inwardly, she grimaced at the thought of being raped by a Scot.

Never! She would kill herself before that could happen. Perhaps even take a few more of the whoresons with her. Yet her most important concern was the safety of the monastery, the Chalice and its Keeper, Brother Stefan and his students, and Morghe and Dafydd.

The irony was that she was being forced to trade her freedom for the lives of others, including one man who knew firsthand what slavery was like.

Gyan thrust the sword point into the nearest Scotti corpse, released the hilt, and lowered her arm. The blade stood upright, quivering. By not delivering the sword directly into her captor's hands, she had only surrendered the weapon, not her inner self. This symbolism would be lost to all non-Caledonians, but it gave Gyan a surge of satisfaction. She froze in an attitude of proud defiance as the Scotti commander jerked her weapon from its grisly scabbard. At his signal, four warriors drew their swords and closed around her.

Surprisingly, the commander showed every intention of honoring his part of the bargain. He ordered some of his men to pick up the score of warriors Gyan and her men had killed. The second-in-command was designated to take charge of the monastery, with half the remaining soldiers.

As the Scots fanned out to take up positions around the compound, the Brytoni civilians dispersed. Several monks went to retrieve their dead. The others began filing into the church in subdued silence.

"Commander Fergus, see what I've found!" One of the warriors held a bundle of auburn hair and flailing fists.

"Let me go, you oaf!"

"Bring her to me," ordered Commander Fergus. As the man shoved her forward, the violet eyes widened in alarm. "Ye be nae monk. Give me your name, lass." He grasped her arm to peer into her face.

Gyan's spirits plummeted. Discovery of Morghe added the final stanza to the dirge of the day's failure.

Morghe drew a deep breath. "I am—"

"Nobody! An orphan." Gyan was pricked into silence by the sword of one of her guards.

Fortunately, Morghe possessed sense enough not to disagree. Perhaps there was still a chance to secure her safety.

"Being sheltered by the good brethren, is she?" Grinning wolfishly, Fergus thrust Morghe back into the warrior's hands. "Then I imagine they willna mind having one less mouth to feed."

"No! You promised—" Gyan's outburst was rewarded with another pointed nudge.

"Chieftainess, permit me to remind ye that ye be in

nae position to protest anything." The Scotti commander strode up to Gyan, eyes sharp as dark daggers. "The lass comes with us. In good time, we shall find out who she really be."

"I killed him, aye," Angusel admitted evenly.

"Why didn't you mention this before?"

"Because I thought sending the signal was more important." He locked his gaze with Bohort's. "Wasn't it?"

"I'll be asking the questions here, lad." The centurion's tone was not unkind. But he regarded Angusel under narrowing brows. "Do you realize that murdering a Bryton is punishable by death?"

A ghostly claw clutched Angusel's heart at the nasty turn this conversation had taken. He drew his best weapon: truth.

"I didn't murder him, sir. We fought, and I won."

"Why did you fight him?"

"Sir, he was a spy."

"A spy?" If not for what Angusel guessed to be at least a decade of military discipline, Bohort's surprise might have forced him back a pace. Instead, he smothered the reaction with another question. "How do you know?"

"I saw him meet with the Scots on the beach. He told them something and was paid for it."

"What did he tell them?" Bohort's face loomed closer.

Angusel's thoughts raced. Should he make up something to lend support to his story? No. A lie might destroy what little credibility he now owned.

"I don't know, sir. I was too far away to hear."

The centurion stroked his chin. "You said he was paid. How?"

"I'm not sure." Angusel bit his lip and frowned, trying to recall the elusive scene. "All I saw was a bright flash as the thing caught the sun. It was small. Maybe a buckle."

"But you never saw it up close? The patrol noticed signs of a fight but didn't report finding anything unusual on the body. You didn't take it from him, did you? Maybe that's really why you killed him, eh?"

"No, sir! I didn't even think about it." Angusel wanted to quip that maybe the men of the patrol didn't make a complete report but decided the suggestion might buy him more trouble than he could afford. "I swear."

Bohort paced to the window, which overlooked the brooding sea. To the north, a dark finger of Brydein thrust above the foam-speckled waves. The commander of the Ayr Point detachment slowly shook his head.

"I'm afraid this doesn't look good. You say the man was a spy, but you have no proof." As he faced Angusel, his countenance was as stern as the gray waters at his back. "I'd like to believe you, lad, but without evidence in your favor, I cannot let you go free."

"Proof! You want proof?" Forgetting his swollen knee, he took a step toward the centurion. The knee collapsed. He stumbled into the worktable, clutching it to brace himself against the agony. A hand came to rest on his shoulder, but he shook it off. Through clenched teeth, he growled, "My word as a warrior should be all the proof you need."

"That might well be, Angusel. But this is beyond my authority now. Do you understand?"

"Aye, sir." Pushing free of the table, he struggled to meet his fate squarely on both feet. He hoped his face betrayed none of the effort's cost.

The door opened to reveal the centurion's aide. "Sir, your pardon for the interruption, but the unit is formed up and ready for the march to Dhoo-Glass."

"Good, Alun. We're taking Angusel with us. Find a bandage to bind his knee." As Alun left the chamber, Bohort faced Angusel. A flash of what seemed to be regret wrinkled his brow. "Angusel of Caledonia, I am placing you under arrest for the murder of the Dalriadan herdsman. Tribune Urien must decide what to do with you."

The Scots breached Tanroc's outer defenses much more quickly than Gyan would ever have imagined. By the time her captors had led her and Morghe across the channel to the Manx mainland, the Scotti army had hacked through all the thorn hedge's portals. She saw no other sign of damage to the hedge, as though they had known exactly where to attack. There was no other explanation for this—and the Scots' knowledge of her value as a hostage—than treason.

"Of course, Chieftainess Gyanhumara. What did ye expect?" The commander of the invasion force gloated. "In my position, would ye not also use every resource?"

Gyan refused to dignify the question with a response. If she lived through this, she would never permit herself to be in his "position." Enemy or not, she bore no respect for any leader who led from the rear and left his subordinates to do all the fighting. And dying.

Well into the afternoon, the two women were forced to watch the assault from outside the general's headquarters tent on a nearby rise.

The ground between the hedge and the palisade walls was littered with Scots who had fallen victim to

Brytoni arrows. But that line of defense had to be abandoned as the Scots used their archers to set the wooden palisade ablaze. A huge section came crashing down amid a great shower of sparks. The greedy flames danced even higher.

One Brytoni archer, faithful to the last, tried to leap clear of the collapsing wall and failed. Of his body there was soon nothing left but a smoking husk. Gyan squeezed her eyes shut but could not blot out the horribly vivid sight. Or the gut-churning stench of charred flesh.

So this was war. In all her winters of listening to the fireside yarns spun by *Seannachaidh* Reuel, conjuring pictures from the glowing words, nothing could compare with this. All the triumphant tales of raid and conquest by Clan Argyll were dead things next to the gasping reality.

Morghe screamed. Gyan glanced at her. Arthur's sister stood pale and trembling between two burly guards, who were all but doubled over with glee at her terror. As Gyan watched, Morghe's face hardened in anger, and her shivering stopped.

The Scots, Gyan vowed, would get no such entertainment from the Chieftainess of Clan Argyll.

The invaders were pouring through the smoldering gaps in the palisade, shields lashed to their backs as protection from the flames. Several times, Gyan watched blazing debris hit a shield and bounce away without setting it alight. Those wooden shields had to be waterlogged, then. It would explain why, when she and Morghe had been taken from the monastery, the soldiers had dragged their shields through the water as they waded the channel.

Through the ragged curtain of fire and smoke, she could only catch glimpses of the fighting inside the fort.

It appeared that anyone who resisted, soldier or not, was brutally cut down. Gyan did her best not to think about what would happen to the feisty Cynda if she tried to defend herself. Or what would happen if she did not.

Both images blanketed her brain. Neither was any comfort.

Sweeping around the palisade, the fire came perilously close to the stables. Frightened whinnies soared above the din. A group of Brytons rushed in to lead the horses to safety. Though appearing to be no bigger than a fleck of dirt, there was only one black horse amidst the sea of browns: her Brin.

A Brytoni soldier vaulted to his back and began slashing at the unmounted Scots. Gyan silently rejoiced to see her horse strike down some of the invaders with his deadly hooves. Then fresh gouts of flame obscured her view. When at last it cleared, Brin was down. A spear sprouted from his side. She felt the wrenching pain as surely as though she had taken the thrust herself.

A great shout arose from the battle. Several Scots were crawling across the roof of the fort's headquarters, ducking spears and arrows as they scuttled toward the banner of Clan Moray. The Black Boar banner fell. A Silver Wolf loping across a pine-green background was hoisted up in its place. The ensuing cheers, magnified by the soldiers on the ridge, threatened to rip apart the very fabric of heaven.

The commander clapped his hands and rubbed them with fierce glee. "Excellent. Now, for even more pleasant business." He favored Morghe with an appreciative stare. "Who have we here, Fergus?"

"The chieftainess says she be just an orphan, General Niall," Fergus answered, "but I think—"

"I am Morghe, daughter of Chieftainess Ygraine and Uther the Pendragon." Her defiance was aimed solely at Gyan. "And I won't stand for this outrage!"

Gyan wanted nothing more than to wrap her hands around Morghe's throat. The two guardsmen latched onto her arms rendered that impossible. So she settled for the next best thing. "Imbecile! What do you think you're—" The accusation died at the tip of a Scotti spear.

"Doing? Trying to save my skin," Morghe quipped. "Since you couldn't manage it." Her words, too, were rewarded with pain.

Gyan's attempt at a retort was drowned by Niall's harsh laughter.

"A good day's work, Fergus. Ye've netted us two noble wildcats instead of just one. Aye, a good day, indeed. Laird Cuchullain shall be most pleased, especially with the daughter of Uther." The coldness of his tone sent chills down Gyan's spine. He leered at the women. "But this day isna over yet, my fine lasses." To Fergus, he said, "Ready the prisoners for the next leg of the journey."

Risking another jab, Gyan growled, "Where are you taking us, General?"

"Leave off with the spears!" Niall ordered. "Let the lady warrior keep her curiosity—for all the good it'll be doing her." He sauntered to Gyan. "I see nae reason for secrecy. Once Tanroc be secure, we march to Port Dhoo-Glass. Ye, my dear"—he caressed Gyan's cheek with callused fingertips—"shall be my bait to draw out the forces of Urien, your betrothed."

Urien studied Angusel as Bohort delivered his report of the Scotti invasion and the lad's involvement. Angusel stood, shackled and unmoving, between Bohort and a guard. His right knee was swathed in a bandage. Save the rare flicker of pain, his face reflected the calm courage of the innocent. It was a most impressive act. And Urien was determined to strip off his mask.

"Why did you kill him, boy?" he demanded again.

"I told you, sir. Because he was a spy."

"That's not good enough. You could have—should have—stayed hidden and let him live so that our own agents could monitor him. Angusel, I want to know what made you attack him."

"Sir, I—" Angusel sucked in a deep breath. "Sir, I was angry at the herdsman's betrayal. With the entire invasion force moving against Tanroc, I just knew it couldn't stand long. Believe me, sir, I was going to go back to warn Tanroc, and to fight with them. With her." He bit his lip.

"Gyanhumara?"

"Aye, sir. I wanted to, but then the herdsman came by, and I couldn't move without being seen. So I waited to see what he would do. That's when I saw him speak with the Scots."

Angusel pounded his left fist against its companion leg. The chains jangled and bounced against the injured knee. A spasm creased his face. Bohort and the guard tightened their grip on his arms.

Quietly, Angusel continued, "I waited too long. And now she's—she's either captured or . . ."

"Dead," Urien finished for him. "Which probably would have happened whether you had been there or not."

Defiance flared in Angusel's eyes. But the truth couldn't be denied. "Aye, sir," he whispered.

"What do we do with him, Tribune Urien?" asked Bohort.

"What, indeed?" Urien scrutinized his prisoner. "A

pity there are no more druids on Mona to train him as a bard. This is the best performance I have ever seen. All it lacks is a harp."

Up snapped Angusel's head. "What do you mean, sir?"

"What I mean, boy, is that I think you've invented this spy nonsense to cover your real motive." Urien's eyes narrowed. "Revenge."

"What!"

"Oh, yes. I remember that fight. That herdsman clouted you but good." Urien saw a different face: a dusty one, scorched by shame. "You killed him to avenge the insult. And you confessed so readily because you thought I would actually swallow your ridiculous story."

"But sir, it's the truth!" His tone was shrill with desperation.

Anger mounting, Urien advanced to within an arm's length of the lad. "Call me an idiot, do you?" He backhanded Angusel across the mouth.

He winced. "No, sir! But I—"

Urien silenced the protest with another blow. "Then where is this supposed payment? Or perhaps this bauble was something you merely found on the body after the fact?" He cocked his hand. Angusel didn't flinch, but that didn't convince Urien of his innocence. If anything, it was having the opposite effect. "So. Where did you hide it?"

Angusel refused to answer. Urien struck him again. Fury kindled in the gold-brown eyes, but no sound escaped the bloody lips.

"Very well. We'll see if the rats can do a better job of loosening your tongue." To the centurion, Urien said, "Bohort, I have no more time for this murderer. I've got to organize the defenses before the Scots come screaming down our throats. Lock him up, and post a guard. Let me know when he's ready to talk."

A thousand pairs of enemy feet pounded across the Manx countryside. Common folk fled in howling terror before the invaders and were ignored. The Scotti soldiers wasted no time at either of the two villages along the route. Their objective was to reach Port Dhoo-Glass as quickly as possible and lay siege by nightfall. On that long mid-June day, it was not an unrealistic goal.

Morghe and Gyan marched with the rest of the soldiers, separated but unbound, each at the center of a heavily armed unit. No other prisoners traveled with the army.

Gyan was amazed at the relatively courteous treatment she had been accorded. She had expected to be stripped of armor as well as sword upon her surrender at the monastery. Her distinctive belt had drawn several greedy stares, yet no one had touched it. Nor had anyone tried to remove the gold torcs from her neck and arms. From what little Gyan could see through the thicket of spears, it appeared Morghe was being treated equally well.

Gyan's guardsmen made no attempt at conversation with each other or with their captive. She was grateful for their impassive silence, for it allowed her to sink undisturbed into her thoughts.

Her brave Brin had died a warrior's death. Did this mean he would join the Old Ones in the Otherworld? Or was there a place for horses in the domain of the One God? She would have to ask Dafydd sometime . . . if their paths ever crossed on this earth again.

The likelihood of her path crossing anyone's seemed slim. Would she learn what had happened to Cynda? Or

Angusel, who in just a few months had become as dear as a brother?

And what of Per and Ogryvan and her clansmen? Memories marched with her, mile upon dreary mile. Some of the strangest moments of her life chose this time to demand attention. Ogryvan bursting with pride as his six-year-old daughter hefted her first wooden practice sword. Cynda bandaging a scraped knee while delivering a scathing lecture to the nine-year-old Gyan on the dangers of scaling Arbroch's walls. Per as a leggy lad of thirteen, howling with laughter as he sprinted away after smearing mud on his sister's braids.

Through all this, her mind kept returning to the face of the only man who could help her now. She clung to it as the drowning person clings to the log that drifts into reach. The gold-haired, sapphire-eyed image buoyed her spirits during the endless trek. But he was lounging in Roman luxury, across a hundred miles of indifferent sea, ignorant of her plight. The hope of deliverance by Arthur's hand was surely a vain one.

Not knowing whether to laugh or to cry, she did neither. Past fought beside present to hold the future at bay. It was the only battlefield she could find.

Chapter

22

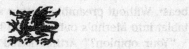

That evening, Arthur read the dispatch and swore, for two reasons. First, for being caught off guard by the Scots' invasion of Maun. He honestly hadn't believed Cuchullain would have attacked for at least another year, otherwise he would have brought Morghe home. She and . . . anyone else who wished to evacuate the island, although the one person he was thinking of probably would never consent to turn her back on a fight. But no, Arthur reminded himself, the Scots hadn't caught him completely unaware. He had sent reinforcements. Just not enough. And the second reason for his frustration was that he had more than three thousand soldiers at his immediate disposal and nowhere near enough warships to transport them.

Arthur opened the door to the antechamber and thrust his head through. "Marcus," he called to his aide. "Get me Merlin, and send someone to Camboglanna for Cai!" After a moment, he added, "Have Centurion Peredur report here, too."

"Yes, sir." Marcus thumped fist to breast and left.

Curse that murdering hound Cuchullain! Who did he

think he was, sending half his fleet to attack Maun? And at night, no less. The dispatch didn't say this outright, but it was the only plausible explanation that fit the timing of the report's arrival.

So. The Laird of the Scots would have to be dealt a hard blow, and swiftly. But how? How?

Merlin arrived to find Arthur pacing like a caged beast. Without preamble, Arthur slapped the dispatch tablet into Merlin's outstretched hand.

"Your opinion?" Arthur asked as Merlin read the tablet.

"With thirty Scotti warships offshore and Tanroc besieged by the invasion force? I'd say Maun is in trouble." Merlin's lips thinned to a grim line. "They were fortunate to get the signal off."

"Quite fortunate." Arthur didn't bother to voice his concern that the beacon sites might even now be in enemy hands; capturing the high ground at the earliest opportunity was a tactic he would have employed in similar circumstances—one of the first tactics Merlin had taught him. "But I've got only nineteen ships here, and two of those are dry-docked. The rest, if they're not on patrol, are on Loch Rigan and the Clyd."

After dropping into the chair behind the worktable, he reached for parchment, ink pot, and quill. And stopped before a single word hit the page.

"Well? Aren't you going to recall the fleet, Arthur?" Merlin laid the dispatch on the table and took his customary seat against the wall. "That seems like your best course of action to me."

"Time is Cuchullain's ally. I must find a way to change that." Staring into the oil lamp's flame, Arthur tried to formulate a solution using distance and time factors. He slowly shook his head. "It's impossible. Even if my courier rides all night, Bedwyr can't get his ships down here before late tomorrow afternoon, at best."

"Which means that even if the troop boarding went all night without a hitch, you still couldn't engage the Scots until the following day." Merlin's dark gaze remained steady. "Barring inclement weather or any other problems."

"Exactly." Scowling, Arthur stood. The pacing resumed. "God alone knows what will have happened by then."

And God alone knew what was happening to Morghe and Gyanhumara now. Visualizing the worst was disturbingly easy. The current task was difficult enough without the distraction of a galloping imagination. Arthur squelched private speculation about the fate of his sister. Banishing Gyanhumara from his mind was much harder, but he managed. Their lives—and the lives of everyone on Maun—might well depend upon the fruit of this night's labor.

The bloody irony of it all was that Arthur had prayed, more often than he could count, for one more chance to see Gyanhumara again. If this relief operation was to be the answer to his prayer, he thought wryly, then God must have a bizarre sense of humor. But if anything were to happen to Gyanhumara or Morghe at the hands of the Scots, he would never forgive himself . . . or God.

"You could sail out now with as many troops as you can squeeze onto the seventeen ships," suggested Merlin, "and have Bedwyr follow when he can with the rest."

Arthur stopped at the window to brace both hands against the ledge and gaze at heaven's vast ebony fabric. No clues glimmered there. Not that he was expecting to find any, but at present he would have accepted aid from any quarter.

"I don't like the odds," Arthur admitted. "Too many things could go wrong. If I have to use that plan, I will. But there must be a better solution."

Merlin closed his eyes to the young warlord's restless circling. The enticing aroma of baking fish from the *praetorium's* kitchen floated in through the open window to become ensnared in Arthur's whirlwind. So there was to be salmon for dinner this evening, Merlin mused. Salmon or . . .

"Herring!"

Arthur stopped in mid-stride. "What?"

"Arthur, the herring fleet is at port. Why not commandeer the fishing boats to transport the rest of your troops?"

As Arthur considered the possible scenarios, he felt his lips stretch into a smile. "Cuchullain's beachhead is probably on the western side of Maun. With most of the army ashore, even if he's left his entire fleet at the beachhead—which I doubt—the Scotti vessels should be minimally manned. Seventeen fully manned warships will be more than a match. Once the Scotti fleet is ours, the fishing boats can bring in the rest of our men. Bedwyr's fleet should sail straight to Dhoo-Glass, in case Cuchullain has decided to blockade the port." He clapped his cousin's shoulders. "Merlin, you're a genius!"

All too soon, Arthur's elation vanished into the gaping maw of economic reality. "But the fishermen will have to be compensated for the loss of at least a week's income. Fifty boats . . ." His voice dropped into a bleak whisper as the excellent plan seemed to shipwreck before his eyes. "My treasury can't take that kind of strain."

Merlin put a hand on Arthur's forearm. "You can count on my help, of course."

Arthur briefly smiled in gratitude at the offer. This wouldn't be the first time he'd be forced to tap into

Merlin's vast personal wealth. And if the fortunes of war didn't improve soon, he suspected it wouldn't be the last time, either.

The Pendragon's summons came as Peredur was dictating the last of the weekly duty roster to the *ala's* scribe. Per's Brytonic had improved markedly since his arrival at legion headquarters, and he no longer needed the services of an interpreter, so these tedious but mandatory administrative chores weren't taking as long to complete, thanks be to all the gods. But Per had to admit that leadership in the Pendragon's army carried certain advantages—not all of them, he thought with a grin, military in nature. The pretty lass who had volunteered to be his Brytonic tutor and occasionally shared his bed, for one. But he'd have traded the status and female companionship and everything else for just one chance to fight a real battle, instead of the mock fights against the other *alae* and centuries.

Per's only consolation was that Gyan's daily routine, emphasizing scholarly rather than physical activities, had to be even more boring than his was. But if he knew his sister, she had probably found a way to turn her studies into a grand adventure and was having the best time of her life.

He dismissed his scribe, donned his cloak and badge, and set off for the *praetorium*. Of the reason for this summons, Per hadn't a clue. Seventh *Ala* had been performing well lately, so he ruled out a reprimand—but not so well that his unit deserved special recognition, either. A mission of some sort, then, perhaps a covert foray into enemy territory? Now, there was an interesting idea; not as exciting as combat, of course, but far better than these endless drills. As he quickened the pace, his heart began to throb with eager anticipation.

The saluting *praetorium* gate guards brought to mind the first time he had visited there, months ago, with Gyan. Nothing much had changed, either in the strange style of furnishings or in his opinion of them. This time, however, he knew better than to gawk in open-mouthed awe.

He turned down the corridor leading to the Pendragon's workroom, as directed in the summons, found the right door, and pushed it open. A courier—one who was on his way out with a message, to judge by the freshness of his uniform and the spring in his step—was just leaving. They exchanged a short greeting. The centurion sitting behind the antechamber's table looked up from his soft clay tablet, gave Per a nod of recognition, and pointed with his short, blunt iron writing tool toward the door leading to the inner chamber. Per gave a perfunctory tug on his battle-tunic, squared his shoulders, and went inside.

The Pendragon wasn't alone. He was standing across the room, near the window, conversing with the garrison commander, the man called Merlin on the battle-field and Dubricius inside their temple. At the sound of Per's entry, both men turned. While the Pendragon's expression was unreadable, the warrior-priest gazed at Per with something approaching . . . sympathy?

Arthur acknowledged Per's salute with a curt nod. "There's no easy way to say this, Centurion. But you need to hear it from me, not the rumor mongers." Per felt his eyebrows lower. "Maun has been invaded by the Scots."

"What!" Per clamped his mouth shut, regretting the outburst and expecting a reprimand. Surprisingly, none came. Dreading what the answer might be, he asked, "And . . . Gyan?"

Merlin spread his hands in a helpless gesture. "We

don't know, Peredur. We just found out about the invasion ourselves. The only thing we do know is the number of enemy ships."

"Thirty," Arthur said, as though sensing Per's unspoken question.

"Gods! That's more than a thousand men. And Maun has . . ." Per ransacked his brain to recall the number Gyan had mentioned.

"Eight hundred." The Pendragon's expression became grim. "If they can make a unified stand. Which, at this point, I doubt."

Per felt his heart begin to hammer its response to his kindling battle-fury. He clenched his fists to retain control. "Sir, what do you mean, if—"

"We believe our forces had very little warning of the attack," Merlin said quietly. "It's a miracle they were able to alert us."

Though no easy task, Per tried to curb his worry for Gyan; she wouldn't approve, if she ever found out. If! That one tiny word raised image after terrible image of what his sister might be enduring as a victim of a surprise attack. He had to do something—anything—to make sure she was all right!

Per saluted again. "Lord Pendragon, I'll ready my men at once."

"No, Centurion," he said. "You will not."

Per felt his jaw drop open in astonishment. "We aren't going to relieve Maun?"

"I will." Per didn't like Arthur's emphasis on the personal pronoun. "You—and your *ala* and the entire Horse Cohort—are staying here."

"What? No! But I have to—" Unwilling to believe what he had heard, and not caring that his breach of discipline could earn him the lash, Per stalked up to

Arthur. Arms folded and face stern, the Pendragon stood his ground. "Sir, you don't understand. She's my sister. You must take me with you!"

"He does understand, Peredur. All too well." The warrior-priest approached Per to grip his shoulder. "His youngest sister is on Maun, too."

Per shrugged the hand away and kept glaring at Arthur. "Then you know why I have to go with the relief force. Sir."

"Yes, I do," Arthur said. "But on this mission, cavalry will be more of a hindrance than a help."

"I can fight on foot just as well—"

"Centurion. You have a unit to command. I cannot—" The Pendragon's vivid blue gaze intensified. "*I will not* start making exceptions for every soldier with a personal stake in the matter." Uncrossing his arms to clasp his hands behind his back, Arthur faced the window. Whether he realized it or not, he was presenting Per with a sorely tempting target. "You must hate me for refusing your request." His shoulders shifted in what might have been a slight shrug, or a sigh. "I don't blame you."

Hate him? Per inventoried his emotions and found anger in great abundance, along with frustration, disappointment, and a boatload of concern about Gyan's fate. But no hatred. Arthur was only doing his job as he saw fit, Per reminded himself. If that meant leaving the cavalry behind, well, it was the Pendragon's decision to make, whether Per agreed with it or not. His promise to Gyan bound him to serve Arthur the Pendragon to the best of his ability, and neither disobedience nor insubordination had a part in that vow. Besides, how could he hate the man his sister so deeply loved?

"Go with the gods, Lord Pendragon." Arthur turned, and Per thrust out his sword hand. "And take good care of her."

Clasping Per's forearm, Arthur's lips twitched in the barest of smiles. "I swear to you, Peredur mac Hymar, as God and Merlin are my witnesses: I will find Gyanhumara and defend her to my last breath."

That Per could believe. But he couldn't resist saying, with a grin, "If she's in any shape to fight, sir, she'll be defending you."

Arthur released his hand. "Of that, Centurion, I have no doubt." Once again, he saw Gyanhumara in her brother's face, and despite his concern for her safety, he couldn't suppress his answering smile.

For several seconds after Peredur's departure, Arthur stared at the closed door, realizing that for the first time, he had ordered someone to do something he himself would not have been willing to do. It wasn't a pleasant feeling.

"Arthur?" Merlin's voice was full of concern. "Is something wrong?"

Arthur shook his head. The burden of leadership hadn't felt this heavy since the day his father died, but he wasn't about to admit that to anyone.

The door burst open, and Cai stormed into the room, dripping sweat from his wild ride from Camboglanna. Just the sight of his longtime companion always buoyed Arthur's spirits, no matter the circumstances. This time was no exception. He greeted Cai with an arm grip and a thump on the back.

"What's all the stir about, Arthur? Rousting a man in the middle of the night like this?" Cai thrust out his lip in a parody of a pout. "And she was a sweet lass."

"If she's that good, you can go back to her later." Cai was the only man Arthur knew for whom eating was secondary to sex. Yet Cai forgot even sex when there was a battle to fight. Arthur had no doubt that his foster brother would support him in this endeavor. "Besides, there should be plenty more just like her where we're going."

"What? Where are we going?"

Grinning, Arthur asked, "My brother, how would you like to captain a fishing fleet?"

The following morning, well before dawn, the Brytoni herring fleet appeared to be putting out to sea. In the hold of each boat crouched a score of soldiers. Cai, swathed in a sealskin wrap of the kind favored by fishermen, stood on the deck of the lead vessel to direct the movements of the fishing flotilla. Arthur and his warships sailed in their midst, the fleet's customary blue leather sails exchanged for undyed sheets to conceal their presence from enemy lookouts. The total size of the relief force was more than sixteen hundred men. And once Bedwyr received word from Arthur's courier, another four hundred troops would be mobilizing to join the operation and, Arthur hoped, seal the victory.

Not long after dawn, the clouds marshaled over Maun to assault the island with their misty moisture. It was the kind of rain that threatened to stay forever, to dampen the spirit as well as the body.

Wearing only the linen tunic and breeches she'd been captured in the day before, Morghe looked miserable. Gyan, still dressed in her leather battle-gear, was not much better off.

Two hooded woolen cloaks were produced for the hostages. Morghe quickly wrapped herself in the cloak offered to her. Though the gooseflesh stood out on both bare arms in the chilly drizzle, Gyan refused.

"But why, Chieftainess?" Commander Fergus seemed genuinely confused by her reluctance.

"I am a warrior. A little cold rain does not disturb

me." In reality, Gyan was determined to resist her captors as much as possible. Any victory, however small, was well worth the fight.

Morghe, huddled in her borrowed cloak, muttered, "Spare me."

"Quiet," Fergus rumbled. "Nae one gave ye leave to speak." He thrust the garment at Gyan. "Ye shall put this on. Now."

"No."

"Lady, donna test my patience. Put it on yourself, or I shall have your guards do it for ye. And I guarantee they willna be gentle. I think they'll like that verra much."

"Call them over, then. That's the only way you'll get me to wear that saddle blanket you call a cloak."

As Gyan donned an insolent grin, murder flashed across the commander's face. He poised his hand to strike. She gazed at him through unwavering, unrepentant eyes.

Evidently remembering his orders regarding the prisoners' treatment, the Scot relaxed his arm. He spun and motioned to the guards. Each man gripped one of Gyan's arms while Fergus draped the cloak around her shoulders and settled the hood over her head.

"Much better. After all, we wouldna want Urien to think that ye've been mistreated, would we?"

"The thought had not occurred to me."

"Indeed." Fergus's disbelief rang clear.

In silence, he escorted Gyan across the camp, followed by the two soldiers. One man carried a coil of rope slung across his chest. Both walked with a spear at her back.

A sharp pounding punctuated the wet late-morning air. Gyan turned her head toward the sound but saw nothing in the immediate vicinity.

Fergus's mustache twitched as his lips twisted into a

smirk. "Ye shall find out about it soon enough, Chieftainess Gyanhumara."

The pounding grew louder as they approached the rear of the camp. Then silence. On the rise beyond the tents stood a platform made of pine logs. Another log, stripped of branches, stood upright in the center of the platform. The soldiers who had built the structure were trudging down the muddy embankment with their tools. Of the Scotti sentries Gyan had seen stationed on the ridge the night before, there was now no sign. She presumed they had been withdrawn to the back side of the ridge.

Encouraged by the spear points, Gyan began the slick ascent, followed by her guards. When they reached the top, the soldiers hauled her onto the platform and shoved her against the stake.

"I always thought you Scots were madmen," she growled as she was bound to the stake. "Now I have proof. If you think Urien is going to fall for such an obvious ploy—"

"We shall see. Comfortable, my dear?" Grinning wickedly, Fergus reached behind her and jerked the hood away. The raindrops began to dot her face and hair. "Well, we canna let it look like ye be enjoying yourself out here."

Commander Fergus and his men walked back down the hill, their laughter muffled by the curtain of mist.

Aboard the Scotti warships rounding Maun's northern tip, the soldiers seemed to ignore the approaching swarm of fishing boats. Perhaps they believed that anyone the fishermen might be able to warn would arrive far too late to prevent them from taking control of the island.

Squinting against the glare, General Caius Marcellus Ectorius watched the more than two dozen Scotti vessels until the headland blocked his view. It wasn't difficult to guess where they were going, hugging the coastline as closely as they were. But Cai did not signal Arthur for instructions. It mattered little if those fish got away; if all went according to Arthur's plan, Bedwyr would be dealing with the Scotti fleet in Dhoo-Glass Harbor soon enough. Cai and Arthur were stalking a bigger catch, one that by now was probably entrenched at Tanroc.

Cai languidly licked his lips as the anchored Scotti ships bobbed into view. Only three; this was going to be easy. He gripped the fishing boat's rail with long fingers, practically splintering the wood. Realizing what he was doing, he relaxed his hold and grinned with fierce anticipation.

Arthur had ordered Cai to wait until the fishing fleet was in position to cut off the Scotti vessels' escape. For a man of action, this was nigh unto impossible when there was real fighting to be done—not all this frolicking about in the water like a gaggle of silly children.

Finally, Cai judged the time to be right and ordered the hoisting of the red signal flag.

On cue, the herring boats dropped anchor. Arthur's warships shot forward, oar-driven, to engulf the remnant of the enemy fleet.

The soaking rain rendered the use of flaming arrows impossible for both sides. Arthur, however, had no intention of conquering the Scotti vessels by fire. He was more concerned with preserving as many of their warships as possible to swell the lines of his own fleet.

As he'd expected, it didn't take long to overwhelm the three lightly manned enemy ships. After loosing a few token volleys of arrows, which caused only minimal injuries to Arthur's men, the Scots surrendered. The worst delays were imposed in the wake of the encounter by having to tend the wounded and secure the captured men and ships. Arthur's most difficult task—that of ridding the island of the invading army, and of making good on his vow to Peredur of Caledonia—was yet to come. Like Cai, Arthur was eager to begin.

The first group of Brytons to make landfall on the Isle of Maun was a scouting party. While the rest of the relief force came ashore, Arthur ordered the scouts to determine Tanroc's status. They returned to the beachhead shortly after the landing of the soldiers and supplies was complete.

While the other men rested and ate, the scout leader made his report to Arthur: "Tanroc and St. Padraic's Island are both flying the Silver Wolf, Lord Pendragon. Tanroc's palisade is badly burned, but the buildings look mostly intact. From what we could tell, the monastery fell without a struggle."

Arthur absorbed the news without reaction. It came as no surprise. "How many are we up against?"

"In total numbers, sir?" Frowning, the soldier spread his hands. "I don't know. The enemy garrisons at both sites seemed rather small. Maybe a hundred men at each."

"Then where are the rest of the stinking beggars?" This from Cai, who had shed his fisherman's disguise on the beach. By the fierce way he was chafing his arms, he appeared to be regretting his decision.

"From Tanroc, a wide path leads southeast, General Cai. The grass is bent flat, as though a great host passed that way."

"Dhoo-Glass. Of course!" Arthur ground his knuckles into the opposite palm. "I should have anticipated this."

"How could you, Arthur?" Arthur frowned at Cai. Ignoring it, Cai clapped hand to hilt. "But while we're here, let's go clean out the Scotti rats at Tanroc and—"

"No." Arthur turned to begin selecting another scouting party for the mission to Port Dhoo-Glass.

Cai clamped onto Arthur's bronze-plated shoulder and pulled him around. "What of your sister? And Chieftainess Gyanhumara—what if the Scots have them at Tanroc or St. Padraic's?"

Cai didn't have to voice the remainder of his suggestion. The concern in Cai's eyes stated his doubt that the ladies were even alive. It was a doubt Arthur refused to share.

"Then they will have to wait." Those were the hardest words he had ever spoken. But once past his lips, the rest came easily enough. "Surprise is our ally. We must deal with the main body of the invasion force first, Cai, before they can strengthen their position and become even harder to defeat."

"Ah, but think of how much more fun we'd have that way, Arthur."

"Right." Despite the swelling tide of worry, the Pendragon chuckled. "Now, send two centuries into the hills east of Tanroc to watch the fort and guard our rear. Then let's hunt some Scots!"

Chapter

23

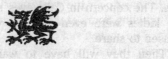

Urien had no doubts about the identity of the prisoner bound, facing him, to the stake on the ridge behind the enemy encampment. There was only one person on the island whose presence in the hands of the Scots could mean anything to him.

How on earth had the swine found out?

He uttered a mirthless laugh. Maybe Angusel's story had had a grain of truth after all. The best lies always did. For Urien refused to believe that the Pict's motives for killing the herdsman had been anything but base. He congratulated himself for having the foresight to lock the murderer away. With a grin, he imagined what the Pict must be doing in the dank darkness, alone but for the rats and his wicked thoughts. All the gold in the land could not save his worthless hide now.

Shoving Angusel from his mind, he studied Gyanhumara's tiny form. He was glad to see her alive and infuriated at the Scots for what they were doing to her. But not angry enough to be goaded into attempting anything as foolish as a pitched battle just to try to win her back. Not against a force that was twice the size of his. Especially not on the enemy's terms.

It was easy to shrug off that temptation for a while. Some time spent under the merciless skies might even teach the ungrateful wench to be a bit more appreciative of his attentions.

Besides, Urien thought, surely the Scots would recognize the failure of their trick soon enough.

Yet, as he waited in his siege headquarters in the guard tower over the western gate of Port Dhoo-Glass, the crawling hours exacted their toll. Two spawned two more. The unseen sun reached its zenith and started to descend behind the sodden clouds, and still Gyanhumara stayed at the stake. She seemed somehow smaller now than when her torture had first begun. Was she buckling under the stress? Urien thoroughly cursed the distance that prevented him from seeing her clearly enough to tell for certain.

Were the Scots planning to let her die up there?

His fist crashed into the timber ledge. Splinters littered the stones at his feet. No man had the right to deprive him of what was lawfully his! Nor was he about to have his long-range plans thwarted by a pack of heathen dogs. If the Scots weren't going to give up, then by God neither would he!

Urien focused his attention upon the steady construction of the Scots' siege engines and scaffolds. To a man, they wielded their tools with gleeful vigor. Many structures were close to completion already. Whether he went after Gyanhumara or not, he would be engaging them anyway. Soon.

Of the fleet that had blockaded Dhoo-Glass Harbor during the intervening hours, Urien didn't want to begin to contemplate, though he knew he must deal with that problem, too. But he judged the Scotti army the more immediate threat.

Thus far, there had been no attack on the city, and

the invaders had made camp safely out of bowshot range of the walls. More than once, a knot of the fatherless sons formed at the forefront of the camp to hop about like mad toads, shaking spears and flinging insults. When the dance reached its frenzied peak, one of them would streak toward the wall, leaping and dodging and rolling to avoid steel-barbed death. Those who reached the gates landed a kick to the unyielding timbers before dashing away.

The masters of this deadly game were carried back into the camp on the shoulders of their cheering comrades. The novices were left to rot where they fell.

Watching one of the more successful attempts—the warrior had sustained only a grazed shoulder—it occurred to Urien that perhaps an assault on the camp before their siege equipment was finished was not such a bad idea after all. If anything, his miraculous success would surely win Gyanhumara's gratitude and warm the chilly attitude she had developed toward him over the past few weeks.

And if he failed . . . well. A woman's feelings didn't matter to a dead man.

The sound of running footsteps in the corridor invaded his thoughts. He turned toward the sound, feeling his lips thin into a scowl. More bad news on the way, no doubt.

A guard clattered to a halt in the doorway and saluted. "My Lord," he gasped. "The—the eastern lookouts—"

"Come on, man. Out with it!"

The guard drew a deep breath, let it out, and drew another. "Our fleet, my Lord. It's on the way! According to the lookouts, it should arrive within the hour."

Urien dismissed the man with a wave and returned his attention to the activity in the siege camp, thoughtfully fingering his chin. The signal had gotten through, then. Good. If the fleet could break the blockade to land reinforcements, that would certainly make Urien's job a lot easier. But he felt his jaw clench as he considered another implication: now Arthur would reap all the credit.

Not if he, Urien map Dumarec of Clan Moray of Dalriada, had his way.

After withdrawing from the slotted window, the commander of the Manx Cohort summoned his officers to plan the attack on the camp.

Though fear clotted the air like the haze of cooking smoke on a becalmed evening, the villagers toiled at their timeworn tasks with grim persistence. Arthur supposed that for these simple folk, the business of daily survival far outweighed any thought of armies and battles, as long as those armies didn't fight across their hearthstones.

He was both relieved and concerned to see that the enemy had left the villages intact. Relieved that the people—and the livestock and wheat fields and apple orchards that were their livelihood—were unmolested. Concerned because it was more evidence that this was no raid. The Scots wanted Maun.

Halfway to their destination, the cohort met the scouts returning from the port. Upon sighting the main column, their smooth, ground-swallowing lope became a dead run.

Arthur called a halt and ordered a ration break. The formation kept its shape as the soldiers reached for water skins and oat cakes and dried beef. Arthur motioned Cai to join him as he strode forward to meet the scouting party.

"Lord Pendragon," rasped the scout leader between

ragged breaths, "Port Dhoo-Glass is still . . . still in Brytoni hands. But the Scots . . . they've laid siege."

"They didn't waste any time," growled Cai.

Arthur glanced at his foster brother. "Would you, if your prime objective was to secure the island?"

"You think that's their game?" Cai snorted in obvious disbelief.

"Cai, I know it."

Hands to knees, the scout leader panted heavily. His men were doing much the same. Arthur waited. Inwardly chafing at the delay, he realized he would get no more answers until the scout leader had recovered enough breath to speak. Finally, the Pendragon judged his man to be ready and launched a barrage of questions regarding the size and layout of the Scotti encampment.

"It's large enough to support a full cohort, sir," the soldier answered. "Couldn't get an accurate mancount. Too much activity, what with building siege engines and all."

"Do you still doubt, my brother?" Cai only shrugged. Arthur continued questioning the scout leader: "Any sentries? Patrols?"

"We saw no patrols, my Lord. Ten sentries are stationed on the back sides of the two ridges to either side of the river, just west of the camp. Weren't troubling to conceal themselves, either. Should be easy marks for our archers."

"Confident beggars," Cai observed cheerfully.

"Indeed." Arthur allowed his tone to run cold. "A pity they won't be able to learn from their mistake." After dismissing the scouting party with a word of praise, he turned to address Cai. "Pick a squad of your best—"

"Your pardon, Lord Pendragon, but there's one thing

more," said the scout leader. "They have a prisoner. A lady."

Arthur's eyes narrowed on the man. "Only one?" Thank God no one else could hear the thrashing of his heart. "Describe her."

"Tall, my Lord, and red-haired. Bound to a stake on the southern ridge. Been there a while, by the look of her."

"In this weather!" Cai flailed a fist at the heavens. His outburst drew several stares. "Those bloody—"

"Easy, Cai." Arthur gripped Cai's shoulder.

Cai's fist unclenched, and the hand dropped to his side. But the amber fire in his eyes did not die.

Arthur knew his foster brother's reaction was born of anger that any woman would be so mistreated. He empathized with Cai, though for different reasons. At least Gyanhumara was accounted for, but what in God's name had happened to Morghe?

"Don't worry, Cai." Arthur kept his voice neutral. "We will get Chieftainess Gyanhumara out of there as soon as we can dispose of those sentries."

While a squad of bowmen ran ahead to fulfill their role in the operation, Arthur and Cai divided the main column, reformed the twin units, and hiked off the valley floor. With Cai's five centuries in the hills north of the river and Arthur's to the south, the advance began anew.

Alone on the ridge, Gyan struggled with her bonds until her arms stung from the rope burns. Her guards had done their work well, but not quite well enough. The hastily erected pine post wasn't anchored to the surrounding platform. It seemed sunk into a hole, supported by the platform logs. And many of those logs did not touch the stake.

Eventually, Gyan was able to work the post loose. Not that it did much good toward getting her free, but the effort kept her warmer and gave her something to do. And her captors, casting occasional smirking glances at her from their encampment below, didn't appear to be overly concerned.

Of the sentries she thankfully saw no sign, although she heard them easily enough. She could not make out their speech, but the frequent bursts of laughter mingled with swearing or occasional groans of disappointment told her they were probably dicing to pass the time. Which was just as well; they'd be too busy, she hoped, to bother her.

By early afternoon, the sun emerged victorious over the clouds' rainy assault. Gyan was grateful for the extra warmth. A few minutes under the soggy skies was one thing; a few hours was quite another. She paused from her labors to bask in the sun's rays. As she leaned back to stretch and gather strength, a new idea formed: the post just might be loose enough to turn.

She had to try. The hours had made her unutterably weary of the view of the bustling enemy camp, the walls of Port Dhoo-Glass bristling with Urien's archers, and the red-sailed Scotti warships clogging the harbor.

A heroic effort wrenched the post a scant few degrees. But Gyan was determined to succeed at this new task, for it helped to relieve the burning anger she felt toward her predicament. The Scots were now completely ignoring her. Their efforts to build the siege engines had redoubled since the rain had quit.

Urien might be arrogant to a fault, but he couldn't be foolhardy enough to lead the city's forces to her rescue against these highly unfavorable odds. She was doomed to rot on this infernal ridge!

As the shadows lengthened, Gyan managed to force

the post through a quarter turn. While not completely devoid of the accursed Scots, the northern vista was a definite improvement.

Then came the unmistakable whine of arrows in flight, and the thumps as they found their targets. A cry of alarm died mid-word.

She twisted her head over her left shoulder in a futile attempt to see what was happening to the sentries. But the ridge fell away too sharply, and she had to guess from the sounds. Or lack of sounds. For now no laughter came from the hillside, only a single weak moan.

Another arrow sang. The moan ended in a wet gurgle. The Scots in the camp continued their work in ignorance.

Gyan expected to be released, but her unknown benefactors did not appear. At first, this only fueled her rage. The passing minutes rekindled the cooler fires of logic. Perhaps the archers had been an advance unit sent to kill the Scotti sentries to preserve the secrecy of the main attack. She fervently hoped this was true. And dared not imagine who their leader might be.

She glanced back toward the port, and her stomach knotted. Another fleet was fast approaching the harbor. Sighing, she closed her eyes and slumped against the post. Even if a Brytoni army had made landfall—and the rumbling sounds growing steadily louder from the west confirmed this guess—the presence of these seaborne Scotti reinforcements could only mean more trouble.

Anxious-sounding shouts from within the camp drew Gyan's attention. She opened her eyes, expecting to discover that the warships were landing, perhaps under resistance from Port Dhoo-Glass. The harbor scene had indeed changed, though not as she had expected.

The newly arrived warships were sporting not red sails but Brytoni blue.

Squinting, Gyan tried to tally the sails. There was so much activity in the harbor that it was hard to get a true count, but the Brytoni fleet seemed to be outnumbered by perhaps five or six vessels. But it didn't seem to matter. Despite Scotti attempts to thwart the tactic, the Brytoni fleet managed to form a line across the harbor's mouth, effectively penning the Scots and evening the odds. There wasn't enough room for all the Scotti warships to engage the Brytoni line.

Dark swarms of some sort of projectile—arrows, Gyan suspected—rained onto the ships of both sides. Smoke streamed from the rigging and decks of several ships as their crews ran to beat out the flames. Vessels tried to ram each other, with varying degrees of success. Some began to founder and sink, forcing their men to leap overboard. Not all of the disabled vessels were Scotti.

The Brytoni line started to lose its cohesion. But instead of breaking off the attack and heading for open sea, the ships sailed further into the harbor to pair with the remaining enemy vessels. Though it was impossible to distinguish individual warriors, the surge of movement made it obvious that the Brytons were carrying the fight aboard the Scotti ships. And winning! Each ship to be taken by a Brytoni boarding party joined the reformed harbor blockade to prevent the escape of the remaining enemy-controlled vessels.

The Scotti army arrayed at Gyan's feet, understandably frustrated at being unable to help their comrades, resumed work on the siege equipment as though possessed by battle-frenzy. Perhaps it wasn't far from the truth.

Her thoughts winged back to the afternoon she had

met Arthur's fleet commander, Bedwyr map Bann. She recalled the respect she'd felt toward his shipbuilding skill. Now, watching him and his men in battle, she found her respect for him increasing tenfold.

Before long, all resistance from Scotti vessels seemed to cease. The blockade broke up, and ships dispersed to fish survivors from among the floating wreckage.

Gyan let out the breath she didn't realize until that moment she'd been holding.

Then another thought hit: what if the Scots decided to kill her, in retaliation? A few minutes' study of the camp revealed they were still engrossed in their labors, but that could certainly change.

She turned her head westward, toward the sound of the approaching army. In her entire life, she had never expected to be gladdened by the sight of a thousand Roman-equipped Brytoni warriors. Yet she felt like whooping for pure joy. She settled instead on a sigh of relief. Captivity bred strange ideas indeed.

Even if the Scots did decide to kill her, she'd die with the knowledge that they wouldn't be long in following her.

Gyan peered over her right shoulder at the Scotti camp. From what she could tell, they hadn't yet heard the approaching Brytoni columns over the din of their axes and mallets and shouts. She suppressed a grin.

The rumbling stopped. A peek westward revealed the troops halted on the pair of ridges immediately beyond her. They began advancing a rank at a time, as quietly as possible and staying clear of the river valley, where they would have been visible to the camp.

A bronze-helmeted head popped over the edge of the rise.

Could it be? Impossible! She had to be dreaming. Too

much time under the elements had made her over-wrought imagination produce this vision. Or perhaps it was a trick of the light. A cruel one.

She blinked, hard. Wonder of wonders, Arthur did not disappear!

Their eyes met. His gaze was every bit as intense as she remembered. The air around him seemed to throb with his strength and courage. Mentally, she drew upon that power with her steady gaze.

He smiled briefly. Her heart danced.

The instant passed. He crawled to the top of the ridge and scuttled through the tall grass to Gyan's platform.

"Any Scots watching, Gyanhumara?" he whispered.

She cast a glance at the camp and shook her head. He rose to his knees, lifted his sword, cut the rope, and ducked back into the grass. Rubbing her stiff arms, Gyan took a step away from the post.

"Get back," Arthur ordered, still whispering. "I'm not ready for you to move yet."

As Gyan backed up to the post, a collective shout rose from the enemy camp. Arthur jumped to his feet, Caleberyllus in hand. But the enemy's attention was focused on the city gates, where Urien was emerging with the Port Dhoo-Glass defense force.

From the platform, Arthur waved a "hold steady" signal to his column and to the men on the opposite ridge.

"Urien can't have seen our approach from his position. What does that fool think he's doing?" he muttered as the two sides rapidly closed across the neutral ground.

"Trying to save me, of course. I've been up here for hours." Fists on hips, Gyan regarded the Pendragon critically. The thought of letting Urien die in this battle to solve her problem was tempting—but unworthy. "Well, Arthur, are we going to help him? Or just sit up here and watch his troops get devoured?"

"We are going to wait until the Scots are committed to attacking Urien." Again, his gaze locked on hers. "Then we will devour them."

His face betrayed no emotion save readiness for the imminent battle. Yet his cool appraisal of her sent a tingle down her spine. And prodded her into action.

"Good." If she was ever going to find out how things really stood between her and Arthur, she realized she would have to take the initiative. And there was no time like the present. "Then permit me to thank you for rescuing me."

She threw her arms around his neck and sought his lips with hers. His surprise didn't last long. He wrapped his arms around her and began questing with his tongue as though trying to probe her secret depths—a response even more passionate than she had ever dared to imagine! Desire too long suppressed welled up within her with surprising yet satisfying force, finding release at last through her ravenous lips. As he ran his fingers through her hair and she pressed her body to his, an exquisite ache flared in her loins. Her heart racing like fire through sun-scorched grass, all thought of enemies and battles fled, only for a moment.

But, oh, what a glorious moment!

Seconds before crashing into the front line of Scots, Urien glanced up to the ridge. And could scarcely believe what he saw. Gyanhumara was free—in the arms of another man. As they parted, the man straightened to his full height. Even without the scarlet-crested helmet, only one officer in the legion could be that tall.

Arthur. Not with the fleet, as Urien had originally supposed, but here at his very doorstep. Impossible!

Then Urien saw the relief troops scrambling to the tops of the ridges behind the enemy encampment and realized he had unwittingly provided the distraction Arthur needed to make the Scots' destruction swift and complete. And it appeared Arthur was going to win the best prize of all: Gyanhumara. Urien wanted to break off the attack and withdraw his troops to make Arthur fight for every inch himself. But it was too late. He was committed.

Urien's howl of rage mingled with the battle cries and horses' screams and the shock of steel on steel as he and his men engaged their foes.

Chapter
24

Arthur's eyes seemed to bore through Gyan. "Can you fight?"

"Absolutely!" She flexed her sword arm. "I have work to do." Fired by anger and chilled by hatred, her tone was hard as steel. "Revenge work."

"Then use this." He unhooked the sheath of the short, double-edged sword from his belt and fastened it to hers.

She would have preferred a longer blade, and one not so blatantly Roman in design. Swords like this had consigned countless Caledonians to the Otherworld. Yet she could either put the weapon to good use or stand by while others reaped the glory.

She drew the sword and ripped the air with a series of experimental thrusts to get a feel for its balance and weight. A well-wrought weapon, though quite unlike any she had ever used before, it would have to suffice. This day, she'd had enough idle standing to last a lifetime.

Arthur nodded, eyes aglow with approval. "We shall attack soon. Where's Cuchullain?"

Cuchullain—of course! With everything else that had

happened, Gyan had quite forgotten about him. Up rose the memory of that first dinner with Arthur and his barely restrained anger at what the Scot had done to his emissary. She left her study of the sword to regard its donor levelly. "The leader of the invasion force is a man named Niall."

Arthur's harsh oath flew heavenward. Like a lock snapping into place, his iron control returned. "Then Cuchullain's repayment will have to wait until later." Again, he gave her a spine-shivering stare. "But there won't be a later for you, Chieftainess, unless you find a shield. And stay with me."

He offered his shield, but she waved it away. Instead, she yanked off the Scotti cloak to pad her left arm, miffed at the suggestion that she needed his protection.

"Arthur, Morghe is with Niall. I can lead you there." As she finished securing the cloak's ends, she displayed a mischievous grin. "If you wish." Her tone darkened as mischief transformed into somber warning. "But that stinking Scot is mine!"

"Agreed." If he was taken aback by her demand, he didn't show it. "Now, get ready."

Holding Caleberyllus aloft, a blazing beacon in the afternoon sun, the Pendragon shouted the charge.

The air hosted a cacophony of yells and cries, the neighing of the horses of Urien's cavalry unit, the thunder of charging feet, the crash of toppling siege equipment, the clatter of steel and bronze and iron. And behind the manmade din roared the raging sea.

Gyan was oblivious to the passage of time and only dimly aware of the growing fatigue and hunger pangs born of her imprisonment on the ridge. Caught in the relentless dance of thrust and dodge, parry and slash, whirl and kick, lunge and stab, duck and cut, she felt no past and no future. Just the present. She could have killed one or a hundred, she didn't know. The fury she harbored toward her defeat at the monastery and the Scots' treatment of her was unleashed with savage strength upon each new foeman she met.

But her blood-lust would never be sated until she possessed the head, with its rattail auburn braids, of the man who was ultimately responsible: General Niall.

She found his headquarters tent. The Silver Wolf banner snapped at the entrance, guarded by the Scots' best warriors. Their ranks swelled as other soldiers recognized their leader's danger and ran to help. The numbers didn't faze Gyan. With Arthur at her side and most of his column at her back, she plunged exuberantly into the enemy's midst.

The general's defenses were shattered in seconds.

Gyan retrieved a longsword from a Scotti corpse and glanced up in time to see Niall's face disappear behind a flap of muddy canvas. Screaming in triumph like the hawk that has marked its prey, she bolted into the camp headquarters.

"What's the matter, General?" Morghe taunted. "Problems?"

The stocky Scot jerked his head back inside the tent and spun to face her. "Problems," he snarled. "I'll show ye who be having problems, lass."

He lunged and snatched her arm, yanking her close. A startled cry escaped as he twisted the arm behind her back. Naked steel froze her throat.

Chieftainess Gyanhumara burst into the tent.

She looked positively ghastly. Her braids ringed her head with a ragged copper aura. Glowing with hatred that burned like wildfire, her eyes matched the flaming cheeks. Cuts covered her shield arm between tattered remnants of a cloak. Yet to Morghe's surprise, most of the blood splattered across Gyanhumara's armor did not appear to be hers.

Despite how she felt toward the woman, Morghe wanted to cheer.

"Any closer, and the lass dies."

The blade nipped Morghe's flesh. Her heart started pounding so hard, she was sure it would kill her before the Scot could.

"Whether she dies or not," growled Gyanhumara, "you are mine. Hiding behind a woman won't save your worthless skin. And when I am finished with you, General, there won't even be enough left for the rats." Raising the sword in both hands, she stalked toward them.

Before Niall could carry out his threat, Morghe raked her booted heel along his shin with all her strength. His yelp seemed to carry more surprise than pain, but it was all the distraction she needed. She whipped her free hand up and pitched forward to push away from his sword. She landed on hands and knees in the dirt and hurried for cover under the field table at the back of the tent.

"You can't seem to keep hold of your captives, Niall." The chieftainess's face twisted into a wicked sneer. "What a pity."

"Bah! I shall deal with her later." Niall's posture shifted into combat readiness. "Ye handled your captivity well, Chieftainess. Let us now see if ye can die as bravely."

As the warriors crossed swords, Morghe peeked outside. From what little she could see through the handspan crack between the canvas and the ground, the battle appeared to be drawing to its bloody close. There were no living Scotti invaders in sight. The air reeked of death. And the name on the lips of every Bryton was: Arthur.

"Morghe!"

She knew that voice. And despised it.

Morghe crawled clear of the table and stood. Brushing the dirt from her knees, she schooled her expression into neutrality. Her true feelings toward her brother were no one else's business—least of all his.

Arthur filled the tent entrance. Caleberyllus was red to the hilt, matching the pommel's ruby. The sun at his back created an Otherworldly glow about him as it glinted off his bronzed shoulders. The gold dragon pinned to the short scarlet cloak seemed to writhe within its round tricolor enamel prison as he fought to steady his breathing. Compared with the chieftainess, his face was calm. Only his eyes betrayed eagerness for more action.

It was the first time Morghe had seen him during a battle. And, she hoped, the last.

He beckoned. She inched around the tent's perimeter to avoid the deadly dance in the center. Tolerating his arm around her shoulders, she gave him a false smile of gratitude before turning full attention to the fight.

While not a warrior herself, Morghe had witnessed enough practice sessions to make a fair evaluation of these combatants. Gyanhumara was taller and had the better reach, but the Scot was heavier. She was quicker, he was more experienced. But she was a woman. Though they now traded blows with seemingly equal force and frequency, she was sure to tire soon and lose.

Yet Gyanhumara was not tiring. Even when Niall opened a nasty gash high on her sword arm, it only seemed to double the ferocity of her attack. It was indeed an incredible display. Morghe could not suppress the upwelling of respect.

She glanced up at her brother. Respect for the warrior woman was etched into every line of his face. Admiration, too. Perhaps something more.

Niall retreated from Gyanhumara's swift, furious blows. He stumbled against the table, and she jammed her sword's pommel into his shoulder with a sickening thud. His arm went limp. The sword slipped from his fingers. In half a heartbeat, her weapon flashed again. His head thumped onto the tabletop. Spurting blood, his body crumpled to the ground.

It was utterly revolting. Worst of all was the look of bald-eyed shock, frozen forever on the bloody, bodiless head. Morghe wanted nothing more than to flee to some private place and retch her guts out. For pride's sake, she stayed.

Chest heaving and head bowed, Gyanhumara dropped her sword to brace herself against the table. After a moment, she stooped to snatch Niall's head by the braids. Arthur left Morghe's side to approach the chieftainess. Trophy in hand, she straightened and turned to him. And collapsed into his arms.

Carefully, Arthur lowered Gyanhumara to the ground. Propelled by her healer's training, Morghe stepped forward. While Arthur peered over her shoulder, she unfastened her borrowed cloak and tore away several strips to bind Gyanhumara's arm.

"Will she be all right, Morghe?"

Morghe studied the unconscious woman. "I believe so, Arthur. The wound is deep, but she hasn't lost much blood yet. The rest are just scratches." A pity the Scot couldn't have done any better. "You may want to get another physician to check on her later, but she looks to be suffering more from exhaustion than anything else."

"No need. I trust your judgment, Morghe. Stay with her until the battle is over and it's clear to move her." He jerked a thumb toward the tent opening. "I must get back out there before the men start to wonder what's happened to me."

"Of course, Arthur." It was far better to be in the tent with only one corpse—even a headless one—than outside with hundreds.

He unpinned the ruby-eyed dragon and knelt to drape his cloak over Gyanhumara's still form. Before rising, he bent lower and gently kissed her lips.

Morghe watched in astonished silence as the key to winning Urien's favor—and, if the Fates were kind, perhaps even retribution against her brother—tumbled into her lap.

When she awoke later that evening, the first thing Gyan noticed was that the canvas of the general's tent had hardened into stone and timber. She was now lying on a bed. Wool-lined furs caressed her bare arms. Then the aches began their screaming chorus. The loudest notes came from her head and her sword arm, though every corner of her body seemed determined not to be left out. Even breathing hurt.

She shut her eyes against the pain and tried to will it away, to no avail. A weak moan escaped her parched lips.

"Gyanhumara?" The voice was gentle, full of concern.

Arthur was holding her hand, the hand not attached to the wounded arm. Gazing into his sapphire eyes, she drew strength from their steadiness.

"Water," she croaked, trying to sit up.

"Easy, now."

Arthur disengaged his hand from hers and carefully pushed her down onto the pillows and furs. Since sitting up hurt worse than lying down, she didn't resist. He reached for the cup and pitcher on the small table nearby and poured a measure. Cradling her head, he held the cup to help her drink.

The water was a cool miracle to her burning throat. She drained the cup and let the pillows embrace her head.

"Are you hungry?" Arthur asked, praying for a sign that Gyanhumara was indeed going to be all right.

He got no answer, for she had already surrendered again to sleep.

Not wanting to wake her, Arthur brushed her lips with his. Her mouth curved into a faint smile. He knew then that she was truly on the mend and permitted himself the luxury of a sigh of relief.

Yet when he rose to leave, he could not will his feet to move from her side. So he yielded to their wisdom.

Her copper hair, now unbraided, spilled over her shoulders and onto the furs. Pale and relaxed, her face still reflected power from the prominent cheekbones and aggressive chin. He was glad to see that her cheeks had lost the crimson flush that had marked her frenzy. Her eyes twitched behind their lids, and her smile deepened.

His lips mirrored a response as he wondered what she was seeing in her dreams.

Her right arm rested atop the furs. He didn't have to raise it to see the mark he knew was there, hidden from view—the mark he had given her. Visible now was a pair of azure doves flying up and over the elbow, one in pursuit of the other. The bandage obscured the wing tips of the lead bird. The only tattoo on her left arm was a braided band, identical to the mark worn by Tribune Urien map Dumarec. And for the identical reason.

Thinking of the heir of Clan Moray forced Arthur to reexamine his predicament. Gyanhumara's action on the ridge before the battle had been no expression of mere gratitude. Despite her claim, the sensual touch of her lips had announced that she wanted him almost as much as he wanted her.

Yet what to do about Urien?

Arthur subdued the urge to pace, lest the clicking of his boots on the flagstones disturb Gyanhumara. Heartily, he wished for Merlin's advice. The man had undeniable experience with such matters, after having helped Uther win Ygraine. But Arthur had entrusted Caer Lugubalion and the rest of the legion's affairs to Merlin's care. Arthur might confide in Bedwyr, if the man could be pried from his work on the captured warships. Cai, who had more women in his bed in a week than most men had in a month, would be no help at all.

Arthur's father had dealt with his rival in an enviably straightforward fashion. Uther provoked a battle with Gorlas and killed him. Rather, his men killed Gorlas while Uther went to Ygraine—with Merlin's assistance and hers. Most of the story was common knowledge, except for Ygraine's complicity. Her position as Chieftainess of Clan Cwrnwyll demanded strict silence.

None of this was any use to Arthur now. Killing Urien would cause more problems than it would solve, for he could not risk losing Clan Moray's support. As Moray went, so went the rest of Dalriada. Many of their vessels sailed in the fleet, and Dalriada held a vital line against the Scots. The events of the past two days were enough to sway the toughest skeptic. Even Cai.

The alliance with Clan Moray of Dalriada had been based upon the friendship Dumarec had shared with Uther, now bestowed upon Uther's son. But Dumarec wasn't going to live forever. Even without Gyanhumara to complicate the matter, Arthur would need some other way of cementing the relationship.

Morghe.

Giving his youngest sister to Urien in marriage might be a viable option, if Arthur could somehow make Urien agree to the match. But that, Arthur realized, wouldn't be easy. The scion of Clan Moray had never been one to give up without a fight.

Arthur stalked to the window and slammed his fist against the unyielding stone wall. The pain had a steadying effect. He spared a final glance for the woman who had become his heart's captor. Gyanhumara slept on, peacefully oblivious to everything save her dreams.

Upon returning to her bedside, he pressed her left hand to his lips and set it back down again. She did not wake but murmured his name. His name—yet not his name. More like "Arteer." The Caledonian equivalent, perhaps? No matter. Coming from her, it was the sweetest sound in the world.

As he left the room, the Pendragon vowed to take whatever steps were necessary to keep Gyanhumara of Caledonia by his side.

His exit from the chieftainess's chambers did not go unnoticed.

In the shadow of another doorway, the corners of Morghe's mouth twitched into a sly grin. After her brother's footsteps echoed into silence, she scurried to the room he'd just left and slipped inside.

Bedwyr map Bann strode the central corridor of the officers' wing, mentally reviewing the details of his battle with the Scotti fleet. Eventually, Arthur would want a written report, of course, though the gods alone knew what he ever did with all that parchment. But Bedwyr had standing orders to give Arthur an oral summary as soon as possible. That is, if Arthur could be found, which seemed to be somewhat problematic this evening. After searching the captured Scotti encampment, the field hospital, and the Dhoo-Glass dignitaries' inn and feast-hall, Bedwyr had finally tracked his commander and friend to this building.

His persistence was rewarded with the sight of Arthur emerging from an intersecting corridor. "There you are!" Grinning, Bedwyr quickened his pace.

Arthur glanced his way and pulled up short. A startled look crossed his face, but only long enough for a smile to take its place. "Bedwyr, well met!" When Bedwyr was close enough, Arthur added to his greeting a firm arm grip and a clap on the back. "Well met, indeed. I was just thinking about you."

Arthur's smile darkened into a more secretive look. And Bedwyr knew better than to try tugging those secrets from him. So, with his lips stretching even wider, he reverted to his usual rebuttal tactic. "Ah, you thought I'd drowned out there today?" His long hair whispered across the back of his battle-tunic as he shook his head. "Sorry, my friend. You can't be rid of me that easily."

As they resumed course for the entrance nearest the feast-hall, Arthur laughed. "Careful. More insubordination like that, and it's to the port barber with you to get that tail of yours hacked off. In fact, I may just save you the trip." His hand groped reflexively for his sword hilt—but he wasn't wearing Caleberyllus. Which in itself wasn't odd. That he had forgotten, though, was.

Bedwyr arched an eyebrow. "So this means I'm safe for now?"

"For now." All trace of humor vanished. Eyes forward and pace brisk, Arthur ordered, "Report."

There was no mistaking what "report" Arthur wanted. While reciting his battle summary, Bedwyr pondered Arthur's actions. Something was obviously amiss, enough so to make Arthur abandon their friendship behind a wall of military protocol simply to hide his embarrassment over being caught in an otherwise insignificant slip. Bedwyr had tolerated a lot of quirky behavior from Arthur over the years, but he sensed something different about this situation. And that Arthur needed to talk about it. Since the corridor was deserted, with most of the building's inhabitants doubtless already partaking in the victory feast, here seemed as good a place as any. Hoping Arthur would take the cue, Bedwyr halted.

Arthur did not.

Bedwyr cast around for a reason Arthur might have visited this wing, one that might explain his unusual reactions. "One of the officers is wounded," he offered into the widening gap. "How bad?"

Arthur gave a short jerk of his head. Ah, Bedwyr mused in silent triumph, a direct hit amidships. Lengthening stride to catch up, he asked himself who might produce such a reaction in the Pendragon, a leader who normally accepted the fortunes—and misfortunes—of battle as well as anyone.

The name that came to mind made his stomach

twist. Bedwyr lunged at Arthur from behind, latched onto his arm and spun him around. Arthur glared. Bedwyr ignored him. A pox on the man's precious privacy; Bedwyr had to know. "Oh, gods, Arthur, is it . . . Cai?"

"No." Arthur sighed, and his glare dissolved. "Cai is fine. Our casualties were minimal."

Minimal, Bedwyr thought, but not nonexistent. "But I'm right, don't deny it. Who, then? Will he recover?"

Bedwyr bore Arthur's inspection for what seemed like half an eternity, with no clue to what Arthur might be looking for. Finally, he replied, quietly, "She should."

"She—Morghe?"

Arthur shook his head. "Chieftainess Gyanhumara."

Those two words made more sense to Bedwyr than anything he'd heard all evening.

Up sprang memories of his brief meeting with the vivacious Caledonian warrior woman, whose position of leadership obviously had been more than ceremonial. Recollection of his response when he discovered she'd feigned ignorance of the Brytoni tongue made his lips twitch in amusement. The incident had caused him to respect her intelligence and abilities all the more.

Bedwyr's smile faded in the face of his concern about her present condition. "What happened?"

"She fought the Scotti invasion commander. During the duel, Niall opened a gash on her sword arm." Arthur's gaze seemed tinged with amazement. "And she relieved him of his head." Bedwyr felt his eyebrows lift as Arthur's tone adopted a more pragmatic note. "But she lost a fair amount of blood, and the physicians decided she should recover here, where it's more quiet and comfortable—and private—than in the field hospital." The sapphire sparkle in his eyes transformed him into the Arthur Bedwyr knew best. "I was just making sure they were right."

Clearly, Arthur felt a lot more toward Gyanhumara than respect. Which, given her relationship with Arthur's greatest rival, was nothing short of a war in the making.

Yet Bedwyr didn't bother forming arguments to steer Arthur from his chosen course. Experience had taught him that bucking a headwind on the open sea was easier than confronting the will of Uther's son. But, experience had also taught him that no matter how dire the situation, Arthur would never let him down.

The least Bedwyr could grant his friend was his loyalty in return. "If there is anything I can do for you, Arthur, for both of you . . ."

Arthur seemed to ponder this for a moment, then shook his head. "But I appreciate that, Bedwyr. More than you know." His smile deepened. "So, I think, would she." As Bedwyr prepared to take his leave, Arthur raised a hand. "In fact, there *is* something you can do for me. And for her."

"Name it, Arthur!"

"Send a ship back to headquarters with a dispatch for Gyanhumara's brother, Centurion Peredur of Seventh *Ala.*" Arthur's secretive smile returned. "Tell him, in these exact words, that she is alive—and well taken care of."

Chapter

25

Kneeling on the cold stone floor of the priory's chapel during compline meditations, Prioress Niniane tried to remain oblivious to the rustlings and whisperings of the other sisters around her as they prayed. A vague sense of unease disturbed her concentration. But other than the muted murmur of the sea and the soft scrape of a branch upon a window ledge, the night was quiet.

"You sent for me, Tribune Urien?"

"Yes, Centurion. I've decided what to do with the murderer."

Her eyes snapped open, and she swiveled her head toward the intruders' voices. Moonlit shadows of the apple trees shifted across the chapel floor. None of the sisters showed any sign of having heard the sounds.

Surely, it must have been the wind. An owl, perhaps. She closed her eyes to resume her prayer.

"He must die. In the viper pit. At dawn."

Niniane was hit by a blast of fury so intense, it sent her mind reeling. She pressed a hand to her temple to still the ache.

To be troubled while sleeping was bad enough, but

this? A waking visitation? Was it possible? Or was she truly going mad?

"But, sir, the Pendragon will—"

"Do you presume to question my authority, Centurion?"

"No, sir."

"Good. Inform the prisoner at once."

This was too much. God's gift or not, the torture had to stop!

Slowly and quietly, to avoid alarming the sisters, Niniane slipped out of the chapel. Once outside, she gathered her skirts in both hands and dashed across the narrow courtyard toward the infirmary. She would fix herself a draught to end these nightmares. Even if it meant drinking it day and night for the rest of her life.

Her fingertips slid across the neat row of fist-sized jars, stopping first at her favorite. She shook a few dried white chamomile flowers into the granite cup that served as a mortar. But she wanted to ensure sleep. Grimacing, she added a pinch of grated valerian root, with a generous portion of apple-mint leaves to counter the bitterness.

As she ground the herbs together, she felt a rush of dizziness. Shaking her head to ward off the sensation, she continued with her work.

She measured a portion onto a small square of cloth, tied up the corners, dropped it into a mug, and bathed it with a dipper of water from the pot by the fire. The water swirled into a mossy brown as the herbs were coaxed into releasing their healing essences. With trembling hands, she raised the mug to her lips.

"But I'm innocent, Centurion Bohort. I swear it!"

"I'm sorry, lad. Those are my orders."

The golden-brown eyes registered a parade of emo-

tions: shock, disbelief, fear, anger . . . and, finally, resignation.

The crash of shattering pottery wrenched Niniane to her senses. Her hands were empty. The sleeping-draught puddled at her feet. Shards poked through the steaming liquid like tiny islands.

She knew that lad. It had been barely a week since he had visited Rushen Priory with Chieftainess Gyan-humara, seeking shelter from the thunderstorm. And the face she had just Seen looked no older.

Niniane found a rag and stooped to wipe the floor.

What had Angusel done to earn Urien's wrath, to deserve death? And when? Six months from now? A month, a week?

Tomorrow. It had to be. When the visions slashed through the veils of sleep, she Saw events that seemed years away. This was the only logical explanation for the Sight's urgent intrusion upon her waking hours.

As surely as she knew her own name, she knew the lad was innocent. And she had to do something—she didn't know what yet, but something—to stop his execution.

In the sunless hour following matins prayers, a lone figure, cloaked and hooded against the damp, guided the half-dozing donkey along the strand toward Port Dhoo-Glass. On their left reared the white-faced cliffs. The moon, a great silver eye, graciously provided all the light they needed for the five-mile trek.

Niniane stopped her donkey on the rise overlooking the port. Around the walls guttered the torches and dying campfires of a sleeping army. She knew the Manx Cohort conducted field drills, but something seemed decidedly odd. Rather than an orderly array of tents and structures, the camp looked like a vast jumble of canvas and timber, as though a whirlwind had passed through.

She made out banner poles in the gloom, but the banners themselves hung limp in the predawn calm. Dear Lord, whose army was it? Had she stumbled on an invasion? In her heart, she believed Angusel truly was innocent of whatever wrong he was to die for. But even if it was not an enemy force that lay between her and the city gates, how was she ever going to get through in time to stop the execution?

"Who are you?"

Gasping, Niniane whipped her head around. The donkey brayed. A pair of archers stood a dozen paces away, arrows at the ready. A third man slowly advanced with a leveled spear.

"Have you no tongue, woman?" demanded the spearman. "What are you doing out at this hour?"

The moonlight bounced off the contours of the man's brooch. It was a dragon.

"I am Prioress Niniane, of Rushen Priory." She played a hunch, fervently praying it was a good one. "I have an urgent message for the Pendragon."

Urien fought from the depths of sleep to respond to the insistent pounding. He snatched his cloak from a nearby chair to wrap about himself before opening the door.

In the dim corridor loomed the hulking shape of Arthur's aide. "Your pardon, sir, but the Pendragon requires your immediate presence."

"Now? What about?" Urien scowled. "If this is some sort of jest—"

"No, sir," insisted Centurion Marcus. "I was ordered to deliver his summons. And not to return without you."

"Wait outside, then, while I dress."

The commander of the Manx Cohort slammed the door and groped toward the table to light the lamp. As he shrugged into his uniform, he failed to think of an even remotely plausible reason for having to report to Arthur before cockcrow. Probably, Urien decided, this was just another excuse to flaunt his ill-gotten authority—authority that should have belonged to Urien from the start.

So be it. The whore-spawn was only digging his own grave. Not to mention, Urien thought with an inward grin, the political embarrassment Angusel's execution would surely cause Arthur.

At the city wall, the tall gates were already cracked wide enough to permit passage of the two men. Urien glanced up at the gradually brightening sky, hoping that whatever Arthur wanted to speak to him about wouldn't take too long. If nothing else could improve his mood, watching the death of that troublesome Pict certainly ought. And seeing Gyanhumara's reaction when she found out.

Afterward, of course.

The guards flanking the entrance to the Pendragon's headquarters tent uncrossed their spears at Urien's approach and saluted. Returning the gesture with no more enthusiasm than could be expected at this uncivilized hour, Urien ducked to step inside.

Seated behind the document-strewn field table, Arthur did not acknowledge Urien's entrance. He remained bent over his work tablet, drawing the iron stylus across the wet clay with swift, decisive strokes. Urien could not make out the figures from his position. Not for want of trying, either.

After a few moments, Urien cleared his throat. And got no response.

"Lord—" The unpalatable words lodged in his throat. He coughed. "Lord Pendragon?"

At last, Arthur looked up to give Urien a long appraisal. "Tribune Urien. Good of you to come. Finally." Anger seemed to prowl at the other end of that intense gaze.

Urien swallowed his surprise. Why would Arthur be angry with him? Had he not fought brilliantly yesterday?

"My Lord, I—"

"Save your excuses, Tribune." The sharpness of the reply killed any doubt. The Pendragon was not at all pleased.

And Urien could not fathom why. Unless . . . "If it's about my battle report, you'll have it by midmorning."

"Good. But that is not the reason you are here." He fingered the stylus as though using it to craft his next words. "I wish to reward the one who sighted the Scotti fleet."

Urien's eyebrows climbed his forehead of their own volition. "I suggest you save your reward, then, for someone more deserving. He is a murderer. And he is to die for his crime."

"When?"

"This morning. At sunrise."

"Really." Arthur slapped the writing tool against his palm. "Who?"

Too late, the real reason for Arthur's summons crystallized. Somehow, he had found out about Urien's plan, and there was no way around the question but the truth. Mentally cursing his stupidity, he braced himself for the worst. "The Pict, Angusel."

The stylus hit the tabletop with a crack. Arthur's eyes glittered ice-blue in the flickering lamplight. "Let me get this straight, Tribune. You are going to execute one of my hostages—the one person responsible for bringing me here to save your neck—without my approval." The Pendragon stood and stalked up to Urien. "Why?" The word was no louder than the rest, yet its bite was deadlier than steel.

Refusing to be intimidated, Urien squared his shoulders and tilted his head to meet his commander's glare. "He killed a Dalriadan cattle herder. Some of Centurion Bohort's men found the body on the bluffs near the Scotti beachhead. Angusel confessed to the deed. He claimed the herdsman was a spy, but—" Urien's palms began to sweat, and he resisted the urge to wipe them on his thighs. "He could not produce any proof to support his story."

"That is no basis for a death sentence."

"There was the body." By this time, his brain was racing to keep up with his runaway heart. "And the confession."

"Motive?"

"Revenge."

"His word? Or yours?"

"He lost a fight to that herdsman last week."

"Answer my question, Tribune. Did Angusel of Clan Alban of Caledonia confess to killing that man for revenge?"

"No."

"I see." Arthur's gaze grew colder, even more intense. "You have overstepped your authority to order the execution of someone who is, by treaty, under my protection, without first consulting me."

"I have the right to dispense justice on matters involving my clansmen," Urien argued hotly. A fresh gust of hatred helped fan the blaze. "And my decision was made before your arrival. Sir."

"Indeed."

As Urien bore the sharp scrutiny, it seemed that Arthur was not going to accept the lie. Yet that was sheer nonsense. Only Bohort knew when the actual order had been issued. Since it had occurred well after the gates had been shut for the night, the centurion wouldn't have had the opportunity to inform anyone in the camp.

"Halt that execution order, Tribune. Bring Angusel to me immediately. If you do not reach him in time, I will have your head." He turned with a swirl of his scarlet cloak, paused, and faced Urien again. "And have the men of that Ayr Point patrol report to me."

Angusel circled his prison cell for what must have been the thousandth time in a day and a half. One pace to the center of the door, another to the corner and the dented, stinking privy pot. Turn. A pace to the edge of the moldy straw pallet, and half a pace to the wall. Turn again. Tramp twice across the rat-gray, rat-eaten blanket under the gash in the stone that passed for a window. Pivot once more, step off the pallet, and take one last half-step back to the beginning.

He could have made the circuit in his sleep—if he'd been able to sleep. The pain in his knee was forgotten as he fumed at the injustice of his fate.

Sounds of the previous day's battle had spilled through the window slit. Gradually, the clamor had changed timbre and volume from the soldiers' war cries and screams of the wounded and dying beyond the city walls to the jubilant banter of townsfolk passing outside his cell. The Scots had been defeated.

To Angusel, it meant only one possibility: his signal to Arthur had been successful.

Yet his reward was to be death. And a dishonorable one at that. Angusel shook his head with incredulity.

Surely, even Arthur—who had beaten the Confederacy, and forced them into an alliance, and wrenched Senaudon from Alban, and ordered Angusel's exile to Maun—surely even he wouldn't act so unjustly if he knew the facts. If he knew. If.

No, it didn't fit. The Pendragon might be many things, but he was not a monster. Aber-Glein and Senaudon had been won by superior tactics, not by treachery. Afterward, Arthur had treated the Caledonian leaders with respect. The treaty terms, while decidedly favorable to the Brytons, weren't completely one-sided. All things considered, Angusel's tenure on Maun had been enjoyable. Until his chance encounter with the Dalriadan spy.

Angusel realized then who had ordered his death.

The strengthening light in the chamber heralded the start of a new day, the day fated to witness the end of his life on this earth. Moving underneath the high window, he searched the domain of the gods. From this angle, he could see only a sliver of the white-blue morning sky. How could any of them possibly see him? Or even know where to look? Or care? The ancient tales of the gods walking the earth to help heroes were just that—tales. Not history, as some folk preferred to believe. Just some worm-riddled bard's fantasy, inspired by too much ale.

Besides, he was no hero. True heroes might be captured in battle and imprisoned, aye, but their actions were never confused with crimes by their supposed allies. And the motives of a hero were never questioned, under any circumstance.

Angusel turned from the window and slid down the night-chilled stone wall. His injured knee sent stabs of pain through the rest of the leg. But he didn't mind the cold anymore, or the pain. For they were signals that he was still alive, signals soon to be stilled by a serpent's sting.

Hugging knees to chin, he gazed upon the small clay drinking cup. He picked it up, summoned the face of Urien map Dumarec, and heaved it. The cup burst into a hundred red-brown shards as it collided with the wall. The satisfaction lasted only an instant. Sighing, he rested chin on knees again.

Angusel's biggest sorrow was that he would die in ignorance of what had happened to Gyan. That she had acquitted herself well against the invasion of Tanroc, he had no doubt. Capricious fate had stolen the one opportunity he would ever have to fight alongside his mentor and friend—and, he realized with no small shock, his sister. Not by blood but in spirit.

Ignoring the thought of being overheard, it was with a kinsman's outpouring of grief that Angusel of Clan Alban mourned the passing of the Chieftainess of Clan Argyll. For if the Scots had indeed thrown the bulk of their force against Tanroc, her chance of survival would have been slim. No matter how brilliantly she might have fought. Even the greatest warriors knew there came a point when skill could not overcome the sheer weight of numbers.

And the Scotti swine had made sure to surpass that point tenfold.

Maybe he would meet her in the halls of the Other-world, and together they could fight unearthly foes forever. Angusel's lips twitched into an echo of a grin as he pictured the battles to come. Hosts of putrid monsters . . . gory fangs dripping poison . . . wickedly curved talons that could rip bones from living flesh . . . unblinking yellow eyes that froze the soul in a single glance. And deep in the midst of this ravening evil, he and Gyan and the Army of the Blest, all clad in dazzling armor, swinging swords forged by the gods.

Death might not be so bad after all!

The slap of sandals on stone in the corridor outside the cell shattered the visions. Angusel raised his head. The door creaked open to reveal a pair of guards. One carried chains looped over his shield arm. Both held spears.

Angusel rose.

"Gitcher arse out 'ere, pris'ner," ordered the man with the chains.

Silently, Angusel obeyed. Nor did he bother to resist as his arms were yanked behind his back and shackled. The lock snapped shut with deadly finality. A spear point jabbed between his shoulder blades, and his last march began.

"Sure is a quiet 'un, Brychan."

"We'll see 'ow quiet 'e is in the pit, Erec, won't we?"

Angusel ignored the coarse laughter. Perhaps he'd even show them a thing or two about courage, the Brytoni curs. And where was the leader of their pack, Urien? Surely, he'd want to be here to gloat. But if the guards knew, they showed no sign, and Angusel wasn't about to ask them.

Each soldier gripping one of Angusel's arms, the trio trudged abreast down the dank corridor. Guttering torches along the walls shed more greasy smoke than light. A small, furry shape darted between their feet and fled, chittering, into the shadows. From somewhere came the *plink* of water dripping onto stone. The men's rhythmic footfalls and rasping voices sounded unnaturally loud, and Angusel began to wonder whether they could hear the desperate pounding of his heart.

Out of the hazy gloom at the end of the corridor

emerged the outline of a door. Its features sharpened as they neared. There was neither lock nor bolt, only a plain handle.

This was it, then: the entrance to the viper pit.

What if—what if Lord Annwn of the Otherworld wouldn't take him into the Great Hall because he hadn't proved himself worthy in battle? Would he be denied a place in the Army of the Blest? Doomed to wander the realm of the living to see and hear all . . . but never to be seen or heard by mortal kind?

"C'mon, boy. In ye go."

Angusel sighed. Nothing could be done about it now.

Erec tugged on the handle, and the door opened on groaning hinges. A blast of fetid air made Angusel's eyes water. It didn't seem to bother the guards as they propelled him across the threshold. They snatched torches and pushed him into the chamber. The door thumped shut behind them.

Roughly circular, the room wasn't much larger than his cell had been. But unlike the cell, the floor was wooden, and those planks were the only things now separating Angusel from death.

Near the door stood a barrel. Beside it, a lever sprouted from the floor. The lever's function Angusel could guess. He might have wondered what was in the barrel, but now his only concern was for this grim business to be ended.

"Lessee wot the buggers be doin'," chortled Brychan as he reached for the lever.

Erec produced a strip of black cloth from a pouch at his belt. "Blindfold, lad?"

Angusel shook his head. No one would accuse him of not meeting the Hag of Death face-to-face. Erec shrugged and stashed the cloth back in the pouch.

Grunting, Brychan yanked the lever. With a screech,

a section of the floor fell away. The hissing of a hundred serpents burst from the shadowy depths. He clamped his hand on Angusel's shoulder and forced him to look down the hole.

"There be yer new 'ome, boy. Lotsa company for ye."

Angusel stared in morbid fascination at the writhing mound of black bodies, glimmering faintly in the fitful torchlight. Company, indeed. And were those really bones scattered among the adders, mute testimony to the fate of the pit's last resident?

Another hand drew him back. "Here now, Brychan, the lad'll be down there soon enough. No need to—"

"I can 'ave me fun, can't I?" Without waiting for an answer, Brychan reached into the barrel and pulled up a bucket. "Time to wake up, me beauties." He dumped the contents into the hole. As the sand spattered the snakes, the hissing grew even louder and angrier. Brychan glanced at Erec. "Where be the key?"

"Tribune's not here yet. Oughtn't we wait?"

"No 'arm in gettin' the boy ready." Brychan extended an open hand. "Let's 'ave the bloody key."

"I'll do it m'self." Erec lifted a ring from his belt. It jangled with a score of iron keys that to Angusel looked identical. One by one, Erec began fitting them into the lock that held the chains.

The door slammed open, and the quest for the key halted. Urien shouldered between the guards. Contorted with rage, his face looked demonic in the shifting light. Angusel stood unflinching under his captor's glare.

"Angusel of Caledonia, you are hereby granted a reprieve." Urien spat the words like venom. "I am here to escort you to the Pendragon for further questioning."

Urien spun and strode from the chamber. Angusel

stared after him, scarcely daring to believe what he'd just heard.

"You deaf, boy? Gitcher arse movin'!" Brychan prodded him with the butt of his spear. "The Pendragon don't like to be kept waitin'."

"Ease off, Brychan!" Erec planted a hand in the middle of Angusel's back to propel him from the chamber. "Come, lad. Brychan, can you secure the pit?"

His only answer was a halfhearted grunt.

Accompanied by Erec, Angusel followed Urien. With each step, his heart lightened. Not even surly Brychan's return could stunt his growing joy.

The procession drew stares from townsfolk and soldiers alike as they quick-marched through town and into the camp. Angusel didn't mind the stares or the pace. He was too busy delighting in the feel of the cool, clean morning air against his skin. Everything seemed somehow clearer and brighter. Even the birdsong, to which he'd never before given a moment's thought, was infinitely precious.

Surely, once the Pendragon heard the true story, he would order Angusel's release. There might be restrictions, true. Probably even punishment. But nothing as irreversible as what he had just faced. For one wild moment, Angusel wanted to join the birds in their song.

The rippling Scarlet Dragon marked the headquarters tent. The men at its entrance withdrew their spears at Urien's command. After dismissing Erec and Brychan with a curt nod, he grabbed Angusel's arm and dragged him inside.

"The prisoner, as ordered. Sir." Roughly, Urien pushed Angusel forward.

"Unchain him."

Urien left the tent, presumably to find Erec and his

keyring. As Angusel stood in silence before the Pendragon, his hopes of being released began to flee. If anything, Arthur looked even more forbidding than Urien had. But there was no hatred that Angusel could see. A flicker of hope rekindled.

Finally, Urien returned with the keys. After a few moments, he located the correct one, and the chains slid to the ground at Angusel's feet. Angusel rubbed his stiff arms.

"Thank you, Tribune. That is all." Without another word, Urien departed. Arthur's brow furrowed as he went on, "Angusel mac Alayna, you stand accused of murder. Explain yourself."

Swallowing thickly, Angusel began.

Arthur remained silent in solemn concentration as he listened to the story, unmoving but for an occasional nod of understanding, his face an unreadable mask. It was unnerving for Angusel to be unable to discern where he stood with the man who held the key to his fate. That unwavering gaze compelled him to reveal everything. Even his deepest feelings of devotion toward Gyan, which he had barely acknowledged to himself, never mind anyone else. At that, the Pendragon's mask seemed to crack a little, letting escape a flash of—what? Sympathy? Compassion? Whatever it was, it heartened him.

He finished his tale and paused. When Arthur made no move to speak, Angusel summoned the courage to continue. "Lord Pendragon, may I ask a question?"

"Ask."

"Sir, what happened to Gyan—Chieftainess Gyanhumara?" As soon as the words escaped, he wanted to call them back. But he had to know. "Is—is she—"

"She is here, recovering. You may see her later, if you wish."

Gyan, alive! But before he could voice his elation, the impact of Arthur's second statement hit him. "My Lord?"

"You heard me, Angusel."

"But . . . does this mean I'm free, sir?"

Arthur's hand closed over a blood-splattered leather pouch lying on the tabletop. He pulled it open and shook something into the opposite palm. The fingers curled into a fist around the shining object.

He rose and approached Angusel, who was still frozen at attention. "At ease." Angusel relaxed his stance a little. As Arthur's hand rested on Angusel's shoulder, a feeling beyond mere warmth tingled in that touch. "Angusel, if I had more men with a tenth of your loyalty and courage, my task would be easier by a hundredfold.

"Yes, you are free," the Pendragon said. "To go home, even, as reward for your efforts. And this is yours, too." He pressed a gold brooch into Angusel's palm.

Angusel studied the intricately wrought lion, feeling his eyes widen in amazement. Finally, he looked up. "Sir, why this? My freedom is reward enough."

"That is your freedom, Angusel."

"The herdsman's payment? But how did you—"

"Come by it?" Arthur's eyebrows twitched, and an enigmatic almost-smile flirted with his lips. "Suffice it to say that my methods of questioning are very . . . thorough."

"Sir, this is far too generous of you. I can't accept it."

"Nonsense. The lion is the symbol of Clan Alban, is it not?"

"Aye, sir, but—"

"All the more reason for you to have it. And it would

please me greatly if you chose to remain in my service. As a warrior."

"My Lord, I thank you. I'm honored. But what I did, all of it—" Angusel drew a breath. "I was only thinking of her. Chieftainess Gyanhumara. With all respect, sir, I would rather stay here and fight at her side. To go where she goes. And to die for her, if need be."

It was not the love of a man for a woman that Arthur saw in the depths of those golden-brown eyes. The emotion kindling there was the love of friend for friend, framed by a good measure of respect, bordering on reverence. Arthur nodded approvingly.

"So would I, Angusel," confessed the Pendragon. "So would I."

Chapter 26

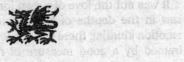

Gyan awoke at first light. A figure was dozing in the
chair beside her bed, and the memory of Arthur's visit
the previous evening drifted back. How considerate of
him to have kept vigil all night. She felt a swelling of
love at the thought.

"Arthur?" Smiling, she stretched out her hand.

The eyes that flicked open to meet hers were not blue
but violet.

"No, Gyanhumara, your lover is not here."

Lover? "Morghe!" Despite the pain lancing her
wounded arm, Gyan pushed herself up. "What are you
doing here? How dare you accuse—"

"How?" Her grin was positively wicked. "By the
evidence of my own eyes, of course."

"It's a lie."

"Is it, now? Then show me a witness who can tell me
what my brother was doing in this room for so long last
night, if everything that happened between you was
innocent."

"A witness?" Gyan laughed. "You must be mad,
Morghe. I am not on trial here."

"No? Your reputation is."

"My reputation, indeed!" Gyan creased her brow. Could Morghe know something? "Who would believe that anything—untoward—happened last night? I was half dead of exhaustion."

"Really? You were obviously awake enough to know that Arthur had been here." Again, Morghe displayed a malicious grin. "And something made you think he might still have been here this morning."

"Answer my question, Morghe."

"Who would believe me? Why, probably anyone I choose to tell. People are always looking to believe the worst about their betters."

A name burst from Gyan's lips. "Urien."

Immediately, she regretted her mistake.

"Why, Gyanhumara, what an interesting idea." Morghe's grin widened. "Too bad I've already thought of it. He's not very happy with you, you know."

"Fine." Gyan strove to hide her plunging spirits behind a casual mien. "Then he can tell me himself."

"Oh, I'm sure he will." Morghe rose from the chair, making a show of fussing with her skirts. "As soon as I inform him that you're awake and appear to be feeling much better." With a giggle, she flounced from the room.

Gyan shook her head in disbelief at Morghe's audacity. What could she possibly hope to gain by pouring her poisonous slander into Urien's ears? His notice, perhaps, or his favor? But why? Did she think she could dislodge Gyan from Urien's side? If so, Morghe was welcome to him. Indeed, it would solve many problems. That is, if Urien would have her, which was highly doubtful. The heir of Clan Moray had never taken his eyes from Argyll lands. Nor was he likely to change his target anytime soon.

Maybe Morghe just wanted to cause trouble for Arthur. Again, Gyan was forced to ask herself why.

An answer presented itself. It made little sense, yet Gyan had noticed that logic always seemed to flee whenever Morghe stepped into a room. So did mention of Arthur. Which led her to believe that, for some reason, Morghe bore little love for her brother.

Whatever came of Morghe's actions now was in the hands of the One God. He would have to help Gyan cope with the situation. With Arthur's help, too, she hoped.

Stretching, Gyan assessed her body's condition. The overall soreness had abated, except where Niall had cut her. No practice blade had ever made her arm throb like this. Even the wound Arthur had given her couldn't compare. It would be several sennights before full strength returned; this she knew from watching the recovery of her clansmen following Aber-Glein. Hugging her arm to her chest, she mentally railed at herself for letting the Scot slip past her guard to inflict the wound.

Excusing that flaw in her performance because of her weakened condition or because of her enemy's superior skill wasn't an option for her. Good warriors had no use for excuses. And after all, she had won the encounter to collect her first battle trophy. Her father and brother would be proud!

Gyan found the trophy wrapped in canvas beside her bed. Gazing at Niall's bloodless face, reliving the fight, she wished she'd also had the opportunity to defeat Fergus, who had been instrumental in her capture. But she had not seen him defending the rear of the camp. That one had been a truer leader than the general he had served. Fergus had probably gone down at the forefront of the battle under Urien's assault.

She rewrapped Niall, deciding not to display him until he could be properly cleaned and embalmed. As she put the trophy back, her stomach rumbled. Small wonder, she realized. More than a day had passed since her last meal.

Cleaned of mud and gore, her boots slumped against a pine chest at the foot of the bed. Inside the chest, she found her battle-gear, also clean, and a dun linen tunic and matching breeches. Since the sun streaming into the bedchamber promised a warm day, she chose the comfortably loose linen garments. But the bronze dragon on her sword belt seemed to beckon.

Gyan picked up the belt, thoughtfully rubbing the ridges and valleys that formed the dragon's body. She truly was one of Arthur's warriors now, properly blooded and victorious. After slipping the belt over the tunic, she fumbled with the fastening thongs behind her back before finding the hooks. She hoped practice would make it easier, as the merchant Al-Iskandar had promised.

Would practice make it easier to say the things she wanted to say to the man she loved? With Urien still looming large in the picture, she wasn't so sure.

She caught the faint but unmistakable aroma of frying bacon, and her stomach again reminded her of her body's immediate need. Bidding a silent farewell to her vanquished foe, she stalked off toward the kitchens.

"Lord Pendragon, you really don't have to go to this trouble," protested the holy woman of Rushen Priory. "I can make it back by myself."

"My pleasure, Prioress."

Effortlessly, Arthur lifted Niniane to the back of her donkey. While she adjusted herself in the saddle, with both legs draped over one side because of her robe, he vaulted onto his borrowed chestnut horse.

"You're not taking any men, either?" Niniane asked.

Around them, soldiers labored to purge the camp of the chaos left in the wake of the previous day's battle. But his brief smile in response to the gentle tease was only for her.

"No, Lady. This"—he patted Caleberyllus's leather-sheathed blade—"is all I need."

When they were well out of earshot of the camp, plodding along the beach at the donkey's sure-footed pace, they shrugged off all pretense of formality.

"A plain leather scabbard? Don't tell me fortunes have been that bad for you, Arthur."

"Not quite." He chuckled. "No, Niniane, it's by choice. Having this apple on the pommel is bad enough. I don't need the scabbard drawing attention, too."

"But I thought that was why I gave you the sword in the first place. As a symbol for your men."

"True. They needed it then." Gazing out over the restless waters, he watched a fishing boat battle its way up the windswept coast. He empathized with its captain. At times, it felt as though he were fighting headwinds, too, and not making any forward progress. "But something I've learned in the past two years is that men don't follow a piece of metal. They follow the hand that holds it. And only as long as that hand brings victory."

"There will come a time, Arthur, when you will not need Caleberyllus for battle because there will be no one to fight."

He gave her a sharp glance. "You have Seen this? Or are you just speculating?"

She smiled ruefully. "With the Sight, it amounts to a little of both."

"And I think it's going to take more than just a campaign or two to make my enemies respect my territory."

Niniane arched an eyebrow in response to the way he had referred to the land protected by the force under his command, but she made no comment. "I'm not saying it won't," she agreed at last. "All I am saying is that when the time does come, you will need to find something else for your hand—and your sword—to do. Perhaps then it will be time to trade the old nicked, scratched battle scabbard for one that's more in keeping with Caleberyllus's value."

"But then maybe the people will need to be reminded of those nicks and scratches, and how they came about."

"Maybe," Niniane said. But having already Seen the battle signifying the demise of Arthur's realm—decades hence, she hoped—she knew that no number of reminders would help him repair bonds shattered by mistrust, disloyalty, and treason.

They lapsed into silence for a time, guiding their mounts through the inrushing waves. Yet they were not alone. Scores of sandpipers scurried after the endlessly rising and receding waters, hunting whatever bits of food the sea cast upon the beach. When the riders approached a flock, the birds scattered, squeaking, only to settle back into their timeless routine once the danger was past.

Angling away from the sea, Arthur and Niniane headed into a deep draw that broke the pale face of the surrounding cliffs. Tucked against the throat of the draw, the pristine priory walls peeped from behind shady apple boughs. Over the surf's bass thunder rose the serene treble of the sisters' singing as they went about their appointed tasks: washing laundry and hanging it to dry on ropes stretched between the trees, harvesting the leaves and flowers of the herbs growing around the compound, tending the large outdoor bread ovens.

A small group of nuns toiled in the vegetable garden, skirts hitched up to their knees to permit greater freedom of movement. Some of the nut-brown calves, Arthur observed, were quite shapely.

Hand to back, a sister straightened and glanced up. Seeing Arthur, she uttered a startled cry and began fumbling with her skirt's knot. The others soon discovered the reason for her distress and followed her example.

He looked away, as much out of consideration for the embarrassed women as to conceal his quiet amusement. In truth, there was no need for them to fear the least bit of unseemly conduct from him—but, of course, they had no way of knowing this. There was now only one lady to whom he wished to devote his amorous attention. The problem was, she had no way of knowing, either.

Apparently scenting home, the donkey pricked his ears and surged forward with renewed vigor. Arthur nudged his mare to match the new pace.

"Thank you for what you did for Angusel this morning, Niniane. I know you didn't have to."

"Oh, but I did. When the signals are that strong, one must obey." Her eyes shone in the soft sunlight. "And pray that it is the right thing."

"Today you did the right thing," Arthur said. "Because of you, I saved an ally's life. And discovered someone who can't be trusted."

"You mean Urien?"

"Yes. I don't like lies, no matter how small. Small ones spawn bigger ones." He frowned at the memory of the meeting, and the fact that Urien had lied about when the execution order had been issued. Urien's cooperation, while never a certain thing, would likely be tenuous at best. "But I couldn't dress him down for it without risk of exposing your secret."

Niniane's smile looked decidedly grateful as he dismounted to help her down. He led the donkey into the pen and secured the gate.

"God be with you, Arthur."

"And you, too, Lady." He pressed her delicate hand between his. "I leave Maun in two days. Is there anything else you can tell me?"

Niniane chewed her lip. With a full life stretching before him, now was definitely not the time to speak of his final battle. But there was the matter of Arthur's youngest sister, Morghe. Nothing that Niniane had Seen, specifically. Just a knowledge of Morghe's deep anger toward Arthur, which might manifest in any number of unexpected, potentially dangerous ways.

She studied his face: so young, yet responsibility was already beginning to etch its indelible mark. She did not have the heart to cause worry to lodge there, too. It would come knocking soon enough on its own. But something had to be said. Lord willing, a few words would be enough.

"Arthur, when you get ready to leave, I think you ought to consider taking Morghe with you." In the silence wrought by his surprise, Niniane explained, "She is terribly unhappy here on Maun. And she hates you for it."

He laughed mirthlessly. "I sent Morghe here for her own good."

"When do any of us see the good in something we despise because we are forced into it?"

"We must all do things we don't like." The subdued assurance made Niniane wonder what unpleasant task was invading Arthur's thoughts. "At some time or another."

The call rang out for third-hour prayer. The prioress cast a glance toward the chapel as the sisters obediently set aside their work to heed the bell's summons.

"She misses her home," Niniane said. "I know you sent her here because you care about her, but she doesn't see it that way. If you let her go now, it may not be too late to change the way she feels about you."

The bell seemed to become more insistent, and she knew she had to hurry. But surely the Lord would forgive her a few minutes' tardiness just this once.

"Arthur, please don't sacrifice your relationship with Morghe this way."

He looked away and did not respond for several long moments. When he finally returned his gaze to her, the brief but unmistakable flicker of pain made her want to weep.

"Very well, Niniane. I will consider your advice."

Smiling her relief, the prioress hurried for the chapel. The tierce bell's echoes were drowned by the crying gulls and moaning surf.

Back in her quarters in the officers' wing later that morning, Gyan had an unexpected visitor.

"Gyan! Gyan, I'm so glad you're all right," exclaimed Angusel as he burst into the antechamber.

They exchanged the warriors' arm grip, before impulse urged Gyan to draw her comrade into a sisterly embrace.

"Well, of course I'm all right, Angus. What did you expect?" Thinking of Morghe's earlier words, she added, "Better leave the door ajar." Angusel cocked a questioning eyebrow. "It's a long story. For later, back at Tanroc." As he went to obey, she noticed the limp. "What happened to your leg? And where were you when I needed you?"

Angusel returned, and they each dragged a chair to the table.

"You mean, you didn't hear about how Urien tried to kill me?"

"What?" Fists clenched, she shot to her feet.

"Gyan, please, it's all right now." He caught her hand and tugged. Reluctantly, she sat again. "But it's a long story, too—for later. Honestly, I'm sick of telling it. Let's just say that I didn't see as much of the action as you did." After a moment, he brightened. "What I really came for was to hear about your fights."

Although his reticence aroused her curiosity, she let the matter drop. He would tell her what had happened to him when he was ready, just as she would eventually explain her aversion to closed doors.

So, for most of the following hour, Gyan recounted the events of the past two days. It wasn't easy to strip the emotions from the facts to give Angusel an accurate description of her capture and the battle. With the help of his persistent questions, she clarified as many details as she felt he ought to know about. Which did not include either her personal encounter with Arthur on the ridge the previous afternoon or the one with Morghe at dawn.

Angusel was visibly disappointed. "But they said you killed a hundred Scots, Gyan, and wounded twice that many."

"Oh, come now! Do you really believe that?"

"I suppose not. But I think you could have if you'd wanted to."

Gyan laughed lightly. "Such faith!" She reached out to tousle his curly black hair. "Angus, what am I going to do with you?"

The spirit of seriousness seemed to descend upon the young warrior. "Let me always fight by your side, Gyan. That's all I ever want to do." He spied her sword leaning sheathed in the corner, retrieved it, and offered her the hilt. "I know this isn't mine, but that doesn't change my feelings."

Angusel carried the potential to become a great warrior, a promise that sang in the glitter of his eyes, the set of his jaw, the pride of his stance. And he was the son of the *ard-banoigin* of a clan nearly as powerful as Argyll. Gyan did not treat his pledge lightly.

Solemnly, she stood and grasped the hilt with her left hand—since her wounded arm could not bear the weight—and drew the sword. Angusel knelt, head bowed, hands clasped behind his back. She laid the naked blade on his right shoulder. The edge touched the base of his neck in the ancient Caledonian ritual of the giving and acceptance of trust. According to custom, the one holding the weapon was at liberty to decapitate the one making the pledge if there were any doubts about the sincerity of the offer.

And through the turbulent centuries, the Oath of Fealty rite had been used for execution as often as not.

Gyan harbored no doubts as she intoned the prescribed words: "Does Angusel mac Alayna of Clan Alban swear allegiance to Gyanhumara nic Hymar of Clan Argyll, even unto death?"

"Even unto death!"

She inflicted the ceremonial scratch on his neck to seal the promise.

The door banged against the wall. Angusel scrambled to his feet. Gyan sheathed the sword. And immediately regretted it as the identity of the intruder registered.

Glowering like the wild boar of his clan's symbol, Urien of Dalriada charged into the room.

"Urien." Gyan glared at her unwelcome visitor. "What a surprise."

"Indeed. Boy, leave us," Urien ordered without taking his eyes from Gyan.

Angusel looked at her expectantly. She firmly guided him toward the door.

"I won't be far, Gyan, if you need me," he promised, in Caledonian.

When they were alone, Urien demanded, "What did he say?"

"Just expressing concern for my health." It wasn't far from the truth. "Which is more than you've done, I might add."

"I did not come here to inquire after your health."

"Of course you didn't. You have about as much feeling as a rock. Less, I think."

Growling, he lunged at her and latched onto her right forearm, below the bandage. She clenched her teeth against the searing pain as he yanked her closer. Then he grabbed her other arm. His breath reeked of rancid ale.

"Damn it, woman! Is he your lover?"

Despite the pain, she couldn't resist the temptation to bait him. "Who—Angusel? Don't be ridiculous."

"That's not who I mean." Urien's grip tightened. "And you know it."

She tried to wrench free. And failed. As her struggles died, a grin of malevolent triumph spread across his face.

She refused to give him the victory. "Who, then?"

"Don't play stupid with me, Gyanhumara. You wear his standard across your belly." His jaw clenched as his eyes flicked down to her belt and back to her face. She could read the hatred in those narrowed eyes. "The Pendragon."

"So. You would believe every lie you hear?"

"I believe my eyes! What I've been told only reinforces what I saw before the battle yesterday. You and Arthur, on the ridge."

By all that was holy, how was she going to sidestep this? Then an inspiration hit: "Why, Urien, I was only thanking him for releasing me."

He spat an impolite invective. "Don't give me that. I saw what I saw. It was not just gratitude." His fingers dug even deeper. "Was it?"

Sheer force of will bridled her outcry. Disappointment lurked in Urien's rage-colored eyes.

When she refused to respond, he continued, "If it had been me, would you have done the same?"

"What do you think, Urien?"

Urien released her arms and strode toward the door. She swallowed the urge to voice her relief. He whirled to face her again.

"Lady, I don't know what to think anymore. But remember this: I am not accustomed to losing anything without a fight!"

The timbers of the door and its frame trembled under the force of his departure.

Chapter

27

General Caius Marcellus Ectorius lounged on the low cot in his tent, conducting the planning meeting. In a wide semicircle on the ground sat the centurions of the cohort to be sent to Tanroc's relief. Ten pairs of eyes regarded him with unwavering respect as he imparted his instructions.

Times like this, Cai thought with an inward grin, were almost as rewarding as the battles themselves.

A shadow darkened the dirt. Cai glanced up at the tent opening, now blocked by the form of his foster brother. One hand clutched the captured Scotti standard. Recognizing the urgency behind that cool gaze, Cai drew the meeting to a close.

Arthur advanced into the tent. As the centurions filed past him, he gave each man a clap on the shoulder and a few words of encouragement for the upcoming operation. To Cai, it seemed the centurions underwent a subtle transformation that manifested in various ways: a lighter step, a swelled chest, a proudly lifted chin.

It was more than just a reaction to the personal recognition of the supreme commander. Cai himself had succumbed to the influence of that touch often enough to know its magic. It always amazed him how Arthur could have that kind of effect on people. The weapon was as powerful as the ruby-headed sword riding Arthur's hip.

When the last centurion had departed, Cai slid over. Arthur dropped beside him onto the cot.

"Good men, Cai. With some of Bedwyr's warships covering the seaward flank, you'll have no trouble tomorrow. When do you leave?"

"First light. As soon as you give us a proper sendoff, of course. Just as long as it doesn't take all day." Cai grinned. "I don't intend to march the men by torch-light."

"I get the hint."

As the shared laughter trailed away, Cai pointed to the banner. "What's that for?"

"This?"

For an instant, it seemed as though Arthur had forgotten the reason for bringing the scrap of green and gray cloth. In all their years together, Cai had rarely seen Arthur act preoccupied over anything. And when he did, usually trouble was soon to follow. Cai's senses sharpened for other warning signs.

But the moment passed, and Arthur continued, "It should be helpful at Tanroc."

The banner fluttered to the ground in two ragged pieces. The loping Silver Wolf was torn precisely in half.

"Of course. More demoralization tactics. You don't think facing ten-to-one odds will be enough, Arthur?"

"I prefer not to take chances. As long as I win. If I can win without spending a single life, so much the better." Arthur glanced up from the Scotti banner. "I know you would rather fight."

Cai shrugged. "Dead men won't attack you as soon as your back is turned."

"They won't help you, either."

"There's no guarantee living men will do that. Enemies or allies"—Cai's tone was charged with warning—"or friends."

"True. My job is to see that they do. Yours is to give the orders to implement my decisions." Arthur flashed an engaging smile. "Which you do so well, my brother."

It was incredibly easy to fall under the spell of that smile, and Cai was not immune. He doubted whether he would ever be. Or whether anyone would ever be, for that matter.

He chuckled. "Shall I ask Chieftainess Gyanhumara for Niall's head?"

It was meant as a joke, but apparently Arthur didn't take it that way. "No. I will." His voice dropped into a husky half-whisper. "And there's a small matter I want you to look into after you secure Tanroc. Her woman, Cynda. If she's alive, send her here. And if not, well, I'm sure Gyanhumara will want to know that, too."

Another alarm bell clanged in Cai's head as he recalled the dinner Arthur had hosted for the Manx centurions—and Arthur's behavior, then as well as now, started making sense. He gave Arthur a critical stare. It went unseen by the Pendragon, who was again studying the rent Wolf on the ground.

Cai uttered a long, low whistle. "Saints preserve us all! The Duke of Brydein is in love."

Up jerked the red-gold head, shaking in violent denial. But Arthur did not meet Cai's eyes.

"Oh, yes. Don't give me that head-wagging routine." His elbow found Arthur's ribs. "Come on, Arthur. You of all men ought to know that I've been in and out of love so often, I can see the signs brewing ten miles away."

Arthur gave a derisive snort. "God, I hope it isn't that obvious."

"Not to anyone who doesn't know you like I do." And Cai knew better than to pass judgment or offer unsolicited advice when Arthur was in a mood like this. Still, he had to try. Getting involved with the Picti chieftainess, who was already betrothed to Urien of Dalriada, would certainly be no good for anyone. "Arthur, do yourself a favor. Forget her. Mark my words, that woman will bring you nothing but trouble. If you want, I can set you up with a nice, biddable girl—"

Arthur jumped to his feet, grinding the Wolf into the dirt as he stalked away. At the tent opening, he whirled. Cai had never seen those eyes burn with such force. He fought the instinct to retreat.

"Do yourself a favor, Cai. Keep your counsel—and your girls—to yourself."

After Arthur left, and Cai's heartbeat returned to a more normal pace, he swung his legs onto the cot and reclined on his elbows to stare at the canvas ceiling. He felt a grin spread across his face.

Poor Urien. Against lust of that magnitude, he stood a beggar's chance in a whorehouse.

Angusel was chatting with the guards outside the main entrance of the officers' quarters when the doors crashed open. The guards snapped to attention as Urien stormed past. He did not bother to answer their salutes but struck off in the direction of the waterfront. It wasn't difficult to guess his intended destination.

"Commander's in a fine fettle." One guard smirked as he eyed Urien's dusty progress. "Wonder what's got 'im started. A bit early for a nip, wouldn't ye say?"

Grinning broadly, the other guard shook his head. "Never. If ye can afford it, that is. Aye, laddie?" He looked toward where their companion should have been. The place was empty.

Angusel dashed down the long corridor toward Gyan's chambers, the ache in his knee overwhelmed by the desire to make sure she was all right. He found the door and knocked. When that prompted no response, he turned the handle and gave a tentative push. The door yielded.

"Gyan?"

Arms wrapped across her chest, she was standing at the window, staring out to sea. But for the slight shifting of her shoulders as she breathed, she might have been carved in marble.

Angusel crossed the tiled anteroom floor to join her. Still, she made no move to acknowledge his presence. Her face was composed, emotionless. Except her eyes. They glistened with unshed tears.

"Gyan, what's wrong? What did he do to you?"

In answer, she lowered her arms. The places where Urien had held her became painfully obvious.

"That *cù-puc!* I'll kill him!" His hand was at his hip before he remembered he was unarmed.

"No. You will not." Her gaze fell upon him like autumn mist, mourning herald of winter. "I will not have your blood on my hands."

"You don't think I could win?" As he thought about his fight with the herdsman, a man who'd outweighed him by at least four stones, her apparent lack of confidence hit him like a blow.

She clutched his shoulders. "Another day, another year, perhaps. Not now. I've sparred with him. He could have easily beaten me. But he always let me win." Her hands fell away, and she turned back to the window. When at last she spoke again, it was with words so soft that Angusel had to strain to catch them. "I should have refused the betrothal. Now . . . it's too late."

"No! Gyan, you can still break it off."

Her unbound hair whispered across her shoulders as she shook her head. "Whether I marry Urien or not, it doesn't matter. The same treaty that made you hostage decreed that I marry a Brytoni chieftain or chieftain's son. The man I love is the—" Her chin began to tremble, and she clenched her jaw. "Does not qualify."

Blinking in astonishment, Angusel waited silently for her to continue. When no revelation of the man's identity came, he quested through memories for clues.

Centurion Elian? Unlikely. They were never together except on the practice field, where mutual admiration of each other's fighting skills was the only emotion they shared. Besides, Elian was older than her father. Not that age seemed to matter to some women. Angusel's mother had done her level best to persuade Arthur, a dozen years her junior, to become her consort.

Angusel tried to imagine Gyan and Elian in a more intimate setting and failed. But who, then? Her tutor, Brother Lucan? Or maybe someone she'd left behind at Arbroch?

"Angusel, I'd like to be alone. Please. Why don't you talk to someone about joining the Tanroc relief column—"

"Will you go, too—to Tanroc, that is?"

"Ha. With this?" Her fingers flicked across the bandage. "You saw how I can't even lift a sword, much less use one."

"Then I won't, either. My place is here. With you."

She stared at him for so long, he was sure she was on

the verge of sending him away. He held his ground. If she truly wanted him to leave, she would have to use force.

At last, a soft smile touched her lips. "Thank you, Angus. You're a great help—much more than you know." She held up an open-palmed hand. "But I must deal with Urien myself. Do you understand?"

"No, Gyan, I don't." He glanced pointedly at the ugly red blotches staining her arms. "I swore to protect you, and now you're asking me to break my oath already."

"You swore to act in the best interests of Clan Argyll. There may come a day when that will mean protecting me. Not today."

"If you won't let me fight for you, at least let me stay with you." He ventured a hopeful smile. "Please, Gyan?"

"All right, Angus. You win." Ruffling his hair, she returned the smile. "Let's go find a couple of horses and get away from here for a while. I could do with a change of scene."

They never made it to the stables. On the way out of the building, they were intercepted by one of Arthur's officers.

"Ah, Chieftainess, well met. The Pendragon would like a word with you."

As Angusel watched a spark ignite in her eyes, an idea began to form.

"Where is he?" she asked.

"At camp headquarters, my Lady."

"Good. Angusel and I are on our way out for a ride. I will meet with Arthur upon our return."

The centurion frowned. "My Lady, he indicated that the matter was of some importance."

"What could be so important that it can't wait an

hour or two?" The centurion spread his hands in a gesture of ignorance. "Oh, very well. I'll go now. Angus, do you mind if we ride later?"

"No, as long as I can go with you to the camp."

She laughed. "You don't give up, do you?"

"My Lady," interjected the officer, "he can stay outside the tent while you're talking with the Pendragon."

"Then can we stop by the kitchens first?" asked Angusel. "If this is going to take very long, I want to be prepared!"

The centurion chuckled. "Just like my nephew, always wanting to eat. You're of an age, too, you and Drustanus." Nodding, he eyed Angusel closely. "Yes, lad, we have time for a stop at the kitchens. A quick one."

In due course, the Chieftainess of Clan Argyll set off for the Pendragon's camp headquarters, accompanied by his aide, who introduced himself as Centurion Marcus. Angusel, a loaf of bread in one fist and a hunk of goat's cheese in the other, tagged happily behind them.

As Arthur read Urien's report of the battle, he curled his free hand around the table edge in a conscious effort to keep from smashing the tablet to rubble. The report was a bloody disgrace. Poor grammar aside, the events were not described in chronological—or any other type of logical—order. Worse, Urien failed to present an acceptable reason for his foolhardy foray against the Scotti camp. Rescuing Gyanhumara was not justification enough against those odds, on the enemy's terms. If not for the timely arrival of the reinforcements, Urien and his men would now be glutting the ravens. And Gyanhumara . . .

No. Such thoughts were useless. She was safe, and on her way over, even now. That was all that mattered.

He glanced past the open tent flap at the long shadows of the guards outside and muttered an oath under his breath. This won an amused look from Cai, who was lounging in a camp chair, feet outstretched, casually paring his fingernails with his dagger.

"Have patience, Arthur. They'll be here soon."

The "they" Cai was undoubtedly referring to—the centurions assigned to the Tanroc relief cohort—was not the "they" Arthur most wanted to see. If only Gyanhumara would get here first. Marcus could be dismissed easily enough, and Cai was good at taking a hint. Then Arthur would really have something to talk to her about beyond the paltry excuses he had fashioned to see her again.

A score of sandaled feet crunching across the sand outside the tent broke his reverie. He looked up as the men trooped in. An eleventh centurion followed them: Marcus, with Gyanhumara. Angusel, too, although Marcus made him wait outside.

The lad appeared to be sincere in his loyalties. Most interesting.

But so much for wishes. Trying to get rid of the men, if only for a short while, would be too awkward. And too bloody obvious!

Arthur rose to approach Gyanhumara, who had made her way to the forefront of the gathering. As much as he wanted to prolong her presence here, there was no need for her to sit through his meeting with the leaders of the relief force. Even to ask would send a silent message he was not yet prepared to support with words or deeds.

Again, he was smitten by her exotic beauty, made all the more alluring by the strength radiating from her proud stance. Even her blue doves had become dear to him. The other tattoo, no. But if Arthur had his way, its meaning would soon be changing. For now, he wanted nothing more than to fold her to his breast, and a pox on what everyone else thought.

Logic prevailed. First, Urien would have to be persuaded to give up Gyanhumara and take Morghe to wife instead. How that was going to happen, Arthur had no idea. Of the options he'd already considered, none seemed promising. But this much was clear: whatever plan he selected would not be an easy one to implement. And no one else could help him.

With a supreme effort of will, Arthur banished all emotion from his tone. "Thank you for coming, Chieftainess."

"How may I be of service . . . Lord Pendragon?"

So coldly formal, so utterly correct. If word of this meeting reached Urien's ears, he would have no cause for suspicion. Just as well. Surprise could be a useful tactic in any situation.

"I would ask two favors of you."

Her eyes widened slightly. What in God's name was she expecting? An open declaration of his love? He would gladly proclaim it from the parapets if he thought it would help. Unfortunately, that action would spawn far more harm than good.

Arthur went on, "The first favor is in support of the Tanroc relief operation, which General Caius will be leading." He spared a glance for Cai, who inclined his head toward the chieftainess. Cai's frosty look appeared to border on outright dislike. This seemed odd coming from a man who worshipped mortal women more ardently than he worshipped any deity. Just as well; Urien was competition enough. "Chieftainess

Gyanhumara, may I have the loan of General Niall's head for Caius to take with him to Tanroc?"

"Certainly, Lord Pendragon. I'll send someone over with it as soon as I can." She paused as though debating whether to say something else. An offer to deliver the head herself, perhaps? But no, as badly as he wanted to see her alone, he knew it wouldn't be proper. Doubtless, she knew it, too.

How could she stand there acting so calm, so reserved? Couldn't she hear his heart thrashing about, trying to get nearer to her?

She asked, "And the other favor?"

What was that light shimmering in the depths of her sea-green eyes? Hope? Desire? Before he could decide, it flickered out.

Again, he fought the impulse to pull her into an embrace. And won, again, but the margin of victory was shrinking with each bout.

"I would like a written account of your involvement in the Scotti invasion. Especially of what happened before my arrival. Centurion Marcus can be your scribe—"

"No need for that," she replied, "if you don't mind the report being written in Brytonic. At present, my skill with Latin is rather limited."

"Brytonic?" Would this woman ever run out of surprises? Probably not, and it made him love her all the more. Reluctantly, he buried the emotion before it could touch his face. "Brytonic will be fine."

She nodded tersely. "Is that all, Lord Pendragon?"

He wanted to shout, "No!" and fasten his lips to hers, to unleash the passion she had ignited within him. But the voice of reason echoed coldly through the corridors of his brain.

Instead, he answered quietly, "Yes." He refrained from adding, *For now.*

At his signal, the centurions stepped aside to let her through. As she turned to leave, a patch of afternoon sunlight streaming through the tent opening fell upon her arm.

"Chieftainess, wait. Those bruises—you didn't have them yesterday. Where did they come from?"

"I had an argument with—someone. It's nothing that need concern you."

It wasn't hard to guess who that "someone" was, and by God's holy wounds, it most certainly did concern him! Betrothed or not, the swine had no right to treat her like that. Urien would pay even if it took Arthur's final breath.

A plan gelled. It carried plenty of risks, but the best treasures in life were never won without them. Now, his only lack was an opportunity.

It was all he could do to keep the triumph from his voice as he replied, "I see."

She stepped out of the tent and was gone without another word. As he watched Angusel bound excitedly at her side like a colt frisking around its dam, Arthur would have given his right arm to be in the lad's place.

The following dawn broke upon the orderly ranks of the Brytoni cohort, formed up and ready to march, as they stood outside the gates of Port Dhoo-Glass. At the front of the column, Niall's head glared balefully from a spear carried by General Caius. The two halves of the Scotti banner were tied to the spearshaft. Beside Caius stood the cohort's standard-bearer. In the man's hand, the gold-framed Scarlet Dragon fretted in the early-morning breeze. The soldiers' eyes were lifted to the parapet beside the gate tower where the Pendragon stood. His heart-stirring voice arrowed out to meet them.

Gyan's irritation grew as she felt herself coming under the sway of his exhilarating encouragement. They were, after all, only words. And they did not apply to her. The injury to her sword arm had left her no choice.

She had donned her battle-gear, but only for show. Rubbing the bandage, she wished she were standing with the men below to receive Arthur's bellicose benediction instead of being on the wall with him, all but chained to Urien's side.

Angusel's presence on her shield side was some comfort. Although he would be missing a chance for combat experience, she was grateful that he had rejected the idea of joining the relief cohort. As her duly sworn supporter, it was his right. Just as it was his right to be with her now. In neither instance had she, or anyone else, tried to deny him.

Her hand rested on the pommel of her sword. The ribbed bronze sphere, cool against her palm, did little to fight the heat raging in her veins. Was it only battle-lust? Or was the sight of Arthur, handsome in his gleaming battle-gear and scarlet cloak, igniting a fire of a wholly different type?

She wasn't sure she could live with her heart's answer. Or without it.

"And so you have been given yet another chance to avenge the valiant deaths of your comrades by punishing the Scotti marauders. Acquit yourselves this day with courage and honor"—Caleberyllus was a silver blaze in Arthur's fist—"and the victory will be yours!"

General Caius permitted the men a few moments' undisciplined appreciation before shouting the marching order. As one, the cohort spun to put the rising sun to their backs and surged forward with barely leashed enthusiasm.

While the Pendragon, the Chieftainess of Clan Argyll, and the heir of Clan Moray watched the departing troops, Angusel of Clan Alban eyed the three warriors.

He earnestly hoped Arthur was the man who had won Gyan's heart. The Pendragon was much worthier of being her consort than Urien. If only she could see it, too, and send the Dalriadan pig back to Dunadd where he belonged.

After the column disappeared up the winding river valley, Arthur sheathed his sword and turned to leave the parapet. His eyes met Gyan's with profound intensity. Hers seemed to draw his gaze in and reflect it back with their steady power. Angusel could practically see the sparks fly to embrace each other across the gap. It proved his suspicions and made him want to cheer.

Instead, he kept silent and glanced at Urien, whose eyes were generating their own sparks. The Dalriadan's hand began to twitch toward his sword hilt.

As in the instant before a lightning strike, Angusel fancied that he could feel the hairs lifting from his head. He just had to do something about the tension crackling in the air before something broke. Or someone.

Donning what he hoped was his most endearing grin, he reached for Gyan's hand. "Come on, Gyan." He gave it a firm tug. "Let's go get something to eat. I'm starved!"

Gyan observed the bustling wharfside activity from the window in her antechamber late that afternoon with unshakable depression.

The captured vessels were moored at the Dhoo-Glass docks to be readied for the return to Caer

Lugubalion. Though they still bore the crimson Scotti rigging rather than the Brytoni sapphire-blue, the Scarlet Dragon snapped from the top of each mast.

There was a hypnotic rhythm to it all. An unceasing parade of workers toted barrels and crates to each ship, stowed their burdens in wolf-headed prow or stern, and came away flexing empty arms. Brytoni crewmen swarmed over every oaken handspan, eyes sharp for evidence of enemy treachery: a cracked oar, a missing treenail, a half-severed rope, a slashed sail, a hidden hole in the hull. Though it was serious work, the men bore it with high spirits begotten of the knowledge that they were soon going home. Snatches of their jaunty tunes and coarse laughter sailed on the salty breeze.

In fact, it appeared to Gyan that the warships would be ready to depart on the morning tide. And one of them would be carrying Arthur.

She sighed and sank into the chair behind her desk. Fingering the stylus, she dragged the clay work tablet toward her and resumed the task of composing her account of the Scotti invasion and the Battle of Dhoo-Glass.

The writing was not going well. Finding the proper words was not the problem; it was Arthur himself. His face kept intruding upon all other memories, rendering concentration impossible. And now he was about to leave, before she could tell him how she really felt.

Under the circumstances, she might not have bothered with trying to write anything at all, but he had asked for her report. Not commanded, asked. Just as he had asked for the loan of Niall, for General Caius's relief operation.

That interview with Arthur the previous afternoon had been monstrously difficult. His headquarters tent had been crawling with his officers. Including Caius, who had glowered at her with thinly disguised dislike. Not that there was a single opinion in that tent that mattered to her, save one. But her true feelings toward the Pendragon were not the business of his men. To keep from unmasking those feelings, she had retreated behind a wall of aloofness. And she had been unable to discern anything from Arthur.

This morning on the battlement was entirely different. Gyan had seen the passion smoldering in the fiery blue depths of his eyes. In a moment of sheer folly, she had returned his gaze, ember for burning ember. But Urien had also seen the wordless exchange. If Angusel hadn't spoken up when he did, there might now be a new heir of Clan Moray, or a new Pendragon . . . or both.

And she had paid for that indiscretion. Urien had made certain of that. He had bombarded her with a hundred excuses to keep her within his sight all morning. Trivial matters, hardly even worth her consideration. Half of it she couldn't—and didn't wish to—remember. Finally, she'd taken enough penance and had escaped to her quarters with a plea of fatigue, which he had readily believed. She had recovered enough of her good sense to refrain from telling Urien that she had to finish Arthur's report.

Now the half-done report lay before her. The completed portions had already been copied to parchment. The smooth ochre clay of the work tablet seemed to mock her. The cold iron stylus felt like an alien thing between her fingers.

Someone rapped on the door. She glanced up, grateful for the distraction. Perhaps Arthur had heard her silent call. "Yes?"

But it was not so. The soldier marching into the

antechamber wore the Dragon Legion uniform of a centurion. She recognized him as the man who had escorted her to Arthur's tent, Centurion Marcus.

He halted in front of her desk and gave her a respectful nod. "Chieftainess Gyanhumara, the Pendragon wishes to speak with you as soon as possible at camp headquarters."

Not that again! She simply could not bear another ordeal like yesterday's.

"Please convey my regrets." Gyan gestured at the tablet and parchment. "As you can see, it will be quite impossible."

As the refusal passed her lips, a thought struck: this might be her last opportunity to see Arthur before he left Maun. She was tempted to recant. But she needed to be alone with him. Not ringed by his men.

"What?" Disbelief cracked Marcus's impassive bearing. "But my Lady, no one refuses the Pendragon."

"In case you haven't noticed, Centurion—" She slapped the leather encasing her chest, her voice adopting an edge that was just as hard. "I do not wear a legion uniform. I am under no obligation to answer to anyone. Least of all your war-chieftain." Palms flat on the tabletop, she pushed to her feet.

"You can tell the Pendragon that if he has something to say to me, he can come here and say it."

Chapter

28

Cai made no attempt at stealth but marched the Herring Cohort boldly up the Dhoo valley toward Tanroc. The unit's name had begun the day before as a joke when some soldiers selected for the relief operation realized that most of their comrades had come to Maun smuggled in the fragrant bellies of the fishing boats. Yet it was fitting, and Cai encouraged it. He enjoyed a good laugh as well as the next man. Anything to foster a sense of unity among his troops was welcome, however unorthodox.

To keep in step, Cai started the men singing one of his favorite tavern tunes, "The Seven Saxon Sisters." The rhyme wasn't quite as good when swapping the nationality of the fabled wenches to match the foes the army was soon to engage. But the men didn't seem to care. Voices were boisterously loud, if more than a little off-key, and spirits ran high, and the miles dropped quickly behind them.

If the Scots could hear them coming from five miles off, so much the better. Their heightened fear as they awaited their deaths would be just payback for the terror they had tried to inflict upon the island.

Their leader had already paid. At the hands of a woman, no less. Cai didn't have to look up to visualize what was riding on his spear point.

Arthur certainly had strange tastes in women. The chieftainess was gorgeous, but in a wild way. Maybe it was the tattoos that made her look so barbaric. The way she'd dealt with her enemy spoke volumes, too. If Arthur couldn't tame her, no one could. And untamable women were, in Cai's vast experience, as dangerous as fire.

Cai hoped Arthur had sense enough not to let himself get burned.

At the top of the rise overlooking the thorn-hedged fort, Cai halted the column to survey the situation. Bedwyr's warships were tacking into position around St. Padraic's Island. Arrows swarmed like flies at a cattle fair. The ships in the strait took advantage of their position to rain death upon the Scots at the fortress as well as the monastery.

As Cai and his men watched, the volleys from the monastery steadily dwindled and finally ceased as the Scots spent their ammunition. The ships pulled in to let the soldiers spill over the sides and wade unhindered onto the islet.

Phase one was complete. Time for phase two: the fun part.

Cai shoved the spear into the standard-bearer's free hand. Brandishing his double-headed battle-axe, he sounded the charge.

The Herring Cohort lost a score of men to Scotti arrows as they burst through the thorny portals and streamed toward the charred palisade. They were met inside the fort compound by a band that could not have amounted to much more than a century. Though the would-be invaders faced overwhelming odds, they fought like mad dogs—until they began noticing their leader's head. Then they threw down their weapons, and it was all over.

The encounter hadn't taken long enough to work up a decent sweat—a colossal disappointment. Yet casualties had been light. Arthur, no doubt, would be pleased.

Now the real work began. Organizing the incarceration and interrogation of the prisoners. Dispatching men to search out the buildings to make sure all the Scots had been captured, and to find Brytoni survivors. Tending the wounded. Detailing a burial crew to dispose of the bodies.

In the midst of his planning, Cai looked up to see a plump, middle-aged woman emerge from a nearby building. She glanced around the compound, appearing to take in what had happened, and strode toward Cai with unswerving determination. Curiosity aroused, he ordered his men not to interfere with her approach.

She stopped in front of Cai, who was still flanked by the cohort's standard-bearer. She made a slashing motion across her throat, pointed up at the man's grisly burden, and uttered one word: "Gyanhumara?"

Her accent was thick, but Cai understood. This had to be the Picti woman Arthur had asked him to find.

Cai nodded. The woman expelled a sigh that was heavy with relief.

"She said *what?*" Arthur's fist crashed to the tabletop. The wine cup rocked. Several drops slopped over the rim.

Marcus winced. "Sir, she—I tried to explain—"

The Pendragon relaxed his hand, snatched the cup, and drained it. "I'm sure you did." When Marcus started toward the pitcher, Arthur waved him away. "I'm not angry with you, Marcus. I know you did your best."

The centurion looked greatly relieved. "She's a real fiery one, that lady, if I may say so, sir. General Cai thinks—"

"I know what he thinks." To soften his words, Arthur forced a smile.

Cai thought she belonged under Urien's thumb. Not that the Dalriadan could possibly hope to hold her there for very long.

"Thank you, Marcus. That will be all for now. Go on to the feast." He picked up the stylus and reached for the work tablet. "I will be along later."

Marcus nodded, saluting. The tent flap fell closed behind him.

Arthur laid the stylus aside and filled his cup, wishing it were something much stronger. Like Abbot Kentigern's *uisge*. After downing the wine in three swallows, he poured another cupful. Volume would have to make up for lack of potency.

Curse that woman's stubbornness! What did she think she was trying to prove? Perhaps he ought to let her marry Urien after all. She deserved whatever treatment the Dalriadan saw fit to give her.

No. She did not.

Pain lanced Arthur's heart as he realized he loved Gyanhumara far too much to surrender her to another man.

Her refusal to talk to him introduced a new element of risk. What of it? Merlin and Uther had trained him to deal with contingencies. Only a fool believed plans never went astray.

All this meant was a prolonging of the charade.

Perhaps he could exact a toll for her willfulness, too. Nothing exorbitant, just enough to communicate his displeasure. He smiled slightly as he finished the wine.

Arthur pushed away from the table and crossed to where Caleberyllus lay sheathed at the foot of the cot. As he regarded the ruby, he considered bringing the weapon to the feast in case Urien decided to cause trouble.

An absurd notion. Urien might be many undesirable things, but he was not an idiot. Even if he suspected anything, he wouldn't dare make a public scene.

The Pendragon doused the lamp and headed for the tent flap.

In the waning sunlight, the great ruby flashed a warning. It went unheeded. Gloom swallowed the sword.

Gyan put down the goose quill to flex cramping fingers. It was much easier to hold a sword. Easier to use one, for that matter, than to write about it.

At least the chore was finished.

The stack of parchment sat before her, the words scrambling across each sheet like black ants on parade. She considered rereading her work and quickly discarded the idea. There'd be time enough for that after the feast, she supposed. Given a choice, she wouldn't be staying long.

The aromas of roasting beef and pork had been haunting her nostrils throughout the better part of the afternoon. For the past hour, laughter and footsteps had filtered into the antechamber through the closed door as the other residents of the officers' wing made their way to the feast-hall. By now, the feast would be well under way.

And Urien expected her to make an appearance.

After removing her sword belt, she exchanged her leather leggings for the linen trews. The battle-tunic caught on the bandage, and fresh pain bolted through her arm. Wincing, she worked it the rest of the way off. The soft linen tunic settled around her body like a lover's embrace.

Because of her injury, Gyan had missed the first two nights of the victory celebration. Actually, she could have gone last night if she had wished. The injury provided a convenient excuse when the events of the day had left her feeling somewhat less than sociable. But after using the same ploy to escape Urien this morning, its usefulness was rapidly diminishing.

Regret gnawed at her like a rat on a rope. Not about Urien—about having refused to see Arthur one last time. A public meeting under any circumstance was better than not being near him at all. Soon there would be no more opportunities. She banished that thought with a sigh.

Surveying her gold-tinted image in a small bronze hand mirror unearthed from the bottom of the clothes chest, she decided to send for Cynda to help rebraid her unruly hair. And almost dropped the mirror.

Cynda was still at Tanroc. If she was alive.

To that specter of doubt Gyan refused to grant admittance. Losing the only mother she had ever known would mean losing a piece of her soul. The depth of that anguish she could scarcely begin to fathom.

Gyan glanced at the sun, cursing her slow wits. Caius must have retaken the fort soon after the cohort's arrival. Even without the benefit of the fallen palisade, his numerical advantage was ten to one. Had the idea occurred sooner, she could have ridden to Tanroc and returned to Dhoo-Glass—with or without Cynda—in plenty of time for the feast. Now it was too late.

Her sigh was born of exasperation as she recalled the previous morning's conversation with Angusel, after Urien had left evidence of his true nature upon her arms.

Too late. It seemed to be her personal watchword these days.

News of Cynda would have to wait until the morrow. So be it. Worry had never hurried a single step of the sun's dance. And it was not going to start having any effect now.

Gyan returned her attention to the chest, where further exploration produced a bone comb. She unbraided her hair and smoothed the coppery waves as best she could.

The bronze dragon crouched on the table, waiting. As her fingertips played across its cool body, she considered Urien's possible reactions if she were to wear the belt at the feast. None would be favorable. She smiled.

This time, her fingers found the belt's fastenings with little trouble. Tugging the wrinkles from her tunic, she stepped from the room. As she descended the stone steps and started across the large central yard toward the feast-hall, a figure burst from the doors and raced toward her.

"Well met, Gyan." Panting, Angusel took his usual place at her side. "I was sent to escort you to the feast."

This wrenched a short, dry laugh from her throat. "By Urien, I suppose?"

He nodded. "Arthur's there, too." This was accompanied by a crooked grin. "In fact, they were both asking for you."

"I can imagine."

Of course, Arthur would be at the feast. It was his victory. How stupid of her not to have realized this sooner! Quickening her pace to give herself less chance to change her mind, she revised her thoughts about being with Arthur in public. With the two men present—and both of them roaring mad at her—this was one feast she was not looking forward to attending.

Hoping Angusel would think nothing of it, she switched topics. "What were you doing there? Aren't you supposed to be eating with the other boys?"

"Since General Cai's cohort is gone, they let us join the feast. Me, I'm done eating." He shrugged. "For now, at least."

"Good." This was one time she would not have traded his company for all the gold in Caledonia. Nor, she suspected, would it be the last. "Then you can be my cup-bearer tonight."

Caledonian men and women feasted together, served by the adolescent warriors. To be cup-bearer for the clan's leaders, if even for a single night, was a highly coveted honor that often sparked vigorous competition. Thus, Angusel's exuberant gratitude was not unexpected.

At the feast-hall's double doors, she paused, lowering her voice. "Make sure my wine is well watered, Angus. I don't need my wits to be any slower than they already are."

Angusel began to ask what she meant, but she dragged open one of the doors and stepped inside. The door thundered shut behind them, prompting a few revelers to look up. As more eyes turned their way, Angusel abandoned the question.

Unconcerned by the attention, Gyan surveyed the thatched, timber-raftered hall. To her far left, the side

entrance leading to the kitchens was recognizable by
the steady flow of women through the open doorway,
bearing platters and vessels of various sizes. More
women circulated among the tables, replenishing food
and drink as the need arose. Mostly drink.

Tables and benches formed long ranks before the
dais, which stood at the end of the hall farthest from
the kitchens. One central and two side aisles permitted
movement between the rows.

Gyan's appearance in the center aisle prompted a
commotion at the dais. Flagons and trenchers were
shoved aside. Bodies shifted along the bench to open a
gap. Right between Arthur and Urien. Marvelous, she
thought dismally.

Both men glared at her as if they wanted to settle
their hands around her throat. The idea of fleeing
crossed her mind. No. That was the coward's way.
Besides, what could either of them do to her in front of
all these people?

Unfortunately, just about anything.

She drew a deep breath, squared her shoulders, and
strode toward the dais. Like a shadow, Angusel quietly
followed.

Her passage between the tables drew stares convey-
ing a wide range of emotions, from lustful leering to
sincere friendliness, through casual indifference to
outright dislike. All because she was a woman.

At feasts, Brytoni women did not eat with the men,
they served them. Even now, more than one suffered
the indignity of a playful slap to the backside. The
officers at the high table did not engage in the same
bawdy behavior exhibited by their men. Rather, most
of them watched in tolerant—and often vociferous—
amusement.

This was one Brytoni custom Gyan could not stomach, and no small effort had inured the Tanroc men to her presence at the feasting table. If their conduct and conversation became a wee bit more refined, then the change she had wrought was assuredly for the better.

The soldiers assigned to Port Dhoo-Glass were aware of her habit and didn't appear overly concerned. To the Caer Lugubalion contingent, it was a novelty. Seemingly an unwelcome one. The only Bryton not assigned to the Manx Cohort who didn't seem put off by her presence was the fleet commander. In fact, Bedwyr was the only officer seated on the dais who looked genuinely pleased to see her. She briefly returned his smile as she neared the high table.

Urien pushed to his feet. In expectation of an announcement, the noise in the hall began to die.

"Well, Gyanhumara, have you finally come to do your duty?" Urien smirked. "I'm sure everything must taste sweeter when served by your lovely hand."

A sharp intake of breath behind Gyan told her that Angusel was reacting to the insult. "No, Angus," she murmured, in Caledonian. "Let me handle this." She displayed a mischievous grin. In Brytonic, she retorted loudly, "Not so sweet, I'm afraid, as from yours, Urien."

The hall erupted into a cacophony of howls, hoots, and screeches, mingled with the thumping of fists on tabletops. A storm gathered on Urien's face as he readied his next barb, but Arthur intervened. As the Pendragon rose, silence descended.

"You're forgetting one thing, Urien." He leveled his piercing gaze at Gyan. Anyone else would have instantly knelt, babbling for forgiveness. Even if there was nothing to forgive. Gyan stood firm. "Chieftainess Gyanhumara attends no man."

Before she could stop him, Angusel stepped forward. "True, my Lord! Among Caledonians, women of high rank do not serve anyone. I have the honor of being Chieftainess Gyanhumara's cup-bearer this night. And to serve everyone at the high table if she commands it." He glanced at Gyan, who returned his look with a nod and a smile.

"Well spoken, Angusel." Arthur extended a hand. "Come, Chieftainess. Your place awaits."

"Yes. On my left, my love." There was no love in Urien's tone. "Where a wife-to-be belongs."

And that was only the beginning. Between Arthur's subtle verbal thrusts and Urien's beneath-the-table attempts at her near thigh, it was a worse nightmare than any ever to attack from behind shuttered lids.

Angusel performed his task admirably well; she scarcely tasted the wine at all. Or anything else. Her eyes and nose told her there was roast pork and partridge on her trencher, surrounded by carrots, leeks, and bread. But for all the difference it made to her tongue, the food may as well have been dust.

Enough was bloody well enough! She rose. As she twisted to climb over the bench, a hand locked around her wrist.

"Surely you're not leaving us so soon, my dear?" asked Urien. "The entertainment is due to begin."

Overcoming the desire to put her meat knife where it would do the most good, she replied, "I'm not hungry anymore." She refrained from pointing out that he had been having his entertainment the entire time, at her expense.

"What a pity, Chieftainess. Perhaps your wound still troubles you." Arthur beckoned to his sister, who had been attending the dais with Angusel. Morghe glided forward, all smiles. "Morghe, accompany Chieftainess Gyanhumara to her quarters, and—"

"That won't be necessary, Lord Pendragon." Gyan

wrenched free of Urien's grip and made good her escape.

After emerging from the kitchens with a newly filled pitcher, Angusel intercepted her at the door.

"No, Angusel, stay here. I—" His hurt-puppy look softened her heart. "Thank you. You've done well tonight. I appreciate it very much. I'm sure the others do, too. I just need to be alone." She squeezed his shoulder and gave him a nudge in the direction of the dais. "Don't worry, Angus. I'll be all right."

She hoped that wouldn't prove to be a lie.

Obedient to her command, Angusel refilled the flagons at the high table. Urien downed his at once, dragged the back of one hand across his mouth, belched, and demanded more. After similar performances by some of the other officers, Angusel's supply was soon depleted. Trudging back for a refill, he wondered whether they even noticed his presence, never mind appreciating it.

He returned to discover, to his surprise, that both Arthur and Urien were gone.

Gyan's restlessness prevented sleep. Nor did she even try. Instead, she stood in the antechamber, looking out over the harbor, which now appeared purple-gray in the fading twilight.

She had made a true mess of everything.

Urien's anger she couldn't give a horse's tail for. She was through with his disrespectful arrogance and would tell him so come morning. Then return home to lead her people to war against Clan Moray. And the death and devastation would begin all over again. All because of her accursed womanish selfishness and stupidity!

Having now experienced combat firsthand, at least she would know what to expect. More or less. For, unlike the Scots, from Urien there surely would be no mercy.

And Arthur—if his glare had been any sharper, she would have bled to death all over the food. Refusing to speak with him this afternoon had been an incredibly childish move. Her first glance at him upon entering the feast-hall had told her that. If he never forgave her, she wouldn't blame him.

But losing him would make life unbearable. Even without Urien at her side like a grinding-stone hanging around her neck.

She leaned against the stone framing the window, absently flicking flecks of mortar free with a fingernail, watching the bobbing points of light on the ships moored at the docks and anchored in the harbor. A cool evening breeze caressed her face but was of little comfort.

The door banged open. Hand to dagger, she whirled.

"Arthur." The dagger stayed in its sheath. She folded her arms. "Don't you believe in knocking?"

"Forgive me." He slammed the door, took two paces into the room, and stopped. Fury blazed across his face. "I am unaccustomed to disobedience."

An angry flush rose in her cheeks as her heart kicked into a canter. Disobedience, indeed! "And I am unaccustomed to being whistled for. Like a dog." Fists to hips, she thrust out her chin in defiance.

"I do not whistle for anyone, Chieftainess. Nor do I issue summonses without reason. Furthermore, as my ally, you are obligated to answer to me. Contrary to what you may think." The scowl darkened. "Why did you refuse?"

Gyan tried to craft a suitable retort, but, confronted

with Arthur's scalding wrath, her wits felt as soft as horse manure. So she settled on the truth instead.

"I could not bid you farewell in front of your men."

"You couldn't—God's wounds, Gyanhumara!" Arthur looked up, gritting his teeth. Much more quietly, he continued, "I have things to discuss with you, and all you can think about is yourself."

Inwardly, she winced at the truth of his accusation. And now, here was the chance she craved: to be alone with him, a heartbeat from his arms, to confess her secret desires. Yet there he stood, unreadable except for the blue fire writhing in his eyes. That fire could mean practically anything. What if she was wrong about him? What if he only saw her as an ally—and a wayward one, at that?

Her instincts screamed caution. For once, she obeyed.

"What . . . things?"

"Good Lord, you mean I have to spell it out?" His surprise seemed genuine. Hope ignited in her breast. "I thought you were more perceptive than that."

He stepped forward and pulled her from the window, into his crushing embrace. Her heart leaped from a canter to a gallop at the explosive meeting of their mouths. Joy surged anew with each beat. With Urien, such a kiss had always made her feel like a pigeon in the talons of a falcon. Not so with Arthur! They were falcons together—conquering the clouds, racing the sun, mastering the winds. All her pent-up emotions burst free on the wings of that one kiss.

His fingers began tugging at the thongs holding her sword belt.

Reluctantly, she pushed away. "Arthur, no. Please. I can't—"

"What do you mean, no? It's what we both want."

Hands cradling her cheeks, he peered into her face. "Isn't it?"

"Yes . . ." What in heaven's name was she saying? "No! I mean, I—" She wanted him so achingly much! But not like this. Other matters had to be resolved first. Biting her lip, she turned to the window, hoping the relentless rhythm of the sea could ease her torment. "Arthur, you don't understand."

Behind her, he slipped his arms around her waist, clasping his hands over the bronze dragon. His cheek rested against hers. "On the contrary, Gyanhumara, I understand many things. Including the implications when an *ard-banoigin*"—he used the correct Caledonian phrase easily, to her amazement—"makes love with a man." He kissed the side of her neck, below the ear. An ecstatic shudder scurried through her body. "But I don't want you only because you're wealthy," he whispered. "Or beautiful. Or because marrying you will strengthen my alliance with the other clans of the Caledonian Confederacy." Arthur ran his hands down her arms, going lightly over the bandage and bruises. He drew a breath. "These reasons might satisfy another man. But even if you were none of those things, Gyanhumara, I would still love you."

She felt her mouth curve into a smile as she faced him again. As though of their own accord, her hands slid up over his leather-clad chest to settle behind his head. He bent his face to hers. The candle spun much of its waxen cloak before their lips parted again.

His hands found their way down her back, pulling her even closer. Firm yet gentle, his touch sparked a flame so intense, she thought her heart would surely burn to a cinder. Every fiber of her being yearned for the fulfillment of her greatest desire: to claim Arthur as *ard-ceoigin* according to the ancient custom of her people. To be his warrior and wife, his battle-leader and lover.

Unbidden, the face of her betrothed loomed in her mind's eye.

"But Arthur, what about Urien? Surely, he will provoke war. Against you as well as Argyll."

"I know what could happen when you break your betrothal to Urien. What could happen to both of us." He began to explore the curve of her throat with his lips, and she murmured her pleasure. When he neared the base of her neck just above the torc, he paused. "Leave Dalriada to me, Gyanhumara. My solution will eliminate the need for bloodshed."

"Really, my Lord?" said a new voice.

Startled, Arthur and Gyan turned and stepped apart. Neither had heard Urien open the door. He stood on the threshold, naked sword gleaming in his white-knuckled fist. The One God alone knew how much Urien had seen.

"I should be most interested to hear how you would solve our little dilemma." Murderous rage flared across his face as he advanced into the room. "If you live to tell it."

Arthur's hand flashed to his left hip, where Caleberyllus should have been. He spat a curse for having left it at the camp.

Urien laughed harshly. "Poor planning, my Lord. Where's that great sword of yours now?"

Chapter
29

Gyan wasn't about to let Urien have the advantage. Before either man could move, she dove at Urien's legs. Momentum carried her to the corner where the weapons stood, and she rolled to her feet. She snatched the long-bladed sword—the one she'd taken from a Scotti corpse to use against the dead man's leader—and tossed the sheathed blade to Arthur.

Urien flailed backward, trying to recover his stance. Arthur whipped out the sword, threw down the scabbard, and closed in. His swift and furious attack drove Urien back through the door. In the lamplit corridor, Urien lunged into a vicious counterattack.

Poised on the threshold, Gyan wanted nothing more than to help Arthur slice Urien into crow bait. The short sword Arthur had given her during the battle burned in her palm. She couldn't recall picking it up; her warrior's blood was singing too loudly.

Yet this time, she was honor-bound to ignore the persistent prompting. Whether he realized it or not, Arthur was engaged in the *dubh-lann*, the "black blade" challenge of Urien's right to become *Ard-Ceoigin* of Clan Argyll. Ogryvan had won Gyan's mother in this manner—although, by everything Gyan had heard, it hadn't been much of a fight. But regardless of differing skill levels or armaments, Caledonian Law decreed that only the *dubh-lann* combatants could affect the outcome. Evening Arthur's chances with the loan of the sword flirted dangerously with the precipice of legality.

With bloodless knuckles, she gripped the short sword as she waged war against her battle-fury and tried to concentrate upon the fight raging before her. Being taller, Arthur had the greater reach. Otherwise, the men were closely matched in skill, speed, and strength. Under different circumstances, she would have enjoyed watching the deadly poetry of the two swordmasters.

But the stakes were too high.

Fervently, she prayed for Arthur's victory. While one portion of the Law permitted her to select her consort, the clause governing the *dubh-lann* overrode it. She had no choice but to accept the victor of this combat. And if Arthur lost, a lifetime with Urien would surely redefine the word *misery*. However short that lifetime might be.

The prophecy of the High Priest of Clan Argyll slammed into her mind, and she redoubled the urgency of her prayer.

The clamor of the duel brought guardsmen running from both ends of the corridor. Without explanation, Gyan warned them against interfering and ordered them back to their posts. But the sight of their commander engaged with the Pendragon in what was obviously not a friendly match seemed to make the guardsmen reluctant to obey. The men crowded into other doorways along the corridor. Though this wasn't complete obedience, Gyan was satisfied. She shouted a new command for them to prevent anyone else from getting in the way. The guards nodded their agreement. Two men edged away from the fight to secure the building's main entrance.

By this time, both warriors were sweating and panting. Blood oozed from countless places where hard leather had yielded to the bite of steel. Yet neither man would relent.

Urien made a low lunge. As Arthur tried to whirl clear, the blade tore a gash in his shield-side thigh. Gyan stared in shock as the injured leg collapsed and Arthur dropped to one knee.

Crowing triumphantly, Urien charged.

Arthur scrambled to a crouch. As Urien rushed in, swinging his sword overhead for the deathblow, Arthur sprang. The sword's point sketched a cut across the Dalriadan's forehead with lethal accuracy. Blood cascaded over Urien's astonished face.

The blinded Boar of Moray roared with rage, trying to dash the blood from his eyes. Arthur struck away Urien's sword and shoved him onto his back against the stone floor. He planted a foot on Urien's heaving chest. The sword came to rest at the defeated man's throat.

All at once, Gyan wanted to laugh, cheer, and sigh with relief. Instead, she sheathed the short sword and grinned her approval at Arthur, who was too busy trying to control his breathing to do much more than nod.

"Renounce your betrothal vow, Urien map Dumarec of Clan Moray of Dalriada." When Urien mumbled his reply, blood sprang out from under the blade. "Louder, Tribune, so all may hear."

"I said, I withdraw my claim to the hand of Gyanhumara, Chieftainess of Clan Argyll of Caledonia," came the sullen response. "And may you never have a day's happiness with her. My Lord."

"Don't wager on that, Tribune."

"And what other treaty terms are you going to dissolve now?" Urien's sneer was grotesque through the bloody mask.

"A wise man does not deliver insults from the business end of a sword," said Arthur coolly.

"And a wise man does not interfere in affairs that are not his," Urien retorted.

"You would do well to remember that yourself, Tribune." The deadly warning rang clear. Without removing the sword, Arthur continued, "Incidentally, the solution to our—little dilemma, as you put it, is for you to take the hand of my sister, Morghe."

Urien laughed mirthlessly. "Have I a choice?"

"No."

"Then I accept your gracious offer, Lord Pendragon." It was obvious that Urien thought Arthur's offer was anything but gracious.

"Excellent decision. We will finalize the details later." Arthur lifted the sword and took his foot from the chest of his future brother-by-marriage. Unassisted, Urien rolled to his feet, swiping at his bloody forehead with the back of one hand. "Back at Caer Lugubalion."

"What?"

"I am recalling you to headquarters, Tribune. Effective immediately."

Urien seemed taken aback by this development. "But who will take over here?"

"I will appoint someone. It is no longer your concern. You are dismissed. All of you," he added to the guardsmen, in a tone that brooked no argument. "Back to your duties."

When the corridor was clear, Arthur dropped the sword and lurched into Gyan's arms.

Urien stopped by the infirmary to have his head wound dressed. Fortunately, the attending physician was wise enough to refrain from asking questions. Nor did Urien volunteer an explanation for the injury.

By the time he reached his quarters, his fury had cooled enough to permit rational thought. After stripping off boots and tunic and breeches, he sank onto the bed. But sleep was the last thing on his mind. He stretched out on his back, hands clasped behind his bandaged head. As he studied the age-darkened ceiling timbers in the glow from the room's only lamp, he tried to pinpoint where his strategy had gone awry.

Why he had lost the swordfight was not difficult to explain. He had never sparred with Arthur before. The few times he had observed the Pendragon in one-on-one action had been in training situations with opponents of vastly inferior skill. Including that accursed match Arthur had fought against Gyanhumara. If he had only known then what was going to happen tonight, he'd have given in to his gut impulse that day to run Arthur through, and dealt with the consequences later. But indulging in that fantasy did him no good. Urien railed at himself for committing the basic mistake of underestimating the enemy. He should have won the encounter. Easily.

But his wrath had blinded him, not his blood. And the source of that wrath had a name.

Gyanhumara of Caledonia.

What he had ever done to drive her into Arthur's arms remained a complete mystery.

Losing the duel to Arthur didn't rankle half as much as being forced to give up the woman. His plan to establish himself as overlord of both Dalriada and Caledonia—and his eventual bid for the Pendragonship itself—lay in ruins.

With one blow, he could have had it all! Now he had nothing. No Gyanhumara, no Caledonia, no command . . . probably no rank at all, for that matter. Nothing.

Rolling over, he caught sight of the bronze dragon brooch glaring up at him from its perch on the discarded leather tunic. He yanked it free, tried to crush it in his fist . . . and succeeded only in spearing his palm with the pin. As he sucked the bead of blood from the puncture, his other hand sent the brooch spinning across the floor. It hit the wall and careened into a corner. The jet eye chipped, but the dragon refused to break.

Urien shook his head in frustration, only to be rewarded by a stab of pain. He spat a stream of curses against Gyanhumara, Arthur, and the world in general. Finally, the pain abated. The curses did not.

And then there was Morghe. Some consolation. Shutting his eyes, he tried to conjure her face. The one to heed his summons had emerald eyes framed by copper hair. That image, he suspected, would never be expunged.

Still, the thought of marrying Arthur's youngest sister was not completely unpleasant. If his bid for Caledonia was temporarily thwarted, this new alliance opened up avenues of a different sort: with Arthur's brothers-in-law, Loth of Dunpeldyr and Alain of Caer Alclyd. Men who, like Urien, had been forced through marriage into alliance with the Pendragon. Kindred spirits.

No, taking Morghe would not be a bad move at all.

But revenge against Gyanhumara would have to

proceed with utmost care. If he couldn't attain his goal through the bedchamber, it would have to be done on the battlefield. Subtly, to make it appear as though Clan Argyll had provoked him. The seeds of a new plan were already beginning to germinate. And the first idea to take root was a way to remove his father from the Seat of Moray. As clan chieftain, Urien could escape from under Arthur's thumb, free to plot the details of his revenge.

With Arthur supporting Gyanhumara, the timing of this plan's execution would be critical.

He could wait. A lifetime, if need be. The woad tattoo encircling his left wrist and the scar he would bear across his forehead were his assurances that he would never forget the humiliation he had been dealt at swordpoint this night.

Arthur's arm lay heavily across Gyan's shoulders as she helped him along the deserted corridor to her quarters. His drawn face now betrayed how much pain he was suffering, which he had hidden from Urien and the guards.

He could have met eternity on Urien's blade. The stark realization echoed and reechoed in her brain, threatening to drive her mad. And he had risked that danger only for her, to set her free.

Inside the anteroom, they paused just long enough for Gyan to bolt the door against more surprises. As she returned to his side, he pulled her into an embrace.

"Let's see to your leg first. Before you bleed to death on me."

"What, from this? I've had worse. This is just a scratch."

"Right." She smiled briefly. "And I'm Iulius Caesar."

"God, I hope not!" They resumed their hobbling

pace toward the sleeping chamber. "I'd hate to think I went through all this trouble for another man."

Despite her concern for his condition, she chuckled. She made him sit on the bed while she closed the inner door and began hunting around the sparsely furnished chamber for something resembling a bandage.

"Here. Use this."

Gyan turned. Arthur's tunic lay in a ruined heap on the floor at his feet, and he was holding out his linen undertunic. His tanned chest gleamed like living bronze in the soft lamplight, like an ancient god. But the netting of white scars crossed by crimson scratches belied his mortality.

Yanking on the reins of her racing heart, she stepped forward to take the garment. While she tore strips from the undertunic, he tugged off his boots and, grimacing, eased off his leather leggings to expose the wound. Blood welled from the gash.

"You really ought to get this looked at by a physician tonight," Gyan advised as she applied the bandages. Rocking back on her heels, she locked his gaze with hers. "Promise, Arthur?"

"Later." He clasped her hands. They felt refreshingly cool. He marveled that there didn't seem to be any task she couldn't do. "Thank you, Gyanhumara." He drew her up to sit beside him on the bed.

"Please—just Gyan." His near-nakedness made her shy. To stave it off, she forced herself to speak. "And thank you. For winning. It was a marvelous fight." Frowning, she considered the darker implications. "But we've made ourselves a bitter enemy. Why did you spare him, Arthur?"

"Because whether any of us likes it or not, I still need Urien of Dalriada." Arthur recalled Cai's advice about dead men being unable to attack and wondered if he had made a mistake by sparing Urien. But no, preserving the alliance with Clan Moray and Dalriada was still vitally important to his plans. And that alliance would surely have died with Urien. He regarded Gyan earnestly. "Believe me, it would have given me great pleasure to drive that sword through his throat. But at present, he is more valuable to me alive than dead."

"He would have killed you." The grim image of a different outcome flashed across her mind, and she couldn't suppress a shudder.

"I know, Gyan." He hugged her close, kissing her neck—and was immensely thankful for this opportunity. Urien had come closer to winning that fight than Arthur cared to admit, even to Gyan. "I know."

"So who is to take his place here?"

"You."

"What? Me?" She pulled away to search his face for signs of the jest but found only solemn sincerity. "Arthur, you can't be serious."

"Of course I am. Why not?"

"There must be others who are much better qualified."

"In terms of combat experience, yes." A dozen names, in fact, occured to Arthur, capable leaders all. "But they will have opportunities for advancement soon enough." He ran slow fingers through Gyan's unbound hair, reveling in its silkiness. "You have proven that you can live and train and fight alongside your former enemies without holding that past against them. If my—" He grinned; with Gyan at his side, he'd have to get accustomed to a whole new way of thinking. "If *our* Brytoni-Caledonian force is to become truly unified, I will need your help. On Maun. And I believe you'll do just fine, Gyan."

"Perhaps." As he leaned to kiss her, she put a hand

against his chest. The heat of his flesh sparked a burst of nervousness, but she mentally shook it off. "But I don't understand why you can't leave Urien here and take me with you instead. I could do just as much good at headquarters—"

He shook his head. "I don't trust him. I want him where I can watch him. As far away from you as possible. And I do trust you to do a good job for me here."

"But we'll be apart for so long, Arthur. Now that I have you, I don't want to lose you again."

"Nor I you." He raised her hand to kiss the backs of the fingers—lingeringly, unlike that first time, on the eve of her departure for Maun. And unlike that first time, the smile that spread across her face was one of sheer joy. "But my decision is made. Besides, it will only be until summer's end."

Smile fading, she lowered her gaze. "May as well be forever."

He slid his fingers under her chin but didn't have to exert much force to make her look at him. "It doesn't have to be, Gyan."

He was right, she realized.

Their lips met as he reached behind her in his second attempt of the evening to remove her bronze belt. This time, he was successful, and it clattered to the floor. His fingers worked their way under her linen tunic to caress her breasts.

An ache flared in her loins. She tensed.

Then it occurred to her why she was hesitant. The training specific to this obligation of her rank had dealt with the selection of a proper consort. No one had ever prepared her for what would happen once she was ready to finalize her choice.

But she knew enough to realize that trust was essential to a strong marriage-union. And that trust had to begin here.

After kicking off her boots, she let him slip off her tunic and lay back on the furs. Staying off the bandaged leg, he eased down beside her. She felt her muscles relax as he massaged her shoulders.

Arthur recognized her tension for what it was and silently vowed to curb his own urgency for her sake. As he continued his ministrations, her eyes drifted shut, and she uttered a sigh. Slowly, with lips as well as fingers, he worked his way over the rest of her body, delighting in its contrasts: firm in most places yet wondrously soft and yielding in all the right ones.

His skill opened to her a world of exquisite new sensations, and his tenderness conquered her fear. She twined her arms around his neck and kissed him, hard. He was pleased to respond with equal force. This time, there was no rage to release, and no frustration—for either of them. Only stone-scorching passion, as, following ancient Caledonian Law, the Chieftainess of Clan Argyll accepted the Duke of Brydein as *ardceoigin*.

Chapter

30

Morghe lay on her stomach on top of the wolfskin,
clutching the russet pillow beneath her chin. She
raised her head to escape the woolen covering's
scratchiness and scowled at the whitewashed stone
wall.

She, Morghe, daughter of Uther and Ygraine, had no
one vying for her attention, while the Pict had two of
the most eligible men in all Brydein wrapped around
her little finger.

And the woman had absolutely no idea how lucky
she was.

Inwardly, Morghe railed at the times over the past
several weeks she had failed to maneuver Urien into a
more intimate setting. She had even resorted to putting
powdered sea holly root in the water she used to wash
her hair, mixed with lavender oil to mask the scent.
And the other day, anticipating more opportunities to
be with Urien once she realized she was going to be
stuck at Port Dhoo-Glass for who knew how much
longer, she had gone to the apothecary for yet another
dose of the aphrodisiac. Sea holly was much more
effective when ingested, of course, but she knew the

chances of getting close enough, unseen, to Urien's food or drink were slim. So she had chosen to rely on the weaker power of its aromatic essence instead.

But she probably could have force-fed him a raw root, and it wouldn't have mattered one bit. When she had visited him with the news of Arthur's apparent feelings for Gyanhumara—hoping it would cause him to abandon the chieftainess in favor of Morghe—her report had seemed to engender the opposite effect. Her father's worst drunken rages couldn't compare to the fury that had contorted Urien's face. It was all she could do to keep herself from being trampled as he charged from the room.

Fingering a fragrant tress, she wondered why she had even bothered with the hair treatment this morning.

Again, the pillow tickled her neck. She sat up and hurled it across the room. It splashed into the bronze washbasin standing on the small table near the window. Water slopped onto the pine tabletop and dribbled to the floor.

Her thoughts wandered back to last night's feast. Morghe would have had a veritable field day playing Urien against Arthur. Indeed, she'd expected the chieftainess to do something—anything—other than mope through the meal. But, for some strange reason, Gyanhumara appeared to be troubled by the whole situation. Still, watching the chieftainess stew had been entertaining in its own way.

Equally puzzling was why Gyanhumara seemed to favor Arthur at all. Urien would one day be chieftain of the strongest Dalriadan clan. A sane woman would leap at the chance for such a husband. Arthur was a soldier. The commander-in-chief of the army, true, but still just a soldier—with no lands and a source of income that was sporadic at best. In Gyanhumara's position, Morghe knew which she'd have chosen. In a heartbeat.

But if the Pict's behavior at the feast was difficult to understand, Arthur's was not. Any dolt with eyes could have guessed what had been on his mind when he left the feast-hall on Gyanhumara's heels. Urien had guessed, judging by the way he had stalked from the hall after them.

Morghe reached for the borrowed emerald linen gown draped across the chair, thankful that she'd been able to coax it from the innkeeper's wife. While not the finest frock ever to grace her body, it was far better than the tunic and breeches she'd been captured in, which had begun to reek. She would have preferred having slippers to match, but the woman's feet were too big. Morghe eyed her doeskin boots. They would have to do until it was safe to return to Tanroc. At least, they'd been scraped clean of the muck picked up from tramping across this overgrown dungheap of an island.

As Morghe pulled the gown over her head and tugged it into place, she wondered what had happened in Gyanhumara's quarters last night. The guardsmen had denied access to the building despite her most provocative pleas.

Curiosity was practically killing her. She just had to find out what was going on!

She donned her boots and stepped into the corridor. The *mansio* was awakening to the activities of the other guests, mostly merchants who had been caught at the port when the Scots attacked.

To her surprise, Arthur rounded the corner. His scarlet and gold uniform was impeccable, as usual, and not one hair on his disgustingly handsome head was out of place. His left thigh was swathed in a neatly wrapped bandage, one that was too clean to be covering a fresh wound. But no bandage had been there during the feast.

"Dear brother, whatever happened to your leg last night?"

"It's not important, Morghe. What is important is the news I have for you. Good news, as I'm sure you'll agree." His smile was utterly captivating. It took more than a little effort to resist its spell. "Shall we find a place to talk that's a bit more private?"

"Why, of course, Arthur." Her curiosity was really afire now. What kind of news could possibly be good for her, unless . . . unless he'd finally come to his senses about letting her come home. She invited him into her antechamber, and he closed the door behind them. "So. What is this good news? And why the secrecy?"

"It won't stay secret for long, Morghe. I just wanted to be sure you heard it from me first." He looked thoroughly pleased with himself, and it was about to make her sick.

"Well?" Pursing her lips, she rested a fist on her hip. "Are you going to tell me or just stand there grinning at me all day?"

"A little patience would become you, my dear." Arthur's smile broadened. "There is someone who wishes to marry you."

"Oh, really. One of your soldiers, I suppose."

"In a manner of speaking, yes."

"Sorry, Arthur. I'm not interested."

"I think you will be when you find out who he is."

A name came to mind: the last man on earth she'd ever consent to marry. "Surely not Cai?"

"No, not Cai." He laughed. "I wouldn't let him get within ten miles of you."

Well, that was a relief. Bored with Arthur's little game, she said curtly, "All right, then. Who?"

"Urien of Dalriada."

Urien and Gyanhumara, no longer betrothed? That, and Arthur's thigh wound, could mean only one thing. "So that's what was happening last night—why the guards barred entry to the officers' area. You didn't want anyone stumbling in on your fight."

"Very good." Arthur nodded. "It was Gyanhumara's order, actually. But yes, that was the general idea."

Marrying Urien, the politically powerful and handsome and virile Urien . . . it was her fondest wish! Except for one important drawback.

"You expect me to marry the Pict's castoff?" Winning Urien away from the chieftainess was one thing. This was quite another. Morghe was not accustomed to taking seconds from anybody. Folding her arms, she glared at her brother. "I won't do it."

Her refusal didn't seem to faze Arthur. "Oh, but think of the possibilities, Morghe. To be chieftainess of the most powerful clan of Dalriada." He waved as though painting a picture. "Perhaps even to rule all Dalriada one day."

For whatever reason, Arthur seemed to want this union very much. So Morghe was determined to remain stubborn. "That obviously didn't sway Gyanhumara. Why should I feel any differently?"

The smile vanished. "Gyanhumara is already a ruler in her own right. You are not."

Simple, brutal . . . and the absolute truth. This reminder caused her to dislike Gyanhumara—and the culture that spawned her—all the more. To achieve status in man-dominated Brytoni society, Morghe would have to wed Urien or a lesser nobleman. Although she despised this rule by which she had to play, she despised even more her powerlessness to change it.

As Morghe fingered her chin, a thought occurred: given the right marital circumstances, perhaps she might be able to work toward effecting changes so that her daughters and daughters' daughters wouldn't have to struggle with this problem.

And why settle for less power when more was ripe for the plucking?

"Very well, Arthur. I will marry Urien." When Arthur began to smile again, she held up a finger. "On one condition."

"Name it."

"Get me off this God-forsaken Scotti steppingstone of an island!"

"Consider it done." Arthur gave her one of his intense appraisals that always made her uneasy. "After you make a public appearance with Urien, for the announcement of your betrothal. He should be here soon, in fact, to escort you to the market square."

Morghe cast her gaze to the ceiling. "Oh, please. Is all that really necessary, Arthur?"

"Come now, Morghe. When have you ever known me to do anything that wasn't necessary?"

She laughed from sheer astonishment. "Exiling me to this place, for one thing." When he didn't reply, she pressed her advantage. "And then letting me get captured by the Scots. Why, I was downright lucky they didn't—"

He raised his hands in mock surrender. "Point taken." He started to reach toward her, seemed to think better of it, and lowered his hands. "Morghe. I'm sorry you had to get caught up in this war. And I'm very glad you didn't get—hurt. More than you may realize." Glancing up momentarily, he sighed. "Putting you at risk like this was the last thing I ever wanted to do." He extended a hand, palm up. "Can you forgive me?"

For the surprise attack over which he'd had no control, yes. For her original incarceration at the priory, no—but Arthur didn't need to know that distinction. Wordlessly, she took his hand with a nod and a smile.

After all, she lost nothing by casting this illusion of cooperation and could potentially gain much by it.

Urien stormed down the corridor toward Morghe's chamber. Sleep had done nothing to improve his temper; in fact, as tumultuous as his dreams had been, he doubted whether he had done much sleeping at all. But a lifetime of sleep couldn't make him any less tired of doing the Pendragon's bidding.

Sweat beaded on his forehead. Without breaking stride—and without thinking—Urien rubbed it and winced when his cut started stinging again. He wished he hadn't ripped off the bandage before leaving his quarters, but thanks to Arthur's order, there was no time to remedy that now.

He found the right door and pounded on it. Beneath his fist, he pictured Arthur's face. It helped dispel only a little of the frustration. From behind the door came an irritated-sounding voice that definitely was not Arthur's. On principle, Urien pounded again.

The door opened just wide enough for a scowling Morghe to poke out her head. "I said I was—" The scowl turned into a sly grin. "Well, well. Look what's escaped from the dragon's lair. He certainly got a claw on you, didn't he?" She opened the door the rest of the way and motioned for Urien to enter.

He snorted. Wondering why he had ever agreed to marry this irksome woman—and in the same breath realizing that he'd never had a choice—Urien shouldered past her into the room and faced her. "I've been ordered to escort you to the market square for Arthur's announcement. So, if you'll come with me—"

Sauntering up to him, breasts jutting and hips swaying, Morghe made a sound of disapproval with her tongue. "Come now, Urien, is this any way to treat your wife-to-be?" Moistening her lips, she ran her fingertips up his arm, across his shoulder, and up his neck to his cheek. But despite the stirring in his loins, he resolved to remain stoic. The idea of becoming intimate with Arthur's sister was just too bizarre to contemplate. She took a step backward, crossed her arms, and frowned. "Well. I can see why Gyanhumara got rid of you. At least Arthur knows how to treat a woman." The sly grin returned. "So I've heard."

Urien clenched his fist but, with effort, did not raise it. Punishing Morghe for her insolence was so tempting, so easy—and so very stupid. Arthur would probably dig out Urien's heart with bare hands and feed it to the ravens. He hoped a splash of honesty would cool her off. "Look, Morghe, I don't want this union in its . . . fullest sense. I can't believe you really do, either. All we need to do is put up an act for your brother's sake. You don't even have to live at Dunadd—"

"Oh, but that's where you're wrong, Urien." She moved in close and pressed her body against his, standing on tiptoe to reach behind his head. "I want to be your wife, at your side in Dunadd and . . . everywhere." Her lips parted invitingly as she pulled his face to hers. This time, he didn't resist. He couldn't. There was something enchanting about the lavender scent of her hair, with its earthy hint of another fragrance he couldn't identify. His pulse quickened as she whispered, "I want . . . everything you can give me."

As Urien wrapped his arms around her and covered her mouth with his, he couldn't prevent himself from visualizing Gyanhumara in Morghe's place. Then again, he could count on one hand, with fingers to spare, the number of times Gyanhumara's kisses had been this arousing. While Morghe could not hold a candle to Gyanhumara's beauty, she was pretty in a darker way—and thank God she didn't look at all like her brother.

He had to admit being glad to have a properly bred and trained Brytoni wife with whom he would not be constantly competing. At least, not on the battlefield. Morghe's lust for knowledge was perplexing, but Urien could deal with that easily enough. Kissing her neck and enjoying the sound of her throaty sigh, he imagined how he would educate her in the art of love-making.

But when he began to caress her breast, she wriggled free, flashing an apologetic smile. "My dear Urien, someone we both know would probably kill us if we were to miss his little gathering." She didn't need to mention the fact that if Urien succumbed to his over-whelming urge to make love to Morghe now—or at any time before they were wed—Arthur would kill him anyway. She combed her fingers through her hair and laid the hand against his cheek. It was warm and deliciously fragrant. "But I do thank you for giving me something to look forward to."

He clasped the hand and brought it to his lips. Her smile was one of pure delight. Another wave of lust jarred his body, more intense than anything he'd ever felt, for any woman. Gyanhumara included. It took every bit of will to keep that lust at bay—and every bit of logic to keep remembering why.

Gazing into her eyes, Urien noticed for the first time what an alluring shade of violet they were. "So have you, Morghe." If last night someone had told him how he'd be feeling this morning toward the sister of his hated rival, he'd have laughed himself sick. But this was nothing to laugh at. "So have you."

With the memory of her consort's ardor still vividly coursing through her mind, Gyan strode the main thoroughfare of Dhoo-Glass at Arthur's side. Angusel, of course, was not far behind as they made their way through the swelling crowds toward the market square.

Angusel had come to Gyan's quarters shortly after sunup, unwittingly disturbing her and Arthur. Smiling, Gyan recalled Angusel's embarrassment, which had quickly turned to gladness when he saw Gyan's choice of consort. Angusel's reason for visiting her, though, had been urgent indeed: several rumors had sprung up overnight about what had happened after the feast. Rumors that, if left unchecked, could have done tremendous damage. Hence this public appearance, to set folks straight.

Urien and Morghe were waiting on the market square's stone platform when Gyan and Arthur arrived.

Morghe smiled at their approach, which seemed odd to Gyan. Evidently, Arthur had found some way to convince her that marrying Urien was a good idea. Gyan felt a twinge of regret that when Arthur had returned to her quarters to escort her to the market square, there had been no time to talk.

To Arthur, Urien gave a salute that bordered on blatant insubordination. Arthur didn't bother to acknowledge it. Urien's scowl, as Gyan and Arthur mounted the platform, looked even worse than usual beneath the long red line across his forehead.

Gyan paid Urien no heed. She would much rather have drawn her sword—left-handed, if need be—to finish the job Arthur had begun. Arthur, she noted with a wry smile as she turned to face the townsfolk, deliberately positioned himself between her and Urien.

As Arthur made the announcements, Gyan studied the crowd. Since this gathering was intended for the benefit of the civilians, not many soldiers were present. The army had its own way of communicating that was faster and much more reliable than gossip.

Angusel, standing at the base of the platform where Gyan had bade him stay, beamed at her and Arthur. But his was the only face in the crowd she knew well. Even so, the people seemed to greet the news of the two couples' marriage plans with unanimous approval.

A shout rose from behind the crowd, in the direction of the Dhoo-Glass gates. "Make way!" A legion-uniformed horseman pulled his mount to a sliding stop to avoid plowing into the people. "Make way for the messenger of General Cai!"

An avenue formed. As the horseman approached, Gyan stifled a gasp. Not because of the messenger but because of the person riding behind him.

"Cynda!" Gyan clutched her tunic, over her heart, as relief and happiness coursed through her.

The messenger reined his mount at the base of the platform, dismounted, and helped Cynda down. She stood where he set her, rubbing her backside as Gyan all but flew down the steps to greet her.

Her tunic was rumpled and soot-smudged. A dark streak marked her brow, and her hair was a mass of tangles. Otherwise, Cynda appeared to be unharmed. And the smile that lit her face brought tears to Gyan's eyes. It was the most precious sight Gyan had ever seen.

Unwilling to trust the steadiness of her voice, Gyan drew Cynda into an embrace.

"Ach, Gyan, my dove . . ." Cynda returned the hug in a fierce, possessive way. "I thought I'd lost you."

Which was exactly what Gyan was thinking—but she couldn't bring herself to say it without the risk that the words turn into sobs. Instead, she whispered, "Not that easily." Blinking away the tears, she offered a silent prayer of gratitude to the One God for Cynda's safe return. Louder, she asked, "Are you all right?"

"Aye, well enough, no thanks to those bloody Scots." Cynda released her hold and fixed Gyan with an all-too-familiar appraising stare. "Better than yourself, it would seem." She gestured at Gyan's wounded arm.

"This?" Gyan glanced at the bandage and gave a small shrug. "This will mend. But something more important has happened." She smiled, unable to contain the news any longer. "Arthur is my consort now."

"Gyan, that's wonderful! For the clan"—Cynda winked—"and for you. Truth be told, he arranged for me to be sent here." She jerked her thumb in Arthur's direction.

Gyan gazed up at Arthur. There had been no time to issue such an order either last night or this morning, which meant he had to have done it sometime before. Before the fight, the feast . . . and before they had confessed their love. As her smile widened, her heart pulsed with even greater love for him. His own smile was brief but no less loving.

"Report," he ordered the soldier.

Thumping fist to bronze-clad breast, the messenger began, "Lord Pendragon, Tanroc and St. Padraic's Isle are free again."

The crowd's cheers flew heavenward. Arthur merely nodded.

The messenger untied a canvas-wrapped parcel from his saddle horn and handed it to Gyan. "Chieftainess Gyanhumara, General Cai sends his thanks. This was a great help."

She accepted the parcel with a nod. Niall had finally done her a good service, it seemed.

"Casualties?" asked Arthur.

"The men of the original detachment were either killed or wounded in the first assault, sir." The messenger drew a breath and let it out slowly. "The wounded soldiers were flogged."

Hand to mouth, Gyan gasped. Arthur said nothing, but his clenched jaw and fists betrayed his fury.

She asked, dreading the answer, "What of Centurion Elian?"

"His leg was crushed when a horse fell on him, my Lady." She felt her eyes widen. Had he been the one riding Brin? The soldier added, "He'll lose the leg, but otherwise he's expected to recover."

She spared a glance for Urien. Not even a ripple of sorrow touched his flinty face—which didn't surprise her in the least.

Head bowed, she silently recited the Caledonian warrior's lament. And commended the souls of the fallen to the One God. For the wounded, especially Elian, she offered a special prayer for the healing of their bodies . . . and their spirits.

Continued the messenger, "General Cai's cohort suffered few casualties. The fight to reoccupy Tanroc was brief. After spending their arrows, the Scots at the monastery surrendered."

"Cai is still at Tanroc?" Arthur asked.

"Aye, my Lord. Awaiting your instructions."

"First, Cai must select a contingent from his cohort to restore Tanroc to its original complement. Second, he is to appoint someone to serve as temporary commander until the replacement arrives."

"Lord Pendragon," began Urien, "may I ask who—"

"No, Tribune. You may not." To the messenger, Arthur said, "Finally, Cai is to take the remaining men—along with the prisoners and any wounded fit to travel—and sail for Caer Lugubalion on the morrow. Repeat it."

And the man did, perfectly.

Gyan left Cynda's side to join her consort on the platform once again. What she had to ask him didn't need to be announced to the crowd. "Arthur, what of the prisoners?" she whispered. "Are you going to—"

"Cuchullain is the barbarian, not I." The intensity of Arthur's glare took on frightening proportions. "My prisoners will be treated exactly as their crimes warrant. But any direct action against Cuchullain will have to wait. To take the battle to his shores and expect to win, I'd need another entire legion." Though he kept his voice low, vehemence shaped each syllable. "One that doesn't exist yet." Gaze softening, he reached for her hand. "Gyan, I'm sorry. It's Cuchullain I'm angry with. I didn't mean to take it out on you."

Images of her too-recent captivity assaulted her mind. How well she understood the frustration of being powerless to dispatch an enemy, and she told Arthur so. "We will build up our forces and deal with that Scotti *cù-puc* when the time is right for us, my love." An irreverent thought occurred, one she hoped would cheer her consort. "I don't know about Cuchullain's language, but in mine his name sounds like 'hound puppy.'"

"I'll remember that." Chuckling, Arthur gave her

hand a squeeze before releasing it. To the soldier, he said, "Get yourself a fresh mount from the stables, and ride back to Tanroc at once."

Apparently sensing the excitement was over, the townsfolk began to disperse as the messenger saluted, collected the reins, and led his horse away. Urien stepped off the platform, Morghe on his arm, and headed back toward the fort without so much as a glance in Gyan's direction.

Gyan descended and handed the bag containing her battle trophy to Cynda, then turned to address Angusel. "Please show Cynda to my quarters, Angus. I'll be along soon."

As Angusel and Cynda left, Arthur joined Gyan below the platform. Few townsfolk remained in the square now, but even if the place had still been packed, Gyan wouldn't have cared.

"Thank you, Mel-Artyr," she murmured, "for thinking of Cynda."

"I'm glad Cai was able to find her for you." His eyebrows lowered. "But what did you call me?"

"Artyr. It's your name in my birth tongue."

"I gathered that. But the other part—*mal?*"

"No, *mel*. It means . . ." She reviewed the list of Brytonic and Latin equivalents, examining each meaning like trying to decide what to wear. The Latin word she finally selected could not convey all the nuances, but it came the closest. "Consort. The consort of the *ard-banoigin.*"

"A title, then. Sometimes I think I have too many already."

A gentle smile tugged at her lips. "You don't have to use it." Not all *ard-ceoigins* changed their names to reflect this status. Her father, for one. "It's the consort's choice. Receiving my clan-mark, of course, is a different matter." She caressed his shield arm, picturing the Argyll Doves soon to be winging across the bronzed flesh.

He raised her hand to his lips. Naked desire flared in his eyes. "God help me, Gyan. I love you so much!" He grinned. "Let's get married right away."

She cocked a questioning eyebrow. "By Caledonian Law, we already are."

"But not according to the custom of my people. For our union to be recognized in Brydein, it must be sanctified by the Church. Any child born too soon after the formal ceremony would not be considered legitimate."

"To Brytons, perhaps, but to Caledonians—"

"I know, Gyan. Believe me, I know. I was such a child myself. And it has caused—problems. I am barred from the chieftainship of my clan." He sighed. "I wouldn't inflict that fate on anyone."

This Gyan could understand. There was another matter, however, that eluded her. "You must return to headquarters soon. And you still want me to stay here to lead the Manx Cohort?"

"Yes. I don't like it, Gyan. But I like the alternatives much less." His grin returned. "So, my love. Shall we go to St. Padraic's and ask the abbot to conduct our ceremony?"

The church at St. Padraic's monastery was . . . the Sanctuary of the Chalice! What had happened to it during the Scotti occupation? The messenger had only reported military details, as duty demanded. But what of her former mentor, Dafydd, and his family? And Father Lir and the other monks? Gyan was smitten with a strong desire to find out. And not from the mouth of any messenger.

Arthur was regarding her expectantly, so she returned her wayward thoughts to his suggestion about the marriage ceremony. And tempting though it was, a difficulty occurred to her. And a solution.

"No, Artyr. I'm afraid we can't." She softened the words with a smile. "That church is too small, and too remote. I imagine many people will want to attend. Caledonians as well as Brytons. After all, it's not every day that the Duke of Brydein marries a Caledonian chieftainess. Caer Lugubalion would probably be best. The event will require some planning—and we'd have to allow time for folk to arrive, especially my clansmen, who'd have the farthest to travel." She searched his face for a sign of agreement and was a bit concerned when she didn't find it. "That is, if the Pendragon thinks the Manx Cohort can do without its commander for a fortnight or so."

His eyes lit with a vivid blue twinkle. "You, Lady," he declared with mock reproach, "can be entirely too sensible."

She felt her smile deepen as he bent his face closer to hers. "One of us has to be," she whispered. When their lips met, it was not with the fiery passion of the night before or the warm earnestness of the morning. But she still felt the full force of his love.

With the sounds of the Dhoo-Glass marketplace clamoring in her ears, it was all she could do to keep her desire in check. One of them, she thought with an inward grin, had to be sensible, indeed.

Chapter

31

St. Padraic's monastery, Gyan was relieved to discover, seemed to have been left undisturbed by the Scots. Physically, that is. By what she could tell from her tour of the compound, the buildings showed no sign of damage.

Of the monks themselves she was not so certain.

Where it had once been customary at this hour of the afternoon to see several small groups of monks strolling about or seated on benches in the orchard to discuss Scriptures or other treatises, now the monastery seemed all but deserted. A few brethren were doing chores: tending the garden and livestock, cutting wood, hauling water, washing laundry. And to a man, they seemed to perform their work with a solemn sense of purpose that was nothing at all like the way they had acted before the attack.

She was still pondering their behavior as she rounded one of the cruciform wings of the church. Stifling a gasp, she stopped. Her visit with the badly wounded Elian had been difficult, but this sight made her heart lurch. Spread out before her was a field of mounds, each topped with a wooden cross. It was the place where she and the monks had made their stand against the Scots.

The memory staggered back in all its agonizing detail. The fighting, the dying, the surrender. The loss. And none of the monks had had to die. That realization struck her like a sword through the heart. She had led these decent men to their deaths, and for what? Her foolish pride. If she had not chosen to resist that day, the monastery would have fallen without a struggle—and this graveyard would not be here to mock her today.

Gaze averted to the ground at her feet, she leaned against the stone wall. She did not fight the tears coursing down her cheeks.

"My Lady?"

She knew that voice. Swiping at her face with her tunic sleeve, she turned. And frowned in puzzlement. The man standing before her wore the black hooded robe of the monks' order. Yet this image did not match the voice.

"Dafydd?"

He pushed back the hood. Even if she had not recognized his face, the fading red mark of the slave collar would have confirmed his identity.

"You're a monk now?"

"Yes, my Lady. Renewed my vows, actually. Ten years ago, I was a monk. Before Arbroch."

His statement didn't sound like an accusation, but as a ruling member of the clan responsible for his enslavement, it was hard for Gyan not to take it as such. Quietly, she asked, "Why take vows, when you can visit as often as you like?"

"It's not the same, my Lady. And . . ." The smile he showed her was suffused with peace. "I had to fulfill my promise to God."

She nodded, although she didn't completely understand. That type of peace, for her, seemed hopelessly far from reach. "What of your family?"

"They will stay here until Tanroc is rebuilt, Katra and young Dafydd. And after that, I will still be able to see them whenever I wish. Many of the brethren have wives and children."

"And your daughter? Is she at the priory?"

"No." Sorrow clouded Dafydd's face, and he lowered his head. "My little Mari is with God."

"The Scots?" He answered with a mute nod. She reached for the yielding hand. "Dafydd, I am so sorry." Since his family had been at Tanroc during the attack, there was nothing Gyan could have done to prevent his loss. But that knowledge was no help to her.

His other hand closed over hers.

Gyan peered into Dafydd's face. There was no bitterness, no blame, no remorse, no regret. Memories intruded of the soldiers and civilians—and horses, like her Brin—that had died to defend Tanroc. So much death that day . . . Gyan didn't know how Dafydd could bear it so well. Tears welled again.

"Come, my Lady." He tugged on her hand. "There is something I think you need to do."

He led her into the church. Though she was convinced of the futility of this visit, she didn't bother to resist.

Yet she had to admit the statues were a familiar, comforting presence: Moira with the Holy Infant and Padraic with the serpent, ever wreathed by flickering candlelight. Fragrant incense permeated the air. The Chalice sat enshrined on its golden platform in front of the crucified Christ. It was as though the Scotti invasion had never happened.

But the graveyard outside would not let Gyan forget the truth.

Dafydd strode to one of the side banks of candles, lit a twig, and used it to light the tapers flanking the Chalice. Their glow made the relic look ethereal, as though not of this world. Perhaps, in a sense, it wasn't.

Gyan approached the altar. "Are you the Keeper now, too?"

He snuffed the twig between moistened fingertips, laid it down, and turned toward her. "No, my Lady. But one day, by the grace of God, I might be." Her eyebrows shot up, and he explained, "The brother Father Lir had been training as his successor died resisting the Scots. Father Lir hasn't chosen anyone else yet, so those of us who remain have been taking turns with this office. It's another reason I decided to stay." His clear blue eyes misted, and his gaze seemed very far away. "I think Father Lir's spirit has broken, my Lady. Even though the Scots are gone, he has not moved from his bed."

First the monks, now Father Lir. More tears threatened. "This—all of this is my fault."

"Oh, no, my Lady. Please don't blame yourself. You did what you thought was best." He reached for her hands. When she tried to pull away, he held them with surprising strength. "Who could have known the Scots had other motives?"

Who, indeed? "They could have killed me in that skirmish just as easily as they killed the others. At some point, I knew they wanted me alive—and I knew it was a hopeless fight. Right then, I should have called off the attack." She lowered her gaze. "Maybe some of the brethren would be alive today."

Some cohort commander she was going to make. Perhaps she ought to confess her unfitness to Arthur so he could appoint someone else and save everyone a lot of trouble. And death.

"My Lady, God uses everything—the bad as well as

the good—to carry out His purposes." He squeezed her hands. "You must believe that, or you will drive yourself mad."

This time, she did pull free and crossed her arms. "And what purpose does the senseless deaths of thirty innocent monks serve?"

"For them, eternal life." He spread his hands; whether in ignorance or helplessness, Gyan couldn't decide. Perhaps both. "But for you, my Lady, I cannot say." Facing the altar, his voice drifted into a reverent whisper. "I pray God will reveal it to you in His good time."

Her eyes followed the line of his gaze. There was something oddly soothing about the plain clay cup that had been used by the Christ. The cup that had held His blood—in more ways than one. Overwhelming awe forced Gyan to her knees. No longer able to look upon His anguished, wounded face, or His cup, she bowed her head.

The rustling of fabric and slapping of sandals told her Dafydd had walked away. For what purpose, she didn't know. She couldn't lift her head. Her burden of guilt weighed too heavily upon her soul. She couldn't even bear to ask forgiveness, for how could the One God possibly forgive her for the needless deaths of His servants and for the grief she had caused Father Lir and the other survivors? More to the point, how could she forgive herself?

The unmistakable aroma of fresh bread invaded her nostrils. "The Bread of Life and Body of Christ, my Lady, broken for you." Opening her eyes, Gyan turned her head to find Dafydd on one knee beside her, offering a dish. Upon it lay a loaf that had been ripped in half. "Take, eat—and live."

Intense spiritual hunger gnawed at her heart. This time, she couldn't ignore the pangs.

Recalling the ritual she had seen Merlin perform, she tore off a morsel and put it in her mouth. As the bread and Body became one with her body, a silent voice murmured to her of betrayal and sacrifice. Betrayal, she thought miserably, was exactly what she had done to those monks, and to their entire community. She bent chin to chest again, tears leaving cold tracks on her cheeks.

Willing sacrifice, the voice softly insisted, *essential sacrifice; not for one but for all . . . for love . . . for all time.*

A hand rested gently upon her head, and Gyan could feel the power of holy love pulsing within her. As she glanced up, Dafydd's hand withdrew to curl with its kin around the Chalice. It wasn't empty.

"The fruit of the Vine, my Lady, in the cup of the new covenant in His Blood." Dafydd held the Chalice a handspan from her face. *The cup of death . . . and rebirth.* "The cup of new faith. Drink," Dafydd said, lifting it closer to her lips, "and be renewed." *And be forgiven.*

As she gazed into the dark depths of the wine, her mind conjured an image of what this cup had held while its Owner endured bloody torture and death on a storm-swept hill called the Place of Skulls. Tears burned her eyes. Squeezing them shut, she jerked her head aside. "I—I can't, Dafydd. I'm not—" Her voice caught, and she released a trembling sigh. Again, she saw the crimson-stained bodies and lifeless faces of the fallen monks. Faces that had looked anything but peaceful. Guilt seared her soul. "I'm not worthy."

"No one is, my Lady," he said quietly. "No one ever can be. Not of our own devices or desires. Only by God's infinite, perfect grace can we enjoy His blessed fellowship." Dafydd placed the Chalice in her hands. "And He invites all to confess their failings, and taste of Him."

From an ordinary cup perhaps, Gyan thought, but this? The very vessel whose rim had known the lips of the Lord of Lords Himself? On the verge of another refusal, she remembered: His inner circle of followers had shared this same cup with Him that fateful night, doubtless not fully understanding the implications. And not realizing they had all been fated to betray Him to some degree, if not by word or deed, then by fearful silence. But days later, their eyes had been opened. Opened to His power over death and life, to His love, to His grace and mercy and compassion. And forgiveness.

Come, Daughter; surrender your burden. Drink and be forgiven, commanded the voice, *and forgive yourself.*

She drank.

With the wine coursing down her throat, the Blood slaking her spiritual thirst as nothing on earth could, the voice comforted her with words of assurance, promise, and hope.

For His own mysterious reasons, the One God had placed a sword in her hand and had gifted her with the strength and skill to use it well. And now she would have the opportunity to lead not just tens but hundreds of others to do the same. As the fruit of the Vine lingered on her lips, she vowed to become the best leader she could: for the Lord of Lords, for Arthur, and for the warriors under her command, past as well as future. To do anything less would mean those monks truly had died in vain. She knew she would never forget the mistakes that had led to their deaths, but as she accepted His forgiveness, profound peace settled over her soul.

She didn't want to destroy the moment. But the sunlight slipping from the sanctuary told her it was time to leave. The fleet was ready to sail back to Caer Lugubalion, and she couldn't keep Arthur waiting any longer. Smiling her thanks, she returned the Chalice to

Dafydd and rose. He continued to kneel, head bowed, the cup cradled against his chest. She gazed at the Chalice, inscribing its features forever in her mind and upon her heart.

Laird Cuchullain reclined in the shade of the great willow, watching his wife collect roses in the small garden beyond the leafy curtain. She glided from bush to bush, waving away the bees to add yet another bloom to her collection. Pert pinks, rowdy reds, splendid salmons, winsome whites, all paled beside Dierda's vibrant beauty.

"Dierda!" She daintily cocked her head toward him. "Come and rest yourself, dearest one."

Sheathing her knife, Dierda favored him with a knowing smile. " 'Tisna rest ye'll be thinking of, now, is it?" The roses held in one gloved hand, she swept aside the willow boughs with the other and stepped into the green bower.

He took her into his arms, and she nestled against his chest. "A man needs something to take his mind off his troubles, even if only for a wee time." He stroked her flaming silken hair.

"Still worrying about our brave ones on Maun, my heart?"

"When have I stopped?" The knuckles of his free hand pounded dirt. "Not knowing, 'tis murder! Having to wait—"

His complaint was cut off by the warm touch of her lips. Having to wait for tidings from Maun might not be so bad if more of his time could be spent with his wife like this. But such moments were all too rare these days.

At the grassy rustle of approaching footsteps, they reluctantly parted.

"Laird Cuchullain?"

Cuchullain scrambled to his feet, burst through the

hanging boughs and emerged, blinking, into the sunlight. Dierda followed, her roses lying where they'd been dropped beside the willow's massive trunk, forgotten.

"Commander Fergus, well come!" Cuchullain smiled at his warrior. "What word? Where's Niall?"

The warrior's face was bleak. "Laird, General Niall is dead. So are most of the men." And he proceeded to explain why.

Cuchullain accepted the news in stony silence, barely aware of the rose-scented hand that had come to rest softly upon his shoulder. Up came his hand to cover hers, a familiar gesture. This time, he derived little comfort from it.

"By Lugh Longarm, I knew I should have gone with them!" Cuchullain shook his head in frustration.

"Laird, may I speak plain?"

"I think ye already have, Fergus. But go ahead."

Fergus sucked in a breath. "Begging your pardon, Laird, but your presence wouldna have helped. The Pendragon struck too quick. Even one more day, and Dhoo-Glass would have been ours."

"Might have been, Fergus." Cuchullain sighed. "Might have been."

Dierda asked, "How many returned with ye, Fergus?"

"A little more than two score, my Lady. Brave men who managed to get away from the siege camp before it fell to the Pendragon."

"And what of our ships?" Cuchullain was almost afraid to ask. But he had to know. Gaze lowered, Fergus shook his head. "Niall gone . . . most of the warriors and all the warships lost . . ."

"My husband, think upon those who've come back to us. Like our brave Fergus here." She asked the warrior, "If the warships were lost, by what miracle did ye escape?"

" 'Twas indeed a miracle, Lady Dierda. I took a spear in the side and was left for dead." Fergus pressed a hand against his loose tunic, and the bandages bulged beneath the gray linen. "I woke in the night and crawled to hide in the trees. To die, I was sure. But some of our own soon found me and carried me away, to a Brytoni fishing boat they'd found in a nearby cove. This they told me later, for I was three days with a fever. We would've come to Tarabrogh sooner but for that."

"Three days—on Maun?" Hand to throat, Dierda gasped.

"Nay, my Lady," Fergus replied. "We left Maun that selfsame night and made straight for Doann Dealghan."

"Well, we must be thanking Lugh for that," Dierda murmured.

"Aye. And then begin rebuilding our fleet and forces." Cuchullain squared his shoulders, feeling yet again the fire of that long-ago lashing. Hatred gushed anew as he struck fist to palm. "Arthur the Pendragon shall one day feel my wrath for this, or I am not fit to be Laird!"

"I'm telling you, Merlin, she is not going to like it."

The Bishop of Caer Lugubalion didn't like it, either. The eve of the most important wedding ceremony in Brydein since Vortigern had married his Saxon princess, half a century before, was scarcely the time to argue an issue that pitted politics against religion, an issue that might carry dire repercussions, depending on how certain people chose to react.

Merlin pushed himself up from behind his worktable, with deliberate slowness to control the anger that was trying to surface, and crossed the tiled floor to join the Duke of Brydein at the window. Arthur stood, motionless, glaring at the cloud-laced azure sky, hands clenched behind his rod-straight back. Sensing his young cousin's tension, Merlin put a hand on Arthur's shoulder.

"What would you have me say, Arthur?" he asked. " 'Fine. Go ahead and have doves painted on your arm. Never mind that the dove is symbolic of the Holy Spirit; you have my blessing anyway'?"

The broad shoulders drew back even further. He withdrew his hand.

"You think people won't notice?" Merlin continued. "I might be able to overlook this issue for your sake. For both of you. But do you think my peers will? Do you think you're too well respected—or too feared—to escape being branded a heretic? If you can honestly answer yes to these questions, even just one . . . well." Head wagging, Merlin stroked his chin. "I've gone through too much with you already to stand idly by while you throw everything away over something as absurd as painting an image on your skin."

A falcon traced slow circles among the clouds. Arthur remained silent, whether watching the bird or not, Merlin had no idea. With a triumphant screech, it dove. Arthur's head shifted in a barely perceptible nod.

Merlin tried to imagine what thoughts must be coursing through that gilt head. Chief among them had to be the realization that another man with any amount of strategic and tactical sense and leadership ability could take over. Another man . . . like Urien of Dalriada. If Arthur didn't recognize this, he would be in serious trouble.

Arthur's fist thumped the stone window ledge. "Any other symbol—bear, horse, falcon—"

"Would be perfectly acceptable, true." He did not mention that Hebrew Levitical law forbade all tattoos. Under the Covenant of Christ, compliance was a moot point. "But we're not talking about bears or horses or falcons. I'm sorry, lad. As your bishop, I cannot condone it."

"And as my political adviser? Or my kinsman?"

A rueful half-smile tugged the corners of Merlin's mouth. He retrieved his pewter cup and refilled it with *uisge* from the pitcher. Raising the cup to his lips, he confessed, "Sometimes I think I'm trying to do too much. I ought to disappear from the eyes of the world. Retire to a quiet cave in the hills somewhere—Gwynedd, perhaps—and be a hermit." He paused to picture what such solitude might be like with nothing more around him than the serenity of nature, to be responsible to no one but himself and his Creator. "This is one of those times." He took a swift, hot swallow.

"What?" Fists on hips, Arthur regarded Merlin. "And give up your baths? Your heated floors?" He laughed, although there was no mirth in it. "Abbot Kentigern's *uisge?*"

"Ah." The scene dissolved into amber ripples within the cup. Perhaps paradise existed only in dreams after all. Besides, with the Lord's war raging on so many fronts—physical as well as spiritual—now was scarcely the time to retreat. "You've called my bluff. I suppose you still want an answer."

"Of course."

Merlin closed his eyes for a moment, silently praying for wisdom. "As your adviser, I would say that refusal to comply with this Picti custom will cause problems. With Argyll. With their allies, perhaps. To what extent, I can't foretell. I imagine it will depend a great deal on Gyanhumara's reaction."

Arthur nodded his agreement. "And as my kinsman?"

"That's easy. Do whatever you think is best, given what your bishop and your adviser have told you. Just remember, you have to live with the consequences. And your wife."

"Great, Merlin. Thanks a whole bloody lot."

Arthur sat at the table in his workroom in Caer Lugubalion's *praetorium*, trying to keep his mind on the task at hand. But the scouting reports looked like so much gibberish. With a single irate motion, he swept them from sight. The persistent vision of Gyan's face destroyed his concentration. Not the face as he had come to love it best, with a mischievous smile dancing on her lips and mirrored in her sparkling sea-green eyes, but the way he was sure it would look when he informed her of his decision about the tattoo.

The parchment leaves fluttered to the floor. His chair grated against the tiles. He stood, bent to scoop up the papers, dumped them back on the table, and began pacing to work off his frustration.

It wasn't the prospect of brooking Gyan's anger that bothered Arthur but the reasons themselves. As much as he wanted to deny it, Merlin had been absolutely right.

The legacy of Uther's final defeat at Dun Eidyn, at the hands of Colgrim and his Angli horde, was a decimated, demoralized army and the loss of an important eastern seaport and surrounding territory. Now, two years later, Arthur was just building up enough strength to begin balancing the scales. Yet he was still a long way from buying any kind of lasting peace for the folk he had sworn to defend. Two years and two major engagements weren't enough to secure the kind of universal loyalty and trust he would need to weather the displeasure of the Church.

The Caledonian Confederates were another unknown factor. Their horsemen increased the Brytoni cavalry squads tenfold and played a vital role in Arthur's long-term strategic planning. If the Caledonians perceived his refusal to wear Argyll's mark as a slight, they might well shatter the treaty and plunge him back to where he had started.

Worse, even. For it also would mean losing the woman he loved more than life itself.

An insistent knock pierced his thoughts. He stopped in front of the door and opened it.

Gyan stood on the threshold. Her joyful smile almost made him forget what he had to say. He beckoned her into the room, closed the door, and folded her into an embrace. But as hard as he tried, he knew his kiss lacked the fire she had come to expect.

She regarded him with a quizzical frown. "Artyr, what is it?"

"Before I tell you, I want you to promise me two things. First, no interruptions."

She nodded. "And second?"

Her hair smelled like a rose garden. Covering her mouth with his again, he was able to unearth some of his buried passion. But not enough to persuade him to abandon his duty.

"And second, Gyan, remember that I love you."

He grieved to watch the emotions battle across her face as he explained his refusal to be tattooed with her clan-mark. But she honored her promise. Toward the end, she stared down at the emblem on her sword arm as it lay folded with its companion across her chest. Even after he had finished, she made no move to speak.

He was mentally girded for a fierce outburst, but her protracted silence sliced through his defenses. He slipped his fingers under her chin and forced her to look at him.

"Well?"

She shook herself free of his touch. "Wearing the clan-mark is the consort's way of pledging fealty to the clan. To refuse is a grave insult." Her voice was low and lethally sharp. "At best."

"I know, Gyan." She didn't have to tell him what the worst might be. Those scenarios still stormed through his head. "You must believe I do not intend it as such." Within the tough shell of the command nestled the earnest plea.

Her cold eyes searched his face. Finally, they seemed to thaw. "I do, Artyr. But my clansmen, my father—"

"There must be another way."

"There is," she replied without hesitation. "But as warrior to warrior, not as husband to wife."

Chapter

32

The Caer Lugubalion *mansio's* dimly intimate dining hall was much as Gyan remembered it from her springtime visit: slabs of salted pork swinging from the rafters, a thin haze wending from the kitchens to curl around the wealth of pitchers and flagons and trenchers scattered across the groaning tables. Her boots clicked on the tiles as she advanced into the hall.

The main difference was the size of the throng. In the spring, the *mansio* had been all but deserted. Now, the innkeeper and his helpers scurried everywhere like mice at a cheese-making to serve their parched and famished guests. There was not a single empty bench or chair to be found.

One group of patrons had evidently abandoned the quest for seats to cluster, goblets in hand, near the cold hearth. Spirited laughter attested to the quantity of wine that had already disappeared.

Gloriously adorned chieftains and chieftainesses, high-ranking clergy and legion officers, fur-robed merchants—a thief's fondest dream in the flesh. And they had all been invited to Caer Lugubalion to see Gyan and Arthur formalize their marriage vows in the Church of St. John on the morrow.

She sincerely hoped they would not be disappointed.

On an intellectual level, she understood Arthur's refusal to wear the Argyll Doves. She could not force him to blaspheme the One God any more than she herself could be tattooed with Epona's Mare. And the depth of his love certainly wasn't in question. Her lips still throbbed with the memory of his most recent kiss.

Yet his passion couldn't heal the hurt, entirely. In a sense, he had rejected the most sacred traditions of her people, and in so doing, he had rejected her. As ludicrous as it seemed, she was unable to dismiss the idea. And it stung like the tongue of a whip.

Motionless, she pondered the swelling sea of faces. Caledonian clan rulers seemed content to break bread with their Brytoni peers, peacefully ignorant of Arthur's decision. What would happen to this newfound camaraderie once the news became public knowledge? Would these warriors exchange meat knives for longswords and sever the trust Arthur had worked so hard to build?

Not if the Chieftainess of Clan Argyll had any say.

The probable reactions of her clansmen worried her the least. Gyan was certain they would support her solution. The trick lay in winning her father's agreement. No chieftain alive was more thoroughly steeped in Caledonian traditions than Ogryvan of Clan Argyll. The One God alone knew how he was going to respond.

And Gyan was about to find out. Grinning, Ogryvan strode through the crowd. "Gyan, my lass!" If he'd held her any tighter, his embrace would have bruised her ribs. Her reunion with Per a sennight ago had been deeply heartfelt by both of them but not nearly as exuberant.

Ogryvan and the Argyll contingent had arrived at Caer Lugubalion less than an hour before. Gyan wished this reunion could have occurred under different circumstances; concern over the matter of Arthur's clan-mark held her other emotions hostage. She strove to keep her tone light, but it wasn't easy. "Father, please!" After returning his embrace, she pushed free and put hands to hips. "I'd like to be in one piece for my wedding night, if it's all the same to you."

That won a hearty chuckle. Then he seemed to notice her bandaged sword arm. "One piece, indeed. And what's this? Are you all right?"

Nodding, she replied, "It's my first war-wound, Father." Despite the more serious thoughts on her mind, she grinned. "You should see the man who did this to me. He was kind enough to give me my first trophy, too."

"I look forward to seeing it." He hugged her again, gentler this time, but not by much. "By all the gods, Gyan, it's so good to see you! Arbroch just hasn't been the same without you and Per to stir up trouble." Adopting an inquisitive look, Ogryvan released his hold and glanced around. "Where is that rogue stepson of mine, anyway? I thought he'd be here to greet me, too."

"Practicing with the best riders of his unit. For the cavalry games." If her father heard the note of disappointment in her tone, he made no comment.

She had hoped to speak to Per about the issue of Arthur's tattoo before Ogryvan's arrival, but by the time she found her brother, he and his team were so intensely engaged in their drills that she couldn't get his attention. Not that she didn't understand the fervor; these cavalry games were to take place the day after the wedding as part of the nuptial festivities, and obviously Per wanted his team to win and bring honor to his sister the bride. If, she thought bleakly, his sister was going to be the bride.

Ogryvan slapped his forehead. "The games, aye!" Arms crossed, his look grew stern. "I was expecting Per to ride on my team."

She felt her lips stretch into a rueful smile. "Then you'll have to take that up with him, Father." Smile fading, she drew a breath for the plunge. "But first, there's a matter I must discuss with you." The tide of laughter-painted faces washed closer, and she lowered her voice. "Alone."

Like the dining hall, Ogryvan's guest chambers in the *mansio* were quite familiar to Gyan. They boasted the same three chambers for talking, eating, and sleeping, the same plain but adequate furnishings, the same timber-ribbed whitewashed walls. But if the floor tiles had to take much more of her father's furious pacing, they would certainly begin to shatter.

"Gyan, this is appalling!" He glared down at her as she sat on the long, low couch. "Wearing the clan-mark to show allegiance is the *ard-ceoigin's* most sacred duty." He tapped the graying doves on his shield arm. "Not to mention the personal benefits."

Common wisdom maintained that a tattoo blessed its owner with the virtues of the creature it portrayed. The Doves of Argyll represented grace and speed.

"I know, Father. So does Arthur. Do you think he would have agreed to my idea if he didn't believe in its importance?" Speaking the words silenced the mental nagging, but she swallowed the sigh of relief. "Do you

doubt Arthur's willingness to swear allegiance to me?
Or to Argyll?"

"Not his willingness. Only the method." Ogryvan
waved a finger in Gyan's face. "Urien map Dumarec
would never have created a problem like this."

"You're right. Urien map Dumarec would have done
anything in his power to secure Argyll lands. Murder
included." She countered Ogryvan's stormy gaze with
her own. "My consort is a man of principle."

"Oh, principle, aye. The sort of principle that calls
for disregarding the traditions of his wife's people."

His angry echo of her secret doubts wounded like a
sword thrust. But she refused to show her hurt. Any
sign of weakness would do no good for her cause, or
Arthur's.

"Would you have him risk the wrath of his priests?"
When Ogryvan hesitated, she pressed on. "Of his
God?"

With a noisy sigh, he dropped to the couch beside
her. Clasping her hand, he seemed to engross himself
in the study of the repeating pattern of her betrothal
tattoo. His thoughts she could only guess. None of
those guesses seemed very promising.

At last, he asked, "I suppose you would not consider
taking another consort?"

"No!" She gentled her tone. "Father, my idea will
work. It must work." Her other hand covered his. "But
only if I don't have to present it to the High Priest by
myself."

"He didn't come with us, Gyan. Proclaimed himself
too old for the journey." Ogryvan shook his head.
"Despite my efforts to change his mind."

"Then obtaining the blessing of his subordinate
should be child's play. That is, if you're with me in
this." She searched his dark eyes for some glimmer of

agreement and found only sadness. "You are, aren't you?"

"I don't know, Gyan. What you've suggested is so— different."

"How so, Father? Warriors—"

"Warriors, aye. But not an *ard-banoigin* and her consort." He rose and helped Gyan to her feet. "I know you need an answer, lass. And I wish I could give you one." Mercifully, his hug this time was not a bone-crusher.

"I'm sorry, Gyan, but I must sleep on it."

At dawn on the first day of the month named in honor of the greatest leader Rome had ever known— the same leader whose plan to conquer Caledonia had failed half a millennium before—a boisterously merry Argyll company rode to the appointed meeting place in the forest beyond Caer Lugubalion. Now and again, horsemen detached themselves from the formation, weapons at the ready, to frighten away flocks of over-curious Brytons. The Caledonians of the other clans knew better than to try to follow but greeted the procession with hearty waves and broad smiles. The ritual bonding of the *ard-banoigin* and the *ard-ceoigin* was a joyous occasion. And meant for no eyes outside the clan.

Gyan, riding beside Arthur at the head of the procession, did not share her clansmen's mood.

Ogryvan had left to oversee the formation of the company before Gyan could speak to him about his decision. And she could scarcely bring up the subject now without having everyone else find out.

In any event, her course was set. She had to go through with her plan. No other option was feasible.

But without her father's support, she wondered if it would be doomed to failure.

Glancing at Arthur, she ventured a small smile. His silent answer warmed her like the sun. If only they could just put this day behind them . . . to be alone to enjoy the pleasures of each other's company! The mere sight of him, so handsome in his freshly oiled and polished battle-gear astride the proud-stepping Macsen, almost gave wing to her doubts.

Almost.

The track veered into the denser reaches of the forest. A faint hum grew steadily louder, like the chorus of a hundred hives. The last time she had heard such a sound was on the day she received the Argyll clan-mark. By their chants, the priests were sanctifying the site in preparation for the ceremony. Although this type of chanting no longer held any influence over her, she welcomed its familiarity and the pleasant memories it bred.

The large, round pause in the march of trees had been meticulously cleared of vegetation. Fresh knife slashes decorated the trunks of the oaks guarding the perimeter. Shaped into the symbols of the Old Ones, the carvings were reminiscent of those covering the stones ringing the Nemeton at Arbroch. This clearing had been specially selected to fulfill the same function.

A rough-hewn rock occupied the center of the clearing. Across its flat top lay the knives and needles for the morning's work, winking brightly in a neat row beside the pot of dark blue woad dye. Small heaps of smoldering ash discharged tangy gray tendrils. Circling the altar's base was a thick mistletoe and ivy braid.

The company dismounted at the edge of the clearing, and most remained with their horses. As Gyan, Arthur, and Ogryvan approached the knot of priests standing behind the altar, the chanting ceased.

"Who is to conduct the bonding?" Gyan asked.

A man stepped forward. "The Master selected me to officiate this ceremony, Chieftainess." Like the other priests, his face was lost in the shadows of his robe's hood. But there was no mistaking the oily voice.

"Vergul. Well met." Gyan resisted the impulse to modulate her tone to match. "This must be quite an honor for one so newly ordained."

"Indeed. Although without the Sacred Flame"—he swept an arm toward the cold altar—"I would hardly call this a proper bonding."

"I have already made arrangements, Priest. To occur during the . . . other ceremony." She raised a hand to still his protest. "Since it's forbidden to remove the Sacred Flame from the temple—"

"Except to carry it to the Nemeton," another priest broke in.

Gyan nodded curtly. "This will have to suffice."

Vergul answered with that vaguely mocking bow she had come to know so well. Straightening, he lifted both arms to command the attention of his audience.

"The *Ard-Banoigin* will commence the bonding by accepting the mark of her consort."

A swift glance at her father produced no more than a wink and a nod. Yet it was enough. Flinging her arms around his neck, she balanced on tiptoe to plant a kiss on his cheek, to the delighted surprise of the crowd.

Vergul was not amused. "Are you quite through with deviating from the ritual, Chieftainess?"

"Priest, I have not yet begun." With her smile, she tried to convey nothing but sweetness and innocence.

Leaving him to puzzle out her meaning, she knelt beside the altar and bared her arm to the rock. Another priest presented himself to perform the work. Under his cunning fingers, a blue dragon took shape. More details would be added in the days to come; for this ritual, only the dragon's outline was drawn. Yet even if not another drop of dye touched her skin, the tattoo would still be impressive. Undulating curves spiraled around her forearm from wrist to elbow. At her request, the priest contrived to make the betrothal-mark seem like part of the dragon's lashing tail. He knew his craft well.

When he was finished and Gyan regained her feet, Vergul reached for the wrist of the newly painted arm. He thrust it toward the brightening heavens.

"Be it known this day that Chieftainess Gyanhumara nic Hymar now wears the sign of the Dragon. No other clan in the ancient history of our people has ever claimed this formidable beast for their symbol." This time, no trace of mockery warped Vergul's tone. "Chieftainess Gyanhumara, may the power of the Dragon guard your days and lend you countless measures of its awesome strength." The sneer returned. "And may you prove worthy of this singular honor."

"No fear there, Vergul. I shall never dishonor the clan."

"Let us hope not." He turned to address the company. "The *Ard-Ceoigin* will now receive the Doves of Argyll."

"No." Over the gasps and shocked murmurs, Gyan said, "By the laws of his religion, he is forbidden to wear the Argyll clan-mark."

"Blasphemy! There is only one true religion!" The other priests vehemently voiced their agreement.

"That is what my consort believes, too."

"Ah." Grinning, Vergul rubbed his hands together. "And do you share this belief, Chieftainess?"

The veiled hint took her aback. How could Vergul know that she had forsworn the Old Ones for the One God and the Christ? Or was he only making a shrewd guess? Either way, she could ill afford to fuel his suspicions. Caledonian priests were notoriously intolerant of anything falling outside the bounds of their parochial definition of truth, and just as notoriously merciless when passing judgment.

"My beliefs are not the issue here, Priest," she growled, praying Vergul wouldn't start asking questions about the Christian ceremony to follow this one—and extremely thankful he and his brethren wouldn't be attending it. "Arthur's loyalty to Argyll is."

"Aye! The Pendragon is prepared to prove his loyalty in a manner that is acceptable to his people." Ogryvan's glare as he regarded first the priests, then every member of the assembly, was charged with warning. "I trust it will also be acceptable to ours."

Facing her consort, Gyan thrust out her open-palmed hand. Because she knew Arthur would not be able to understand the Caledonian tongue, she had forearmed him with the knowledge of what would be happening. Caleberyllus emerged from its scabbard. He offered her the hilt and went to one knee at her feet.

This sparked another round of muted murmurs.

"You swore never to dishonor the clan, Chieftainess." Vergul trembled with the effort to retain control. "Yet what do you call this—this blatant disregard for—"

"Enough, Vergul!" At Ogryvan's roar, the priest shrank back a pace. "I have no objections. Neither should you."

With an impatient wave, Vergul gathered his brethren around him. Their whisperings reminded Gyan of so many snakes competing for the same stretch of sun-baked stone. At last, the hooded heads nodded. As the priests parted, Vergul stepped forward again.

"So be it. From this day forth, let Artyr, *Ard-Ceoigin* of Clan Argyll, be known by the mark of the Oath of Fealty. Chieftainess, you may proceed."

Gyan grasped Caleberyllus's hilt with both hands, ignoring the pain in her wounded arm and bridling the urge to stand agape before the magnificent weapon. Its physical beauty was complemented by its perfect balance and flawless twin edges. Something remarkably akin to a rush of power flowed into her fingers to course through her body. No surprise there; Arthur's sword was imbued with his vital essence.

Truly a sword worth dying for.

This was the quintessential core of the Oath, the ultimate surrender of self. With Angusel, who had made his pledge with a borrowed sword since his had been miles away at the time, it had been different yet sufficient.

Now, with Caleberyllus burning between her palms and Arthur's steady sapphire gaze locked to hers, Gyan was smitten by the full impact of understanding. This insight destroyed her doubt.

She raised Caleberyllus to within a handbreadth of her face in salute and lowered it to his left shoulder. A shaft of sunlight pierced the circle of oaks, caught the blade, and exploded into a brilliant silvery flash. The company's hushed reaction conveyed naught but approval for what they clearly considered a manifestation of divine blessing.

Perhaps, she thought with a ghost of a smile as she tightened her grip, they were not wrong.

Arthur map Uther had knelt in ritual submission once before: to the conclave of Brytoni chieftains, presided over by Merlin, who had sworn him into the office of *Dux Britanniarum*. But Merlin had not commanded him to bow his head. Nor had the man of God—not bishop then but priest and one of Uther's few surviving generals—pressed Caleberyllus against his neck.

"Does Artyr mac Ygrayna of Clan Cwrnwyll of Brydein swear allegiance to Gyanhumara nic Hymar of Clan Argyll of Caledonia, even unto death?"

Gyan had rehearsed the ritual with him the night before, so these Caledonian words were no mystery. Nor did he have any question how to respond.

"Even unto death!"

With his head still bowed, he could only imagine the pale scar on the underside of her right forearm, the mark that had been wrought by his hand on the sword she now held. He recalled that day in all its exhilarating, confusing, frustrating detail. The irony forced a smile to his lips. That was the mark that had first bound his heart to hers, not the one she was about to bestow upon him.

For her ears alone, he repeated the vow in his birth tongue. He meant every word, to the depths of his soul.

If Niniane had ever told Arthur that she had Seen him on the morning of his wedding day kneeling before his wife, feeling the terrible, wintry tooth of his own sword, he would have thought the prioress had taken leave of her senses.

Chapter
33

"How am I supposed to weave these blasted twigs into your hair if you won't sit still?" Cynda fussed.

"I can't help it, Cynda." Gyan began to rub the new tattoo again. "My arm itches."

Cynda sighed in obvious annoyance. "Keep that up, and you're going to make your arm all red and ugly." She set down the comb and laurel cuttings and selected a small clay pot from the clutter on the nearby table. "Here, use this. Mind you don't get any on your gown."

Gyan uttered a short laugh as she spread a dollop of lavender-scented ointment across the rampant blue dragon. The cool salve soothed the itch miraculously well.

"There." Cynda pressed the polished copper mirror into Gyan's palm. "What do you think?"

Cynda had twisted Gyan's hair into a single plait and wrapped it like a dragon's tail around her head. The laurel twigs were braided into its blazing coils as if to camouflage the beast.

This was no Caledonian bridal crown but a Roman symbol of victory. Arthur had suggested she wear the laurel by right of her triumph over General Niall at Port Dhoo-Glass. And Gyan, who once had despised even the mention of Rome, had been pleased to comply.

"It's lovely, Cynda." She smiled, still looking into the mirror. Her former nursemaid's teary-eyed face appeared over her shoulder. Gyan turned. "Cynda?"

The older woman seemed to lose her struggle, and sobs erupted. Gyan set the mirror aside, rose from the chair, and drew Cynda into an embrace.

"No, no—your gown!" Cynda tried to push away.

"Don't worry." Gyan refused to let go. "You won't hurt it. Now, tell me, why are you crying?"

Drawing a shuddering breath, Cynda dried her eyes with trembling fingertips. "Oh, Gyan, my wee dove, you look so much like your mother did when she—she and your father—" She bit her lip and buried her face in Gyan's shoulder.

An image flickered in her mind's eye. Whether a true picture or not, Gyan would never know. As she patted Cynda's back, she regretted that she had been denied the chance to know the woman to whom she owed her first life-breath. But regret was soothed by the balm of confidence that Hymar would have been proud of her daughter. For at last, Gyan had managed to forge a union that meant not only peace for Argyll but peace for herself—something that, several months ago, she never would have dreamed possible.

With a final squeeze, the women parted.

"And look at me." Cynda reached for a cloth to dry her face. "Bawling like a bairn when I should be helping you finish dressing."

She marched to where Arthur's gifts lay on the bed and picked up the first: Bronsaffir, a long double-bladed sword commissioned of Wyllan, the same Manx smith who had forged Caleberyllus. Cynda laid the sheathed weapon across Gyan's outstretched palms and went to retrieve the sword belt from the oaken armor-chest.

Gyan grasped the sapphire-pommeled hilt with her left hand, since the half-healed wound on her sword arm was still troubling her. The blade whispered free of its bronze scabbard. Though not as long as its cousin by a hand's length, Bronsaffir still owned the keen edges and delicate balance and fierce beauty that distinguished Wyllan's finest creations.

Sheathing the sword, she tried to imagine the thrill of feeling the awesome blade shear through enemy flesh. It wasn't difficult.

Her bronze dragon sword belt had been cleaned and polished for the joining ceremony. Cynda gave the dragon's head a final swipe with her tunic sleeve before cinching the belt around Gyan's waist over the high-necked azure gown. Gyan beamed as Cynda fastened Bronsaffir, couched in its dragon-etched scabbard, to the belt. Most folk doubtless would regard the armor and sword as odd accessories for a bride. But she would never have considered being parted from them this day.

To complete her wedding attire, Gyan had ordered a special clan mantle. Though it was woven of the traditional Argyll saffron and scarlet pattern over midnight blue, its edges were scalloped with threads of gold. She stooped for Cynda to drape the cloak about her shoulders.

A sharp rap rattled the door.

"That'll be your father." Cynda pinned Arthur's final gift, an enamel-ringed, sapphire-eyed golden dragon brooch, to the cloak and smoothed the last wrinkles from Gyan's gown.

Ogryvan stood in the antechamber, darkly resplendent in his clan tunic and ebony leather leggings and boots. His mantle was fastened at the shoulder with a gold dove brooch. The golden neck and arm torcs, like his daughter's, also bore the Argyll Doves.

Greeting Gyan with a wide smile, he offered his arm. "Come, Gyan," rumbled the Chieftain of Clan Argyll as the woad doves on her right forearm settled over the identical design on his left. "Let's not keep the Pendragon waiting."

"What the devil is keeping her, Merlin? I've been waiting here for hours!"

Arthur's seemingly endless circling in the robing room adjacent to the chancel reminded Merlin of a similar interview three months earlier. The topic then, as now, had been the Caledonian chieftainess. But Merlin knew that anger did not drive Arthur this time, only typical bridegroom nervousness.

"Peace, Arthur. You have not." Merlin reached out to intercept the armor-clad shoulder. "Now, be still. Watching you makes me dizzy, and I can't sing if the room is spinning." With a wink, he added, "And if I can't sing, you won't get married."

Arthur shot him a hard glance but stopped pacing anyway.

Merlin sighed his relief. The escalating chatter seeping into the closed chamber told him that St. John's was nigh to overflowing. He asked the acolytes to help him don his outer vestments.

The first measures of the *kyrie eleison* drifted from the choir to herald the entrance of the bishop and the groom. A gradual hush settled over the sanctuary.

Without warning, Arthur went to one knee at Merlin's feet. Smiling, Merlin placed both battle-scarred hands upon the red-gold head in silent blessing. When Arthur rose, all traces of anxiety seemed to be gone.

The acolytes lit their candlesticks as Merlin opened the door. Side-by-side, the boys advanced to the altar to light the candles at either end. The fat center candle was a stranger to the Christian wedding mass. The chieftainess had requested its addition to the ceremony to honor Caledonian tradition as an ancient symbol of unity. In this case, so her argument went, the unity was not just between two people but between two nations. And she had been absolutely right. So, for the sake of diplomacy—and with his own words about the Argyll tattoo secretly needling him with guilt—Merlin had agreed.

Now, the unlit candle crouched behind the chalice and loaf, like a demon among the blest. Merlin wondered, not for the first time, whether he had done the right thing.

The acolytes finished their work and marched to their bench behind the altar. Pushing aside all thoughts save the task at hand, Merlin picked up his cruciform crosier and led Arthur, the Duke of Brydein, into the chancel.

Standing at the back of the church beside her father, Gyan paid little heed to the glittering array of guests: her kin and Arthur's, other Caledonian and Brytoni clan rulers and their retinues, clergy, merchants, craftmasters, and anyone else who could produce a legitimate invitation. She barely noticed the army and naval officers, dressed in shining parade uniforms and gripping silver-tipped spears, shoulder-to-shoulder in two long ranks to form an aisle down the center of the sanctuary.

Her gaze was riveted to the door opening onto the altar area.

The Chieftainess of Clan Argyll witnessed the entrance of her consort with great joy. As always, she delighted in the sight of his ceremonial regalia. His gold breastplate gleamed in the brilliant rays bathing the chancel. Unlike the first time she'd seen Arthur in this uniform, Caleberyllus hung at his side from a gold-studded leather baldric. The knee-length gold-trimmed scarlet cloak was pinned by a brooch of the same design as hers. His gold dragon challenged the world through a blood-bright ruby eye. Like hers, Arthur's bare head was crowned with laurel.

Arthur spun smartly toward Gyan. Even across the twoscore paces separating them, she could discern the barely contained excitement emanating from his gaze and wondered if he could sense hers.

As Arthur beheld his bride, he fought to control the emotions that must surely be threatening to dominate his expression. Never had she looked more beautiful or more regal. Yet she seemed to wear her beauty and her power easily, like a favorite cloak that was flung on and scarcely given a moment's thought. And he loved her all the more for it. As much as this ceremony meant to him, he simply wanted it to be done, so he could be alone with her to express his love.

Merlin's solo voice began the *gloria*. The officers raised their spears, and every civilian head turned to watch Gyan and Ogryvan approach the altar. Muted gasps of admiration raced before the bride and her father, punctuated by the rhythmic thumps of spear shafts meeting flagstones as the couple passed each honor guard pair.

Without moving his head, Arthur studied some of the other faces before him.

Beside Bedwyr stood Arthur's mother, Ygraine, Chieftainess of Clan Cwrnwyll of Rheged. She regarded her only son with a fiercely proud smile. Her daughters and their families clustered around her—Yglais and her husband, Alain, scion of Clan Cwrnwyll, and Annamar and her husband, Chieftain Loth of Dunpeldyr.

Morghe, Uther's only other child by Ygraine, stood a little apart from her mother and half-sisters, leaning on Urien's arm. She seemed to accept her betrothal willingly enough, but Arthur couldn't forget Niniane's warning about Morghe's anger. Perhaps now that she was betrothed to the heir of Clan Moray of Dalriada, that anger was a thing of the past. Arthur hoped.

Urien map Dumarec glared at Arthur with thinly veiled hatred. And not just because of Gyan. As long as Chieftain Dumarec pledged to support Arthur with Clan Moray troops, Urien's options were severely limited. He could either remain under Arthur's command or resign his commission and return home—neither of which, Arthur presumed, was an attractive choice for someone whose ambition outpaced rational thought.

Arthur rested his hand on his sword hilt. Urien glanced away, whether taking the hint or not, Arthur couldn't tell. Perhaps he had, for when Urien looked forward again, his expression seemed decidedly more subdued—which was fortunate for Urien.

Across the aisle, beside Cai, who was serving as honor guard commander, stood the Caledonians: Clan Argyll first, of course, followed by the other clans. Chieftainess Alayna of Clan Alban was not present, though Arthur didn't find that surprising. She was probably none too pleased that she had lost him to the chieftainess of a rival clan. But with most of her warriors committed by treaty to Arthur's army, she was in no position to retaliate, except by refusing to attend this event.

But her son Angusel stood proudly in Argyll's front rank, between Cai and Gyan's half-brother, Peredur. Upon Angusel's crimson-and-green-streaked sky-blue cloak prowled the gold lion brooch, the symbol of both his clan and his freedom from being Arthur's hostage. That freedom, in response to the young warrior's courage and loyalty, Arthur had been more than pleased to grant.

At first, Angusel seemed to regard Arthur with a puzzled frown. Then the frown became a smile as Angusel's hand touched the scar on his neck—a similar mark to the one Arthur himself now bore, the sign of fealty to the Chieftainess of Clan Argyll. Not that Arthur needed such a mark to remind him of the oath he had sworn to Gyan—or the oath itself, for that matter. Neither, Arthur suspected with an inward grin, did Angusel.

Gyan and Ogryvan reached the end of the aisle and parted at the base of the steps. At Cai's command, the honor guard pivoted to face the altar as Ogryvan took his place beside Peredur.

Turning, Arthur held out his hand to Gyan. As she clasped it and squeezed, her gaze locked to his. She smiled, and for a moment, the rest of the world and its problems seemed very far away. With his smile, he tried to convey at least some measure of the love that burned within him. Hand in hand, they mounted the steps to the altar, where Merlin waited to finish the ceremony.

*　*　*

Gyan's heart was so uplifted by the glorious music and by the steady presence of her consort that she felt it must surely take wing.

Every detail seemed infinitely precious: the lulls and crescendos of the harmonious monks . . . the snowy altar cloth embroidered with crimson Christian symbols . . . the bishop's mellow voice and stately movements as he performed the duties of his office . . . the warm, fragrant bread . . . the flickering candles reflected upon the golden chalice . . . the wine's rich sweetness . . . the pungent aroma of incense from the acolytes' censers . . . the shafts of westering sunlight blazing across the wounded face and body of the dying Christ . . . the brilliance of united flame as she and Arthur lit the center candle . . . Arthur's smile before bestowing the ceremonial kiss . . . the thunderous jubilation of the crowd when their lips finally met.

The bejeweled moments tumbled one by one into the treasury of her mind.

"God, what a day!" Arthur plucked the laurel wreath from his head and flung it across the room. It hit the wall and burst into a shower of greenery.

Gyan laughingly agreed. "All those toasts—I thought they'd never let us escape from the feast." She laid her cloak aside, retrieved the copper mirror, and began tugging twigs from her braid.

"Here, let me help." To Gyan's pleasant surprise, he worked quickly yet gently.

"Thank you." Most of her thoughts raced ahead to the moment when she and her consort could douse the lamps and lose themselves in the pile of sleeping furs. But one matter required immediate attention. "I really appreciate what you did for me this morning, Artyr."

Arthur paused. In the mirror's flame-tinted face, she saw the fingers of his left hand trace a slow course over the fealty-mark.

"I did not swear an empty oath, Gyan."

"I know." The memory of Caleberyllus's power was one she would never forget. His hands cupped her cheeks. She tilted her head back as he bent to cover her mouth with his. The fires of her passion roared to life, hotter than ever. Such a pity to have to interrupt, but . . . "Shall we finish with my hair, so we can make ourselves a wee bit more comfortable?"

He chuckled. "Agreed." More twigs pattered onto the tiles. "You seemed to enjoy yourself in St. John's, my love."

"Of course. Why shouldn't I?" He pulled the last laurel leaves from her hair, and she turned toward him.

"Well, I just thought you might not understand everything. I don't mean the words," he amended, silencing her protest with a finger to her lips, "but the—"

"Symbolism? I understood more than just the words, Artyr." Smiling, she clasped his hands, glad for the chance to share this secret. "You see, the same man who taught me your tongue also taught me about your God. At my request."

Arthur didn't hide his astonishment. "But the candle lighting—"

"I asked Merlin to add that Caledonian custom for the benefit of Father and the rest of my clansmen. Not for myself." She recalled the private conversation in the bishop's workroom, scant minutes before riding to the bonding ritual. Swept along by the tide of events, she hadn't noticed anything odd at the time. Now, hindsight was telling a different tale. "I'm amazed he agreed so readily."

"Maybe it was his way of apologizing for advising me against accepting your clan-mark."

"Maybe."

Doubts again rose within her. This time, their target was not Arthur but herself. Gyan disengaged her hands and walked to the window overlooking the inner courtyard of the *praetorium*. But from the mental tirade there was no escape.

"I know I have a lot to learn about the One God. But I find it hard to believe that He would care so much about a mark on the skin." To silence her doubts, she decided to enlist her consort's help. "And what about me? Does this mean I'm really not a Christian?"

His chest pressed to her back as his arms twined about her waist. His lips were warm against her neck. The aromatic essence of his victory crown lingered like a halo.

"I think God cares more about what's in our hearts than what's on our bodies. But some people"—he sighed—"clergymen, especially, can get strange notions sometimes."

Strange notions, indeed. It was all too confusing.

"I have to be careful," Arthur went on. "So do you now. The Church holds a lot of sway. Not so much over the regular army but the common folk. Our auxiliaries." He started massaging her shoulders. "I think allowance could be made for you, that you received the mark before you became a Christian. But me—well, we've already been over all that." The kneading hands stilled. "One day, I will wear the Argyll Doves for you."

"No, Artyr, you don't have to—"

"I will find a way. I promise." The steel in his tone melted as he asked, "What made you turn to Christ, Gyan?"

Contemplating the moonlit courtyard, she grappled

not with the answer to Arthur's question but with the idea of whether she should say anything at all. Regret over her conversion was not the issue. In fact, her most recent taste of the sacramental wine had again affirmed in her heart the rightness of the decision. But what would her consort think of a warrior and leader of warriors who had forsaken the religion of her people because she had been afraid to face her prophesied destiny?

She leaned against his chest, feeling his arms tighten protectively around her, grateful that he seemed willing to let her take her time. But she knew he wouldn't be put off forever. At last, she replied, "It is the way of my people to ask help from the god who is most able to grant it." The darker secret threatened to lodge in her throat. Resolutely, she pushed it out. "Only the One God proved strong enough to help me face my doom."

"Whoa, Lady." He clamped a hand on her arm and spun her to face him. "What do you mean, your doom?" She saw no reproach in his eyes, only profound concern.

Gyan translated the words of the prophecy into Brytonic for her consort.

"I'm certain the High Priest meant Urien." The doubts fell silent at last. She reached up to caress his cheeks. "Now that I have you, Arturus, my Roman love, that fate no longer awaits me."

Her lips parted in an invitation he wasted no time to accept.

After their lovemaking, Arthur lay awake beside his peacefully sleeping wife, pondering what she had said. His Christian upbringing made it difficult to pay heed to a pagan prophecy.

Yet some small part of him refused to shrug the

matter off. Though his father was Roman, he was the son of a Brytoni woman. And Caledonians traced their lineage through the mother . . .

No. It was absurd. He was a soldier, not a chieftain. Nor likely to become one. Thanks to his father, his feet trod a different road: Roman-built, and dusty, and hard. But now, this traveler had a companion to share the trials and triumphs of the journey. As Arthur ran his fingertips over the azure lines of the dragon that ramped around Gyan's forearm, his heart surged again with the great love he felt for her. She was incontestably his now. Just as he was hers. Caleberyllus would never let him forget that.

And as long as he had breath in his lungs and strength in his body and fight in his soul, no one was ever going to come between them.

Explicit Liber Primus

kdh, MCMXCVIII
Psalm 139:9–10 NIV, Soli Deo Gloria

Author's Notes

Precious little is known about the period following the withdrawal of the Roman legions in about A.D. 410. From the only surviving contemporary British source, a sermon of woe written by Christian cleric Gildas "the Wise" in the mid-sixth century, one can infer that it was a period of political, economic, social, military, cultural, and religious chaos. The British fought not only amongst themselves for leadership to fill the power vacuum they inherited from the Romans, but also against the various invaders from the Highlands, the Continent, and Ireland. Everybody had a different agenda, and a different means of pursuing that agenda, covering both ends of the moral spectrum and points in between. Faith flagged—not just faith in whatever divine power one chose to worship, but faith in their leaders, each other, and themselves.

Tradition asserts that roughly fifteen hundred years ago, a leader arose from the tumult to weld the sundry factions into a strong, prosperous nation, buying a generation of peace for his people. Tradition names him Arthur. Tradition also acknowledges that he had help in many forms: prophets, advisers, heroes, and friends.

I postulate that Arthur's assistance came, first and foremost, from his wife. And not merely to weave his cloak and embroider his shield cover and use his banner to dry her tears while languishing in the cold castle, wondering whether he was going to return alive.

Over the years, as I devoured every Arthurian title I could find, fact as well as fiction, one thing became clear to me: Guinevere has taken a bum rap. And she's in good company, along with Cleopatra and even "Good Queen Bess," Elizabeth I, who had a fair share of detractors. The female Pharaoh Hatchepsut, who habitually wore a fake beard, was all but lost to us until recently. And the ninth century's Pope Joan, who held the office for two years, has been the subject of one of the biggest coverups ever instigated by the Roman Catholic Church. A woman of true power, it seems, is anathema to her male peers, chroniclers, and historians.

But it is not my intent so much to exonerate Guinevere as it is to present a version of her story plausible enough to explain how the medieval and later stories, rife with themes of lust, adultery, and treason, might have come to be. To that end, I have striven to create as accurate a picture of late-fifth-century Britain as possible, avoiding such words as *potato* and *tartan*. This is by no means a claim of perfection, and if I've overlooked something obvious, I welcome the opportunity to learn from readers' comments.

A warrior-queen Guinevere is not as farfetched as it might sound. Writers of antiquity, men like Diodorus Siculus and Ammianus Marcellinus, traveling in what was then known as Gaul (modern-day western Europe), recorded their observations of Celtic society at about the time of the birth of Christ. These writings included commentary on Celtic women, who were noted to be at least as strong and fierce in battle as their husbands, if not more so. By this time, some Celtic tribes had already begun migrating into Britain. There they encountered an ancient aboriginal race, the Picts, living in what is now the Scottish Highlands.

What is known about the Picts is sketchy at best. Historians are even unsure what they called themselves. *Pict* is derived from a Latin term for "painted people," a reference to the custom of painting their bodies with woad (blue) dye. The stone carvings these mysterious people left behind are either hieroglyphic or runic in appearance, and as yet no Rosetta Stone equivalent has been unearthed. This is a mournful situation for the historian and anthropologist but gives rise to all sorts of fascinating possibilities for the novelist.

It is generally believed that the Picts were a proud, warlike race, not unlike their Celtic neighbors. Evidence suggests that over the centuries, they intermarried extensively with the Scotti (Irish) and various continental Celtic tribes, engendering a unique cultural blend. This blend can be seen in the sharing of physical characteristics, deities, modes of dress, warfare, and language. I have taken the approach that by the opening of *Dawnflight* in the waning years of the fifth century, this blending process is well under way.

One distinctly Pictish aspect that seems to have remained intact is the nature of their society. Evidently, women shared clan leadership responsibilities with their menfolk, and descent was usually traced through the mother. Theirs was an integrated society, unlike the Celts, who, by all reports, were highly segregated.

With regard to the Picts' language, of which nothing is known, I have used Scottish Gaelic as a starting point, usually with modifications as the need arose. Thus were born terms like *ard-banoigin,* not found in any Gaelic dictionary but roughly translated as "exalted woman heir-producer," and her consort, the *ard-ceoigin.*

On the subject of names, I decided that my classically educated Romano-Celtic Arthur deserved a sword with an inherently Latin name—a combination of *calere* ("heat") and *beryllus* ("beryl"), yielding *Caleberyllus*—rather than using the Latinized *Caliburnus* of disputed etymology.

I also took the liberty to invent or borrow distinctive names for many of my characters; in particular, *Ogryvan* (Leodegrance), *Angusel* (Lancelot), and *Gyanhumara* (pronounced "ghee-an-huh-MAH-rah"—Guinevere). Ogryvan is derived from the Welsh Gogfran, who appears in an ancient triad as "a giant" and the father of one of the three Guineveres *(Gwenhwyfar* in Welsh) to whom Arthur was supposedly married. Angusel is based on King Auguselus of Scotland, mentioned in Geoffrey of Monmouth's twelfth-century *History of the Kings of Britain* as one of Arthur's staunchest supporters.

As for my title character, arguably the oldest known form of her name is *Guanhumara.* But my character needed a version that would yield a suitable nickname, and *Guan* just wasn't it! Neither was *Guin.* She also needed a name that would not conjure preconceived notions in the mind of any reader with a passing familiarity with the Legends, which in my opinion *Guinevere* does, and so, to a lesser extent, does *Gwenhwyfar.* Hence, *Gyanhumara,* or *Gyan* ("GHEE-an"), as she's known to friends and kin: chieftainess, warrior, leader of warriors, the barbaric foil to Arthur's civilized Roman ways . . . and the best portion of his soul.